"*Ritual* murder?" Vanessa repeated, sure she had misheard.

"The corpse has been subjected to some considerable heat, and drained of various bodily fluids. It has also been disembowelled, and castrated, like some kind of medieval execution. What's even more frightening, I had a call this morning - a crank, I thought at the time - who actually told me to expect to find just that. 'Dismembered' - the very word he used."

"Jesus Christ," was all Vanessa could find to say. Finally; "I hope you can track this 'crank' down."

"Better than that, I have his number, and he's on his way in as we speak. He's a Doctor of Medieval European Literature at Oxford University. He's convinced that this all has something to do with the Holy Grail legends…."

Copyright © C. Wood, 2008

Illustrations © C. Wood, 2008

The following is a work of fiction, and any similarity to real persons, events or institutions is purely coincidental.

First published by Fenriswulf Books, 2008.

1st. Impression

ISBN 978-0-9559751-0-3

Fenriswulf Books
C/o Dubton Farm Flat
Brechin
Angus
Scotland
DD9 6RA

info@fenriswulf-books.co.uk

www.fenriswulf-books.co.uk

Chaz Wood was born in 1973 and currently writes for a living, though not the kind of material he would prefer. His day job involves responding to technical queries via email for one of the UK's biggest supplier of Broadband internet services, and 'Maranatha' was partly composed and edited during lunch breaks on quiet back shifts.

In 2000, after 6 years studying graphic arts and media, he released a self-published comic 'Yokelore', which re-told Celtic fairy tales and myths for a teenage audience.

In early 2005 he published a four-part graphic novel 'The Black Flag' through Brigid's Hearth, Idaho, a cottage industry press. The books retell an ancient Irish myth cycle, set in a darkly futuristic but very recognizable Britain.

'Maranatha' is his first published full-length work of prose, and brings together many of his personal interests; the development of the Western Church, esoteric mysticism and medieval history.

Mr. Wood currently resides in the heartland of Scotland, rural Angus.

MARANATHA

The First Book of the Trinity Chronicles

C. Wood

Illustrations

She was a sad, miserable bitch, and she looked it.   Page 14

"Let's just say you may have woken me out of a silly little daydream."   Page 61

Khalamanga tried hard to focus his mind and form a practical opinion...   Page 120

"...a dweller in the underground, unseen, but always under your feet, listening and watching in the darkness."   Page 164

...a human canvas painted in red, white and black...   Page 201

MARANATHA

(Aramaic, *māran athā*) *"Our Lord cometh…"*

"But one of the soldiers with a spear pierced His side, and forthwith came there out blood and water..."

(John, 19:34)

OVERTURE

The streets of Zvornik lay broken, the black outlines of buildings mere cutouts against a grubby smudge of sky. The bombs, the shooting and the screams had all subsided to the still of the grave. Only the dead remained to see the pale grey morning and all 100,000 acres of this Hell.

The silence was broken by a regular rhythm; steel ringing against stone, the scene given movement by a tall figure striding. His dress was black, from beret to boots. Leather gloves slid an expensive foreign cigarette from a breast pocket filled with trophies and lit it with an American lighter as Captain Gavrilo Silajdzic snaked his way through the remains of the old City of the Bell Tower. The smoke of undying fires merged with mist which crept over the River Drina and veiled the tops of the tallest buildings which huddled together like homeless children. The beauty of the mountains and the river valley was blackened, all nature banished. He saw no evidence of any historic towers now as he turned a corner, nor would he have cared if he had, for ahead of him lay his final destination, the end of his six-day journey from Sarajevo.

The Church of St. George crouched at the end of the road, its half-open doors revealing blackness beyond, but still the most welcoming sight he had seen that past week. As he entered, he brought shafts of cold daylight with him to stimulate sounds of life inside, the first he had heard all day. Patches of blotchy skin shuddered beneath ragged shawls and blankets, mumbling sorrow. *Peasants.* Unpleasant, pestilent.

Crouched in front of the altar was a tattered vestige of a human being, grey-bearded, muttering prayers into the scabrous remains of his hands.

"Milan?" Silajdzic asked. And again, louder.

The priest looked up from his fingers to the figure which cast its shadow upon him. "Who's asking?"

Silajdzic stepped aside into a pool of light and drew a five-pointed star in the air with his left hand. Milan found his feet and hugged the other man like a brother. "Oh, you've come. Thank God. A terrible time we've had of it but somehow, the Church still stands. I see it as a sign from God. It's the only reason I'm still here."

"For divine protection?" Silajdzic surmised with a laugh.

"Yes, exactly." Flustered with excitement now, Milan began rummaging through bags and bundles beside the altar. "I have it here." He produced an old leather holdall and removed a tight gathering of rags from within, about two feet long and bound up with string. "Men died getting this out of Montenegro. Take it to our people, help them bring victory and peace in God's name." Silajdzic took the gift and began to pull away the bindings, but Milan's knotted fingers intruded. "No. Don't show it. Just get it out of here, to our brothers, as fast as you can."

Silajdzic spared the other man a defiant glance as he continued to pull the object into general view. "Just a brief confirmation. Is that permitted?"

The priest was outraged. "You think I'd deceive you? We're all in this together, aren't we?"

"This *is* a war, Father. Besides, Father Rattus said no-one can be trusted."

Milan's voice hardened. "Well, I don't trust that English Rat either. He has knowledge he won't share, and feeds us scraps like the hobo's dog whenever he sees fit."

"He is a man of God, I understand. Like yourself." He finished uncovering the prize and held it up. It was a strange item; a metal spearhead over twenty inches long, enveloped in sheaths of gold and bound with wire, with a vertical slot which held an iron nail.

Satisfied, Silajdzic bound it back up and slid it into his backpack. "Thank you. Hope that losing possession of this doesn't bring disaster upon your Church." The thought carved Milan's face with furrows of concern. "Don't worry, Father. I promise you, the Holy Spear will be in good hands."

As he went to leave, Silajdzic heard a sharp breath pierce the air behind him.

"Your uniform...you're SDG. Who - why are you - working for *them*?"

Silajdzic turned, a deep snarl pulling his face into angular chiaroscuro.

"In times of war, one must make hard decisions. If you don't like the idea of that, Brother – *Father* - then you shouldn't be here."

"Well I don't like the idea of Zeljko Arkan holding that spear, and his fascists seizing victory."

"*Mors stupebit et natura, cum resurget creatura*, Father. These are dark days for us all. And Commander Arkan doesn't hold the spear, *I* do. Anything else you want to add, or are you finished trashing my leader and my comrades?"

Fear painted Milan's complexion. Silajdzic's quotation from the Dies Irae - the Latin hymn describing the Day of Judgment - had struck a discord within him. The *diabolos* had entered the *musica* of Milan's hope, for there was no denying that death had struck, and all nature shaken - mostly thanks to Arkan's SDG.

"Tell me – truthfully, Brother – that you are faithful to us. Tell me I am doing the right thing here."

"I know what is right, for I know what my people have suffered over the last thousand years. Slaughtered by Turks as they fought for their freedom. Massacred and burned at Montsegur, raped and enslaved by Stefan Nemanja."

"They were heretics – Cathars, Bogomils –"

"They were my *ancestors*. And now you, who I do not see leading anyone, or raising a gun in defence, tell me that I am wrong to fight for *my* country, my beliefs, and to avenge all that blood spilt by Papal decrees and Muslim scimitars?"

"I didn't say you were wrong." Milan argued.

"Five hundred years ago, we could have ruled Bulgaria without any Roman clerics vomiting lies from their pulpits. For they would have been on their knees, crying to their God and to Satanial." Spots of spittle, trailing his words of fury, landed across the priest's forehead. "All *your* kind."

"What are you saying?" Milan choked on his despair, his realisation wringing glistening grief onto his cheeks.

"I'm saying, the Black Sun is rising, Father. But you're not going to live to see him, and nor are your holy brothers going to stop him."

The unseen 9mm semiautomatic spat five rounds through the priest's chest, throat, and stomach, five wounds which formed the points of a five-pointed star, a pentagram or pentangle. Silajdzic thought it an amusing gesture, branding the corpse with the symbol of its own order. His satisfaction was disrupted by cries and groans from the pews.

"What are you doing!" the woman howled, a lacerated soprano rising to the rafters. "Stop it, stop the killing!"

For a second Silajdzic contemplated putting her down where she stood. Then he saw her child, a boy of no more than ten or eleven, follow fearfully in her footsteps.

"Please, don't hurt my boy. Don't hurt him," she begged as her fears washed out her anger. "Do what you will with me, but leave him alone."

He saw her gaze wander downwards, where Milan's blood flowed in five rivers toward the altar. He drew down the headscarf which covered her matted yellow hair, ran his fingers through long wispy strands of soot and dust. She hadn't lived long but hard, and the toils told on her skin and in her eyes, red-rimmed and weeping. The gold crucifix around her neck made him smile; so much for the power of the Lord. He tested her reaction, grabbing her heavy breasts through her shirt, and she closed her eyes in tired resignation. She had suffered this before, and was numb to it now, a deep-throated groan of surrender her only acknowledgement of his frantic actions as he pulled up her dress and bent her over the back of the nearest seat.

The boy stood confused, wondering what the pair of them were doing. He was very afraid of the man in the black uniform and had no wish to anger him. He looked a lot like the men who had shot his father and watched him die screaming, eaten alive by wolves.

A minute later Silajdzic stepped back, wiped her blood off himself using the hem of her skirt and adjusted his clothing.

"Please, leave us be now." Her voice held the reedy undertone of agony barely restrained. She had taught herself not to scream, not to cry, and to save her breath to thank God for continued life.

"I'm not going to touch your son." Silajdzic assured her. "Rather, I want him to grow up knowing how useless his God was at this moment, and force him to ask; where was my saviour, my Christ, when I needed Him? Where was my God? And one day, I hope, he shall learn the truth."

She raised her head from the shadows to look upon her son again, to steal a grain of love from the hand of pain for one moment. The child had advanced nearer, happy to have heard his mother's voice again when something wet and warm slapped him across the face. He wiped at it with his hands while Silajdzic strode past him to the door, sheathing his hunting knife as he went. Just before he stepped into the dusty white chamber of daylight, he turned back to look at the boy, a muddy Breugel orphan beside the corpse of his mother, whose slashed and ruptured throat spewed crimson puddles around his feet. Silajdzic tossed the woman's bloody crucifix onto the bleeding floorboards and laughed aloud, the sounds breaking the peace of the tomb.

"Suffer little children, and forbid them not to come unto me: for of such is the kingdom of heaven, eh, *Father*?"

DAY ONE: Monday

A monotonous sequence of electronic beeps tore through the dreams of Vanessa Descartes at 0830 precisely. She stirred in bed, angry at the intrusion to her fast-receding fancy of kissing Omar Sharif on the steps of the Taj Mahal. She hoped the telephone would ring off quickly, allowing her to rejoin her lover in a few minutes' time, but the caller was in no mood to grant her any mercy on this wet April morning.

With an anger reserved usually only for ex-lovers and aggressive salesmen, she hurled the quilt away and threw herself across the room, almost falling flat in the process as her pyjama bottoms slipped and snagged around her ankles. She had lost a stone and a half in her last three months of self-induced loneliness and hard dieting, daring to hope that her recent drought of romantic interest was due entirely to her being a size 14. Now a slim 9 stone, she was still valiantly holding out for her exotic Middle Eastern adventurer to invite her on board his private yacht, but she was not yet of a mind to hope that this call was from him. She pushed the handset to her head and yawned into it, blatantly broadcasting her weariness.

"Frau Descartes?" A strong local accent prodded her consciousness, crackling in her ear, physically pushing her away from the earpiece.

"Yes."

"Please forgive this intrusion. I was given your number by a mutual associate of ours...."

She didn't feel in a particularly forgiving mood, certainly not to strange men who spoke English with an almost comical German accent. "My name is Weber, assistant to Dr. Steiner, our head curator. I am from the Hofburg Museum, and your colleague, Dr. Michael Reed, assures me you could be of great assistance to us. And, given that you are still here in Vienna, it seemed appropriate to beg your help once more."

She yawned again as she sat down on the floor, unhappy now that it wasn't a crank call, something she could easily hang up on and forget. It sounded serious, urgent. It sounded like work.

She and a small team of researchers had been summoned by Steiner at the beginning of March to carry out extensive tests upon a number of holy relics, to establish if any of them were all they were cracked up to be. The answers had, without exception, been an overwhelming negative, with one tantalizing exception; a particularly famous item from the Hofburg's treasure vault, the so-called Spear of Destiny, the Holy Lance, the Spear of Jesus, which it was said had been the very item to have plunged into the side of the crucified Messiah. *Lancea et clavus domini* proclaimed the engraved blurb on the gold sheath which clothed part of the spearhead, and the 7-inch crucifixion nail, alleged to be from the Cross, which was set within the upper third of the object.

Vanessa's preliminary results on the nail had more or less discredited the likelihood of such an audacious claim, but the intriguing fact remained that, merged with the nail, were fragments of a possibly much earlier example. Steiner had banned all further investigation as if to preserve this last shred of mystique and keep the credulous crowding into his treasure vault. For Vanessa, that had been the most frustrating part of the investigation. Coming from a forensic background, her secret hope had been to analyse the shards of the ancient nail for traces of 1st Century DNA or blood, a prospect so controversial that it was almost destined to be denied.

Publicly, she respected Steiner's wishes and the need to maintain a level of mystery about matters of religious significance; as an irreligious scientist, privately she had railed against his lack of courage. Dr. Reed, the head of the operation, agreed with her sentiments and recalled the rest of his team the day the Holy Spear was locked safely back up in the Hofburg's Schatzkammer or treasury to be presented once more to public view. She had remained in Vienna, nestled in her Holiday Inn apartment in the Margaretenstrasse, appreciative of the cultured city itself if not the attitudes of custodians of priceless treasures. It was an alien species she was living amongst, a race of walking cut-outs from fashion and beauty magazines. Within days of her arrival, she had learned to spot the tourists at a hundred metres – and even they seemed to dress better than most people she knew back home.

She saw no tracksuits being worn by squads of shuffling, cursing, smoking young men, no dirty old trainers. Women didn't squeeze themselves into ripped jeans three sizes too small in Vienna, nor flaunt their stretch marks and their offensive lack of personal grooming. Only in dirty common Manchester, and Britain in general, had she seen such squalid sights, and as she thought about it in that dark, half-awake moment of the morning, she realised that over the past month she had almost forgotten what a chav looked like.

"My help..? So it's something important?"

"Yes. Around midnight last night, someone broke into the Hofburg and destroyed one of our most valued exhibits. Have you seen the news?"

Vanessa shook the dust and drowse from her head, trying to understand the hard-edged words.

"No, I haven't. Why, which exhibit?"

"The Holy Lance. The very Spear of Jesus you are so familiar with."

She groaned aloud. The results of her work on the spear were still something of a sore point. She had seen her efforts praised in scientific journals and insulted in 'fringe' magazines, occult web forums, and other media which refused to accept the empirical truth over what they had already decided were the facts. Before the work began, Vanessa had held a particular view on the item. Fashioned by pagan hands probably during the lifetime of Christ, dedicated by its cursing blacksmith to Mars or Victoria or possibly no god at all, yet its point was thrust by the hand of a common legionary into the side of God Himself, in flesh incarnate and the saviour of Man. She was not overly disappointed to learn the truth, though Steiner certainly was. The Stone-man had crumbled in the face of her facts, which were harder and colder than he had ever expected. And now here was his colleague, begging her assistance on his behalf once more, pushing her for another commitment:

"Frau Descartes...?"

"I'm sorry to hear that." If the spear had been damaged beyond repair, she didn't understand what possible use she could be. She was a metallurgist, not a blacksmith. "But to be honest, sir - I didn't enjoy my time working on that artefact. The thing has haunted my dreams ever since and I really wish I had never accepted the job in the first place. No offence intended." Despite the unlimited attractions of Vienna and all it had to offer, she had been looking forward to returning home soon, to getting away from narrow-mindedness and controversy and be around familiar things, even chavs.

Weber hesitated, wondering how to continue. "I assure you, your involvement will be very brief. You'll be paid at the full rate, if you could come along to the museum this morning and assist the police with their enquiries. For our sake as well as theirs - our Director is keen to have this matter resolved."

"Is that it? I'm not trying to be funny, but-"

"Well...you see...when I say 'destroyed', I mean - pulled to pieces, the spear has been. It is very bizarre, but the circumstances have made it rather difficult to be sure. That is why I wanted you to come down and recreate the spear." He paused. "Please don't be offended, Frau Descartes. This call is only because I trust your hand. If you do not wish to participate further, then we will accept your decision graciously and not bother you again."

Vanessa gulped. She felt honoured and embarrassed at the same time, yet annoyed that she was not being required for any greater work than the collecting and cataloguing of pieces of metal. But the tone of Weber's voice suggested another agenda at work, an unspoken motive.

She tried to be as blunt as possible. "So what are these 'circumstances' ?"

"The problem – ah, you see – the spear was found in the middle of a crime scene. One of our security guards is missing. We can't assume as yet it is he who is responsible, but the police are investigating the connection nonetheless."

She sank back with a sense of relief at having finally forced the facts out of him. A missing man was unfortunate, but unlikely to mess with her head. There would be no blood, no forensic investigation or morbid photographs to examine, no human entrails to be scraped into evidence bags. No problem.

"Alright, Mr. Weber. Give me a couple of hours."

"Thank you, Frau Descartes. Thank you so very much for your help, we fully appreciate it."

She hung up and stomped off to the bathroom where she stood and gawked at herself in the mirror, a crack in the glass severing her head from her neck at a strange angle. She peered closer, pulling down an eyelid, sticking out her tongue, ruffling the tousled mass of Titian hair which looked more dirt-brown in the pale light. It had been a bad night again, her old fears having nibbled and gnawed at her until the grimy dawn crept around the edges of the curtains.

She was a sad, miserable bitch, and she looked it.

She had stood on the brink of oblivion more than once in her life but had always managed to crawl back from the abyss. This was why she was single, she realised. Not because she had a saggy arse or didn't burn off enough calories every day, but because her outer personality was being warped by her own endless reflections on a childhood brought to an abrupt halt by the sight of the family bath filled with the blood of her beloved Francesca.

She was a mess, and she knew it.

What a hot shower and scrub couldn't remove, the contents of her makeup bag would just have to cover up, as always. She couldn't face the idea of going back out into that beautiful city of beautiful people looking like one of the Great British slobs she so despised. She would have to make the effort, kid herself on that she looked wonderful, until she returned to Manchester and the land of ripped jeans and trainers. Soon, she would be on that 'plane back home, and it would be goodnight, Vienna.

For Professor Tomas Emilio Baltasar Bartolomé de Carranza, the Austrian capital would soon present a very different appeal. He sat alone in the History department staffroom, shovelling his way through a heap of examination papers with the zeal of a man looking for a penny in a cowpat. He was a writer, he reminded himself; one of some international importance in the field of Biblical scholarship if the magazines, newspapers and internet discussion boards were to be believed. He had collaborated on restoration work on the Nag Hammadi gospels, had assisted Dr. Geza Vermes with translations of the Dead Sea Scrolls, and had long since seen the market for learned speculative journalism on such subjects.

It had seemed strange to him, how as the Western world's faith had eroded, so its desire for alternatives had arisen to fill the void. Since the days of the 'God was an alien astronaut' craze in the '60s, he had understood the public's need to know that there was something beyond their grey, grinding existence. And he had given it to them, in four increasingly-bestselling works which covered the possible truth behind the city of Jericho; the 'reality' behind the Christmas story and how Herod had been dead before Christ had been born; and his own re-enactment of the Book of Exodus in which he described his two-month trek under desert sun in the footsteps of the Tribe of Judah. The fourth title, 'Who Was Jesus?' had entered the Spanish bestseller list four weeks ago at the number 2 spot (a bit of news which made de Carranza feel like something of a pop star), and confirmed his appeal as a local celebrity among the students, the housewives, the seekers of strangeness. Autographs had become a regular occurrence on his public outings, and it had been the bright idea of his personal secretary to secure him a series of high-profile book signings across Europe, culminating with a trip to Paris on Easter Sunday in six days' time.

He was a writer and an historian, he reminded himself again; with a busy schedule of travel, appearances and interviews to face in the coming week. He was a scholar, and yet he was spending this Monday of Holy Week reading through other people's rambling, self-important dissertations on the book of Exodus. He should have been drinking wine and smiling with glamorous women and old but very influential men in exciting European cities, not pursuing some idealistic notion of education for ungrateful upper-middle class boys who had nothing better to do with their time.

The chair creaked as he leaned back against thickly-painted brick walls that had once borne graffiti scrawled during the civil war, mocking Franco and promoting the ideals of liberty and brotherhood from the days when battles were fought on that very campus and University buildings were contested like castles. The bullet holes and slogans, the stains of history, had long since been erased from the sight of the staff. But for de Carranza, who had lived the best years of his life under dictatorship, memories proved much harder to paint over. He had known friends from his own university days, men and women more outspoken and radical than he, who had suffered under the state, and who paid for their protests with their liberty or with their lives.

A timid knock on the door went unheard.

"Professor?"

Even the voice of his devoted secretary failed to stir him. He had examined over half of his second year class's mid-term papers and failed all of them so far. Nobody had understood the question he had set them, nobody had done the research, and several had blatantly copied the answers from each other. He was beginning to despair for the future of Spanish youth.

Pablo Sandoval sidestepped into the room and tried to attract the older man's attention.

"Professor. You...er, you're due in class."

"I'm a what?"

"Your class, Professor. You're already five minutes late."

"Late?" the word was spat back at Pablo like a cherry stone. "I am never *late*. I am 'unfortunately delayed'. That's what you always tell them, Pablo. Whether it's the journalists, the agencies, or the editors, de Carranza does not keep people waiting."

"I know, but this is your second year class-"

The head of the Ancient History department stood up and cast the pile of unmarked papers onto the floor. Though not tall, he had long since learned to compensate with the swagger of a perpetual drunkard, tempered with the bluster of a man who had fought for everything he had achieved, and jealously guarded those victories with the passion of a she-wolf protecting her cubs. For good reason was he known to the teaching and administrative staff as '*Perro de pelea*'.

"No, Pablo. This is my second-rate *donkeys*. I spend half my weekend reading their drivel. They insult me, they insult themselves with their laziness." He gestured dramatically to the scattered sheaves of paper at his feet. "This is fit for compost, yet they expect it to allow them passage to a third year under my tutelage. Had I pinned my hopes of an academic career upon work such as this, I would be cleaning your streets by now, Pablo. Possibly your toilet. So I will keep them waiting; they don't deserve my time."

He strode to the coffee table where a drink began to be brewed, sin-black and bitter. The echoes of his anger having subsided into the bubbling of boiling water, de Carranza's voice again rose to fill the small room.

"You seem miserable, Pablo. Why? Real Madrid didn't lose at the weekend; Ronaldo saw to that. His 100th goal so I heard, according to the fans outside my apartment who decided to inform me of the fact at 3am."

"I know, Professor. But I heard strange news on the radio this morning. It made my mother weep. Somebody has desecrated the Spear of Destiny. The most priceless relic of Christendom. What is wrong with people? I fear for the world sometimes, the things I hear."

For the first time during their conversation, de Carranza's sweeping stare connected with his secretary and narrowed sharply upon him, as if he were delivering more plagiarised exam papers. Pablo Sandoval was a man in his mid 30s who still lived with his mother. She doted on him, and Pablo in turn spent most of his time doting on de Carranza. He loved Jesus with slightly more passion than *los Galacticos* of the local soccer squad, and the passion with which he spoke of his Lord and the eleven white-shirted disciples drove de Carranza to distraction, for he spoke of little else.

"Desecrated? Unlikely, as no *consecration* ever occurred in the first place. Medieval relics, Pablo, this one like every other – fakes to fool the faithful, and fuel faith. Don't be taken in."

But Pablo wasn't listening, pointing and babbling instead. "Here it comes now. On the television. Look."

de Carranza faced the TV screen as instructed to see panoramic views of Vienna, followed by a close-up of the Hofburg museum as explanatory subtitles scrolled across the screen. He skimmed the text, frowned at the burly, blond-haired detective who mouthed silently into the camera. Something in the man's manner, in his Teutonic bearing, made de Carranza think briefly of the Aryan supermen who had ravaged Europe in his father's day, and whom he had been warned as a boy would one day rise again.

"So someone is dead. A man has been killed – murdered - over this thing, this piece of metal, that was never near Christ or the Holy Land in its life."

Pablo turned away. "He would never have wanted any of this."

"Who?" de Carranza stooped to collect the scattered examination papers.

"Our *Lord*, Professor. What does any of this have to do with His simple teachings?"

de Carranza crushed the papers back into their binder. "That, Pablo, is something I've been asking myself for 30 years now." Walking to the door of the staffroom, he added; "And no doubt I'll continue asking it, until the day I meet Him."

Despite her heart's every wish, Vanessa found herself dressed, groomed and hurrying across the Michaelerplatz toward the Hofburg Museum by 11am that morning. The rain had cleared up and the tourists had come out with the sun, bringing their animals, their undisciplined children and their loud-mouthed ancestors with them. Having pushed her way up the endless heaving highways of human traffic and tripping over skittish, scuttling Dachshunds, she was finally met at the great Swiss Door by a horse-faced and balding man whose baggy suit suggested he had recently been the victim of sudden weight loss.

Built in 1552, the grand archway led them through to the Schatzkammer or state Treasury of the Hapsburg empire, but there was nothing grand about the sight which faced them across the pale desert of the Schweizer Hof courtyard. Half a dozen uniformed officers guarded the entry doors, keeping tourists at bay with shoulder-slung Heckler & Koch MP5s. Whatever else the Austrian police were, they had certainly come prepared.

"Thank you again," Weber greeted her urgently, a brusque handshake ending their re-introduction. "We fully appreciate your assistance, Frau Descartes."

Something about that manner of address irked her. Perhaps its association with *hausfrau*s and the image of fat German women cooking cabbage, or its suggestion of the ridiculous notion that she may conceivably be married. She ran a hand through her hair, reassured by the unyielding dryness of the hairspray that she didn't look a complete mess, and smiled despite her inner feelings. Weber was acknowledged by the policemen at the doors with a nod and the pair of them entered, their footsteps adding resonance to the soundtrack of urgent activity within the vaulted hall.

"No problem. Where's Dr. Steiner?" she had expected the head curator to have made his ominous presence felt by now.

"He is working in Italy at the moment, recording a television programme about the Spear. Very unfortunate timing. He will be on his way back soon."

With any luck, she hoped, her job would be done by that time. It might also be the perfect opportunity to motivate herself into getting out of Austria. That perverse twist in her soul was still longing for foul-mouthed taxi drivers, half pints of Boddingtons and fish and chips.

"By the way, why the guns outside? What do they think this is, bloody 'Die Hard'?"

"Outrageous, isn't it. But the police insist that this event may only be one of a series of similar planned actions. They're certainly prepared for the possibility."

"To do what, shoot holes through the first person they think looks like a burglar?"

"This way," Weber urged her, turning toward a densely-carpeted exhibition room off the main hall, an all-too familiar scene to her. As she followed the thin man in the rustling jacket, the display room announced the scale of the operation in which she was now enveloped; *consumed* by it, like Weber, lost within his suit. A dozen uniforms and several more plain clothes mingled and murmured in the middle of the hall, illuminated in bursts of white from crime scene camera flashguns, figures and faces folding across the glass angles of display cases as they conducted crucial business.

"What the hell is going on here?"

"The pieces have not been touched; left just as they were found." Weber pointed generally to the floor of the inner Treasury. "We hope you find them all intact."

As they approached, Vanessa's attention shifted from the scattered parts of the Holy Spear to a commotion of some kind at the other end of the Treasury. Two officers hurried through the central path between rows of exhibits, furtively carrying a sealed plastic bag between them. She knew what homicide evidence bags looked like, and her heart tightened.

"Any news on your missing guard yet, Mr. Weber?"

"Well...I'd rather not say. It's all quite dreadful, but none of it makes any sense yet. Er-" he extended a shaking hand toward a tall, broad man who had just appeared behind them. "Let me turn you over now to Kommissar Wilhelm Petersen. I have some things to attend to." With that, Weber turned and fled the scene, as rapidly as a man could without actually running.

She watched him go before turning to look up at the man with the centre-parted fair hair and impressively chiselled jawline. A day or two's growth of beard showed that he had found even less time for sleep and grooming than she. His shirt collar was askew, a button was missing from the middle and spots of spilled coffee dotted his cuff. Despite all that, her first impression was that if he pulled on a peaked cap he'd look ready to invade Poland.

"So what hasn't he told me?" She was already expecting the worst. If that little rat Weber had told Petersen of her past career in forensics, she would personally remove his testicles with her bare hands. There was no way she was going back to that kind of work, not a chance in hell. "Who's dead, and how?"

The trenchcoated Norseman jerked a thumb behind him. "His missing security guard's turned up. Cleaning women in the Chapel next door discovered his severed head sitting on a silver dish this morning. The Rektor's having hysterics. The Wien Boys' Choir probably won't be singing today, unfortunately."

Her old fears began to recede in the face of reason. There would already be a pathologist assigned to this case; after all, Vienna must have dozens of people better-qualified than she to investigate a gruesome decapitation. Weber, she decided, would probably be able to keep his chances of extending his family after all.

"Severed...head." she repeated slowly, making certain she understood.

"Yes. Caused by a heavy and sharp implement. Clean stroke. Still haven't found the rest of the body or the murder weapon, but we're assuming it's somewhere on the premises. Wherever it was carried out, there would have been a lot of blood, but a few drops in the vicinity of the Holy Spear display case is all we have so far."

"Head on a plate. Like John the Baptist?"

Petersen nodded. "Very elaborate for treasure thieves."

"Any clues?"

"None. The whole situation is chaotic. Strange details, such as the wristwatch: it was found stuffed in his mouth and shows a time of twenty-five to six. For some reason, the killer wants us to note that particular time. But it has no significance that we can see, as yet."

"Maybe they want you to take note of 1735 tonight?"

"Possibly. We have men on standby across the city at other museums, in case something similar happens there. Interesting you mentioned the Baptist as well. We've checked out possible Biblical references - chapter 5, verse 35 perhaps - but there is nothing there either. The victim was 50-year old Josef Siegel. Pretty unremarkable character. Not married, member of the local church of St. Michael's. Came into this job with impeccable references. That's all we've got on him at the moment. The way this scene has been arranged shows considerable planning. There is an answer here, if we knew how to read it...but we don't, yet. So our immediate hope is to pull something from the spear itself."

Vanessa sucked her lower lip between her teeth, making little squeaking sounds as she contemplated the mess Weber had gotten her into. "Ah. And that's where I come in, eh."

"Yes. Mr. Weber preferred to allow you to supervise that. Given the unique and sensitive nature of the artefact, and the fact you are so familiar with it."

"Kommissar, a man has been killed and hacked up - we shouldn't be holding back the investigation for the sake of the sensibilities of a few devout Catholics." Petersen looked uncomfortable for the first time since their meeting. Discussing the details of a murder was one thing - personal beliefs was obviously quite different. "I'm sorry," she floundered, her cheeks betraying her embarrassment. "I didn't mean...are you religious at all?"

"I enjoy the pageantry." He allowed the first shadow of a smile to cross his tight mouth. "And the wine." After another uncomfortable moment of silence, he led her to the pieces of the spear. "Here. We'll allow you time to gather the parts."

But Vanessa's attention was arrested by an altogether different form of dismemberment. "Is that the blood?" she asked, guessing something in the region of half a cupful had been dripped across the floor in five large blotches, half a metre or so away from the display case. The glass had been penetrated with some kind of industrial cutting instrument, leaving a neat round hole the size of a saucer.

Petersen nodded. "We thought at first someone had lacerated themselves on the glass of the case when it was cut open, but there's no blood near enough to suggest that. And as I said, not enough to be from the decapitation either. Looking at the pattern, it's been let out slowly and deliberately - no arterial spray, nothing to suggest any violent wounding." He saw her looking away, registered her growing discomfort. "Anyway. I'll send you an analyst to assist with the dusting."

"I can do that myself." She began to pull on a fresh pair of cotton gloves. "I spent eighteen months in criminal forensic investigation in England. As I'm quite sure Mr. Weber has already informed you."

One day, she told herself, she hoped to lose that big rotting albatross which hung around her neck. It was something she had thought about erasing from her CV for years now, and she resolved to do just that as soon as she returned home. If it meant that she would end her days working behind the delicatessen counter in Asda's, then so be it. As long as she wasn't squeezing anti-depressants down her gullet three times a day.

Petersen shrugged awkwardly. "Well..." he began, gave up.

"Never mind." she pointed to the half-dozen security cameras covering the part of the hall they stood in. "Have these recorded anything worthwhile?"

Petersen looked down at the floor, unhappily studying the lack of polish on his shoes. "The tapes the cameras record onto are the responsibility of the guard on duty in this area. That, unfortunately, happened to be Mr. Siegel."

"So, they're all blank then?"

"No, they have recorded okay, up until 2355, when they run out. Siegel did not replace the tapes at that time, maybe because he heard the intruders and went to investigate, and forgot about them. I have sent the tapes to be digitally analysed in case there is something hidden on them that we've missed, so it's in the hands of the experts now." Petersen pocketed his hands and glanced urgently towards the exit. "Look, if you need anything - staff, supplies - call me. I'm going out for a cigarette. This place is starting to get on my nerves."

She allowed herself the luxury of a smile as she removed the parts into folded pieces of protective fabric. She knew exactly how he felt.

The legend behind the spear at the Hofburg was a colourful one indeed. Said to be owned by a blind Roman legionary named Longinus, whose name would later be inscribed on the weapon, the business end found its way into the side of *Iesus Nazarenus, Rex Iudaeorum* and the resulting flow of holy blood across the pagan's face cured his blindness instantly.

Following its use to test whether the crucified Messiah was alive or not, the long man's *lancea* was enshrined in the Holy Land for 300 years, so they said. After the death of Christ and the birth of his new faith, the first Emperor of Rome to adopt that faith obtained the weapon, brought back from Judea by his mother Helen, whose pious act of souvenir-collecting would later see her canonized. Constantine the Great used the spear to mark the boundary of his territory and for as long as he carried it he laid waste to his pagan enemies, and the Roman empire became Wholly Christian, as it would later become Holy Roman, the First Reich, under its First Emperor Charles the Magnificent, and subsequent holder of the spear. Napoleon, destroyer of the Holy Roman Empire, had sought it but was denied that one piece of the old Imperial crown jewels, and it came down to Adolf Hitler to succeed where Bonaparte had failed; to hold the Holy Spear, albeit for little more than a decade.

Yet after two millennia of gloss and glory, it came down to a small group of modern-day iconoclasts in the third month of 2006 to wipe away the colour and tear up the legends. St. Helena had not recovered the treasure for her son; no blind Roman had ever stabbed the side of the Son of God, at least, not with that particular artefact. And even after the public disclosure of her team's research into that fact, the faithful still shuffled excitedly through the halls of the Hofburg, to gawp at the wonder that was the Spear of Destiny. That is, until that morning.

Vanessa walked briskly down the corridors of the laboratory she had virtually lived in for two weeks during March. She was chased all the way by the assistant curator of the Hofburg Treasury who clung to her every step, like one of the annoying little Dachshunds she so dearly longed to kick out of her path, his wide black suit swishing around him with a will of its own.

"The full facilities are once again at your disposal," he assured her as they approached the doors of Lab 9. "We need you to make a full examination of the components. I believe a part may have been substituted with a forgery of some sort, hence the dismemberment of the piece. We're looking for a complete test of authenticity."

Vanessa was still at a loss. "What makes you think they would substitute a piece of the spear? I would have thought it more likely they were looking for something. The crucifixion nail, for example, which could only be got at by stripping the wire wrapped around it?"

"I know. I thought that too. But there was a nail found out there, wasn't there?"

"We found *a* nail. Whether it is *the* nail...we'll soon know, won't we?"

They stopped at the doors of the laboratory and Weber swiped his security pass, allowing them to enter. His hand slapped down on a panel of light switches and a trinity of overhead strip-lights buzzed into life.

"Very soon, I hope. Dr. Steiner called from Milan earlier. He is very anxious we get this issue resolved."

"Which issue?" Vanessa asked, surprising herself with the hard edge she heard in her voice. "The problem of the broken spear, or the very inconvenient beheading of one of your employees? I can help with the first. But the second problem is, I'm afraid, in the hands of Mr. Petersen." she stepped into the lab, inhaling the dry, clinical smell of the room. She placed the steel case on the nearest workbench and removed the lint wrappings held within. "*Thank you*, Mr. Weber." She stretched a stare back at the man who shared his name with the SI unit of magnetic flux, and who had already brought such unrest into her own repellent existence. But he lingered, unwanted, waiting for her to begin her duties, and once again she found herself dancing to the demands of bald Austrian men for money. She felt nauseated for a second, as much as if she was about to lift her skirt and spread her legs for him.

Soon the whole business would be over and she'd be back home before she knew it, with a few bottles of wine and a video of 'Dr. Zhivago' to look forward to.

Doctor Emanuel Wole Khalamanga passed through the Oxford University parks at a sedate jogger's pace. The rush hour had subsided, the swarms of cyclists and Labrador-walkers now thinned out to a few individual strays, and the occasional groundsman or park curator. He rounded the corner of Napper's Arable to be welcomed by the roof of the cricket pavilion rise between the treetops; familiar sights from years of having run these same paths, and yet they never bored him.

He knew when to expect to see the men of Keble playing cricket in the field which lay in front of him, where shrubs and saplings poked their heads above the fence like nosey children. He knew to within a few days when the daffodils would be opening up along the verges of Thorn Walk, the tree-lined avenue which bisected the parks from North to South with its handsome pines and yews, twin symbols of death and immortality.

And on this run, his first for over a month, they were as they always had been over the past three decades, happily reassuring him that for all the twists and turns of life and history, there were at least some things which remained. Like the English Springtime weather; Khalamanga could feel rain in the air now, and he lengthened his already considerable stride to avoid another soaking like last time. The sky was barely grey but he knew it would be changing soon, unlike the great numbers of persons he passed earlier in their short-sleeved shirts, cotton dresses or t-shirts, oblivious to the threat.

He had been good at athletics at school and regularly featured in regional cross-country competitions, never winning but often coming a close second or third. Even now, in his fiftieth year, it was something he liked to keep up simply for the chance to exercise his body rather than his mind for a change. It was strange how one of the few times in his life Khalamanga had seemed to conform to any sort of fad or fashion was in the early 1980s when jogging became suddenly popular, and he who had regularly entertained the habit since the late 1960s found himself among panting, red-faced businessmen and housewives who had never run the length of themselves in their lives, all struggling to look smart in their designer tracksuits and colour-coordinated Walkmans. He had never dressed to look the part, preferring instead a loose sweater from his days in the Jesus College Cross-Country Club, and white slacks which inevitably arrived home soaked in mud, sprayed with water and smeared with the stains of the undergrowth. It was a testament to Khalamanga's persistence that the whites were laundered at once and painstakingly attended to afterwards with stain removers, if required.

The new gateway onto Parks Road welcomed him and saw him moving back in the direction of the city now, the sound of traffic pushing against the background of birdsong. People, in groups and in pairs, mainly students, emerged into view, converging upon him. He swerved and dodged them at every turn, dancing on and off the pavement to keep his rhythm up. Belligerent clouds soared into view overhead, forcing him into a sprint for the final leg. It was less than a quarter of a mile to the house on Crick Road, a large detached affair spread over three floors of Victorian grandeur and rather excessive for a single man with Khalamanga's tastes.

His familiar red brick walls and apple trees swung into view as he loped off Bradmore Road and just as he reached the door, a swollen cloud overhead burst with noise, the primal wrath of God. Khalamanga sensed the thunder before he heard it, and as the door banged shut behind him a shower of rain lashed down across the centre of Oxford. A rainstorm that would last for the next seven days.

He stripped out of his running clothes and added them to the laundry basket in the hall. There was enough of a wind to be heard through the double-glazed windows of the living room. He closed the curtains on the deluge, orange and green chequered nylon relics from his first student flat in 1975, the year he met his first and only girlfriend, during a field trip with his class to the holy Externsteine stones in Germany. Women had never featured in his life since, though often his family would make jokes that he hurry up and 'do his bit' to keep the bloodline going strong.

Though the curtains looked like an old tablecloth cut in half, they served their purpose and Khalamanga had never seen any cause to replace them. He didn't understand the concepts of fashion, trends, or even taste in furnishings and interior design; he had kept them for their warm colours which reminded him both of his native

Nigeria and the exciting days of his early University life. The green had originally been much nearer the colour of the Nigerian national flag, and over the years he had come to accept their fading vibrancy in the same way as the memories of his home city of Enugu. He remembered impressions, sensations, feelings of warmth from both family and sun, feelings he still longed for and wished he could return to. Perhaps he would, one day soon.

But first, he allowed himself a few minutes of complete inactivity in front of the television news before returning to his chores and thereafter, his studies, his research, the papers and words which filled his life and his thoughts.

The international news was coming to an end, the final report concerning some holy artefact in Vienna. He grabbed several key phrases of interest: *"...pieces of the priceless artefact scattered in an act of seemingly random vandalism...police have no leads...severed head of a missing security man has been discovered in the Chapel, but as yet no body...investigations are continuing..."*

By the time the news had finished, he had already convinced himself of dark and arcane motivations behind the terrible events. The symbols were too suggestive to ignore.

He telephoned the international operator and, through the next twenty minutes of sitting on hold and being transferred from one line to another, found himself invoking every shred of the saintly patience his friends and family had often said he had been blessed with.

"*Wien Kriminalpolizei, Mordkommission.*" a brusque native voice shook him out of his dreamy morning warmth.

"Ah....bitte, sprechen sie englisch?" Khalamanga stammered, feeling suddenly foolish and very out of his depth.

"Excuse, please."

There was background talk, noise and movement, the phone was passed to somebody else.

"Wilhelm Petersen." Another voice announced, sounding stressed and impatient.

Khalamanga swallowed hard. "Good morning to you, sir. Please forgive my contacting you like this, but I've just seen the report of the crime at the Hofburg museum-"

"Who are you, sir? English?"

"Excuse me. I'm Emanuel Khalamanga, Doctor of Medieval Literature from Oxford University. I have spent a lifetime working with medieval manuscripts concerning alchemy, the Holy Grail and other mystical traditions."

There was a pause as Petersen waited for him to get to the point. "How can I help you, Herr Doktor?"

"I was hoping I could rather help *you*. The news stated you had no leads."

A deep sigh travelled down the line from Vienna to Oxford, suggesting that help from a Holy Grail enthusiast was about as welcome as a dose of herpes. "No, Herr Doktor, we have no leads at this moment but we are, I assure you, looking into it. Was there anything else?"

"Only that I believe this matter may have a deeply symbolic context. The concept of dismemberment is common to stories featuring the Grail, which is also closely associated with the Spear of Longinus. To me, the significance of the artefact and the bizarre and gruesome method of murder may well be connected."

"The body has not yet been discovered. What makes you think this was done by people with interest in such matters?"

"I can't rightly say, sir. I have this feeling..." Khalamanga now realised how ridiculous he was sounding, and decided to bring an end to his ill-considered attempt to seek a new direction in his life. Perhaps, he thought, it really was time for a holiday. He looked down at the scribbled notes he had made earlier, seeing now only wild conclusions drawn from the vaguest of facts, and crushed them up into a ball. "Look, I'm sorry to have wasted your time. If you find anything, call me on this number..."

He heard Petersen scratching with a pen at the other end. At least the detective was not dismissing him out of hand.

"Well thank you for your concern, Herr Doktor. If any new developments come up, I shall have someone call you."

"Good luck." And with that, Khalamanga hung up. There would be no more developments, no-one would call him, the murder would remain unsolved and the case put down to a maniac of indeterminate nature. Petersen would move on to his next case; drugs or street crime, and the whole matter would be dropped and filed away in a vault somewhere, Khalamanga's name and home telephone number a mere footnote to an obscure, motiveless crime.

He considered his next move. Physically tired and now mentally drained as well, he resolved to go to bed for a few hours and sleep off the disappointment and embarrassment of the morning's brief adventure. And as he trudged up the stairs, his grass-stained trousers and damp sweater lay forgotten in the hall.

While Khalamanga snored through the afternoon, for Vanessa, the time flew by in a hazy blur of examination, finally free from the lurker until her work was done. Weber now hovered like a baggy vulture, desperate to pounce upon any scrap of news that his beloved spear was genuine and entire, and bit by bit this was proved to be the case. The iron wings, the gold sheath, the silver sheath bearing the dedication to St. Maurice, the wire, all turned out to be genuine.

"And what about the spearhead?" he begged, desperate to be told the truth, although she reckoned by his demeanour and tone that he had already made up his mind. She almost felt sorry to have to prove him right.

"The spearhead dates to the Carolingian period. 7th Century at the absolute earliest." she flashed up on her computer screen the XRF results of the metallurgical composition of the original spearhead from the archive. "This is what we once had. But this is what we now have." She moved the pointer and dragged an image of the new spear's data over the top of the original. The two sets did not match, the peaks on the graphs out of step. "Our original had a much purer iron content, as you can see; other elements show considerably different readings. But had I not scanned this under your direction, Mr Weber, we may never have discovered this."

"And the nail?"

She said nothing. Her mind switched onto another level at that moment. Finger fluttered over the mouse button, her brain processing a dozen simultaneous thoughts related to his question. She chewed on her lipstick, caught a glimpse of her screwed-up reflection in the monitor screen. She looked wasted, frightening. Her pale freckled skin was dark, the wide childlike eyes which ex-partners had always found so fascinating now looked sunken and heavy, and her attractively firm jawline just looked hard and manly.

"Frau Descartes...?"

Sweat tickled the side of her neck, slithering beneath her collar. She flashed up the scan of the nail now in their possession, and the crumpled face disappeared. "I'm sorry, not even an attempt at a fabrication here. This is a rusty old iron pin which is at the most fifty years old. But, there is something I found that may give us a clue, or may make things even more complicated."

"What?"

The door opened behind her, a draft of cool air from the corridor beyond ruffled across the backs of her legs, and as she looked up she found the large frame of Petersen filling her vision. His head momentarily eclipsed the lights in the corridor, throwing him into shadowy relief and lending him a glowing white halo. Feeling very cramped suddenly, Vanessa drew back against the laboratory bench, making a few precious feet of space between them.

Petersen stepped inside. "It's five forty-five." He announced. She glanced at her watch, a couple of minutes fast, it seemed. She had completely forgotten the significance of the time of day. "1735 has come and gone. Our presence was kept completely undercover, but there's been no second break-in anywhere, no thefts. Now we're still looking at a random and elaborate act of murder and desecration to no apparent end. A few crank phone calls this morning to my office, and nothing else."

"Any word on the body?"

Petersen shrugged. "No, it's only just turned up, found dumped under some bushes in the Burggarten. The murder weapon appears to have been found as well, a 52-inch, 14th Century German greatsword, in one of the Schatzkammer basement storerooms. I don't know any more details, I've been around at Siegel's apartment for the past two hours. But I'm not expecting anything in the least bit helpful, from either the weapon or the body. Everything about this matter seems designed to be as frustrating as possible." he gestured vaguely to the workspace behind her. "Have you had any luck?"

Weber groaned, "Yes, Herr Kommissar; all of it bad. The spear – the Holy Nail - fabrications."

Petersen sucked his cheeks. "Any prints?"

Weber touched her arm excitedly. "You said you had found something?"

"Oh, yes. So I did." she cleared the computer screen and brought up a close-up scan of the spear. "Whoever made this spear left us a message. This is engraved in the iron of the weapon itself, and lies underneath where the sheaths would normally be." The men crowded in behind her, desperate to see anything which could shed a glimmer of light on their dark enigma. "It's very small. Whoever did this used a fine engraving tool. This cannot be read with the naked eye - it's not visible on the surface, except as a series of fine squiggles and scratches."

She rotated the image through 90 degrees. Five lines of lettering appeared there, incomprehensible symbols which had nonetheless been put there with some purpose in mind.

"What is it?" Petersen asked.

"Looks like Greek to me."

"It does, yes." Weber agreed, "But what could anyone hope to gain by this?"

"The engraving is also of a high quality," she added. "No tentative scuff marks, he's started the engraving straight away and without any hesitation. It looks to me as if this was done very recently, and by a professional at that."

Petersen pointed to the screen. "Can you give me a hardcopy of this? We need to get this translated immediately."

"I thought you'd say that," Vanessa replied with a sweet smile. She handed a slim document folder to the Kommissar. "All your scans and prints are in there. Also on CD-ROM."

Petersen took the document gently, allowing a grin of respect to break his face. "Thank you. I'm very impressed." He shared her stare for a moment, finding himself drawn into her green-eyed gaze.

"So I see." She lowered her head to look into her handbag, breaking the thread which linked them.

The telephone in his pocket burbled out its polyphonic ring tone. He listened to the message, nodded urgently to himself and returned the phone to his coat. "Initial post-mortem's complete. Doctor Rosenfeldt says some very strange things have been done to the body, but she wanted me to see them personally."

Vanessa smiled. "Well, it looks like we all have our things to do. If you gentlemen are satisfied with my work for today, I'll be getting away."

Petersen waved the folder she had given him as he stepped through the door into the corridor beyond. "Thank you for this," he called back. "I'll call you to let you know what I find out."

"No trouble," she replied half-truthfully. All that intensive work had forced her to miss lunch. As she gathered her coat and bag, she felt the long-suppressed need to find a shop selling decadent cream pastries packed with calories and carbohydrates.

When he finally awoke, Khalamanga felt drained and flaccid, as though something had sucked out his vital energy during his nap. The need to expunge his negative feelings in the most productive way carried him up to the attic, two storeys above where the fading daylight poured through a dusty and webby skylight window which was more rust than frame. The bare wooden floorboards groaned beneath his tread, his long-legged shadow bending up bare walls and contorting around the beams as he moved to the easel at the far end. He snatched the dust sheet away and stepped back to familiarise himself with his current project; a painting in acrylics of Saint Maurice, the original Christian knight and Khalamanga's first childhood hero, draped in Roman armour and holding high a *gladius* streaked with the blood of holy victory as he looked upon the object of his quest - the Holy Grail itself.

It was heroic legend which had long inspired him, ever since his discovery of a Victorian illustrated book of knights in a Charing Cross Road bookshop as a young boy. From then on he had tried to give shape to the sense of wonder these stories brought him with drawings and sketches, and during his University days he had forged a naive but colourful painting style, influenced by the distant memories of his homeland with browns, greens, yellows and reds featuring prominently. His favourite pieces decorated the walls of the middle and upper hallways and bedrooms; the rest lay stacked in cupboards, covered by blankets, collections of canvas too personal to throw out, too childlike or idealistic to risk anyone else seeing.

It had been a joke on his part to portray this Saint Maurice in his own image; as a tall, thin-faced individual with chocolate complexion, wide-eyed with perpetual discovery, now gazing upon the greatest secret of all. He had thought about adding on his trademark steel-framed spectacles as well, but thought that might push the joke into the realms of absurdity. It was a sardonic fantasy at his own expense, for throughout his life and career he had felt unfulfilled in almost every way. As a result, Khalamanga's quest for a greater understanding had taken him into the many arcane and sometimes absurd byways and dead-ends which now filled modern Arthurian and Biblical scholarship. It seemed that almost every week a new and more exotic theory about the Grail, or Jesus, or the Bible grabbed his attention. He had dismissed the 'Bible Code' in the 1990s after finding similar patterns of 'hidden prophecies' in a copy of one of his own dissertations, which predicted his house would suffer a plague of locusts and the loss of his entire foodstock within the week, neither of which came to pass although he did recall a tense moment when he found himself almost out of toilet paper.

As an old-school Christian, he viewed the more prurient examinations of the private life of Jesus as unnecessary and meaningless, and he discarded any attempts by so-called scholars to turn His life into some kind of soap-opera. He was intrigued by investigations into the alleged corruptions in the Vatican, and had read with interest but growing scepticism the fat corpus of popular works on holy relics. None of these went any way towards bringing him peace of mind. He had wondered for a long time if a pilgrimage of some kind would help to allay his anxieties, to kill or cure his sense of spiritual longing, to find something which would make him feel complete and to convince him that it really was still worthwhile calling oneself a Christian in these strange days.

He switched on the radio that sat on the floor beside his chest of art materials. He poured a twisting gurgle of water from the ancient porcelain sink into an old mug and swirled brushes around in it. Crackling interference from the transistor gave way to a Mozart overture, galvanising Khalamanga into mixing up bright, garish concoctions of orange, red and yellow to create a holy radiance reflecting off the knight's armour. It was a brightness he wished he could experience even a little of himself; outside the sky was still grey, vomiting its endless stream upon his house and the city around him. It was going to be a long day.

As Mozart dissolved once again into a wave of static, a high-pitched warble broke over the noise. He dunked brushes into water and plunged on down the stairs three at a time before the telephone caller hung up.

"Yes, uh, hello?"

There was a series of crackling sounds and then a voice demanded,

"How did you know about the body, Herr Doktor? Tell me. *How did you know?"*

Khalamanga froze on the spot. It was the detective from Austria, the man he had told himself he would never hear of again. His voice was edgy, nervous even; it sounded as though he were shaking as he spoke.

"Er, I'm sorry?"

"It's Petersen, Wien Police department. How did you know about the dismemberment of the body?"

Khalamanga dragged his chair to the telephone table and fell into it, trembling with anticipation.

"I...I didn't know. I had a hunch, a feeling that there was more than met the eye. That was all."

"Well this is what met my eye this evening. This body has been disembowelled, castrated and cooked."

"*Cooked?*"

"Cooked, yes. And drained completely of blood, bile and cerebral fluid. These acts were carried out post-mortem and could not have occurred at the museum. You mentioned 'dismemberment' before - I distinctly recall it. You told me you were a specialist in ancient literature, Herr Doktor. I want to know how you guessed the modus of a murderer through your studies of the Holy Grail, how you guessed details of this crime that we have only just discovered. And I need something more convincing from you than your 'hunch', I am afraid."

Khalamanga caught his breath, lost it again, felt his head pulse. It was terrible, yet thrilling at the same time; his vague sense of intuition had, somehow, borne the strangest fruit.

"I'm sorry. I'll try to explain. The connections may only make sense on a subconscious level of symbolism - think of C.G Jung. Are you with me so far? Although, there are some literal similarities. In one of the early Grail romances, called 'Peredur, Son of Efrawg', there is a procession which involves a head on a platter and a bleeding spear. I presume it was the connection between the spear and the head that made me think. The spear you had there is also the artefact which is specifically mentioned in several of the legends and also by Wagner in his opera 'Parsifal' - where the maimed Fisher King is wounded sexually, castrated, until he is healed by that same spear. I did not know the body would have been cut up in such a manner. I simply considered it a possibility, if your perpetrator was acting out some aspect of the Grail legends. I suppose I could come to Vienna to meet you in person, if that wouldn't be any trouble for you. Would you want that?"

"Yes." There was no hesitation in the policeman's voice. "Call me as soon as you arrive. I will send a car to collect you. We must discuss this further."

"I will. And thank you," `Khalamanga signed off. Well, he thought, Vienna in the spring would not be as welcoming as his homeland, but the visit might prove to be a lot more productive.

Vanessa was still thinking hard about Vienna and herself as she clattered through the the city. The sights of the street and the traffic made her feel slightly drunk; car headlights smeared into streaks, tourists laughed and talked in a dozen languages as she crossed onto Leopoldsgasse, location of the Eastern District Police Headquarters where Petersen's group of the Kriminalpolizei was housed. The mosaic of architecture, built centuries apart, collided with the sky, blotting out stars and heaven and grounding her in the world of man and all his evils. Stone and glass cut her off from nature, the city closing in on her now, taunting her to make a move, to strike down her fears.

She crammed the last crust into her mouth and sucked sugary crumbs off her fingers. Boot heels clicked like an old clock breaking down, her intermittent pace echoing her stuttering thoughts. Her shoulder smacked into somebody and a stream of abuse in Italian followed after her, but she did not look back. Within a minute she was there, clacking and scuffing up the stone steps to the massive doors above. People flowed past her, immersing her once more in the normal current of life. She was safe in sanctuary, surrounded by distractions and freed from the pressures of the world and her own inner conflicts again. Life trickled back into her numbed consciousness, the shameful pleasures of the pastry now warming her belly.

After enquiring at the front desk she found her way to Petersen's office, which was located at the far end of a large open plan office at the top of several flights of stairs. The stern stencilled signs pointing her there proclaimed *Mordkommission*, and even with her limited command of German she realised this indicated homicide – the murder squad. Petersen's investigation of the spear was incidental to his dealing with the decapitation, not the other way around.

All the same, he had called her with the news that the miniscule inscription had been translated, and she felt compelled to see with her own eyes the meaning behind the symbols she had uncovered, and with any luck conclude her involvement in the whole nasty messy affair.

"Can I help?" asked a young officer in shirt sleeves and shaven so cleanly his jawline shone, rose pink.

"Er, Inspector Petersen's office? He's expecting me." She felt very out of place amid the sharp white shirts and uniforms which swarmed through the landscape of heavy old desks, flatscreen monitors and precision-engineered deskchairs which propelled their occupants back and forth like carnival rides. The one stationary figure among the dozens around her, Vanessa felt as if she physically impeded their investigations simply by standing there.

"This way." The man got up and led her to the door set in the wall of a wooden enclave. Petersen's name was etched thinly in the glass door, which was pushed gently aside to reveal a dark oak-panelled room, illuminated mainly by the tall, thin window opposite, rosewood-framed and paned. Shelves, head-high, and drawers lined the room on all sides. Centred on the floor stood a massive desk, probably once used by a senior barrister or judge, which could never have come through the thin doorway and must have had the partition walls built around it to create the Kommissar's working space. The 19th-Century decor and rich furnishings suggested more the drawing room of a gentleman's club, a feeling enforced by the low-key conversation which drifted between the two men who were slow to acknowledge her presence. There was only one picture on display, at the edge of the desk; a stocky, pale-looking teenager standing proud in an immaculate uniform. Petersen on or just after graduation, she deduced. The air was thick with the dry smell of Gauloises, his French cigarettes, and she coughed hard as she edged further inside.

"Sir? Lady to see you."

The Kommissar himself stood by his desk, leafing through a bundle of photocopied notes.

"Glad you could come," he said as her guide closed the door. "This is Dr. Karl-Heinze Gruber, from the University Languages department." Petersen introduced the bearded blonde man sitting beside him. "We weren't quite correct with our assessment of the inscription, it turns out."

The large man in the tweed suit explained, "What you have here is not written in Greek, but Coptic."

Vanessa frowned. "That's Egyptian, isn't it?"

"The last phase of the Egyptian language, it flourished from around the 2nd Century AD to the 12th. It is still used today in the Coptic Orthodox Church for its liturgies, in much the way that Latin continues to be used in ours. But leaving aside the alphabet-" he put on a pair of large plastic-framed glasses, relics from the 1960s or some German designer's idea of retro eyewear; "This inscription you have here is taken from a part of the Nag Hammadi scrolls. Ancient Coptic documents recording Gnostic mystical works, which date from around the 4th Century AD. This fragment of text is a condensed form of a passage from Codex VII, known as 'The Second Treatise of the Great Seth'. This work purports to contain sayings from the mouth of Jesus Christ Himself."

"So what does it say?"

Gruber cleared his throat and ran his finger across the scribbled translation notes he had made for himself.

'And I was in the mouths of lions...but I was not afflicted at all, for I did not die in reality but in appearance. For my death, which they think happened, happened to them in their error and blindness, since they nailed their man unto their death...for their Ennoias did not see me, for they were deaf and blind...yes, they punished me...it was another, their father, who drank the gall and the vinegar; it was not I...they struck me with their reed; it was another, Simon, who bore the cross on his shoulder. It was

another upon whom they placed the crown of thorns. But I was rejoicing in the height over all the wealth of the archons and the offspring of their error, of their empty glory, and I was laughing at their ignorance.'

Petersen nodded. "It's not quite your orthodox Easter story, is it?"

Gruber spread his hands in agreement. "There were schools of thought which advocated the idea that Christ had a twin brother. But Gnostic works are, by their nature, steeped in allegory. Some say Jesus Himself was a Gnostic. It is a complicated belief system, and one I confess to having little understanding of, other than that found through my translation work."

Vanessa asked nervously, "What...er, what was that other word, 'En'...something?"

"Ennoias," Petersen filled in, suddenly an expert after forty minutes in the company of Gruber. "In a Gnostic context, it seems to mean a kind of mystical, divine thought. But literally, the Greek word 'ennoai' means a deliberately obscure kind of speaking or writing which still hints at the real meaning underneath."

"So, do you think this is all some kind of puzzle that we're expected to solve? Like a cryptic crossword clue?"

"I hope not, because my head is aching already. I was never good at puzzles, least of all ones based on mythologies I don't understand."

Gruber agreed. "Nor I. This passage, and indeed, some of the more controversial works in the Nag Hammadi library, have long found favour among occultists, conspiracy theorists, seekers of the Holy Grail and such. It is often held up as proof that the Gospels are wrong and Christ survived the Crucifixion to bring up a family."

"Fringe societies." Petersen concluded. "The kind of people who would be interested in the Spear of Jesus, and may be inspired to commit ritual murder to obtain it."

"*Ritual* murder?" Vanessa repeated, sure she had misheard.

"The corpse has been subjected to some considerable heat, and drained of various bodily fluids. It has also been disembowelled, and castrated, like some kind of medieval execution. What's even more frightening, I had a call this morning - a crank, I thought at the time - who actually told me to expect to find just that. 'Dismembered' - the very word he used."

"Jesus Christ," was all Vanessa could find to say. Finally; "I hope you can track this 'crank' down."

"Better than that, I have his number, and he's on his way in as we speak. He's a Doctor of Medieval European Literature at Oxford University. He's convinced that this all has something to do with the Holy Grail legends and ancient mystical symbolism."

Gruber coughed gently, reminding the others he was still present. "Er, as my work is strictly in the translation and study of language, I fear I am not going to be of further help here, Kommissar."

"No, no." Petersen said, "On the contrary Professor, you've been very helpful. And thank you for coming in at such short notice."

"However, if your investigations are drawing you into the strange world of the occult, I can recommend a colleague of mine who has worked on, shall we say, more arcane and obscure matters than I. He is an excellent historian and he has applied his talents to a number of good-selling books that explore the less orthodox possibilities surrounding the Christian faith. In fact, his latest book is a serious investigation into a number of the Nag Hammadi codices, and this one-" he tapped his translation notes, "in particular."

Petersen sighed with relief. "Where can I get in touch with this man?"

Gruber had already pulled a pen from his breast pocket and was scribbling down details on one of Petersen's sticky note pads. "His name's Tomas de Carranza, from the University of Madrid. Bit of a jet-setter, likes his publicity. I'm sure he would relish the chance to get his teeth into a case like this. Here's the number for his department." He tore off the page and passed it to Petersen, who accepted the offering with gratitude. "If there is nothing else...?"

"No. Thank you again, Professor. Shall I show you out?"

The two men shook hands warmly, but Gruber was in a hurry. "Thank you Kommissar, but I'll find my own way. And I do hope my work turns out to be of some help to you."

He shuffled briskly past Vanessa and silence fell across the office. Her visit had seemed fairly pointless after all, serving only to confuse her mind further. Now she realised she would not be of any further use to Petersen's case; it was in the hands of academics and Professors now, not field scientists, no matter how well-meaning or enthusiastic they may be. After a moment or two of silence, something clicked into place in her mind. She pointed to Gruber's sticky note. "That name...I have a book of his, that new one. I bought it at the airport when I arrived here. Mainly for its blurb - 'The Most Controversial Biography Ever!' Well, it made a change from 'Bridget Jones' Diarrhea', y'know?"

"What's it about?"

"It's about..." she stopped, realising the significance of what she was saying. "It's about the idea that there were two Christs, one who lived and one who was crucified."

Petersen had already swiped his coat from the old-fashioned coat stand in the corner. "Then let's go and pick it up. It sounds like as good a place to start as any."

Tomas de Carranza had strode into his room ten minutes that morning late to find an expectant and unusually reverent class. Pausing only to slam the exam papers on his desk, he turned to the whiteboard, uncapped a marker and wrote a large letter 'D' on it. He stepped back, looked at it sideways, and added a bit of 15th-Century gothic illumination before sitting down, arms folded, feet up on the desk in front of him.

The class stared back. They were used by now to their celebrity tutor's slight eccentricities, his wild mood swings, his passionate enthusiasm for his subject which often resulted in his lessons veering off on strange tangents. But this was truly bizarre behaviour, even for a Monday morning.

"What you see behind me is the grade I have given you all for last week's assessment on the Book of Exodus." An outbreak of shocked murmurings fluttered among them. "Not one of you has answered the question I set. You were not invited to speculate wildly upon the origins of this text, nor were you advised to reference my own somewhat radical investigation from over thirty years ago. Greying I may be, but I am not so senile as to miss my own words hacked up and re-assembled by an amateur forger. That I take as the deepest insult.

"Normally I would refer such a matter to the Dean, but because you have already spent one and a half years of your lives here, and I do not care to stand solely responsible for destroying your future careers with one single action, you all have one opportunity for redemption. You will take the remaining time for this lesson to visit the library and to compose, independently of each other and without reference to popular internet encyclopaedias, the essay I demanded and expected last week. Those of you who accomplish this may remain in my class for the rest of the year. The others had better speak to the head of Tuition about a transfer to a less-demanding course."

Silence, mostly stunned, seeped into the room of whitewashed walls. "Gentlemen, you are wasting time."

Chairs and desks scraped and squawled as shuffling feet carried their owners out of his sight. The door was not closed behind the last man; there were not even muttered curses and crude jokes to be kept from his earshot. Such meek submission to his will brought de Carranza both alarm and satisfaction at once.

He cuffed the door shut behind them with a resounding bang designed to carry all the way down the corridor, and returned to his seat with his copy of *El Mundo*. Daylight painted him blue and red and yellow through the stained glass window, projecting hazy portions of the figure of Cardinal Jiménez onto his face in a mottled organic mosaic. As he began to read, a strange sense of peace filled him. He had never had a fortunate upbringing like any of his class; his father had worked very hard all his long life, and had always provided for them. He did not despise the youths for their privileges, only their misuse of it, but there had been something perversely satisfying about the whole event.

He turned to the international news to find it as predictable as ever; holy wars still continuing in the Middle East, another bloodbath, more bombs. It seemed that faith, both in God and in gold, seemed destined to make a bloody mess of the Holy Land indefinitely, or until some new Messiah came who could banish all religious differences forever. And when that day came, hell would be an ice rink and Tomas de Carranza would find himself skating across it on his way back to church.

He skimmed articles concerning the newly-appointed Pope Pius XIII, offended at the blandness of His Holiness' utterances. His personal respect for the papacy as an institution had ended following the sudden and surprising death of John Paul I in 1978. In the man who had been Albino Luciani, de Carranza had seen a figure so charismatic that, for a month, the Spaniard had found himself proud once again to proclaim himself a Catholic and to follow a Pope who finally understood the needs of his people, the world, and the Church as a whole. de Carranza had read with excitement of his proposed reforms, had watched the television transfixed and in tears as the new Pope smiled out upon the world, and de Carranza felt the warmth of that smile within himself too.

His new-found fervour was destined to be as short-lived as the new Papal incumbent. It was the assassination of John F. Kennedy all over again. A popular, able leader cut down in his prime; unanswered questions and bungled investigations; a gaping hole left where a strong man had once stood, and the dreadful sensation that evil had in some way triumphed, and that the whole future of the world had turned a shade darker with his passing. de Carranza still recalled that day in late September, 1978. He had just finished one of his first lectures at the University, delivered to a rather bored group of first years when a female colleague came rushing up to him outside the classroom, tears pouring down her cheeks as she wept, "Papa is dead! Papa is dead!"

It had taken him some minutes to realise she had not meant her own father, but the happy Pope who had single-handedly forged a conduit between Tomas de Carranza and his God after fifteen years of spiritual crisis. And as he held the howling woman tightly in his arms, he cried along with her, not least over his dying belief in cosmic justice and his fading hopes of his own eternal salvation. Before September had ended, de Carranza had written an emotional letter to the Archbishop of Madrid requesting Luciani be canonised. When no reply was forthcoming, nor any such action taken, de Carranza considered that letter his final act of faith.

As he chewed over these painful fragments from his past, he was abruptly returned to the present by his telephone buzzing in his jacket pocket. The newspaper crashed to the floor as he struggled to extricate the thing before the answering service kicked in.

"Yes."

There was a short delay, indicating an international call, then he heard a faint but familiar voice. "de Carranza? How are you doing, you old reprobate?"

"Karl-Heinze Gruber, is that you? What a surprise. What can I do for you?"

"You could do with getting a less zealous secretary. You're a very hard man to get hold of. Your secretary was convinced you would not be available all day."

"Oh, Pablo? Yes, he fusses too much. He has my best interests at heart, but seeks to prevent me being overburdened with engagements. I still can't convince him that it is these very things which save me from total insanity. Is this business, or pleasure?"

"Maybe both, if you play your cards right. A police detective in Austria wants to speak to you."

"Is this something to do with this Spear of Destiny affair?"

"I spent an hour tonight with Kommissar Wilhelm Petersen of the Viennese Police Department, discussing with him a section from 'The Second Treatise of the Great Seth', of all things."

"So what do they want me to do about it? I'm an historian. That text is written in Coptic, and I don't read Coptic very well. You're the expert on that."

"Thank you, but it's already been translated. They want to understand how and why the..."

"You're breaking up."

The line swooshed and crackled, then Gruber's voice returned, with a deep echo. "Sorry. They want you to go to Vienna. Look at the spear, the murder scene, help them understand why this inscription has been placed on the Spear of Destiny."

"A quote from a Gnostic Gospel on the Holy Lance?" de Carranza laughed aloud. "Is this some kind of joke?"

"No joke, Tomas. Petersen believes it's a cornerstone of his case. A museum security guard has been found, separated from some of his major body parts. The police are clueless, although Petersen did try to convince me otherwise."

"Fair enough, but I haven't received any messages."

"I would quiz your devoted secretary, if I were you. Just in case he's trying to protect you from the horrors of an international religious conspiracy, I have the number of the Viennese police department."

de Carranza scribbled down the number on the back page margin of *El Mundo* as he cradled the 'phone in his shoulder. "That's wonderful, Ka-Hache. You never know, I may drop in on you for coffee while I'm there."

"Thanks for the warning. Oh, and one last thing. There is a rather attractive young English lady assisting the police as well. Have a good trip, won't you?"

de Carranza pocketed the phone and in the time it took him to gather up his paper from the floor, his plan for the next twelve hours was complete.

Through the rest of the day and into the evening, de Carranza sat in his office, poring over hundreds of Internet web pages; Viennese travel guides, streetmaps, hotels, airport times, until he had filled his desk with printouts and booking receipts. The business had taken longer than expected, pushing the time almost to six o'clock. He stuffed the information into his satchel, locked up and hurried down to the reception desk. Pablo, the dutiful guardian of the faculty, was still there, refusing to leave the premises until de Carranza himself departed and Pablo could ensure that his beloved master was going home safe and sound.

"Ah, Professor. Are you finished for the night then?"

"For tonight, and for some time to come, I fancy. Cancel everything. Lectures, signings. Call them all off. There is vital work to be done, more important even than my book and those clowns I call a class."

Pablo's voice rose half an octave. "Every...*thing*? Professor, what's happened?"

"That business with the Spear of Destiny is what's happened." He leant his weight over the desk. "Any calls for me?"

"No, not lately."

de Carranza cocked his head enticingly, like a mother trying to coax the truth out of a little child.

"Are you quite sure? No anxious Austrians looking for help with famous religious relics?"

Pablo's hands shuffled guiltily across the papers spread in front of him. "There was...somebody. His accent, you know, I didn't think- I mean, he was hard to understand."

de Carranza patted the other man reassuringly on the shoulder. "It's alright. The message got through to me nonetheless; your caller was quite genuine."

He stretched over the desk and poked his finger into the power button of Pablo's laptop. The younger man watched his solitaire game turn to black and the computer shut down with a soft descending sigh which was echoed by its user.

"But I'm only thinking of your own good. And your condition."

"Forget my condition. My condition does not interfere with my work. And tonight, my work requires me to travel to Vienna. People there need my help. They have a murder case to be solved and I have been asked to assist."

Pablo clenched his fists beneath his chin, as he always did when upset. "But this is *murder*. This is not your normal work. Why on earth should you want to become involved in something so horrible?"

de Carranza snapped off the main lights at the panel above the desk. Pablo chased him down the dark corridor towards the exit.

" Precisely *because* it is so horrible, Pablo. And before long my name shall be in the news, and they will understand. Tell your mother to stop crying for I, de Carranza of Navarre, am on the case of the Holy Spear of Vienna. And if these events are inspired by anything more than mindless vandalism, I shall ensure that my contribution brings rewards."

"I won't be at your side to call upon in an emergency, you know?"

Finally, Professor Tomas de Carranza stopped, succumbing to his secretary's insistence. He placed his hands on the younger man's shoulders and spoke quietly, reassuringly. "Pablo, you are a wonderful secretary and a true friend. I love you like a son, and you have been my right arm these past five years. But sometimes you worry far too much about me."

"I have every right to. You shouldn't be rushing off like this. Your condition...you know what the doctors said."

"Doctors say all sorts of drivel, Pablo. One week doctors say eating sugar is bad for us. Next week, they say drinking milk is bad for us. Soon, everything will be bad for us, according to doctors. I haven't lived sixty-four years listening to what doctors say." he thumped his chest with his fist. "I listen to what my *body* says."

They stepped out into the cool evening and the insistent singing of crickets. The moon was fat and clear, washing the campus buildings in streaks of milky white and turning the whirring moths into tiny hovering ghosts. When Pablo still looked glum, the other man slapped his cheeks between his hands. "Come on, think of the wonderful opportunity - for the greatest book of my career. A real-life treasure hunt, with murder and mystery to be solved. I cannot let this chance pass me by, and when it is all over, you will see that I was right. You'll have more appointments and appearances to deal with than ever before - this will be the pinnacle of my success."

Pablo stood alone and deserted in the gaze of the moon. "But what am I going to do while you're gone, Professor?"

de Carranza climbed into the driving seat of his 1972 white Alfa Romeo convertible. "Enjoy the peace and quiet, I should hope." and with that, he fired the engine and left Pablo looking at a pair of black tyre streaks on the glowing asphalt.

DAY TWO: Tuesday

Wilhelm Petersen had spent the night in his office, scouring Vanessa's hardback copy of 'Who Was Jesus?' with her. The concept of time had more or less ceased to be relevant during their studies; when one of them drifted off in a doze, the other took over, scribbling notes, running Internet searches, checking references. It wasn't until the knock on the door that either of them realised what time it was.

" 'Morning," a voice called into the room.

Petersen jerked up in his seat, looked around himself with bug-eyed alarm. There was a woman sleeping with her head on his desk, and for a moment he couldn't remember how she got there.

"Er...sir?" the man in the doorway queried his superior.

"What the hell time is it?" Petersen snapped, convinced it was far too early for any of his team to be doing the rounds.

"You asked me to let you know about the museum security tapes as soon as they'd been studied, sir. Sorry it's a bit late, but Knobloch said he's been up all night working on it."

Petersen waggled the mouse to deactivate the screensaver and peered at the clock on the computer monitor. It was 0819.

"Oh. Thank you, Kupfer. Is there anything useful on there?"

Kupfer glanced aside at Vanessa, now stirring, disturbed by the voices and activity around her. "I haven't been told anything yet, sir. They want you to come down now."

"Frau Descartes, this is Sergeant Kupfer." Petersen announced as he stood up and wriggled into his jacket.

She stared at her watch, yawned and wondered how crumpled she must look. She felt clammy and very groggy. Her mouth felt dirty and her throat rough, and she tasted Petersen's French cigarettes. "Morning." She mumbled in reply.

"Sir," Kupfer announced, "There is also a visitor to see you. Said it was most important."

"What do they want?"

"Said he was a Professor of something. From Madrid."

Petersen tried to rebuild his thoughts. He grabbed de Carranza's book, 'Who Was Jesus?' and held up the back of the dust jacket to show its author's portrait. "Him?" Kupfer squinted, nodded. Petersen stretched and made an effort to make himself look official. "Bring him in. If I'd known he'd be here this soon, we could have taken it easy last night." He offered Vanessa a sideways glance but she failed to pick up the hint that with hindsight, their evening could have been less business and more pleasure. He angrily tossed his scribbled notes into the air and knocked over his desk tidy, scattering pens, paper clips and assorted desk junk everywhere.

As Petersen began stuffing things back into their plastic compartments, the office door opened jarringly, admitting a breathless blast of Spanish leather and Cuban cigar smoke. Petersen stared in the direction of this intrusion to find the figure of Tomas de Carranza illuminated there. "Kommissar Wilhelm Petersen?" the visitor presumed in a voice thick with the resonance of Southern Spain, not dusty but vibrant, exotic and appealing, like a mature wine. He stretched a hand across the desk. Petersen shook, feeling the other man grip him hard in return, a warm, confident touch which communicated openness, trust, and the underlying desire to impress.

"I am."

"Tomas de Carranza, Professor of Biblical Archaeology at the Universidad Complutense de Madrid." The Spaniard indicated the half-smoked cigar in his mouth. "Do you allow this...?" Petersen replied by shaking his own packet of Gauloises. "Ah, thank you. Shall I take a seat-?"

Petersen nodded toward one of the spare chairs. "Kupfer!" he called, summoning the sergeant to the doorway. "Tell them downstairs we'll be five or ten minutes."

The door closed, leaving Petersen and Vanessa to become better acquainted with their visitor. Their first reaction was that de Carranza was even larger than life than his publicity portrait suggested, in personality if not in height. His skin was arid and lined like a Moroccan desert yet he exuded a sense of freshness and vitality which belied his years. His shoulder-length hair was iron-grey, tied back with a length of black ribbon, his beard trimmed into an immaculate, pointed goatee and signified a man who took great care with his appearance, and enjoyed doing so. Gold rings adorned the three middle fingers of his left hand. A burgundy polo neck sweater and a fashionable black leather coat lent him something of the look of a film star or artistic enfant terrible, an appearance enforced by his Cuban-heeled boots and designer label jeans.

"Thank you very much for seeing me so early, Kommissar. I wanted to announce myself before you got into your day's routine."

"To be perfectly honest Professor, I've only just woken up."

The Spaniard sucked thoughtfully on his cigar for a moment, making deep hollows in his cheeks. Then he burst out laughing. "Excellent indeed, Kommissar. But I do not believe that for a second." While Petersen continued to round up paper clips and pins, the visitor's attention turned to Vanessa, and on her it lingered for a period of time beyond mere curiosity. "And to whom do I have the pleasure...?"

"Dr. Vanessa Descartes," Petersen muttered without looking up. "She's assisting us with our research. Did the initial analysis of the Spear."

"Ah yes indeed, I recall the name now. May I say, what an honour and a pleasure to meet you, my dear." He stood up and took the liberty of kissing her hand. The warm smell of leather and expensive aftershave filled her senses, exciting her mind with thoughts and images far removed from reality or even possibility. The traces of his saliva lingered on her skin as he drew back to his seat, a tiny yet intimate contact she felt unwilling to wipe off. From being a moody, mysterious portrait on the back of a bestseller to making Continental advances towards her in the space of a few seconds caused Professor de Carranza to make a deep and instant impression.

Silence followed, disrupted only by the plinking and plonking of pens and paper fasteners into the desk tidy. Petersen started, "Professor de Carranza-"

"Please, just 'Tomas'. Two syllables instead of seven - saves time and breath."

"Well, Tomas. As you may have noticed, we have made an attempt to study your book. I confess, a lot of it is over my head, but there is some material in there that I believe has significance to our case."

"Indeed. My analysis of 'The Second Treatise of the Great Seth', especially."

Petersen paused his game of desktop hoop-la for a moment. He had no idea how to handle this boisterous, egotistical character who exuded charm like perfume, and was clearly aware of the fact, too. "You're very up to date with the facts of our enquiry."

"You were speaking to an old friend of mine, Karl-Heinze Gruber, yesterday evening. He called me to say I should expect a message from you. Well, I must confess I did not wait for the message. I dropped what I was doing and came over straight away – after all, a murder has been committed, and there will be more to come."

Half a dozen paperclips pinged against plastic, one after the other, fired home with deliberate accuracy, before speech resumed. "And what makes you think that, Professor?"

"Come, sir. This is no random act of violence, but – truly – a symbol, a bold statement of deepest – even historic - significance. One does not risk discovery, nor jail, to carry out such an atrocity for mere thrills."

Petersen shuffled through some pages in front of him which he passed across to the visitor. "I've put together a draft report of what we have so far. If you need further details, just ask. I also have another expert scheduled to arrive from England. Take a few minutes to acquaint yourself with this information."

"I'm to have an assistant?" de Carranza was sceptical. He had not considered the possibility of other minds working concurrently on the investigation. But after all, every sleuth had to have a sidekick. "What's his field?"

"Medieval European literature, religious esoterica. And other things I've never heard of."

The Spaniard pondered deeper on the arrival of a partner, then accepted the notion with a hearty shrug. "Hm. Well, I can see some relevance there to our case, I suppose."

"Sir?" Kupfer pushed open the door again with an air of urgency. "Are you–"

"Yes, we are ready now. Let's get down to the viewing room and take a look."

"Me too?" de Carranza asked, surprised at the general invitation.

"Why not?" Petersen said on his way out. "Seems you're one step ahead of the rest of us already."

de Carranza found himself at Vanessa's side as they both went for the doorway at the same time. She threw him a sympathetic smile.

"It's okay," she explained. "He really has just woken up. And so have I, so I apologise if I'm a bit..." she looked for the right word, scratched her head, covered up her temporary mental paralysis with a broad mooncalf grin. "Vague."

"Must have been a beauty sleep." de Carranza returned the smile, which evolved rapidly into a hearty laugh. "Please, ladies first."

"Thank you. Though I'm probably not that much of a lady."

"That, my dear, is something I would prefer to be the judge of myself."

That learning process began while he hung back inside the office to watch her walk away from him, chewing thoughtfully on his cigar as he carefully studied her swaying locomotion.

As Petersen and his guests marched in two by two formation through the second floor, they passed bronze busts and portraits of notable members of the legal profession going back to the 1700s, to the days when that part of the police building had been a judicial courthouse. The endless procession of elderly, stone-faced arbiters made de Carranza feel as if he were under intense scrutiny, and he felt sudden and overwhelming guilt for all the misdemeanours he had committed in his life. At the end of the corridor a marbled spiral staircase twisted down into the dark bowels of the building, which Petersen and Kupfer began to descend. de Carranza turned aside to look into the contents of a large glass cabinet filled with blown-up photographs and relics from some recent and notorious crime, probably borrowed from the nearby Kriminalmuseum. "Who's Jack Unterweger?" he asked, pointing to a life-size head and shoulders portrait.

"A serial killer of prostitutes," Petersen explained over his shoulder. "I was on that case back in '94, my first taste of real homicide. Somehow it failed to put me off."

The two policemen pattered down the wooden stairs ahead and disappeared from view.

de Carranza lingered in front of the case, unable to break the thread which held his gaze, the portrait of the handsome middle-aged man behind the glass. He was eye to eye with a murderer, albeit only a picture of one, and it troubled him.

"Hey." a hand tugged at his sleeve. As he drew himself away, he wondered what it would be like to face a real killer, a possibility he had never considered until this moment. Murderers could look like bank clerks, like policemen even. The distinguished flecks of grey at Unterweger's temples and his confident, open smile helped to suggest a corporate executive or businessman in the Spaniard's mind, not someone whose behaviour had been compared to Jack the Ripper and who had made a career out of those crimes.

The stairway took them down into the lower level of the back end of the building, a place where the air was cooler and the decor much plainer. No wood panelling here, no pictures, not even of multiple killers. Instead plain internal notices pinned to cork boards, flashes of colour provided only by green emergency exit signs and bright red fire extinguishers. Their surroundings consisted of plaster walls and mould-green linoleum like that found in state schools and old hospitals. A much later addition to the original architecture, functional and cold. This was the side of the building unseen by general visitors, where evidence was studied, suspects dragged into interrogation rooms and plain closed doors hid the inner mechanics of justice.

de Carranza and Vanessa walked together in silence, listening as Petersen continued to quiz Kupfer. "So, have you finished with all the other security men?"

"Yes, sir. They assure us they found nothing out of place on Sunday. The way the guard patrols work, they tend not to see much of each other, except during shift swaps and rest breaks. Which are staggered, of course."

"And no evidence of any forced entry?"

"No, sir. We've completely dusted all windows, doors, and other openings inside and out of the Schatzkammer. It is clean. So clean we can't believe somebody did not actually erase all signs of there ever being anything there."

"Unless we really are looking at an inside job. Which would by its nature, require a conspiracy."

"Oh," Kupfer went on, "And we got the results of the sword back from the lab. No prints. Plenty of blood, however. Seemingly it wasn't that sharp after all, which you'd expect from something 700 years old, so whomever swung it must have had real strength to take the head clean off."

Petersen expressed his contempt with a grimace so dark that de Carranza felt briefly unsettled to be in his company. The sudden shift in expression made him wonder how quickly the Kommissar's temper could be inflamed, and the possible consequences of that. Given his size and weight, he hoped dearly he would never find himself on his wrong side, and pitied anyone else who had done so in the past.

"A sword?" de Carranza piped up. "Fascinating. What theories do you have for the use of such a weapon in this day and age, Kommissar?"

"Absolutely none so far, Professor." Petersen declared loudly, his tone roughened by irritation. "That was something I was rather hoping Doctor Khalamanga could shed some light on."

"Khalamanga? Interesting name for an Englishman."

"Well, he sounded as English as the Prince of Wales when I spoke to him. Ah, here we are."

They were met at the door of the video room by a fat, curly-headed young man of about twenty-five wearing a denim jacket and a 'Guns n Roses' T-shirt. He faced the policemen with a tired smile, until he spotted Vanessa, when he suddenly perked up.

"Kommissar Petersen, good morning." he opened the door and led them into a room filled entirely with television monitors and a bewildering array of VCRs, digital media players and computer terminals. The multiple monitor screens, all showing the same image, looked like part of the eye of some enormous insect.

"Where are the rest of your team?" Petersen asked as he scanned the otherwise empty viewing lab.

"They had to go home, sir. Too tired. We had 24 hours of video recordings here to process from six sources. And it's not exactly 'Playboy TV', you know?" He pulled up some seats and paid special attention to Vanessa as she came in rather reluctantly behind de Carranza, as though sheltering behind his physical presence. "But I kept going, thanks to Gummy Drops and Pepsi. Just means I'll be swinging from the lights tonight, is all."

The young man's tired eye continued to linger on Vanessa until Petersen's hard-voiced impatience snapped him out of his dreams. "So what do you have for us, Knobloch?"

The large lad pressed some buttons on a remote control and four monitors in front of them flickered into life.

"To be perfectly honest, practically nothing."

The sound of Petersen's forehead connecting with his fist filled the entire room.

"Although, let me quantify that...we have *practically* nothing, but there is, I've noticed, a discontinuity in the guard's routine that occurs towards the end of the recording from Camera IV. None of the others have picked this up. That in itself may be significant, a deliberate evasion of the other cameras, maybe. From the plans of the treasure room you gave me," he gestured to a photocopied floor plan with 'X's indicating the cameras, angles of vision shaded in, and multiple coffee rings obscuring everything else, "I deduced this was probably the case, hence him trying to dodge the camera at the end of the tape. Look."

Knobloch played the tape. An image of the treasure room swam into view. A line of static flickered up the screen, then a dark figure walked slowly from left to right and passed out of shot.

"By the way, what you're seeing is the director's cut; I edited this down to show the highlights of our movie, the only sequences where something actually happens. This is our man here, I believe."

Petersen squinted hard at the screen. "Difficult to be sure. Do we actually have an identifiable shot of the victim?"

Knobloch nodded. "Yes, sir. We do. But only at the point of deviation I mentioned before, when he isn't on his patrol route you see here. This was the first thing we tried; to get a positive identification out of an enhanced image from one of the tapes. But the lighting isn't good. His peaked cap throws nasty shadows down over his face, and he wears it quite low. All we can say for sure is that our man is Caucasian, stands between 5 ' 9 to 5'11 and weighs about 180 pounds."

Kupfer nodded. "That fits, but it's a very general profile. It could be any of the security men, apart from Pfeifenberger."

Knobloch went on, "We took as many angles of his face as we could and emailed them onto Fischhof in Linz. He did his best to construct a three-dimensional virtual model based on the main points of reference we could provide him with, and this is what we got." He snatched a sheet of paper from one of the shelves and passed it to his audience. Petersen frowned at the images; a computer-generated head seen from the front, side and 3/4 angle. The features were bland but unknowable. "He also took a comparative reference from the crime scene pictures of the head," Knobloch went on. "Even using that to build on, you can see he couldn't confirm very much of what we have here. You want my opinion? I think this character is trying to be deliberately obscure."

Petersen flicked the printout back onto the bench. "Show me this deviation from the patrol route."

Knobloch fast-forwarded. "As I say, what we have is this routine, in which he passes back and forth, back and forth...until we were all just about ready to fall asleep, when we get-" he pressed a button and the picture slowed down to one quarter speed. "-this."

A dark blob appeared at the bottom left corner, just behind the camera's time and date code. As it moved on, it formed into a face in profile, the peaked cap still in place but this time illuminated more clearly by nearby display lights.

Petersen pointed excitedly at the screen. "That is Siegel. Alive and walking – there he is, dammit."

The sequence ran to its end, was rewound and played again. "That's what we thought." Knobloch said. "But funny how he finally decides to confirm his identity so late on in the night. Right before the tapes run out."

"Yes, strange indeed." de Carranza pondered. A sensation of dread was crawling through his stomach, a parasitical worm feeding upon his confidence.

"Maybe somebody else was impersonating him earlier," Vanessa guessed. "That's why he kept at an optimum distance between the cameras. So as not to arouse suspicion."

But Petersen was insistent. "That still demands a conspiracy. Only a veteran guard of the Schatzkammer would know the exact route to take to keep himself so far from the cameras' range. A conspiracy that some knew about, and others didn't. Otherwise, why this deception? And after this appearance - you say the tapes run out, right? Except he should have changed the tapes five minutes before. So whatever he was doing, he wasn't doing his job."

Vanessa's meagre understanding had faded. "But all this time, the cameras plainly show the spear safely in the case. Why send a substitute guard to walk around a display item, to have the real guard turn up at the end? It's not like anything's happened to the spear. It's still there, right beside the jewelled cross."

Knobloch added, "We watched out for furtive glances, or lingering looks...he doesn't spend any time hanging around any of the exhibits. Obviously there are periods where he's not picked up at all. But for the rest of the time - back and forth, back and forth. Like a pendulum, and just as boring to watch, believe me."

de Carranza shuffled nearer the screen. "Maybe that was the point. Play the last clip again." The worm was gnawing, nibbling.

Knobloch obliged. "What are we looking for?"

The Spaniard was peering intently at something as yet unseen by the others. "You're right, it is him. But he is not alive, and nor is he walking."

Petersen gawked, aghast. "What?"

"Roll the tape back to 03:59:27."

Knobloch obeyed, desperate to see what he had missed all this time. "Now watch. He moves across the screen from bottom left. Goes out of shot before he reaches the bottom right. Fine. But watch the glass cabinet that stands to his left, in the centre of the picture. Mr. Knobloch...back again, this time a frame at a time, please."

As they all watched, Siegel appeared in shot at the bottom left corner as he had always done, moved across the bottom of the frame until only his cap was visible. de Carranza's finger appeared over the middle of the screen, tracing out an image reflected in the glass which was definitely not that of the security guard.

Petersen stared, terrified and excited at the same time as he realised he was looking at the first piece of hard evidence in the whole case. "Freeze it."

The tape clicked and held on that frame, allowing the pattern of dots to assemble itself into a dark and terrible suggestion.

"What the hell is that?"

"Our first breakthrough." Petersen said, "that's what it is. Well done, Professor."

There was a figure there, dressed in dark clothing, hunched and furtive, the back of its head facing the glass. And carried in front of it was a plate of some kind, and on that plate was a severed head wearing a peaked cap.

de Carranza fell back in his seat, silent. He blinked, but the image did not go away. It was not so much the idea of the murder or its grisly details which held him there, body and mind both frozen; it was the half-glimpsed image in a blurry arrangement of pixels on a monitor screen, carrying a dead man's head before him in some revolting kind of procession, the fact that he had *seen* the monster capable of this act, albeit a grainy shadow.

He was coming closer to the realms of the unknown. The veneer of self-publicity and excitement had already flaked off his personal triumph. Like his marriages, like every difficult situation he had got himself into in his life, he would now have to see it out to the end, whatever the cost.

Vanessa's chair scratched on the floor.

"Have to get out of here," she whispered, and threw herself headlong out the video room.

On one level, she felt ridiculous for her reaction. During her 18 months working in forensic investigation, she had seen the results of the worst aspects of the human condition, had fought in vain against the feelings of anger and helplessness that she could not shake. Only her decision to step away from modern crime and turn to archaeological investigations saved her from a Prozac habit, months of depression-related sick leave and a total nervous collapse. The half-forgotten nightmares continued to corrode her reason, the innuendos which pointed to things beyond the mundane and had almost convinced her of the existence of true physical evil, of divine agents of vengeance, of angels, and the origins of sin.

Fuelled by the horror of what she had just seen, her mind began to terrify her further with the esoteric imagery she had crammed into it over the past day. *The Great Seth who was Jesus I was in the mouths of lions the genitalia are missing the most controversial biography ever on a plate like John the Baptist the whole situation is chaotic 1735 dates to the Carolingian period, the 8th Century...*

She found herself sliding down the wall of the corridor, her eyes impaled on the sharp striplight above. Her thoughts became more scrambled the harder she tried to collect them, like a broken egg in her hand. The white tiles and murky gray-green floor reminded her of a public toilet, the kind of place where one could expect to get mugged or raped. She wanted out as quickly as possible, but she had nowhere to run to. Nowhere, except back where she came from, to the room with the severed head on the screen and the fat sweaty lad who couldn't take his eyes off her knees.

In a sudden surge of terror, she found herself tearing back to the door of the room just to be away from the isolation of the fluorescent blue corridor where her thoughts ran red like the murder victim's blood and the darkest, most arcane secrets of mankind began to glimmer through rips in the fabric of her own reality. She felt the claws of panic rake her skin through her clothing, saw her flesh cut by shimmering razors and lines of blood snaking up her arms like crimson serpents. As she reached the door handle, she was thirteen years old again, a terrified child waking from a nightmare and running into her mother's bedroom for comfort and the reassurance that everything was all right.

The handle was snatched out of her grasp, the door ceased to be and in its place a headless, naked corpse stood before her, a fountain of blood gushing from its wounded neck which had been 'severed by a very heavy and sharp implement'. She tried to turn away but she was held where she stood, facing this hermaphroditic thing with no genitals, in their place an uncoiling length of intestines which slid to the floor from its slit belly to form a steaming pile around her feet. Then there was only suffocating blackness as the hands of the corpse gripped her tighter, squeezing the vital fluids out of her, screaming at her as she screamed back, *Please, mum, wake me up!*

"Vanessa!"

She blinked, the horror faded, found herself trembling in the grip of Tomas de Carranza. She tried to meet his gaze but could not, humiliated more than she could bear. She was chilled with fear, burning with flushes of embarrassment. She hadn't suffered a panic attack like that since her teens. What the hell was happening to her?

"*Vanessa*? Can you hear me?"

Her throat bulged. It felt tight and dry, not only due to last night's passive smoking. In her sleeping nightmares, she found she could never cry out or scream for help, forever gagged by her own fears and destined never to be rescued.

She managed to summon enough muscle power to nod her head in reply.

"It's okay," the Spaniard's voice told her, "It's gone now, it's over. Do you want a drink?"

She nodded vigorously, wishing she could stop feeling like a child. He let her go and started to walk away to the drinks machine, and she stuck to his side, too scared to let him out of her sight for a second.

"Coffee?" he asked. She nodded again. "What happened to you there?"

She leant back against the wall as he made his selection.

"I..." she squeaked, coughed, and started again. "I had a bit of a...a funny turn."

"*Turn*?" he raised an eyebrow, not understanding her usage. "You mean, you-" he stopped to stab the stubborn sugar selector button. "-you felt ill, afraid at what you saw?"

"Yes. I've been thinking too hard lately," she tried. "That thing on the video just brought it all to a head."

"An unfortunate choice of words, my dear."

Petersen quietly emerged from the viewing room and stood in the doorway, keeping a discreet distance but making himself available if required.

Vanessa found herself fighting back a guilty smile. "Sorry. But I got the sensation, for a moment, that we're facing something that is very wrong, very frightening. Something that has the power to commit an act like this, and leave us with almost no evidence to pursue. And it made me feel so helpless." She looked across anxiously at Petersen. "I'm sure you can understand that."

"Yes," he agreed. "All I have is the statements of half a dozen men who say they saw nothing out of place until they found the spear cabinet cut open. They all have each other as an alibi, and we are facing a closed case if we can't break that silence, or confirm or deny their story." The machine gushed and whirred beside her. de Carranza studied her calmly, that head to foot look she had seen him give her in the past, summing her up, judging her.

"You fellows must think I'm a ridiculous, scatty bitch." She laughed.

The Spaniard handed her the cup of coffee and she sipped it gratefully. "Not at all. And I don't know 'scatty'. Now drink up."

Petersen confessed, "And I'm sorry to have pulled you so deep into this investigation. If you want out, Frau Descartes, just say so. Murder is very wrong, and the circumstances can often be intimidating. I've worked on homicide now for thirteen years. You never get used to it. You can never say, 'It's just another body'. It's always somebody's life taken away, somebody who will soon turn to dust because of another's hand."

"I know. When I was a girl, I lost someone..." she choked on her own breath, finding the words difficult to say, almost passing out with the emotional rush which came over her. "Someone who was very dear to me. I had loved her more than myself. When she went..." she paused to dry her eyes. "I felt as though someone had thrust a hand into my body and torn out my heart - deprived me of something that I needed to survive." The men nodded, didn't speak, grunted at the right points to assure her only that they were listening. Neither had any wish to interrupt her catharsis. "Well, I tried to live on, for her sake. And slowly, the pain began to subside. But sometimes, I find myself asking all those questions again, and feeling that same way, and I feel like I'm bleeding, like from a wound that's always open..." she scratched anxiously at her wrists, as though trying to erase some unpleasant mark.

Petersen understood. He wouldn't seek details, nor ask more than she was willing to tell, but he had reasons of his own for sharing her emotions, her troubled sense of desolation at the image on the screen.

"Yes," he agreed, "It's hard. And when there is no logic, no motive, like this, then it's not difficult to imagine a great evil force at work, an evil that would take pride in terrorizing us. And for me, that is why it must be fought, why I must devote every waking minute I have to this. I owe it to the world to bring it to an end."

Vanessa cradled the cup in her hands, warming her sticky palms. "We all do. And we owe it to Siegel, as well."

Petersen looked at the two of them. She seemed comfortable around the Spanish academic, more comfortable than she had been around him in all the past ten hours or so.

"Why don't you two go off somewhere pleasant and find some nice things to talk about?" he suggested brightly. "I'll get to work on the full report and call you when Doctor Khalamanga arrives. Then we can all get down to business."

"Sounds like a splendid idea." de Carranza grinned. He offered Vanessa an arm, which she took after a moment's consideration.

"As long as you're buying."

"What made you think we were going anywhere that sold fine foods and wines?"

"Because right now, I'm not going anywhere that doesn't."

As they walked to the stairs, arm in arm, Petersen stared after them. He tried to fight back the bemused smile which was creeping across his face, failed, and returned to the video monitor room.

"Everything okay?" Kupfer asked.

Petersen jerked a thumb behind him. "She's falling for the Granddad. Woman must be on the edge, alright."

Kupfer pursed his lips. "Oh dear. Well, I suppose-"

"Kupfer, you didn't think-?" Petersen pointed to himself, and laughed aloud. "Oh, no. Not at this time of year, so close to Maria's death. Besides, I think I make her nervous." He pulled his jacket around himself and looked intently at the monitor screens, still frozen on the macabre scene from the Schatzkammer. Kupfer saw a dark look fall across his superior's eyes, a look he had not seen for a long time. "Play it again, Knobloch."

Outside, the city waited beneath a pale hazy sunlight filtered through the gauze of vehicle fumes. The sky was a fuzzy blur and de Carranza resolved to enjoy the light while he could, much like the general philosophy he had carried with him through his adult life. With any luck, he hoped, he might even be able to imbue Vanessa with some of that optimism.

As they emerged from the shadow of the police offices into the warm daze of mid-morning traffic, both drew simultaneous breaths of relief. He caught her off-guard with a grab and ran with her down the street, pulling her along behind him.

"Whoa - wait - hold on. Where are we going?"

"Somewhere where the sun is shining. Somewhere I'm sure you'll appreciate."

He led her a brisk dance to the kerb and opened the door of an olive-coloured 2-seater Peugeot as she skidded to a halt, barely keeping her balance on the smooth paving stone. "Drab, isn't it." He apologised, "But the hire company didn't have any Lamborghinis. Plus, I was in a hurry."

She looked into his face, wondering if he were serious, and indeed just how serious he was about life in general. He seemed frivolous, lightweight, almost her polar opposite. And yet his attitude was proving infectious. She felt herself flowering in his company, revived by his sunny personality. He knew he was right, and she was more than willing to believe him, for she knew only too well what the alternative entailed.

They sat inside and he fiddled with controls on the dashboard. Vanessa closed her door but still sat tight in her seat, staring ahead as though waiting for some great revelation to manifest across the inside of the windscreen. In truth, she could hardly believe that so little time in the company of this man who was still a stranger could lift her soggy spirits so high. And the more she thought about it, the more she realised how she had known de Carranza in little ways before their meeting. Her enjoyment of 'Who Was Jesus?' had been enhanced by the author's amusing asides and wry footnotes, the kind of smooth writing one did not usually experience in such works. Some nights, too tired to read any further, she had spent her last few waking moments contemplating the author's portrait on the back of the cover, drawn into that wise and worldly gaze and this alone had probably contributed toward some of her more exotic sleeping fantasies, and a few of her waking ones too.

The strong smell of new car and air-freshener made her nostrils tingle, especially when she detected the insidious undercurrent of cigar smoke. And here once again she found herself playing through a wild and improbable scene in her head, so bizarre it brought a flush to her skin and made her chew on her lip. The man was old enough to be her father, and here she was entertaining more crazy dreams.

"Go on," he urged. "Settle back, relax. And do strap yourself in."

He turned the engine over and slid down the windows to let some air circulate within the stuffy cabin. She caught a glimpse of herself in the side mirror and realised she was still sitting bolt upright in the stiff, new upholstery with her bag clenched defensively in front of her, ready to deflect any oncoming horrors.

He started up and pulled out into the traffic. "Forgive my asking," he said gently, "But you talked about having lost someone back there. Was it - dare I say the word - murder at all?"

"No. But it was horrible, and very sudden." She stared through the window at the passing scenes. She knew she should have felt more for what she saw; the historic streets that had seen the march of Hitler, the waltzes of Strauss and the genius of Mozart, yet she was left cold by the 18th and 19th Century facades, seeing no further than her own bleak reflection in the car window. Vienna was wasted on Vanessa Descartes now. With this exciting, exotic man beside her, Vienna could have been Stockport, or Amsterdam, or anywhere.

"You know," he mused as he shifted gear and careened around a bend, "Back in the 1980s, I used to have a Maserati GT. This was after my second marriage broke up, and I realised I had better things to spend my money on than someone else's debts. For a while, I really believed I was a true European playboy." He patted the steering wheel. "Well, it was a nice dream while it lasted."

His macho driving style drew her attention but did not unduly bother her. She was still living inside her mind, in her own past, her spoken words mere lip-service to the rest of the world around her.

"What happened?" she asked. "To make you split up."

"I thrashed the engine too hard. Couldn't afford the repairs."

Vanessa's mind struggled for a moment, then she burst out laughing. "I meant, you and your wife..."

"Oh, *that*? We were simply two selfish people who both expected the other to give in to their every whim. Who knows, one day I may even get around to testing the old maxim of 'third time lucky'." He looked at her with a smile designed to assure her he meant no such thing, but she saw the merest shadow of truth within his stare. "We probably deserved each other. I think I required some serious debunking. It certainly helped bring me down to earth."

She twirled a lock of hair around her finger, pondering. "Are you into wine at all?"

Tomas de Carranza's smile became a beaming grin. "Dear lady, for me, wine is one of the few pleasures that I thank God I am still fit enough to enjoy, and the fruits of the vineyard probably the only justification I still have for even believing in His existence in the first place."

Flight BA0700 from London Heathrow deposited Dr. Emanuel Khalamanga at Vienna International airport at 1410 that afternoon. The tired, caffeine-fuelled 50-year old let himself be brushed along with the streams of sightseers and business people until the first blast of Austrian air blew across his face, bringing with it the scents of car exhaust and take-away food. Much like Oxford, really.

He had no idea what to expect when he arrived in this strange country, and as such he had dressed himself in the way he would always do to face a wet, windy spring afternoon back home. A crumpled blue and white checked shirt lay under a rather worn sports jacket with leather elbow patches, a garment which had been remarkably fashionable when he graduated and had become a permanent outdoor accessory ever since. Khalamanga didn't own a car, and had always been forced to keep his wardrobe practical over any other considerations; his bicycle had fallen into disuse recently in favour of taxis and buses. He still wore his college scarf, now providing over thirty years of service, and his sports shoes were one of a dozen identical pairs which he had accumulated over the years for their comfort, simple Velcro fastenings and low price tag.

He dropped himself into the back seat of the first available taxi, mumbled the name of the hotel and proceeded to doze off as the great and historic sights of Vienna flashed unseen past the car windows.

"Mr. Pfeifenberger," Petersen addressed the Schatzkammer's head of security. "Tell me again of your movements on Sunday the 14th from when you arrived at the museum."

The short, stocky man behind the interview desk adjusted himself nervously. "I've been through all of this before."

"I'm aware of that, and I'm sorry to have to detain you further. I assure you, you'll be free to go as soon as I am satisfied with your statement." He nodded aside to the audio recording machine which sat on the end of the table. "For the record."

"Am I being charged with anything? Because I've been here for over a day. I'd like to state that *for the record*."

Petersen looked at his watch carefully. "Actually...23 hours, and 14 minutes. And if you don't start telling me what I want to hear, I shall be detaining you for a further 48 hours, and this time I *will* be charging you, Mr. Pfeifenberger, for wasting police time."

"I think I need a lawyer. I don't like the way this is going."

"Nor do I. Having studied the security tapes of Sunday night, I'm afraid to say that the statements from you, and your colleagues, do not add up. A murder was committed in your treasury; a glass case which is connected to a complex alarm system, broken open and an artefact taken from within. No camera in the Schatzkammer recorded any of this, and nobody - not one of you - saw or heard anything. Now either you're all in this together-"

"Hey!"

"-or none of you are worthy of the description 'security guard'."

Pfeifenberger leaned in close. Petersen didn't like the way his protruding brow kept twitching, etching deep crosses and swastikas into the middle of his forehead. "Listen to me. None of the men employed there have been taken on without the most stringent security and disclosure checks, and I trust each and every one of them implicitly, as does our director - however, we cannot all be everywhere at once. That is why we have a battery of security cameras covering every inch of all our exhibits."

"Well. Not quite every inch." Kupfer countered.

"What the hell do you mean?" by now, the security chief's outrage had displaced any cool-headed notions of his rights to a lawyer. It was now a personal battle of wits between him and the policemen.

"We have found that in the group of six cameras which covers the general area where the Holy Spear is held, it is possible for an individual to keep almost completely out of sight. If he knew exactly where to walk."

"That's rubbish." Pfeifenberger snapped. "I set up that CCTV coverage myself. I ran tests for three days to ensure we had a complete 360-degree coverage of every area in the Schatzkammer."

"Are you religious?" Petersen cut in.

"No. We have priceless works of art in there. We have the treasures of the Habsburg Empire, we have artefacts worth millions-"

"Who is the Great Seth?"

"What?" Pfeifenberger finally succumbed to the Kommissar's insistence. "What are you asking me? I don't know what you're talking about."

"Just answer the question. Who is the Great Seth?"

Pfeifenberger's chest heaved with breathless incredulity. "I don't know of any Great Seth. I don't understand what this has to do with a murder, or my job or my colleagues, or security cameras, or the Spear."

"Did you kill Josef Siegel?"

"Damn you, I did not murder anybody, and nor did any of the men I work with. That was my statement when you first dragged me in here, that is my statement now-" he leaned especially close to the recording machine. "*-for the record.* And now you ask me ridiculous questions that mean nothing to me? If anyone's wasting police time here, it's yourselves."

Petersen shuffled some papers in front of him and nodded. "You're right. I'm sorry. Please, carry on."

"I started my work at 8pm on Sunday night. I went to the toilet at about 22 or 2215, I came back, sat in the office and ate my sandwiches and some sliced meat for twenty minutes, then made a coffee. Time passed, and the next thing I remember was Heinrich running shouting into the office to say the Holy Spear had been trashed, and Siegel was nowhere in sight."

"You called us at 0015 on Monday morning, Mr. Pfeifenberger. Conveniently, the tapes of Siegel's area ran out at 2355. That leaves over a quarter of an hour which is completely unaccounted for. Did you not see that the six cameras in his area had turned off?"

"They don't turn off." Pfeifenberger snapped. "What use would that be? The cameras continue to operate in close-circuit mode - all that happens is a light on the recording units goes off. Evidently, no-one noticed this."

"And *evidently*, no-one noticed a severed head being paraded through the middle of the floor, in full view of these still-operational closed-circuit cameras. And *evidently*, no-one saw the break-in and vandalism which occurred sometime between the tapes running out at midnight and when you called us fifteen minutes later. So what the hell were you all doing? Drinking beer and watching porno?"

"I can't explain it. Maybe someone looped the circuit, did something to the visual feed. I don't know."

"But you trust all your men implicitly, Mr. Pfeifenberger. And if none of your men fixed the camera feed, and Siegel didn't do it, then there would have to be an intruder in the museum, right? So no matter what, things have occurred which you and your trusted and valued colleagues should have seen. Unfortunately, we are unable to prove any failing on your part other than blind negligence, which in itself is hardly a crime, but in this case could well have allowed one to happen."

"Then I'm sorry. I truly am. Can I go now?"

"You told us there was no possibility of a blindspot on your cameras. We're going to show you one now. Follow us, please. "

Pfeifenberger refused to move. "That's ridiculous, and I won't accept such lies."

"This won't take a minute." Petersen tapped him on the shoulder. "Just give us your opinion of these video recordings, and then you can go. You see, *we* think there's a blind spot. If we're wrong, then you can tell us so. But either way, we would like you to confirm it."

Reluctantly, Pfeifenberger hauled himself out of the seat and trailed after the policemen to the monitor room. Petersen activated the video players. The six monitors filled with pictures of different angles of the treasury, then a black shape moved across the bottom of the fourth screen, disappeared, and the picture returned to normal.

"Something moved on that one," Pfeifenberger objected, pointing to the screen for camera IV. "That's wrong," he objected. "It's only showing up on one of the screens."

"And why's that wrong?" Petersen asked.

"Because - because it's a blind spot, that's why. That person's head just shows up on monitor IV, and nowhere else. That is not the coverage I set up, nor the one I'm used to. That should have been picked up by the camera opposite as well...in fact, the whole area. No, this is completely wrong." Pfeifenberger crouched in front of the screens, analysing each one in turn. "They've been set too high. They're covering blank wall space when they should be looking lower down." Kupfer stopped the tapes, leaving their interviewee to stew in silence for a minute. "Someone has interfered with our cameras."

"Someone has, yes. However, that's for us to investigate now. Sergeant Kupfer will show you out. Thank you for your patience, Mr. Pfeifenberger."

"But - this is my job-"

"Yes, Mr Pfeifenberger. But a crime has been committed, and that is *our* job now. If we need you to help us in future, we will call you."

As Kupfer led the unhappy man away, Petersen picked up the phone and dialled through to his incident room.

"Kebl? It's Petersen. I want every one of those security cameras dusted for prints and checked for DNA. Get Stroebel and everyone together and meet me there in one hour. If we're going to learn anything more before our experts start poking around, this is our chance."

Two miles cross the city, the second of those experts had already arrived. Khalamanga stepped out of the taxi and squinted up at the floodlit stonework which reminded him more of an international embassy than an hotel. The pavement surged with walking fur and flashes of gold. Laughter and talk in ten tongues penetrated his muddled mind, bursts of school language lessons flooding his memory. He looked down at the letter in his hand; yes, this was the Hotel Sacher, one of the most luxurious hotels in the world, which he had booked into simply because it was central and had vacancies. He hadn't even thought about the cost. Once again he cursed the strange system of fate which always seemed to dump him on the top floor of every hotel he had ever stayed in over the past 30 years.

Taking a deep breath and filling his slender chest with resolve, the tall, thin black man carried himself listlessly towards the red-coated doorman to begin the next stage in what had so far been a contorted week.

And it was only Tuesday.

He only hoped that the lift was in working order, unlike that time in Marseille in '83.

Walking through the Hofburg treasury, Petersen and Kupfer had much to discuss in the light of Pfeifenberger's interview. Kupfer had noticed a distinct change in his boss's demeanour, from tetchy irritation to exuberant optimism. In the five years that he had worked with Petersen, he had never seen the man so baffled by any case before, and was very glad for Petersen's sake for the recent breakthrough. It also made Kupfer's life a lot easier, as dealing with Petersen's mercurial emotions was often a task in itself.

"I still don't get it, sir. If Siegel had gone wandering, he must have passed someone, or shown up on the other cameras at some point along the way. Knobloch's people said there was no sign of him on any of the tapes apart from the ones in his area. Is there a secret exit somewhere in here? Did he sneak out for a walk around the Michaelerplatz, or what?"

Petersen finished eating the beefburger he had bought on their way over to the museum and stuffed the greasy wrappings away in his overcoat pocket. In a strange way it was amusing to see how quickly Petersen had slipped back into the bachelor lifestyle since the end of his last, brief relationship the previous autumn. Gone were the sharp suits and carefully-ironed shirts - back came the casual jackets, the scuffed shoes, the chain-smoking and the wine gum wrappers lying around in the car. He had never been the same since his wife Maria had driven her sports car into a tree one Easter. It was almost as though after losing her, he seemed incapable of seeing anyone else fill her place. Four years later, he still made weekly pilgrimages to her grave to lay fresh flowers.

Petersen wiped his mouth on the back of his hand, saying, "And the only evidence we have that Siegel was ever there at all while alive is through the testimony of his colleagues. To all intents and purposes, the man is invisible until he appears as a severed head on a plate. We have to assume, Kupfer, that the man we see walking is definitely not Josef Siegel. Personally, I still favour the conspiracy theory. The guards, or a cabal within the group of guards, did it."

Petersen looked at the investigators who were still measuring, triangulating and recording. "I've asked them to monitor the movements of a person walking around Siegel's area with the cameras set in the current configuration. I get the feeling we are going to find more than one blind spot here."

"You believe Pfeifenberger, then?"

"I believe his reactions were genuine, yes. He was shocked the cameras had been tampered with. Whether that was the shock that we discovered the fact, is another matter. As for the other guards, I have men assigned to watch all of their movements over the next 48 hours. And if nothing else turns up, I'm going to grill those bastards until one of them bursts."

"And what about the Great Seth?"

"I don't know. I'm going to have to discuss this with our Professor, and when we know a little more about it, put some more pressure on Pfeifenberger."

"Are you thinking some kind of cult, or religiously-based group? Radical Freemasons, Rosicrucians, or something?"

Petersen scratched his neck, knowing he really had to shave soon. "What the hell have you been reading, Kupfer? What's a Rosicrucian when he's at home?"

The sergeant shrugged, slightly embarrassed now. "Just a bit of research, sir. Mystical, magical societies. Possible connections. Doing what you always tell me I should be doing: trying to understand the killer's mind."

Petersen watched intently as an officer was walking back and forth in a bizarre impersonation of Groucho Marx, following parallel lines of chalk marked on the floor.

"You reckon there'll be enough of a gap to allow someone to pass almost undetected?" Kupfer asked.

The crouching officer stopped, stood up and stretched his spine, clearly relieved that it was all over.

"We're done here, sir," he called to Petersen, "Steinberg wants us to check out the results now in the security room."

Petersen turned to his sergeant, smiling. "Let's find out."

"This is what we have, first of all," explained the short, thin officer named Steinberg to the gathering behind him, "Four of the six cameras have been adjusted vertically and horizontally from what would have been an ideal set-up. In one case-" he pointed to monitors VI and II - "-as much as a 45 degree angle away from each other. Without that adjustment, both of those cameras would show a perfect combined view across the width of this area, possibly even with an overlap."

Petersen asked, "So how much of a blind spot do we have there?"

Steinberg turned from the bank of monitor screens and scratched his moustache. "About two metres, sir. Wide enough to allow someone to slip through unseen, even someone taller than Siegel. What's even more exciting is this..." He pressed some buttons on the playback machines. "Here's Rieser moving along at the exact middle point between the two sets of cameras, crouching, like the figure we saw in the reflection on the tape. Within that 'dead zone' created by the adjusted cameras, Rieser has disappeared. Whoever moved these cameras knew exactly what they were doing."

"Excellent." Petersen said. He turned to Kupfer. "You know, looking at this now, I don't think Siegel's head was supposed to have been caught on film, after all. I think someone slipped off their path."

"If he had been alive, sir," Steinberg said, "With the current camera configuration he would have had to have been walking on his knees. I definitely concur with that - the head was a mistake."

"Good spot of luck, eh?" Kupfer laughed.

"First bloody one on this whole case." Petersen retorted. "Now all we need to do is figure out how the hell they broke into the display case without getting seen. Alright, people. By close of play today, I want a hypothetical route through the entire Schatzkammer. I also want checks done on the walls and floors of this place for concealed entrances, doors, false walls. This building has been an Imperial treasure vault for centuries - it must hold its share of secrets. I want X-rays, I want sonar, every clever thing you can bring in here."

As they left the museum into the cool floodlit evening, Petersen's telephone rang. He was answered by a nervous, quiet voice, which sounded as if it belonged to someone who was not used to speaking on the telephone.

"Ah, hello Inspector. Emanuel Khalamanga here. You asked me to call you when I arrived. Well, eh, I've arrived. In my hotel room now."

"Good for you, Doctor. Spend the rest of the night settling in. I'll call you in the morning and we'll meet up for a talk. Rest up, and thank you again for coming at such short notice."

Khalamanga was about to thank him in return when the line went dead. He tried not to be too disappointed that his services were not immediately required, that there was no car to collect him, no urgent meeting. The man was obviously very busy and would probably be working into the night, doing all the tiring, difficult things he was sure policemen had to do.

As he placed the telephone handset down, he found his eyes drawn to the local television news, which reported a brief update on the matter of the Holy Spear. There followed a story on another matter of religious significance; the inquest into the recent and mysterious death of the Archbishop of Paderborn in Westphalia, wherein the venerable cleric had been discovered a week past on Sunday, drowned in a vat of yeast in his own brewery. The police had not ruled out foul play, although once again they seemed unable to find any evidence. Though saddened by the story, Khalamanga was also inspired by the great praise heaped upon the late Archbishop by his successor, reminding him that good men still existed in the world, a fact which made their passing all the more tragic.

Switching off the plasma screen, he lay back on his bed and let his gaze wander to the ceiling. He had never been fond of hotels, finding them rather impersonal, but this one was more agreeable than most. The Sacher stood just behind the Imperial burial vault on the Maysedergasse and opposite the Hofburg itself. He had deliberately got as close to the scene of the crime as he could, hence his relegation to the top floor. Reading again the information leaflets he had grabbed from the tourist office, he was irked to find out he had arrived on the one day of the week that the Schatzkammer was closed. And since the policeman was busy, and the museum locked up, he resolved to get a feel for the local area and get his bearings, as Petersen had suggested.

He began his evening of discovery with a stroll around the immaculate Burggarten which stretched out behind the Nationalbibliothek building. The library was closing, it being nearly six o'clock, and was the one place that Khalamanga had decided he would have to visit before he left, to examine the ancient collection of papyri and the original writings of Martin Luther, as well as the more esoteric manuscripts stored there. He spent a few moments basking in the baroque glory of the white-stoned building, a testament to the brilliance of its architects, the von Erlachs, and the inordinate sense of exuberance on the part of Holy Roman Emperor Charles VI who had commissioned this addition to the Imperial Palace in the early 1700s.

He wandered the grounds for a while before moving further into the sprawling courtyards of the Hofburg, now swimming in warm amber floodlights which highlighted this majestic keystone of the Habsburg Empire and filled the Doctor with a sense of the true grandeur of history. Standing before this monument to the will and power of central Europe granted him a fleeting view of times less sophisticated scientifically but infinitely purer artistically, when wonders were created not for gain or infamy but for the greater glory of the celestial empire. Of times when knights rode and made a battleground of the fields and towns of Europe, and when religious divisions inspired papal excommunications, murder and persecution. The excitement Khalamanga felt with this insight into his fanciful vision of the Middle Ages, ebbed rapidly as he realised how little the centuries had done to change the Old World's attitudes.

The splendour of the museum dispersed before the doctor's sad eyes, forcing him to turn away from that symbol of secular authority and dominion, and for a second he fancied himself as a monk, refusing to catch the eye of a beautiful temptress, fleeing the temptations of the Hofburg.

An accordion man sat on a wall a short distance away, a feathered hat and lederhosen painting a quaintly amusing picture for the visitor, who nonetheless felt compelled to toss a few coins into his silver-lined case. Khalamanga was perfectly used to being the clichéd innocent abroad, but something had now crept over him which filled him with a deep discomfort. It was in the symbolism, not the actuality, of the imperial majesty around him; the sensation that for every empire built, there are thousands or millions of individual lives crushed in the process, walls and palaces built not with stones but with the souls of slaves and soldiers, the foundations the bones of the vanquished.

He walked away, unheedful of the gangs of sightseers which mingled around him, and headed off to his room to read, to be back again in his familiar world of chivalry and romance, heroism and humility, where deeds were done for God and quests were always fulfilling.

By contrast, de Carranza's day had passed pleasantly in the company of Vanessa and a bottle of Chianti. The setting was a small cafe between the Rooseveltplatz and Sigmund-Freud-Park, an intimidating pair of neighbours who had de Carranza jokingly expressing his own inadequacy.

"Careful, Tomas. Doctor Freud might hear, and start telling you things about yourself you didn't want to know."

He laughed that off at the time but her words lay lodged in the seat of his consciousness like a speck of dirt, and forced him into objectifying the afternoon more than he had planned. It was rare that Tomas de Carranza spent time with a woman and spoke from his head more than his heart, yet that was how the dinner conversation progressed.

He found the meal particularly heavy-going, despite it being recommended by the waiter as Franz Josef's favourite; Tafelspitz, or thundering great slabs of beef with what looked (and tasted) exactly like hash browns although the waiter referred to them as Rostkartoffeln. Despite the spinach dressing, it was just like the things served up in the University canteen, a fact which made him laugh out loud when it was delivered to the table. The apple horseradish sank like a brick within him, and as the bill was brought for his attention, de Carranza reflected sadly that for all their culture, architecture, art and music, the Viennese still cooked up dinners like Bavarian pig farmers, and expected you to pay up for the privilege as well.

They hadn't discussed the Hofburg case either, although they had talked a little about him and a lot about her. She had opened up to him without the laxative of alcohol, confessing her own inner fears in a purgatorial overture before the drink had even arrived. With the depths of her soul laid bare, the discussion then brightened to take in art, literature and favourite television police shows. He learned that she loved classic films but she would not say which actors she preferred.

The encounter was proving pleasing, promising even, but he still didn't know what to make of her. She was fragile and damaged in some ways, yet strong and hardened in others. She knew her own mind, perhaps too well - he knew the signs of neurotic introspection after five years in the company of Pablo Sandoval. She was somebody who needed somebody, for her own sake and safety. And while he was more than willing to be her chaperon throughout the investigation, he was wary of being drawn too far into her world. He had spent the best part of a decade baby-sitting his emotionally-damaged first wife, a woman who held the world to blame for all the pain she had suffered in her past and who gave back nothing in return for all the care and pampering she received.

She was an undeniable attraction, Vanessa. In her colouring and looks she reminded him a lot of his most beloved film actress, Nieves Navarro, about the time she made '*La Muerte Acaricia a Medianoche'*. The brightest thing about Vienna he had seen so far, as he had found little time for sightseeing. And yet like the city herself, he knew she was a deadly attraction. He hoped she would find her rational scientist's mind again soon, and show him her normal self so that he might be the better judge of her as a person, free from fear and pains, and enjoy her company out of pure friendship or more, not pity or sympathy. He thought of Dr. Freud again, his memory invested in the neighboring walled gardens and their symbolism not only of enlightenment but of the feminine and all its mysteries.

And now they moved together, unhurried and relaxed through the deep shade and sun-spotted colours of Freud's Park of the Eternal Womb, she with her handbag now swinging casually at her side, no longer the shield of defence it had been in the car, and he with his hands clasped behind his back to demonstrate his openness, his oneness with Her Realm.

"That was wonderful, thanks." she told him as the descending sun wrapped itself around the dark outline of the Votivkirche. "I can't think of a better way to round off a dinner than with a walk in the park. Especially one as gorgeous as this."

He sucked a long breath into his chest, enjoying the clean air which rushed to his head. "Yes. Indeed, delightful. Perhaps not *the* garden of delights...no, my dear, no other earthly garden can compete with that of the Alhambra Palace in Granada. To the Moors who built it, a garden was the closest thing to heaven on earth. The symbol of paradise and eternity. Have you ever...? Well, you would cherish the experience, I promise. It is truly like another world."

"Next time I'm in Spain, I'll remember to look it up."

"Careful." He took her elbow and sharply steered her around a mound of illegally-deposited dog turd on the path. "This city can be a minefield."

"I know. I blame the owners."

"No, I'm quite sure it's dogs who are responsible. You won't find *that* in the Alhambra."

She laughed at his unintentional humour then fell serious again. "I can't help but notice, though - we haven't even mentioned the Hofburg case yet."

"I didn't feel it appropriate, given your state earlier-"

She pulled him to a halt and for just a second, he was convinced she was going to take him all the way into the bushes behind them. "Tomas, I want you to *listen* to me. I appreciate you trying to do the best for me, but you shouldn't try to protect me from the real world. I can handle it, believe me."

"You can handle it? I'd love to believe you, but when I held you outside the police video room, you were trembling like a rabbit."

"That was mainly because...you were *holding* me," she smiled guiltily, knowing she had thrown him a line and been more honest than she had intended. That would be the Chianti talking then.

He caught whiff of the bait but turned his nose up at it. "Nonsense. I know true fear when I see it. And I will not be responsible for sending you back into that state. Not when you've been so..." he paused, flicking the hook back in her direction. "...so good today."

They stood beside the car before either of them realised they had come to the end of their stroll. He waited for her reaction, physical or verbal, but she seemed keen to be his passenger again, to let him drive her home.

"Vanessa, let me be honest with you. Even I am already starting to have doubts about my place here, about whether I'm as well-equipped as I think I am to handle what may be waiting around the corner. I know that we have not seen the last death in this case. Can you face up to that? Can you face more bodies, more blood? Because I don't know if I can."

"Now you're sounding like me," she laughed. "Have I infected you with my bad vibes?"

"Let's just say you may have woken me out of a silly little daydream."

"Out of the two of us, Professor, I would say I'm the one who's been sleeping." She patted the roof of the car. "Well what now, Sir?"

"You said you wanted to get back to your rooms, get a bath, and relax. And I did say I was going to call upon Professor Gruber tonight, remember."

He saw her peering at a distant point somewhere over his shoulder, frowning. "Oh yeah. I remember." a mild sigh drifted past him. "Well, let's go, then."

He drove her to the Holiday Inn through the evening traffic, stripes of white and amber light gliding past them to the radio accompaniment of Berlioz's 'Symphanie Fantastique'. No verbal dialogue passed between them, but he detected more of her ambiguous physical signals. Her hands moved from behind the headrest of the seat, to her knees, to a clasped position over her lap, and back again to behind her head.

"Holiday Inn." He announced as he pulled up on the handbrake. "That'll be fifty Euros."

She laughed as she gathered herself together and pushed open the door. "Sure. Not even London cabbies are that bad." She leaned in close, "And thanks again. I do hope we can do it again sometime soon." She had almost kissed him on the cheek for his trouble, he fancied, just before she pulled herself out of the car.

He waited for her to get inside the hotel, waved at her in reply as she turned to wave at him from the doorway. Then she was gone. He sat and waited a minute longer, weighing up the previous few hours, before punching in the details for Laudongasse on the sat-nav.

de Carranza stepped out the car and adjusted his jacket, checked his hair in the mirror and strode smartly across to ring the doorbell of the semi-detached house at number 174. Unseen in the driver's seat of a black Volvo estate car, parked half a block down the road, a slim figure in priest's clothing watched de Carranza as he waited on the doorstep. He scribbled down some notes on the writing pad on his lap: "*DC to G's, 942pm, prob. spear-related biz?*"

The car had smoked windows, making it all but impossible to see inside, an accidental piece of luck which suited the nocturnal activities of its driver very well. The car had been chosen primarily for its heavy steel construction and lack of crumple zones, making it a useful high-speed weapon or getaway vehicle in an emergency. And even if anyone had been able to notice him within, very few would stop to question a man in priest's clothing. It was a useful distraction as well as a means to get others to drop their guard. In the days to come, however, he knew he would need a lot more than a suit of clothes and a car to get him through the impending storm and the dawn of the Black Sun.

A light went on behind the window in the front door. The priest swiftly drew up the 35mm camera from his lap and snapped off half a dozen shots as de Carranza was welcomed by Karl-Heinze Gruber and ushered inside. The door closed and the priest wound up the window again. He turned on the CD player and sat back to listen to the thin voice of Roy Harper singing 'Burn the World', a song he had first heard while serving out in Bosnia. The lyrical beauty of the words held dark portents for Europe and the world as a whole, bringing a flood of mixed emotions for the listener. The circumstances had not improved greatly since the Balkan war. The wars of faith and freedom still raged. Europe faced another genocidal holocaust, more terrible than had ever been imagined or attempted in the past. The priest realised there was very little time left, and he knew his own actions would have to be carefully considered. All he could hope to do was what he had always done - what had kept him alive in the seventeen years since Iraq, Bosnia, Palestine and Israel - to be faster than them, to run, to hide, to draw them out of their shadows while he hid in his own - to line up his telescopic sights on the right head at the right moment, should the need arise.

"Why burn the world, indeed." he echoed in a voice thick with passion.

"Come in, come in. I'm so glad you could come. So, is this visit pleasure or business?"

de Carranza followed Gruber down the narrow hallway of pinewood panelling and spotless white carpet, concerned at the possibility of leaving little deposits of dog turd in his wake.

"Both, as it happens."

"I'm afraid I'm all out of women at the moment," Gruber laughed upon opening the door of the living room. "So you'll have to put up with me, a few drinks and a game of chess, if you fancy."

de Carranza accepted the invitation heartily. Gruber was a compulsive chess buff, even to the point of attending international contests which seemed to de Carranza's mind the most ludicrous waste of time. He could understand the need for people to attend a football game or athletic event, but not to watch two old men pushing pieces of carved wood around a board. To Gruber, it was as exciting as a Madrid derby in La Liga, but to de Carranza it was on a par with watching the houseplants wilt.

de Carranza looked around the living room, silently absorbing details. Neat and minimal, arranged with a perfectionist's fuss and ordered by someone who clearly lived alone and had a little too much time on his hands. He noted that the few dozen DVDs beside the television cabinet were arranged in alphabetical order. The living room table held a silver-plated Napoleonic chess set, Gruber's pride and joy. While Gruber prepared drinks at the sideboard, de Carranza crossed the deep faux fox rug to the fireplace and surveyed the line of pewter and silver figurines displayed there. "I've been introduced to the lady you mentioned. You're right; she's very impressive."

"Slim, supple redhead. Just your type, I thought."

"Quite." de Carranza agreed, unwilling to continue the banter he had always enjoyed so much in the past. It didn't seem appropriate to reduce that sincere, troubled woman to a series of schoolboy opinions. He picked up a statuette of a silver dragon from the mantlepiece, put it back again.

Gruber noted his guest's idle curiosity. "My daughter gives me those things at Christmas. I happened to express interest in them once in passing, and she's got it into her head now that I'm just crazy for dragons. There's a whole collection of them gathering dust upstairs."

"Dust?" de Carranza retorted, "I see no dust in this house, Ka-Hache. You have an excellent maid. Do you pay her well?"

"No, this is all my own work. But don't worry, I don't go dancing around the place with an apron on and a feather duster." he passed de Carranza a gin and tonic. "Now, you mentioned something about business?"

They sat down either end of the leather sofa, a well-worn brown three-seater which squeaked and creaked beneath de Carranza's restless body. "I'd like to ask about the inscription on the spear," he began. "It doesn't look like any of the original versions of the 'Great Seth' that I'm used to."

"Very well spotted, Tomas. You're quite right, it is written in the Sahidic dialect. That form is usually associated with the region of Hermopolis Magna, once a major shrine of the Egyptian god Thoth, and the inspiration for countless alchemists and magi through history."

"And modern-day clowns like Crowley, so I recall." de Carranza added. "I read some of that rubbish as a young man, in the days when I thought myself rebellious and radical."

"Crowley may have been a poseur, but his influence lives on to this very day. And many educated and respected persons still buy into magical beliefs."

"And what about you, as an educated and respected person, Ka-Hache? Do you buy into that mumbo-jumbo?"

"I like to keep an open mind. I don't believe that everything that exists can be satisfactorily explained by science."

"Keeping an open mind of that sort just makes it easier for your brains to leak out. Magic, and religion: the two are equally redundant in today's world as far as I can see."

"Yet both would seem to feature in this case of yours." Gruber looked at him over the tops of his glasses. "Do you not believe that there could be a link to the esoteric in there somewhere?"

"My new partner from Oxford believes all sorts of things, according to our Inspector. I suppose I'll find out when I have the pleasure of meeting him tomorrow."

"I asked what *you* believe, Tomas."

de Carranza pulled himself out of the depths of the sofa and strode to the table. "I believe we should play some chess," he announced brightly. "I'll even let you play white."

Outside in the parked Volvo, the priest awoke sharply, chilled and sweaty. The CD had long since stopped playing; silence surged around him. Shadow, cold and thick, blanketed him from the dim streetlamps. Movement cut across his vision twenty yards ahead, a pale flash of skin, and his body jerked instinctively into action.

Someone had just walked into No. 177, the house directly opposite Gruber's. A taxi sat at the kerb, idling. He caught a hint of a long overcoat and shining patent shoes, but the figure vanished through the front door before he managed to confirm even the individual's gender. As the taxi pulled off into the night, he cursed himself. He had nodded off, thanks to the soothing melancholy of the music. He angrily ejected the CD and swapped it out for something louder, and much less mellow. It was after 11pm, and he was prepared to make a night of it if need be, fuelled by the clattering guitar of Pete Townshend. He wondered if the flask of coffee in the back seat would still be warm after four hours.

de Carranza was still regretting giving Gruber the option of playing as white, and was struggling just to force the game into stalemate. Gruber had successfully fragmented his forces, luring de Carranza into sacrifices, pins and counter-attacks which had kept the Spaniard on the back foot almost since the start. The game had been going for over an hour, and de Carranza found himself backing further into a corner.

"Your move." Gruber reminded him.

The Spaniard studied the board a final time. His eyes had become blurry with black and white squares, and he was almost glad it would soon be over. He realised that whatever move he made, his king was lost. Refusing to allow Gruber to make the killing move, he toppled his king with a flick of his finger and stood up.

Gruber moved his queen into place, ending the struggle. "Shah mat," he declared with a satisfied smile, but de Carranza was already pointing to his horizontal king, symbol of his resignation.

"*Shah mord, zendeh bad Shah.*"

"Come along, Tomas. You know as well as I do that the King does not die. He is simply paralysed, *ambushed.*"

"He does when I order him to drink hemlock." The conversation paused on that note until Gruber laughed, breaking the silence.

"Best of three?"

"Perhaps next time. I have some research to catch up on."

As he walked through the hall, de Carranza's head was turned by a painting he had failed to notice before, due to its place on the wall behind the front door. It sat in a simple clip-frame but the subject matter kept his attention; a rather bored-looking woman in a red and white gown holding the severed head of a man on a silver plate. Gruber appeared behind him with a glass of wine in his hand.

"It's a Titian," he explained. "*Salome with the Head of John the Baptist.*"

de Carranza continued to stare, struck by the pertinence of the picture and its reflection of cruel reality he had witnessed that morning in the police station, so far removed from the romanticized myth. "So I see. Poor old St. John. He's usually shown being decapitated by a sword, isn't he?"

From the corner of his eye, de Carranza thought he saw a shadow of alarm darken the other man's features.

"He what?"

"Nothing, Ka-Hache. I'm just mumbling into my beard. Let me thank you for putting up with me at such short notice. Perhaps I shall come again soon, if only to catch you in the act of conducting a black mass."

Gruber laughed heartily. "That only happens once a year, at Walpurgisnacht." He drained his glass and put it aside on the hall table. "Go on, get out of here, before I start pelting you with useless dragon ornaments."

de Carranza departed with a cheerful wave and a laugh, but the laughter died on his face as soon as the front door closed behind him. As he walked down the path de Carranza felt angry, inferior. Not because he had lost a simple game of chess to a man who played the game obsessively and studied the tactics of the grandmasters, but a more general feeling of surrender and submission to another mind. He had come to Vienna to promote his own mental prowess, to unravel clues and help to solve a mystery, but more than anything to challenge the mind responsible for creating the mystery in the first place and prove himself superior to that cruel intelligence.

So far that had not happened and de Carranza was reminded of his own fallibility, even if only in the field of chess-playing. He would have to be more careful, think more tactfully, look further ahead. The face of Jack Unterweger swam out of the mental muddle of the day's events, reminding him to be on his guard at all times. Like his chess game, his attitude to life was still impulsive, self-focused, not enough thought given to the stronger forces that could easily manoeuvre him into positions he did not want to be in.

Inside the dark Volvo, the priest stopped the CD player and scrawled down "DC out: 2354. All clear." As the Spaniard opened the door of his car, a set of headlights flashed into view around the corner, momentarily turning him into a glowing silhouette. A tyre whined, the sound scratching hard across the priest's consciousness. His right hand went down to the side of his seat and drew up a Glock-17 semi-automatic. de Carranza jumped into the Peugeot and the other car flashed past, revealed to be a large jeep driven by a middle-aged woman. The priest watched its tail lights turn to firefly flashes in his rear-view and slid the gun away inside his coat, into a custom-built holster that also held a quiver of crossbow bolts. He breathed out slowly, expelling the adrenaline which had just burst within him, instinct and training giving way again to calm.

de Carranza's idle fingers found a radio station playing Spanish gypsy music, and with those bright jangling sounds to cheer him on his way, he started up and headed back to the city centre in the direction of his hotel. He did not see the dark Volvo slide out after him and follow him at a discreet distance, nor did he see Gruber peering out into the street from his upstairs window.

News and badly-dubbed films which he had seen many times before proved to be the only televisual attractions for de Carranza as he sat in his guest house, flicking between channels with the remote controller. He was not bored nor especially tired, just restless and unable to settle on any particular activity. He had scribbled some ideas based upon the information in Petersen's dossier but his mind was starting to reject serious thought and wander away down thorny paths of its own.

He thought back to Gruber's painting, the macabre Biblical tale of the Baptist. He knew of the Johannite sects through history who had worshipped John over Christ as the true Messiah, yet the circumstances of the crime didn't ring true. The head by itself in the chapel made sense; the strange bodily mutilation didn't. Nor did the spear, or the 'Great Seth' inscription.

He was at a complete loss now. So far his attempts to further his own intellectual standing had proved fruitless. He had committed himself to this case; people were counting upon him to deliver the goods, and so far he had nothing to offer anyone, not even himself. He left the armchair and crossed to the bed, meticulously made and hard, so unlike the rumpled four-poster heap in his own apartment which had not been properly made up for months. Nobody else but him ever spent time there, he reasoned, so why bother?

He bounced himself against the bed a few times in an attempt to soften up the mattress, felt his chest flap heavily as he did so. The childish amusement engendered by the bouncing gave way to saddened self-loathing. He had put on weight again, against all doctors' orders. He pulled up his vest and watched his abdomen collapse down into four rounded segments. Some random imagining crossed his mind – what would Vanessa think of that, should the wildest possibilities ever fulfil themselves - would she still find him the intriguing subject of her drink-fuelled fancies, despite the floppy padding and sparse grey clumps of hair? The faded eyes of the black bull tattoo on his left bicep stared boldly up at him, reminding him of younger days when such cares were beyond a lifetime away. Now repelled by the personal inadequacy he had joked about earlier, he grabbed at the remote controller and stabbed the search buttons in search of some late-night adult channel. What looked like a promising trailer for a film featuring a trio of blondes in fishnets and fetish attire turned out to be only an advertisement for an online dating site, followed by pulsating attempts to promote gay chat lines and other extortionate services.

His thoughts idled back to Vanessa, alone and tired just like him, probably, or asleep beside an empty bottle. He had cast his line and she had bitten, but he remained unwilling to reel her in, reluctant to taste the blood that rained from her lips. For then, the sport would have ended and the morality would begin. Would he end up casting her back alive for someone else to tease, or crush her brains out beneath the rock of his will? The games he and Gruber had so long enjoyed as younger men now looked so cold and cruel. Something in that fiery-haired woman, her sea-grey eyes brewing storms, had tamed his old and primal instincts. Either she was an angel of harmony, or he really was growing old and inadequate, he decided.

His thumb squeezed the rubbery 'off' button before propelling the controller across the room to the middle of the sofa, where it bounced onto the rug. If there was nothing to occupy the id, then he might as well try again with the intellect. If nothing else, Petersen's businesslike prose might send him to sleep.

Three lines into the description of the crime scene and his mobile phone rang, fracturing his fragile line of thought and forcing him to stretch across to the other side of the bed to answer the call.

"Professor, you there?"

"Vanessa! Hallo. I've told you - 'Tomas', please."

"Sorry, Tomas. What are you up to?"

"Not very much. Lying here trying to make sense of this damn case." He slapped shut the dossier. "And I'm getting nowhere. You?"

"I'm sorry to butt in on you like this. I fell asleep earlier, and woke up, all groggy like." she trailed off, sounding as if she did not know where to take the conversation now. And pleasing though it was, de Carranza was not feeling open to smalltalk. There was a reason behind this call, and he wanted it.

"Not a problem. Is there anything you want to share?"

"I'm not sure if it's important. But when I came into my hotel tonight after you dropped me off, there was a man in the lobby. Just hanging around, it looked like. He was a priest - big hat, long coat, collar. The works. I just thought he looked out of place. I've been living in this hotel now for weeks and never seen anyone like him before. Looked as though he was searching for something, or someone."

"You know what priests are like these days. Probably waiting for his boyfriend."

She snorted down the line at that. "Now you know I'm crazy. Phoning you up at midnight to tell you I'm getting paranoid."

"Do you want to talk?" he asked, knowing that she did.

"You know what - yes, I do. And I didn't really ring you up just to mention that priest fellow, although he did kind of spook me for about two minutes. But maybe I should save it for another time. When we're face to face and maybe not so tired." She pulled his hooks from her lips and cast them aside, for the meantime at least. "And - I guess – when we've got to know each other a little more. I'm sorry. You know I've had a bad day. I just wanted to thank you again for helping to make it better."

"It's quite alright. I do aim to please. Even if the telescopic sights sometimes need adjusting."

She found that funny, a hard and full-on laugh which almost startled him. "Well, you certainly hit me between the eyes, Tomas. That's for sure. Have a good sleep, and take care. I mean it."

She put her phone down and rolled over the bed onto her belly where she lay for a few breaths, inhaling the perfume of her pillow. It was sweet but should have been sweeter, soaked in male sweat and aggression. She had lost her nerve on the call, just as she knew she would. The Dutch courage of the Chianti had long worn off, leaving her afraid to come out with the words she had planned earlier in the evening, before he had insisted on taking her home, before her exhaustion caught up with her.

Yet there remained a restlessness in her body which kept her alert, driving her to fulfil those lingering longings. Her right hand slipped under the bed and wormed its way along the floor until the fingers found the straps of leather hidden there. For a minute she lay still, pondering, focusing on the moment with a rising swell of expectation. She closed her eyes and brought the lash up onto the pillow beside her, the scent of the leather filling her attention as her pulse galloped and thundered like the 'Ride of the Valkyries'.

Her other hand scrambled out to the bedside unit and grappled with the radio, finding the classical music channel she often listened to at night. This night she turned it up louder than usual.

DAY THREE: Wednesday

de Carranza sat with Khalamanga in Petersen's office at 0940 the following morning, listening as the policeman explained the latest details in what de Carranza had already dubbed 'The Case of the Holy Spear'.

Khalamanga had completely failed to live up to any of the Spaniard's expectations. For a figure standing over six feet tall, de Carranza's first impression was that he was grossly underweight, a condition not helped by having legs which looked far too long in proportion to the rest of him. England was also clearly a country of short men with no dress sense, to judge by the laughably poor taste and cut of his clothing. For a man who was alleged to know so much he said very little, and what little he did say seemed to be quoted verbatim from some medieval text or modern critique, and de Carranza had to wonder if his new colleague had ever conceived an original thought of his own. Apart from anything else, the new visitor seemed in awe of his surroundings, and had hugged his bony knees throughout the entire meeting as though he were a schoolboy facing his headmaster across the desk, taking his cues to talk only from Petersen himself and smiling nervously when spoken to.

Petersen flickered through the grease-smeared pages of 'Who Was Jesus?', now defaced with black ink and coffee stains. He placed it aside and turned to the small pile of books beside him which Khalamanga had delivered earlier that morning.

"An interesting collection, Doctor. I'm still working my way through these, but I do see a little light at the end of the tunnel. Now, I'm pulling together my whole team this afternoon for a review of our case so far. I think it would be very valuable if you gentlemen could attend and present to us, in simple layman's terms, what motivations you feel may be at work here. I'm not looking for a lecture. Five minutes from each of you?" Both men agreed heartily. "Thank you. Here's everything we have." Petersen handed out updated files. "We have a psychological profiler in Salzburg assisting us best he can. However, I am hopeful that any light you gentlemen can shed on this matter will aid him in determining what sort of person, or persons, may have carried out this act."

Khalamanga looked up from his brief study of the file. "I know you said this isn't your priority, but what is the current condition of the spear?"

"It has not yet been reassembled, given that the spearhead itself and the nail are both forgeries."

de Carranza flicked back a page in his file and re-read some notes. "It says here the spearhead found was from the Carolingian period, the same as the original Holy Spear."

"According to Frau Descartes' data, yes."

"So. Who's to say which is the original artefact?"

"Look further and you'll see the inscription was very small, barely a millimetre high. When she first showed me the Coptic engraving, she was very doubtful that this was anything other than a completely modern addition, left on the spear as a kind of cryptic message."

de Carranza crossed his legs and read on. "I think we all need to meet and talk about this in some detail. She says this Seth inscription is not visible with the naked eye. Would it be possible for us to view the spear to verify this? Preferably with Vanessa present."

Petersen hesitated. "I'm wary of keeping Frau Descartes on this case, even in a peripheral role. You saw her reaction yesterday morning."

"Yes, I did. And I saw a lot of her afterwards, and I know she still has a great deal to tell us but she needs time, encouragement, to open up to us. We all need her, Kommissar, because she knows more about the spear than anyone."

"As long as you know what you're doing, Professor." Petersen connected with the other man's stare, and held it. "I don't want anybody's judgement becoming compromised here."

de Carranza slowly reached inside his jacket and removed a cigar, which he proceeded to unwrap as the resonance of that allegation lingered. "You asked me here to help." He replied, rustling crinkly cellophane. "And that is what I shall do."

Petersen finally broke the line and returned to his notes. "Frau Descartes has been given sole access to the spear by the assistant curator. I can call him now and arrange a meeting with all of us, if you want."

The Spaniard smiled broadly. "That would be wonderful." He turned to his new associate. "Then we can all get to know each other better, eh Doctor?."

Within the hour Petersen and the two scholars stood inside Lab 9 with Weber, making quiet small talk until Vanessa arrived with the spear. The thin, angular black man with the grin full of too-white teeth unnerved her slightly, only because he did not fit her stereotyped idea of what an Oxford don should look like. Standing beside de Carranza, he looked a lot like the straight man of a comedy double act. That made her smile and ensured that she had her happy face on by the time people started to speak to her.

Petersen made the formal introductions, Khalamanga shaking her hand gently by the fingers only, as though he feared contamination. Once again, de Carranza took the liberty of kissing the hand the Nigerian had feared to touch.

"The gentlemen wish to examine the spear at first hand," Petersen explained. "To clear up a little matter over the modern inscription."

Vanessa shrugged. "It is just what the analyses show it to be, a very small piece of engraving, carried out with modern etching equipment, I would say." She placed the spear's security case up on the bench behind them and unlocked it.

de Carranza nodded. "Ah, yes. That was rather the part of the report I was looking to corroborate."

"Corroborate what, Sir?" she replied gently. "It's all there. There's nothing to see with the naked eye, just a line of squiggles and scratches. It would have passed completely unnoticed if we hadn't been looking for anything amiss."

de Carranza leaned himself against the workbench as though it were a cocktail bar.

71

"How good is your eyesight, my dear?"

Vanessa found herself physically taking a step back from so blunt a question.

"My what? My eyesight? Pretty damn good, as it happens."

He turned to the assistant curator. "Mr. Weber - what about you?"

"I wear these, all of the time." he tapped the half-moons that rested at the end of his long nose.

"Yes, but are you short or long sighted?"

"Long. Why?"

"I see. And Kommissar Petersen?"

"I have one of the best target shooting records in my department. What exactly is going on, Professor?"

de Carranza smiled inscrutable smiles to himself, walking in circles as if to reflect the turning of his mental cogwheels. Or holding the attention of the others, knowing he was the centre of it. "So, has anybody else ever handled the spear since it was found on the floor?"

"Certainly not." Weber snapped, getting irritated now. "I made sure of that myself. Not even the police went near it, until the lady here had been called in to remove it. The dusting and forensic routines were performed by her alone, under my supervision."

de Carranza laughed at the news he had been hoping to hear. "Could you pass me the spear please, my dear."

After a moment's hesitation, Vanessa opened the steel case and slid it along the bench. "So out of everyone who has so far handled the spear, none is short-sighted."

de Carranza took off his spectacles and placed them aside, leant over the case and peered down into it until his nose almost touched the spearhead. "I, on the other hand, am blind as a barn full of fruitbats. Normally I wear contact lenses for reasons of vanity and practicality, but currently these glasses are more comfortable. I am extremely myopic, as you will see from the thickness of the lenses. What you may not know is that myopia is a natural magnifier, and in the case of the males in my family, equivalent to a 2.5 or 3x power lens at very close distance. I know this as my father was a jeweller, and his father before him, and I too trained for the profession as a small boy..." he screwed his face up further as his head twitched from side to side. "...until I found history more interesting than engraving."

He turned to Vanessa, who was now staring at him with utter incredulity. "My dear, you cannot, but I assure you that I can, read the individual characters in this inscription." He moved his head back down into the case and scrawled down the first line on the back of an envelope which he then passed to Khalamanga. "This is certainly the strangest sight test I've ever undertaken, but how does that compare, Doctor, with the enlargements?"

Khalamanga shuffled papers within his dossier, checked them, and checked them again. "An exact match." He said at last. de Carranza straightened his back, exhaling sharply as he did so. He closed the case again and collected his spectacles.

"Most ancient engravers were probably as blind as me," he explained. "Polished clear stones and crystals for magnifying were known among Roman artisans in New

Testament times. Your tiny inscription does not demand modern equipment of any kind, my dear. Just a half-blind old man with a steady hand and a needle-point chisel."

Petersen laughed at that, the first time anyone had seen him do so. "Let me leave you gentlemen and lady to it," he said. Without any discernible hint of irony, he added; "I'm sure you will all get on very well together."

Weber urgently regained custody of the spear, locking up the case before one of those foreign treasure-hunters got their hands on it.

"I..." Vanessa stammered, now feeling very foolish, something she was becoming used to in the presence of the Spaniard. "Well, I assumed..."

"Assumption is the mother of all disasters," de Carranza grinned. "I should know, having created enough of my own. My second marriage was based solely on assumption: that it would be somehow different from the first one." Khalamanga buckled with laughter and even Vanessa found herself smiling at the situation. She had been proved publicly wrong, even humiliated, but she did not care.

The three of them shared a bench on the banks of the Danube, where snacking and smalltalk filled the time before the meeting with Petersen's incident team. The Augartenbrucke stretched out of the trees across the whispering Donaukanal and with her eyes closed and the sound of city traffic an almost subconscious hum, Vanessa could imagine herself away somewhere else, distant in time and space. She sensed de Carranza at her side, imagined him dressed not in fashionable designer labels but swathed in black Bedouin robes and the warm wind which washed over her arose from a desert twilight rather than the Viennese Spring.

So the city did have her corrals of silence, away from tourists and traffic, where the light of calm could still penetrate. de Carranza looked at Vanessa stretched out in the seat, head back, eyes shut. Unwilling to disrupt her, he gently placed her portion of the snack on her lap.

"Your sandwiches, when you want them."

"Thanks." she continued to watch the sun paint pulsing patterns on the insides of her eyelids and wished that she had packed her sunglasses in her bag. "So what do you fellows think happened on Sunday night then?"

de Carranza removed his spectacles and sat back, his usual prelude to an explanation. "The lack of material evidence so far makes things difficult. All that we really have is this spearhead and a text which highlights the ignorance of others, and can be read only by the half-blind. It's tempting to say that someone is trying to tell us something about the foundations of orthodox Christianity. Don't you think?" he turned to the long, dark figure to his left. Khalamanga shuffled pages within his police dossier, frowning. He had occasionally mumbled to himself but so far said nothing of any consequence to either of his new associates. "Doctor Khalamanga? Who do you think did it?"

"We have no need to know the name or personal details of the murderer," Khalamanga opined. "That is irrelevant. What we need to pin down is the motivation, the psychology, and the reasoning behind the act – for it is a symbolic act. Naming the murderer is a formality for the police."

de Carranza looked back out to the canal, where a passenger cruiser drifted calmly past, its human cargo a wave of sunglasses, hats and cameras on the deck. The Spaniard watched them slide out of his vision and out of his life. He wondered how many thousands of people had passed through his life to date, all the bit-part players each with their own destinies and paths, and how many other lives he had similarly touched in the tiniest of ways.

"Is that your analysis so far, Doctor?"

When a frustrating silence continued to pass for a reply from Khalamanga, rustling to his right returned his attention to Vanessa, now wide-eyed and opening up her sandwich pack.

"Are you joining us tonight for the team talk?" he asked her.

She took out the first sandwich and felt it flop in her hand. It was that cheap, limp bread which would break and tear under its own weight, never mind the filling.

"I'd actually planned to do a little sightseeing. Try to clear my head, and get away from spears and mysteries for a few hours. I wouldn't be adding very much to your presentation, anyway. Though if you want to give me a call, or send me a text, when you're finished...?"

de Carranza noted the girlish glint in her eye. He nodded deeply. "I shall. In the meantime, my dear, can I ask what exactly you were asked to do with the spear this second time around?"

She bit hard into the sandwich, dropping filling over herself, and failed to catch it before it hit the ground.

"Dr. Weber asked me to come and confirm it was genuine..." Mouth full, pronunciation muffled by ill manners: "And to perform fingerprint and DNA swab testing on it, probably because he was concerned the police would screw it up."

"Why did he ask you to confirm it was genuine?"

"Because..." It had never actually occurred to her until now why Weber had ever assumed the spear to be anything less than the genuine article, given its identical appearance. "I don't know, actually."

de Carranza flicked pages aside in his dossier. "These pictures," he shoved a couple of 10x8s in her direction, "These are original crime scene shots of the pieces of the spear, prior to your arrival?" She scanned them briefly. They looked familiar, yes. "And let me confirm, that no-one moved them until you arrived?"

"No, Weber wouldn't let the police touch it."

"Well, has it not occurred to anyone to ask why Mr. Weber was so suspicious of the spear's authenticity?"

She tried raise a clever objection, but found it faltering before it reached her tongue. "No, I guess it hasn't. He certainly seemed convinced there had been some kind of substitution."

"So we must ask, why was Mr. Weber so keen to have the spear examined so closely? He could never have known the inscription was there, had he looked at the thing as it lay on the floor. By his own admission he is long-sighted, so even if the inscription was visible, it would still have seemed to him only as a series of surface scratches. Which *may*, had he been lynx-eyed, have made him suppose the spear had been damaged in some way during its dismemberment." He stopped peering at the photographs in front of him and put his glasses back on. "But I cannot shake the notion that he knew that inscription was there, and wanted you to find it. Mr. Weber's actions aren't easily explained. If he doubted the spear's authenticity, why prohibit police forensic testing on it? And if he didn't, why push you into verifying the fact?"

She turned to look him straight in the face, silently signifying her inability to answer. He smiled back at her, pleased to have made his point.

"You're a very bright fellow, Professor de Carranza. I'm sure you'll find the answer soon." She nodded toward the figure at the far end of the bench. "And the good Doctor too, I bet."

Khalamanga had reclined peacefully, his heels up on the seat of the bench to form a study surface with his legs. While de Carranza spoke, forming the melody of the conversation, Khalamanga had so far supplied the interference in the form of paper rustling, occasional scribbling and the visual distractions of holding up graphic crime scene photographs in broad daylight for any passer-by to catch sight of.

"Doctor?" de Carranza tried, once more pushing the other man to become involved and show what he was made of, prove he was up to the challenge, justify his involvement in the case with some words of insight.

"Yes, sorry. I've been thinking about this statement from the Treasury security head, Mr. Pfeifenberger. And I know Petersen says he cannot suspect him on any evidence, yet it occurs to me that this man could be telling the whole truth, and still remain the guilty party."

Intrigued, de Carranza found himself paying attention to the Oxford man for the first time. "Please, explain."

"Well, take the Commandment 'thou shalt not kill'. It may be an argument of semantics, but Pfeifenberger, and any number of accomplices could easily have slaughtered Siegel in some way that was not, to their minds, an act of murder. It could have been an execution, demanded by some arcane law known only to the victim and his associates. He could have been a rival member of some extremist political group, whose life was taken in an act of war. He could have been a member of a religious or para-religious cult, and was chosen, or even offered himself, as a human sacrifice to some great or noble ideal. Then again, there is the most horrible possibility of all. That those who killed Siegel did not view him as human."

Vanessa raised an enquiring eyebrow. "You mean, like the Nazi idea of 'sub-humans'?"

"Yes. Any of these arguments could be proposed by people with an oblique view of reality, or moral conduct. To admit to murder is to admit to doing wrong. And if these people deem themselves to be right, then they cannot accept what they have done to be wrong."

"Hang on, let me check something." She beckoned de Carranza pass her his file and scanned the forensic reports. "Yes, I thought so. Siegel's blood type was A-positive, one of the most common types. The blood on the floor was B-type negative, one of the rarest...found only in about 2% of the population. As I recall, the B-type was common among German Jews, and something the Nazis made a big deal out of with their blood screening programmes. So maybe there's a racialist angle to all this."

"Nothing in the background report said Siegel was Jewish. In fact, I'm sure it said he was active at a local church."

"Yes," Vanessa agreed. "Doesn't mean he couldn't have converted in earlier life."

"That might explain the castration," de Carranza suggested. "A gruesome exaggeration of circumcision? And let's not ignore the symbolism of the two phallic components of the holy spear which have been stolen."

"I would still treat the castration as more of a symbolic gesture." Khalamanga argued quietly. "It certainly has great significance in the Osiris myth, and to the Holy Grail story of the maimed Fisher King."

Vanessa's mind had already wandered sideways from the case, pulling her mouth into a vague and restrained smirk. Everything so far had been about pricks, all manner of things designed to pierce human bodies. Spears, nails, phalluses real and symbolic, symbols of manhood and aggression - metaphorical pricks as well, in the form of Steiner and to a lesser extent, his lieutenant Weber. It was predictable, almost clichéd, how everything came down to sex, sooner or later. Freud, it seemed, had been right about that at least.

"So what made the pri...the male member so relevant in these myths?" she asked finally.

Khalamanga simply smiled without looking up from his notes. "The theme is common in ancient mysticism and magic. It also occurs in alchemy, in the form of the hermaphrodite or rebis – a symbolic man who is dismembered and re-assembled but for that one piece, signifying a new form, or two separate forms in one. In some works this hermaphrodite represents the union of opposite principles, whether philosophical, chemical, or spiritual." He thought for a moment, and in that brief time realised he had already bored the other two into silence. He added finally, "There are some texts related to these very themes in the Nationalbibliothek, which I have wanted to view first-hand for many years. I'm rather excited that I'll finally get to see them."

"That's excellent, Doctor." de Carranza turned away. "I'm glad your trip here will be worthwhile."

Vanessa flinched at the bite in the Spaniard's tone, but the other man did not react to it any way. She almost wished she could be at the incident briefing later, just to see how he and de Carranza would cope with each other.

"Ladies and gentlemen, good evening. Sorry I'm late – 'phone rang just as I was leaving."

The voice of Peterson preceded his arrival in the incident room, heavy footsteps carrying him through the open doorway. Still agitated from the telephone encounter with the Schatzkammer's curator, Petersen slammed the door behind him and tried to urge his mind back to the case in hand. At one end of the room stood an easel holding a large flipchart. The wall behind was covered in photographs, scans, maps, and diagrams related to the Holy Spear. Beside the flipchart sat de Carranza and Khalamanga, while Kupfer pinned up photographic enlargements of the 'Great Seth' inscription, creating a mosaic of mystery and murder. Sitting and standing opposite were the rest of Petersen's incident team; Steinberg, Rieser, and half a dozen others.

"I've done all the introductions, sir." Kupfer said. "We were, er..."

"...just waiting for me, I know. Well, now that we're all here, let me turn the floor over to our experts, who will attempt to shed a little light on the possible motivations behind this crime." like a cabaret MC, he gestured broadly to the two men behind him before taking his place at the head of his team. Khalamanga and de Carranza exchanged glances, each gesturing to the other to go first.

"No, please lead on," Khalamanga insisted, and with a deep sigh de Carranza took his place beside the easel and turned to face the gathering of curious stares and folded arms.

"Thank you, gentlemen. You will already be familiar with the work of Vanessa Descartes on the two so-called Holy Spears, I am quite sure." He waved flamboyantly toward the photographs on the far wall. "The inscription you see there is written in a late form of Egyptian, from a document entitled the 'Second Treatise of the Great Seth', although in a different dialect to that normally used in scriptures of this age and character. Whether this is significant or not, at this stage is hard to say. However, first let me introduce you to the character of Seth himself.

"In the Hebrew Bible and other religious texts, Seth is the third son of Adam and Eve and the ancestor of Noah. Among the Gnostics who wrote this 'Treatise', Jesus Christ was viewed as the reincarnation of Seth, and the gift he brought to the world was the knowledge of salvation. Now, these Sethians are not recorded much after the 4th Century. The Church burned their writings, drove their followers underground, but a lack of evidence for the existence of something does not confirm its annihilation.

"Following our discussion over lunch earlier today, we have come to agree on the theory that our spear has been left in the museum by members, or supporters of, some Gnostic or neo-Sethian group. Taking the theory a little further, we wonder if the meaning of this action is to draw attention to the contradictions and mystery surrounding the Crucifixion, and the accepted dogma of the Western church."

Nice of you to pass these ideas onto me, Petersen thought, but I am very happy that you all had a good lunch. He thought of the three cups of coffee, the take-away beefburger and half-eaten tube of wine gums which had sustained him for the whole day so far. He would need another cup of tea to see him through this session.

"Let us bear in mind that the spear is the one wound which is not mentioned in the inscribed passage from the 'Great Seth'; and in orthodox Scripture, only the Gospel of John makes any reference to it at all. The fact remains, whoever made one of these spears obviously had the other one available for reference. The copy need not have been made in the 8th Century, of course. It could have been customised to look exactly like the other at any time since that date."

"What do you make of the staging of the wristwatch in the victim's mouth?" Kupfer asked.

"Indeed, a very curious gesture, that. I briefly toyed with the theory it may be an attempt to draw attention to the year of 1735, but as yet I cannot see the relevance of the date to the matter in hand." he moved back to the flipchart and wrote down the numbers '5' and '7' on the pad. "57 as a number by itself has no special significance. But taking 5 and 7 separately, we have multiple meanings. 5 fingers on one hand. 5 points to a pentagram. 5 wounds suffered by Jesus. Then 7, standing for the original 7 planets, the 7 heavens, 7 Hebrew names of God, 7 Deadly Sins, 7 days of Creation..."

"Heinz's 'baked beans' have 57 varieties," Khalamanga interjected.

For a few seconds nobody dared speak or even move. The other policemen sat motionless, convinced that they had mis-translated something. Khalamanga looked up from his prep notes, wondering why de Carranza's lively brainstorm session seemed to have ground to a halt.

"Baked beans - Doctor - may not be so relevant." the Spaniard replied, doing his best to navigate swiftly around that surreal tangent. "Unless we care to interpret the head as a solitary bean, and the spilled blood as tomato sauce. However, if we add 5 to 7 we get 12. 12 Apostles, 12 Tribes of Israel, 12 zodiacal signs. Or it may stand for something else entirely. Like the positions of the letters in the alphabet - neo-Nazi groups, for example, use 1 and 8 to signify the position of the initials of Hitler's name." he drew these on the flipchart, admired his handiwork for a moment, then paused for reflection. "Well," he said at last, "I think that's probably enough to be going on with."

The officers as a group were beginning to wonder what kind of sideshow Petersen had dragged in and kept them all waiting so long for. The man currently studying the flipchart seemed to be under the impression he was addressing a junior high school class, and only God knew what awaited them all when the awkward-looking black man decided to elaborate upon his theories involving English baked beans.

As de Carranza walked back to his seat, the only sound to be heard was the scratching of pens on paper and the rustling of notes. Petersen switched on the kettle on the bench behind him and hoped the Oxford eccentric would be quick with his presentation.

Khalamanga took his place at the easel and unclipped a marker pen. In the process he got ink on his fingers, which he tried to clean off with the corner of Petersen's flipchart page before realising the ink was indelible, but not before he crumpled up half the pad in the process. He took a new page, muttering apologies as he went.

"First of all, please allow me to concentrate on the physical aspects of the crime which originally drew my attention to this case. Here is our body." He drew a stick man on the left of the board with an unhappy face. "And here is what was done to it..." He scribbled over the head and re-drew it on the other side of the board, with a curvy line underneath it to represent the dish the head was found on. He drew a dotted line through the tops of the legs and a small, wiggly line at the bottom right of the board. "The parts which have been removed."

Thanks for stating the obvious, Petersen thought. He had a battle to win against the odds of time and stubborn museum curators and knew the press would be looking for a statement of some sort before the end of the week. Hundreds of visitors had already been turned away from a large and popular part of the museum, a situation which could clearly not continue indefinitely, even allowing for a respectful period of time for the deceased. Petersen knew that the first amateur occult sleuths would be tramping around in the Schatzkammer within 48 hours of the place re-opening.

Khalamanga capped his pen. "Now, in the Holy Grail legends of the Fisher King, we have the ruler of a wasted land who has been maimed sexually, fulfilling the ancient belief that the fertility and health of the king is the same as that of the land. As the Egyptian god Osiris rules the land of the dead, so the Fisher King rules his dark, barren wasteland. Osiris, having been murdered and dismembered by his brother Set, is re-assembled and restored to life, but with one vital piece missing." He tapped the squiggly line on the page beside the stick man. "With relevance to our own investigations, the maimed Fisher King appears most famously in Wagner's opera 'Parsifal' - pierced through the thighs, a euphemism for castration, the King and his land suffer until he is touched by the holy Spear of Jesus. The King is healed, and the land with him.

"Now, in many of the great chivalric romances about the Holy Grail, there is a scene where a questor, a knight, witnesses a procession carrying the Holy Grail, and usually a lance or spear. In several stories, this lance even bleeds. Some say it is the blood of Jesus Himself that flows into the Grail chalice."

He tapped the drawing of the head on the plate. "In this scenario, the divine solar head set upon the silver - *lunar* - dish, signifies night and day. Broken, speared and bloody, Christ dies - entering the realm of darkness - and returns to bring the light of salvation, the cycle of death giving new life - but this can only be achieved through sacrifice. *Duality*, gentlemen; light versus dark, good versus evil. The very essence of the Gnostic heresy."

He stopped, yielding silence. Eyes had glazed over, writing hands had long since given up trying to take notes. Petersen sugared his tea. This was shaping up to be a session of one-upmanship between two undoubtedly learned minds, both untempered by humility or any familiarity with the concept of moderation. He tasted the tea and nearly choked on the bag he had forgotten to take out.

Kupfer said, "To me, the head on the dish suggests a very Christian idea, that of John the Baptist."

"This severed head may not be in an orthodox Christian context," Khalamanga answered. "One of the accusations against the Knights Templar was that they worshipped a male head, named Baphomet. Some writers say they see the hand of the Templars at work in the early Grail stories, especially those of Chretien de Troyes, one of the most important writers of his era. In the Welsh story of 'Peredur' in the

Mabinogion, we have a bloody head on a dish that is paraded in the Holy Grail Procession. So there are many possible meanings, or interpretations."

Rieser asked, "So what about the boiling of the corpse and the draining of the fluids?"

"My initial feeling is that this was done as some form of ritual. The stories and fables are merely signifiers of a greater and deeper truth, to be understood only by the initiated. The bizarre post-mortem cooking may or may not be related to the mutilations, but I would wager it is also an act of deepest symbolic meaning for the perpetrator."

"Why do we need symbols to explain this?" Reiser challenged. "With a psychopath, he makes up his own rules. You may never understand it on anything other than his own terms. Or then again if we are dealing with a criminal organization, it is simply a grandiose warning. To show who's boss. Scare people, grab headlines."

Khalamanga admitted this possibility with good humour. "In which case, he's succeeded. In conclusion, I should like to present the suggestion that the killer has performed a ritual sacrifice, re-enacting a primal scene of creation, or transformation. The answers to this case rest, I believe, within the mystical realms of thought such as found within works of classical alchemy, and its interpretations in some kind of unorthodox Christian context. Well, let me thank you all for your patience."

Petersen squelched his eyeballs, glad that it was all over. "That's it, team." He announced. "Thanks for your time."

Khalamanga went to sit down again, and the room emptied faster than a group of students at the end of their final class before the summer break.

"What now, Kommissar?" de Carranza asked. "Are you through with us, or do you wish us to stay on here?"

"Given the work the both of you have put into this, I should like to keep you around for a while yet, in case we find the need for more explanations. If you don't mind?"

"We'd be honoured." The Spaniard grinned. "I must admit, I am gripped with fascination in this matter. I have a book signing in Germany tomorrow, which I shall cancel immediately. The whole process of this investigation is something I find quite exhilarating."

As they left the room together and Petersen set about locking up after them, he explained; "Professor, in my job, exhilaration very soon gives way to fatigue and cynicism. But if there's anything I can do to assist, let me know."

"I shouldn't mind seeing the body, if that would be at all possible."

"Fair enough. I'll call Dr. Rosenfeldt, arrange a viewing for tomorrow morning. In the meantime, I must get some dinner before I faint. Until tomorrow, gentlemen, let me bid you good-day."

"Dinner, eh? Sounds like a perfect idea." de Carranza said with a slap on Khalamanga's back.

The early evening found de Carranza and Khalamanga in the courtyard of a mock-medieval tavern on the Rotenturmstrasse, a fairy-tale place indeed that to de Carranza's mind should have been populated by curvaceous wenches and shepherdesses, retired dragon-slayers and young men of questionable reputation seeking fortune or redemption. Though neither of them drank beer, de Carranza had been drawn by the cosmopolitan clientele; from square-headed, thin-mouthed individuals of local character to noisy American students, Israeli backpackers, Japanese businessmen and Australian coach parties. Khalamanga was fascinated by the bustling barmaids who carried three litre-sized tankards in each hand, even when they stared at him quizzically for ordering carbonated water, while de Carranza's fascination was focused more on the tightly-laced bodices and blouses as they hurried past.

The weather was still pleasant enough to allow them to enjoy the fresh air, though Khalamanga had announced that rain was no more than an hour away. He felt it in the air, the same feeling he often got whilst running which told him he should turn home immediately, although that view was clearly not shared by the dozens of tourists who sat on the lush grass in the shade of the pine trees and wandered up and down the white gravel paths which made a charming patchwork out of the lawn.

"Well, enough small-talk for today, I think." The Spaniard concluded with a check of his watch, semi-consciously counting down the time until the rain struck. "What is your explanation for what happened out there?"

"I think I bored them." Khalamanga confessed sadly.

"Not in the police station...I mean, at the crime scene. You must have a preferred scenario in mind."

"I have one or two, yes. That the decapitation was a vital part of the ritual. Perhaps even a re-enactment of the beheading game you find in the great Middle English poem, 'Sir Gawain and the Green Knight', where Gawain and the mysterious stranger trade blows to the neck. I'm sorry I didn't have time to mention that earlier."

"And what do you see influencing the boiling of the dead body, the removal of the blood and other liquids?"

"It is confusing, I admit. I think we are dealing here not with an individual, but several, with their own agendas. If the video tapes of the spear run out before the spear is taken, we must assume the worst and decide that it is because someone wanted the tapes to run out. Perhaps we have two rival groups active in the museum, both wanting the spear for themselves. Maybe one of the groups was represented by one or more security guards."

"Fascinating indeed, D...look, I can't keep calling you 'Doctor' all the time."

"It's Emanuel, but you don't need my permission. The name my parents gave me, and the name which Isaiah gave to the Messiah."

"Your family are strongly Christian then?"

"Yes. We're of Igbo descent, from the Southeast. My immediate family moved me to London when I was only a few years old. My birth-place was Enu Ugwu, the City on the Hill, in the part of the country which claimed independence as the Republic of Biafra and which was starved nearly to death at the war's end."

de Carranza sighed, reminded again of the cruel war which had divided his homeland and blackened his own early life.

"I still love my country, corrupted and torn though it has been over the years; even the name is a joke, given to us by a colonialist's wife, but my feelings go beyond politics. God made all men equal in his image. My father lost two brothers in the war, my mother her entire family to the starvation which followed it. Though I had never known those who died, it still affected me, creating a void in my soul where I knew others had once been. However, it made me thank God for the family and the luxuries I did have, and I have never lost that sense of gratitude."

It occurred to de Carranza during this reflective pause that he had encouraged the other man to speak freely and openly about a non-academic subject for the first time.

"So you kept your faith? You're a remarkable man. Are you then, truly as pure as the knights you study?"

"Hah. Only one man was ever pure, and he died on the Cross. All the rest of us can do is try to live up to that example."

"I once thought...I mean, I truly believed that there could have been one leader in my lifetime, perhaps this century, who could have given a better life for millions, and made the Western Church into a truly respectable institution."

"Who was this man?"

de Carranza stretched himself out against the black iron railings and recounted his faded memories of Pope John Paul I. "He was too good for the Church, I feel." the Spaniard said as he closed his recollections. "Too good for the Vatican. Well, let them keep their Humanae Vitae then, and all the hunger, pain and overcrowding that it brings."

His attention was drawn by a brass band striking up in the far corner of the biergarten, surrounded by an enthusiastic audience. The musicians were dressed in traditional attire, all lederhosen and feathered hats. Spectators linked arms and moved in time to the music, a lively piece in waltz time which invited tipsy singalongs and watered the manicured grass with warm beer. The boisterous atmosphere was already getting under de Carranza's skin and forcing him to regret his decision to show Khalamanga some typical local entertainment.

"If I could ever see, or hear of, a man like that again - a man who could promise to bring our Church, and its world, out of the darkness, then I might believe again. I might believe that there is space for such men in this world, after all." The Spaniard raised his glass with a sunken smile. "But until that day, my friend, you and I will remain opposites. You will pray to your God, and I will pray that my next royalty cheque doesn't go missing in the post."

Khalamanga remained unmoved while the band blared out the coda of their current number to whistles and cheers of appreciation, but de Carranza could take no more. He threw back his seat and stood up.

"Damn this bloody music." He jostled his way out of the biergarten to one of the pavement tables at the far end, out of sight of the oompah-merchants. "From the country which gave us Mozart and Strauss, and what do we have now? Farting trumpets and the sound of dustbin lids being bashed together. God, it sounds like fascism."

Following behind, Khalamanga laughed aloud at the other man's sense of outrage. "It's only a brass band, Tomas. It's perfectly harmless."

"Fine for you to say, but I lived for 31 years under Franco, not in safe little England with her dreamy spires and afternoon tea. Many things in this country would have seemed 'perfectly harmless' 70 years ago, before the boots of the Third Reich marched down these very streets." He recalled the words of his father on the day the Spanish monarchy was restored: 'Remember this day and enjoy it well, my son, for the ghosts of the fascists will not stay buried forever'. His gaze drifted into the clouds overhead which had slid in front of the sun, bringing shadows upon the Viennese Spring. From beneath, the spire of St. Stephan's Cathedral pierced the drab sky, man's tribute to God dwarfed by the unbounded sphere of His heavens.

"It is not the same-"

"Is it not. Hmph. Well, we'll see." de Carranza pointed down the huge concourse of Rotenturmstrasse. "Behind there, in the Morzinplatz, stands a monument to the survivors of Mauthausen. The site was once the headquarters of the Gestapo. Such darkness does not easily recede. And there is something unpleasant in the air, something worse than your approaching rainstorm. Something so real I can almost feel it. And all those ants out there, in their cars and their offices and their churches and shopping centres, have no idea what is rising above them."

It was not the city that he was beginning to fear, but rather what it seemed to contain within its darkest recesses - the powers responsible for murder, terror, bringing fear in its oldest and most potent form - the fear of the unknown. She was a two-faced temptress, this city of such dark beauty and grotesque secrets; a troubled schizoid with a colourful but murky past, enticing him into her deadly world.

Khalamanga made himself comfortable in the white wrought iron chair, of the sort usually seen decorating middle-class lawns in Oxford during summer months. "I'm not sure I follow."

"Religion, mysticism, magic, history...all these things surround us in our case. And these were the things that created the first fascist states."

The brazen sounds of the band stopped again and a great cheer went up, applause and whistles.

"Well, I don't believe all those happy people keep swastika armbands in their dressing tables," Khalamanga smiled. Seeing the Doctor's point, de Carranza finally accepted the folly of his words, and laughed along with him.

Neither man saw the slim figure wearing a priest's collar and coated in black Italian wool who stepped out of the group of listeners and moved after them, his hands deep in his coat pockets and his face all but hidden beneath the shadow of a wide-brimmed hat. Edging his way forwards, he slipped his hands under his coat and removed a 35mm Hasselblad. He raised the camera and looked around himself as though casually searching for some interesting landmark to capture. He lined up the wide angle lens with the back of de Carranza's head and idly fired off several shots. Winding on the film, he raised the camera to his face and scanned the gray Gothic heights of St. Stephan's.

Khalamanga suggested, "Perhaps you're tuning in to old ghosts, Tomas. Maybe Hitler used to drink here as a youth. Who knows?"

de Carranza examined the palms of his hands as though expecting to see bloody stigmata burst from them at any moment. In truth, he was wondering why they were glistening silver with sweat.

"Maybe he did."

"We're not seeing the best of Vienna so far, are we? It's like we're standing in the nightside of Eden."

"Every rose has her thorns, Emanuel. And every beauty, her scars." He thought of Vanessa as he said that, the image more apt than he realised.

"Well, this is all most pleasant, but I had planned to visit the Nationalbibliothek before it shut tonight. Do you want to come with me?"

de Carranza removed his mobile telephone from his pocket and punched out a text message to Vanessa's number: 'All done. Dr. K bored them and I mystified them. Looking for a little light relief?'

The face of Emanuel Khalamanga blurred in and out of the viewfinder as the English priest's fingers slid around the focus wheel of the camera. He fired the shutter a half-dozen times then moved smartly off toward a pavement table where a young woman was sitting by herself. He noticed the English-German dictionary lying beside her handbag and approached with a hesitant, slightly backward air.

"Lovely afternoon, me dear?" a thick Southern Irish brogue eased its way towards her. She looked up from her glass of cola to find the priest standing in front of her, raising his hat in polite greeting. "Shame we seem to have lost the sun and all, though."

"Yes," she laughed, "It suits me, actually. Been a bit too warm for me, I'm afraid." Her accent was North-Western England, from somewhere around Lancashire.

"I'm so sorry to bother you," he went on, "I shan't take up a minute of your time. But I'm only here for another day, y'see...an exchange visit with me church back in Dublin. I wonder- could you possibly do me a favour and take a few wee snaps of me, just here, with the cathedral spire behind me there?" He placed the camera on the table in front of her and pointed to the shutter. "Just look through the wee screen and press that when you think it looks alright."

The woman picked up the Hasselblad and squinted through the viewfinder in his direction.

"Oh, it all looks a bit blurry to me, Father. How do I change it?"

"Oh hang on a wee minute, I've been daft again, have I not. No wonder my holiday snaps always look like they come from the Moon." He took back the camera and pointed it down the street to where de Carranza and Khalamanga began to go their separate ways. His thumb triggered the shutter several times before he made a play of checking the focus. "Aye, that'll be fine now, so it will."

He handed her the camera again and she stood up, happy this time with the composition, and snapped away.

"Lovely." He sang. "Thank you for your time, my dear. Bless you."

"No trouble, Father." She replied as the priest walked off across the road and disappeared from view down a quiet residential side street. He slung the camera back under his coat and got into an elderly black Volvo estate car, which he proceeded to drive off at speed.

Having arrived at the library later than expected, Khalamanga resolved to get on with his research as quickly as he could. He had chosen a spare booth with an Internet terminal so he could quickly check online references. He didn't know where de Carranza was going, but it was not his business to ask. The little game with the inscription on the spear had been amusing, but Khalamanga couldn't shake the notion there was less depth to de Carranza's understanding than he liked to think.

He pulled up his seat in the booth and switched on the desk lamp, dragged the pile of books and documents into the circle of light and began flicking pages, bound Photostats of originals over five hundred years old. He had come to the Nationalbibliothek to see these surviving quotations from the works of Zosimos of Panopolis, the earliest recorded alchemist. And the more he read, the more similarities he saw between the crime scene and the ancient Gnostic mysticism of Zosimos.

The cooking and draining of the body's fluids or humours was frighteningly suggestive of some kind of spiritual or mystical purification. Hints and cryptic *ennoias* teased his mind through the words of Zosimos:

'*I am Ion, priest of Adytum, and I have borne an intolerable force. For someone came at me headlong in the morning and dismembered me with a sword and tore me apart...and having cut my head off with the sword, he mashed my flesh with my bones and burned them in the fire of the treatment until, my body transformed, I should learn to become a spirit...*"

"The head...the *head*." His lips vibrated against his finger, purring, as he furiously rummaged through his thoughts for an answer. He slipped the crime scene pictures from his bag and furtively flicked through them. The sequence of close-ups suggested possibilities. It had been placed upon the altar, staring up at the crucifix as Christ stared back down in His agony, enduring another intolerable force for the ultimate spiritual transformation.

In spiritual symbolism, the head is gold, and gold is the ultimate goal of alchemy, not just in physical terms, but in spirit, and in mind also. The Knights Templar had long stood accused of worshipping a *head*, known by the mysterious name Baphomet - a recurring theme at their trials in the early 14th Century. If the Baphomet was, as some claimed, the face on the Turin Shroud folded up and framed, then the meaning was clear enough. 'Baphomet' could have been a code-name for this holiest of relics, stained with the holy tincture of Christ's blood and image. The severed head, the spear, the mystery of Christ...the connection was there to be made. Was the clue in the name?

"Baphomet," he wondered, rolling his lips around the phonemes. "Baph –omet..." He scribbled letters, syllables, homophones in all the languages he could read. Greek:

"batha...metis..." he paused. "Ba thomet?" Egyptian? Pen hovered above paper as a thought struck him. *Arabic?*

On a whim, Khalamanga turned to the computer terminal beside him and logged onto an internet metasearch: "ba'ath", "baath".'

Among the descriptions of the Arab socialist party, Khalamanga's alert mind pounced upon the explanation, repeated throughout the results: 'resurrection' or 'rebirth'. He input a new search, purely on a whim: 'Meaning of Arab name Haamid'. Literal translations varied but the general gist Khalamanga understood was 'the praising, or loving God'.

The tall, thin man stretched himself out to his full length in the seat as he mouthed the foreign words, over and over again.

"Baath Haamid. Baphamid. *Baphomet?*" he asked his dark reflection in the monitor screen. " *'The Resurrection of the loving God*.' " It was a wild, intuitive stab in the dark. Haamid or Hamid was never a name applied to God in any orthodox religion. Yet it remained a feasible alternative to the accepted explanation, that the mysterious name was a corruption of 'Mohammed'. As far as Khalamanga was concerned, the Knights of the Order of the Temple were clever enough to know that name when they heard it. They mixed freely with Arabs, and understood Islam better than some of their descendents 1,000 years later. There was no good reason why the name of the Prophet should have become so garbled in the mouths of Christian knights.

Khalamanga grew giddy in the heat, felt the high bookshelves above closing in on him. He was afraid and excited all at once, as though he had tapped into some conduit of forbidden knowledge that common men were not supposed to know. Perhaps 'Baphomet' was simply a code-word designed to guard the secret of what it represented. Perhaps the Second Coming of Christ was the true gold these alchemists sought - their cover story simply one of material gain, when in truth they were working towards ultimate spiritual enlightenment. And did that imply the Templars had uncovered some of the original Gnostic gospels, maybe even the 'Second Treatise' itself and incorporated it into their belief system? Was this why Philip IV had tried to exterminate the order so ruthlessly - for having practiced the same heresy as that of the Cathars, the Albigensians and the Bogomils? Was the engraved Spear of Seth some attempt to unite the two opposing schools of Gnostic and Orthodox Christianity? Was it this new philosophy, this unification of opposites, which the Templars adhered to, and which brought their downfall at the hands of an unenlightened and jealous monarch?

"*Was it?*" the pencil tap-tapping against his notebook. Tears of joyous frustration misted his vision, drawing out the baroque opulence around him into glowing streaks of colour, inlaid paneling and architraves becoming fluid until his eyes ran with liquid gold. He took off his spectacles and raised his face toward the chandeliers several stories above, the seven points of light blurring and congealing into one brilliant white star.

He closed his eyes and the white star became a pulsing black hole, boring through his retina to the back of his brain. As he continued to think, a gentle hand on his shoulder roused him from his rest.

"Excuse me, sir - but the library is closing in ten minutes."

Khalamanga grabbed at his notes and began clearing things away. "Yes, of course. Thank you."

As he set about returning his books and documents, his thoughts churned with dark suggestions and things he would have to share with de Carranza as quickly as possible.

de Carranza and Vanessa met up at the corner of the Schleifmuhlgasse, a fashionable street in the Freihaus district and a stone's throw from the Burggarten and the Hofburg. Part of an extensive area to suffer heavy bombing during the war, it was now restored with facades which reminded them both of London or Paris, but which had only been in existence ten years or so since being bought by a group of local developers intent on radical renovation and the elevation of a onetime urban desert into an exclusive, upmarket precinct.

Vienna had not looked kindly upon de Carranza's abandonment of Khalamanga, bringing down the expected rain upon him almost as soon as they parted, but the Spaniard was determined to carry on despite it. The evening was still young, and his mind needed a rest after the day's intellectual burdens.

He found her sheltering in the doorway of Alphaville, the massive DVD retail store, her jacket spotted with dark blotches as she held it around herself.

"Thanks," she sniffed as he arrived at her side. "They were closing, so they threw me out."

"I'm sorry the weather has turned against us."

"Don't worry about that, I'm sure it wasn't your fault. And even a wet April evening in Vienna is better than a summer day in Manchester."

"So how do you suggest we make this wet day bright again?"

"It already is bright. As of about two minutes ago." The pavement was slippery and silver, and she pulled him out into the middle of it with only a little resistance. "I had thought about buying us a copy of 'It's a Wonderful Life' and finding somewhere quiet to watch it. Maybe we can make do with our own impromptu version of 'Singin in the Rain' instead – what do you think?"

Being no lover of rain, de Carranza was reluctant to be led a dance through the continuing shower. "I don't know, I think deserts may be more my scene."

"Deserts?" She chewed her lip thoughtfully. "Well, in that case I would vote for 'Lawrence of Arabia'. Find me a sandbox, and I'd be all yours."

He wasn't too sure how to take that comment. They were walking hand in hand down the street, sheltering in doorways as they went with no particular place to go, and that was reality. It had already occurred to him that the natural next step would be to adjourn somewhere warm and dry, an hotel room or guest house suite being the most obvious examples.

"The car's parked back that way," he pointed out hopefully. "We're heading the wrong way."

"I think we've both been heading the right way so far. Don't you?"

They stopped under a large canopy of the Drei Kronen hotel, drawing looks from attendants and staff within.

"We should be careful," he told her. "This is the side of town where only the cool people hang out." He laughed nervously, asking; "Is that still a word you use, in English? Is 'cool' still cool?"

And that was her now at a loss for words. Remarkable, she thought, how just being around this man had the effect of retarding her mental age by about twenty years. Not that she minded feeling like a gormless school kid when such possibility hung in the air, but it didn't do a lot for her pride.

She wiped a wet hank of hair out of her eye. "It is. It's cool."

He raised his hand toward her, thinking to touch her or draw her close, make a statement of some kind; he couldn't decide whether to speak with words or let his actions do the talking, and as she straightened her spine, lifting her head closer to him, he realised she wouldn't seem to mind either way. As she waited for the first touch, giving way to a tighter clinch and the inevitable first kiss, the mobile phone in his jacket pocket rang with a beepy rendition of the 'Anvil Chorus', leaving her thoughts unspoken and her speech faltering into silence.

"Dammit, I thought I turned that off." He ripped the phone from his pocket and nearly dropped it in his rage. "Yes?" he barked into it, ready to deliver a torrent of abuse, when the voice at the other end proved to be depressingly familiar.

Vanessa spun away and contemplated punching her fist through the nearest window. Had the man not been involved in a murder case with serious social and legal responsibilities, she would have walked away and thrown herself into the first available taxi.

He grunted irritably, not actually speaking, then he exhaled a long, deep breath from the pit of his chest.

"...yes, I remember I have an appointment to view the body with you tomorrow morning. Thank you."

He replaced the telephone in his coat pocket. Now that the moment was over, he fulfilled his decision to touch her on the shoulder, seeing her downcast expression reflected in the hotel window. "That..." he stopped to scratch at his beard, his turn to feel awkward now. "That was Petersen."

"Something important?" she muttered, thinking it had damn well better be.

"His men are at Siegel's house. They've found some documents and other things among his personal effects which involve the Holy Spear."

"So he says." She murmured. "I think he's just jealous." She pushed herself to smile, hoping he would see the funny side, but de Carranza wasn't even looking at her. He was thinking ahead to the future, to the following morning, to the remains of the evening. "Tomas? Does he want you over there?"

"It'll wait 'til the morning. I'm quite sure he finds me a distraction, poking my nose into his work."

"That's not what I said. If it's important-" she was silenced by a sharp look from the Spaniard's dark eyes. A vertical finger, wagging father- or teacher-fashion, told her there was no argument. "I was only asking."

"And I am only being selfish. But it is all in a good cause."

She squared up to him, wanting, no *needing,* to get her thoughts out. "Please, Tomas. Don't let me keep you from anything vital here. I mean, I'm flattered you seem to care about me. But-" now she stopped, realising the thoughts wouldn't sound so good spoken aloud. He had told her before about her self-esteem issues, and she could see him building up to another objection, another telling-off.

"I preferred where we were three minutes ago, playing in a sandbox." he said.

That made her smile again, and for a brief second he was Sherif Ali ibn el Kharish.

"You're right," she admitted. "I preferred that, too." She offered him her arm, which he took graciously, and together they walked on in the general direction of the Margaretenstrasse.

Josef Siegel's apartment was a ground floor slot just off the Berggasse, the street where Sigmund Freud himself had lived and died. None of the tenement buildings here looked straight, as if each was pushing the one next to it to encourage a monumental collapse not only of masonry but of the neighbourhood and society in general. Life had never seemed real to Petersen since Maria's death. It had often felt as though he was doing penance in some purgatorial nightmare from which he might soon awaken, stretched out in bed with that shy, long-legged brunette beside him in a loving clinch. Penance which, for sins unknowable, included being subjected to the verbal bullets from his own bosses on a daily basis and, currently, from Steiner and Tomas de Carranza. He had taken enough bullets – now he was determined to throw some back.

He parked the Audi behind the patrol car which sat across the road from Siegel's block. Lights were on inside and he could see dark figures moving about, hear two-way radios crackling.

He had driven through a collage of landscapes to that street of grotty grey boxes as dull and blunt as their inhabitants, passing by centres of learning with pillars and archways dedicated to the eternal glory of the mind, bright modern towers housing the latest generation of apprentices. The white brick testament to the father of modern psychoanalysis reminded Petersen of the influence of the subconscious and the tricks it played on the frail human psyche. de Carranza's absence he put down entirely to the man's infatuation with Vanessa – probably just as well, as both of them now seemed to have served their purpose in the investigation. He would honour his meeting with the Spanish playboy and the headless corpse tomorrow, and that would be that. He couldn't help but wonder, briefly, if the strange castration in the museum was motivated by some similar primal urge or sexual jealousy. And for the first time in his investigation, he found himself startled to consider the possibility that the perpetrator, or one of them, may have been female. He didn't know what manner of demons had scarred Vanessa in her past, but they were clearly still with her, and he doubted de Carranza's talents as an exorcist of any sort. As he released himself from the seatbelt, he wondered if there was anything more unfathomable to man than the female mind.

Vienna had started to smell old to Wilhelm Petersen, as though the city were in some way beginning to putrefy around him. It might have been the drains in this street or one of the less well to-do areas he had just travelled through, but on this early hour of Thursday morning he feared what he might uncover next. Like the city outside, the house seemed mouldy and unwelcoming, an entrance to the world of an individual who seemed almost to have abstained from existing. One door to the left stood open, showing a single unmade bed, and an opened cupboard with nothing inside it. He turned right into the living room, and the heart of the action.

Kupfer was sorting through documents from a small iron box and passing them to a uniformed colleague. It was as drab inside as the undecorated hallway and the poorly-attended outer facade had indicated. A television sat beneath the front window, a single armchair in the opposite corner. Basic essentials like a clock on the wall and an electric heater stood out in the otherwise empty scene, looking more like decorations in a furniture store display room than the essentials of life for a quiet and single middle-aged man. The scent of decay was stronger here, like the end of a trail which Petersen had been following all the way in, the rotting corpse of his quarry.

"We went through all the papers we took from here on Monday," Kupfer explained. "And I was suspicious that there weren't any personal details of any kind. No address books, no notes, nothing beyond utility bills, wage slips and mountains of shop receipts."

Petersen pointed questioningly to the .303 rifle propped behind the sofa. Kupfer explained, "It's a category 'C' rifle. The registration papers for it are back at the station."

"Hunting rifle, I guess." Petersen suggested brightly, trying to buoy himself with optimism. "There's probably up to a million registered guns in this country, and the last estimate put the total stock as high as 3 millions. So he's one of the minority who has actually done the right thing, eh?"

Kupfer coughed. "Unfortunately sir, he's also done the wrong thing. We've found two unregistered .375 Desert Eagles, and several full magazines, inside a box where we found the rifle."

"Oh." Petersen remained afloat, but adrift. "Well, there's no answer to that then."

"Also three SPAS-12 shotguns, with magazines..." at that, Petersen's eyes widened. Such firearms had been completely banned for years. "...smoke and CS cartridges, half a dozen fragmentation grenades, tripwires and other equipment to build anti-personnel traps and bombs."

" 'Quiet security guard. With no military record?' " Petersen's attention was drawn briefly by the officer in the bedroom opposite, holding up two of the shotguns. "Member of some kind of paramilitary group, more like. I think we should bring the GEK in on this."

A uniformed officer handed Petersen a small notebook. "Read through this," he urged. "Tell me what you make of it."

Petersen flickered through what was mostly an empty diary, until the last few pages revealed their secret, scrawled down in large letters:

'SOD offers.
G. Calamari - final offer, 5m US d.
Metzger, no bid.
Vilosivich: trade/transport+3.5m Eu'

Kupfer said, "Calamari is probably Giorgio Calamari. He's a known antiquities dealer and treasure hunter. He could certainly put up a sum of 5 million American dollars, from what I've heard."

Petersen agreed. "I know who you mean. The character who tried to buy a Van Gogh for 60 millions."

"It was a Van Eyck," Kupfer corrected quietly, unheard by his boss.

"Yet it looks like he's gone for this Vilosivich's offer, which is less but with some kind of trade-off, and I would guess, a safe route out of the country." He snapped the book shut and punched the air. "I damn well knew it. It was an inside job. But somebody else knew what he was up to, and killed him for it. Now the damn spear could be anywhere."

Petersen opened the book again, turned to the final page. Scrawled across the inside back cover were several strings of numbers. "These are bank account numbers." Petersen tapped the book against his hand thoughtfully. "I think we'll start by speaking to our financial investigators tomorrow." He handed the book back to Kupfer. "Alright, get all of this stuff tagged, bagged and taken into storage. We'll look at it in closer detail first thing in the morning."

"After your meeting with Mr. Siegel and the Professor." Kupfer reminded him.

"Well, after all of this, and thinking about what our Doctor Khalamanga was saying, I might have a closer look again at him myself. Now we know he was behind the robbery, and in contact with some very wealthy and powerful people. He certainly has a past that is undocumented anywhere, and which demands investigation."

"Sir? We also found this." A sergeant held up an opened envelope and letter. "Delivered here today. The first insight we have into Mr. Siegel's private life."

Petersen took the letter and read it. *"The Grand High Order of the Silver Dragon,"* he laughed. "Is that for real?"

"Very real. It's an esoteric order of magic, membership by invitation only. We've already made our enquiries."

"And what do they get up to? Apart from trying to charge the late Mr. Siegel 150 Euros for an annual membership."

The officer explained, "According to our research, their views seem to centre on the psychological works of Carl Jung, heathen mythologies of Northern Europe and esoteric Christianity. It's very hard to gather a single doctrine from their publicity material, but we're still looking into it."

"Could this have any connection to the Spear?" Petersen queried.

Kupfer shrugged. "The one that was left behind, possibly. The common link seems to be Gnostic mysticism."

"Damn that de Carranza. We could have done with him here, just now. Typical: the one time I actually request his presence, and he's busy."

"Busy?" Kupfer repeated, surprised.

"I have no idea. Probably screwing Vanessa up a back alley somewhere." He rolled the letter up and placed it inside his coat. "I'll run this past him tomorrow. Is there anything else here?"

"That's everything of interest so far, sir."

Petersen was already heading for the front door, without any parting words of thanks or encouragement. He wanted to get out of that rotten little corner of the city as quickly as possible.

"Something bothering you?" Vanessa asked, having become aware that their conversation had faltered again. de Carranza seemed preoccupied with something other than her, despite the friendly noises and reassuring touches. He had succeeded in making her feel a little happier about herself, but she was still wondering why the loud, confident man had become so quiet since Petersen's phonecall.

"No," he lied, knowing she would not believe him, and hoping she wouldn't press him for the truth.

"Have you ever looked at a dead body before?"

That took him aback. "I'm sorry? What an odd question."

"Do you think so? You're all set up to go and view a corpse tomorrow which has been boiled, decapitated, castrated and disembowelled. I'm only making sure you know what you're letting yourself in for. It's not like the cop shows on the TV. It's a dirty, degrading experience, to see the worst that humanity can inflict upon its own kind."

de Carranza smiled grimly to himself. "I appreciate your concern. And I understand that even with your past experience, it is something you would not wish to undertake lightly. But don't worry about me, my dear. It's all for the good of the investigation."

"It's more you I'm worried about." She stopped him with a tug on his sleeve, turned him around to face her. "I don't want to see you..." she bit her lip. "...dragged too deep into this. And it's getting very deep now."

"Yes, it is. But I was summoned to Vienna by the Kommissar, and I will not let him down. I admit I have had my doubts about this whole adventure. But I now feel such an experience can only make me stronger." He added with a half-laugh, "That's if it doesn't kill me."

They headed past the Sigmund-Freud-Park and its tranquil memories of the afternoon before, back in the direction of the Margaretenstrasse and Vanessa's little haven of the Holiday Inn. Walking the dark streets of Vienna by herself was not something she had done very often, despite the city's reputation for being safe for women. But with de Carranza beside her she felt she could walk all night, into the dawn, a childish notion perhaps but one which filled her with hope. She had never felt it much in the past with anyone, that sensation of comfort, protection, since the days her parents had decided to part company and left Vanessa and her sisters to fend for themselves.

He felt her touch his wrist, gently tracing the stern veins that arose from the back of his hand, tickling the fine hairs on his fingers, interlocking with his. She felt no outward reaction from him, almost as if he had been expecting it. Hand in hand, they passed by the facade of a restaurant, from which the strains of a Bach toccata could be heard above the drone of dinner talk.

"There's a question for you," he pondered. "Music. We haven't got around to discussing music yet. Who's your favourite composer?"

"Oh, Wagner. With Tchaikovsky a very close second."

de Carranza drew a long face. "Well, well. Not whom I would have expected."

They were almost at the Holiday Inn now, fifty yards or so from the door. de Carranza led her onto a wooden bench where they sat, side by side, facing the bleak black windows of shut shops. He saw her figure twitching in the reflection, uncertain again, wondering what he *had* expected.

He pulled in a deep breath. "I'm sorry. I'm not trying to be flippant. It's strange, though; the Doctor mentioned Wagner a couple of times to me. 'Parsifal', in fact. The story of the Spear of Longinus and how it heals an injured king." He turned to face her. "Is that one of your favourites?"

"No, it's far too holy for my taste." She started laughing. "Nothing beats 'Tristan and Isolde'. Every time I hear the 'Liebestod' it brings tears to my eyes. Maybe it's my subconscious desire to be a doomed heroine, I don't know."

She reclined in the seat, stretching her tired legs out before her. The sight attracted de Carranza's attention, she noticed, despite his every attempt to disguise the fact.

"Getting a bit chilly, out." She observed. "I suppose I should turn in for the night."

"Well, I hope you have a good evening. And may the rest of your stay be more pleasant than it has been so far."

She felt something heavy sink inside her, as though she had just swallowed a lead weight. She felt disappointed, angry even, at this attempt at a brush-off. "What do you mean?"

"This case. I'm sorry we couldn't have spent time under more pleasant circumstances. And I wish we had been able to see a nicer side of Wien. She must be a beautiful, cultured soul when you get to know her well." He sucked a deep breath of damp warm air up his nose, caught a distant tinge of Vanessa's fading perfume. A Chanel, his second wife's favourite. Sweet and sour lightning flashes of a past life returned – ruffles of a black velvet dress, crystal ear-rings at a University function, harsh words in the bedroom of his old villa - impressions until then forgotten, and all reawakened by that fleeting hint of fragrance, a true Marcel Proust moment.

"I was thinking of staying around for a while yet," she admitted. "We could still meet up under nicer circumstances. And tonight was very nice. Don't think I've even thanked you properly yet."

He shook his head against her politeness, laughing. "You don't need to thank me. It's all cool."

Sometimes she felt the language barrier was more than it seemed. Though his spoken English was near-perfect, it possibly didn't express his inner feelings as well as his native tongue might. "I'm glad it's cool," she agreed. "But we could still make things…more cool."

"I'll be honest," he said, turning to face her. "I agree with you. We could have very good fun, I think. But I feel we're approaching a critical juncture in this investigation, and I don't think any of us can afford distractions."

She chose to ignore his suggestion she had been a 'distraction' so far. And why exactly had he turned down Petersen's request for his presence, if he wasn't going to make something out of the evening?

"But that doesn't mean we can't work together."

"What makes you want to involve yourself with this now, Vanessa? You said your work was done, that you wanted no more of it, that you-"

Her hand grabbed his, pulling it across to her lap and nearly wrenching his shoulder out of its socket in the process. "I'm committed to this," she said, taking time to form her words despite the fact her intestines were making knots out of themselves now. "Because I *caused* this bloody mess. That man in the Hofburg is dead because of me."

de Carranza didn't even blink. "What?"

"When I first completed the work on the spear and the nail, I received calls from people asking me to do 'the right thing' for them. They wanted the nail, and wouldn't take 'no' for an answer. I tried to be polite, told them it was not my job to make such decisions, and they should speak to Steiner if they wanted to study the nail for themselves.

"Then the calls came again - never threatening, never shouting or nasty - just designed, I think, to cause me maximum discomfort. My work suffered, I think Dr. Reed noticed, but I couldn't tell him the reason why."

"Why didn't you tell the police, for God's sake?" He could feel her fingers sweating within his, became conscious of how small her hand seemed in comparison, like a child's.

"I don't know. I didn't want to bring our work into disrepute, have it associated with cranks, maniacs or whatever. I thought it might cast a cloud of controversy over our results. So I let it go.

"Then I received a call giving me a PO Box number and telling me this was where I should send the nail to and they were counting upon me to do the right thing. It was always that phrase, 'do the right thing'. I asked them why they didn't want the spear. They said I should know why, because the spear isn't genuine. Well, they sounded like fanatics to me, so in the end I said I'd send it onto them. And they said that if the nail didn't arrive, they would 'take up arms' and remove it by force."

"So what happened?"

"I sent them a fake. One rusty old 7-inch spike looks pretty much like any other, so I thought. Nobody in the media was much interested in the nail, apart from these weirdos. It was the spear that got the attention because it's famous and full of legend, so I thought it would shut them up and they would never know the difference. Obviously, they knew more than I thought because there it was, back in my hands again on Monday morning, thrown right back in my face, as if to say, 'You cheating bitch'. And I realise now what I did was wrong. And I know I can't go back and change any of it, but I can maybe try to help make up for it."

de Carranza turned his attention away from her to the road in front of them, to where a small group of young people were messing around, laughing, without cares or worries.

"Do you have any idea who these people were?"

"No. It was a different person each time. An Englishman the first time. Then a Frenchman, then a German, the one who gave me the box number. And I don't know any more than that. Only that I've buggered this up, and these fellows have 'taken up arms' as they said they would and I'm probably in serious shit because of it and I knew I should never have come here in the first place." She buried her face in her hands, still clutching his, and warm tears trickled between his fingers and up his sleeve.

"You did what you thought would satisfy everybody," he said finally. "In the end, it may have satisfied nobody, but at least you didn't give in to them. You were strong, brave." He released himself from her grasp and gave her a reassuring squeeze. "You did the right thing after all."

Her face glistened silver in the nightlight, smears of makeup in the tracks of her tears. "Do you think they'll come after me?"

He took a handkerchief from a jacket pocket and wiped away her misery. "No, I don't. They'll have the real nail now, that's what they wanted. Maybe they just left your nail behind to make it look like nothing had been stolen, and to hamper the investigation. Did they ever threaten you?"

"No. Not directly. They all sounded well-educated, and very calm. The first man - the Englishman - seemed almost casual. He didn't actually ask me for the nail, but he did say to expect other people to show a great deal of interest in it, and that I should be careful."

"I want you to call Petersen tonight, and ask him for protection. Will you do that for me, Vanessa?"

"No. I don't want to draw attention to myself anymore." She let his hand go and threw herself back against the seat with a final groan. "I just don't want anyone to cut my head off, that's all."

"You're not Josef Siegel. God knows who the man was in league with, or why."

She understood he was doing all he could to put her at ease. In fact she was probably lucky that he hadn't slapped her on the spot, for being a stupid thoughtless scatty bitch and getting people hacked to bits and causing so much grief to everyone.

"I guess I'd better get in and try to get some sleep, then." She said sadly. "Even though I know I won't."

She glanced towards the hotel but made no move toward it. de Carranza waited, feeling the silence stretch. After a while he became acutely aware of her rapid breathing, still wet and troubled; tears were not far from the surface again. Under any other circumstances he would have drawn her close and kissed her, held her, wrapped her tightly in his arms and told her it would all be okay. Just as he had done almost every day of his marriage to his second wife, just as he had always promised himself he would never do again. He almost cried with the pain of the dilemma, a despair so deep it turned his spoken words into stammering confusion.

"Do you want me to..." he began, hands gesturing in the air to complete the sentence.

She shook her head. Five minutes ago there would have been no argument, but now she had let her fears and tears bubble to the surface, she knew she would not be good company. "I'm sorry for spoiling everything. Another time, another place – maybe when I've got my head back together. And I hope that's sooner, rather than later."

"Shall I walk you to the door then?"

She laughed, sniffed, wiped her nose. "Only if you hold my hand."

He took both her hands in his, stood up and pulled her to her feet.

"Feel free to laugh," she said as they walked together. "I look a bloody mess, I know. But right now, I don't really care."

"Neither do I." he assured her. And before they knew it, they were at the Holiday Inn, facing the main doors, facing each other, facing another 'goodnight'.

"Well here we are again, Tomas. You've done so much for me, and in return all I've given you is hassle. 'Spose I'm due you a hell of a payback sometime for all your patience."

"I ask only that one day soon I get to see you truly happy. And I hope that is sooner, rather than later. If you need anything, give me a call. It doesn't matter what time of night. Just do it."

She drew him in and placed a hurried, nervous peck on his cheek. "For a guy who said he wasn't a gentleman..." She sucked back another surge of tears, felt her face crumple. She just fought back the impulse to kiss him on the cheek for his trouble.

"Look after yourself, Tomas."

He watched her enter, saw the doors close behind her, waited for her to look over her shoulder and wave, smile, blow a kiss. She didn't; instead she faded into the semi-opaque reflections, a receding shimmer behind the double-glazing.

He turned away from the Holiday Inn and meandered back to his guest house, his boots playing a dejected nocturne against the paving stones. He got as far as the corner of the Maysedergasse when his cellphone burbled its way into his attention. He plucked it from his pocket, knowing who would be at the other end, and his heart jumped with excitement.

"That was quick, my dear." he laughed, to be answered by the completely unexpected voice of Emanuel Khalamanga.

"Ah, hello. It's me. Er, can you come to the Sacher, if you're not too busy? I think I've found something. Something rather important."

Vanessa hadn't walked twenty paces inside the lobby when she imagined she heard a voice whisper her name. Now she knew she was delusional, tired, and probably more than slightly paranoid. She had already established a priority of things to be done when she reached her room: get those damn boots off, run a bath, drink wine, find some boring but pretty-looking foreign film on the TV and fall asleep in front of it with the light on. It didn't sound like a bad end to an evening, she told herself, although she would much rather have spent it wrapped around someone warm and comforting - strictly for security reasons, of course.

"Vanessa Descartes?"

That stopped her dead in her tracks. The voice had called her name sure enough, and from a few metres behind her and to her right. She found herself turning in that direction, slowly and fearfully, as if caught in a dream where she was being chased and could not escape.

Here was a man in his mid-40s dressed in black from head to foot, occupying one of the armchairs in the lobby as though he were in the drawing room of his own country house. The voice held an edge of familiarity due to its English accent, something she had heard almost nothing of since the departure of Dr. Reed and his team.

But the voice was familiar for more than just its ethnic origin. It was the first voice which had spoken to her on the telephone about how she should expect others to show interest in the Holy Nail. And now here he was, flesh and blood, an open magazine on his lap. It was the same priest she had noticed on Tuesday night, sitting almost in the exact same spot. And this time there was no mistake, no imagination at work; he was looking straight at her.

He had spectacles around his neck on a chain, a wide, broad-brimmed hat above a set of dark, elongated features. The mouth held a permanent twist of sarcasm, the eyes a hint of boyish cheekiness. A very long coat flowed around him and only the white collar broke the total blackness of his outfit, a minister of God who looked more like the emissary of death. Surely, if he was a hitman, he wouldn't draw attention to himself like this, in such a public place?

"A moment. Please." He whispered urgently.

She dithered, something she realised she had become pretty good at by now. If he did have a gun hidden under that magazine, he could have emptied it into her already. Reassured by this unexpected flash of reasoning, she took her first tentative step towards him. When about two metres separated them, the priest leaned forward and brought his hands together, as though about to pray.

"Miss Descartes, I don't wish to alarm you, but we do need to talk again. You've recently been contacted by some people who wished you to send them something very valuable. Is this not so?"

The game was up. The telephone calls and the demands hadn't been a joke. They had really meant it. People had wanted that nail so badly they were willing to kill for it, and now here was one of them, come to serve judgement upon her for not doing The Right Thing.

"Now..." he brushed dust or dandruff from his shoulder, "You've managed to make things very awkward, shall we say. A fact which, by now I assume, you are probably well aware."

She bent down until she was almost in his face. "Good. If you think you can go about beheading people-"

"Don't." he raised a firm, authoritative finger in front of her. "You don't have the foggiest about what's going on out there, so don't try to presume the motivations of anyone. I regret matters have become complicated. You have not helped things, but I will give you a piece of neutral advice. This is over your head, and over the heads of your learned acquaintances. Now get out of it before you get hit in the crossfire. The last thing any of us need is more - what's that horrible term the Americans use - 'collateral damage'."

She shifted her weight onto one hip, feeling her fears give birth to a nervous kind of swagger within her. The man smelled of vinegar, and she found herself with a longing for fish and chips.

"Well, as heads seem to be very much on the agenda at the moment, I have no intention of losing mine, cheers."

"That's good. You *will*, however, if you keep sticking it above the parapet."

"Really. I thought the Church was supposed to be peaceful these days. Didn't the crusades end a long time ago? Or are you just trying to be metaphorical?"

"No, this is a war as terrible as any other, more so by the fact that so few know of it. It is a war that has been fought through the dust of Jerusalem to the mud of Montsegur, to the streets of Bosnia and to here, this very day. It is a war that was born from a schism, that grew out of lies, heresy and greed. Two factions who were once united under one God and one noble ideal, now so bitterly opposed."

"Sounds much like the history of the Church itself."

"More than you could know. The repercussions of your work on the Holy Spear have sent shockwaves through the ranks and now that we are nearing these final days when everything hangs in the balance, I for one don't want to see innocent bystanders getting in the way."

Vanessa moved cautiously forward, sat down in the armchair beside him. She hugged her bag to her chest, her old shield against the horrors of the real world.

"What are you?"

"Just a humble man trying to hold true to my God, and to what is right."

"You 'phoned me up to warn me, didn't you? That something like this murder would happen?"

"I didn't predict the murder, no. I wanted you to be careful, to expect others to start putting pressure on you. I had no idea what form that pressure might take, or what events might result from it."

She leaned closer. "Tell me what is going on. For God's sake, all I wanted to do was help, to do the right thing, as I understood it. Can't you see that? I never wanted any of this."

The priest laughed and raised his magazine. It was a copy of the German edition of 'Penthouse'.

"You're begging me to divulge secrets in an hotel lobby, which men have killed for, been burned for, gone to war and built and destroyed empires for?" he stopped abruptly, realising his voice had raised more than he intended. He pulled the brim of his hat down, perhaps conscious now of the hotel security cameras which recorded their every move. "Some things are better left unknown. Trust me."

So that was it, she realised. No answers, just a 'friendly warning' and goodnight. Her fear, her bravado, her curiosity all surrendered to outright indignation. For a minute she sat and raged in silence.

The priest lowered his magazine. "You're in this, by the way." He indicated the article he was reading, illustrated with photographs of the Holy Spear and a smiling portrait of someone called Doctor Vanessa Jane Descartes – a relic of another age, depicting a woman who looked proud, confident, successful. A woman she no longer recognized. "I like the way you apologise for not finding the spearhead to be genuine."

Vanessa continued to stare across the lobby. "I'm not taking that crap. You've put me through hell these past weeks, screwing with my head, like I wasn't screwed up enough, ever since I first came into contact with that bloody spear-" she noticed his mouth stretching into a smirk, possibly amused at how strong her native accent was coming through. "-and I'm glad you think it's funny, mate, so how's about some answers, like what the hell your pals want with that fucking piece of rusty old iron?"

He flicked over a page, unfazed by her outburst. "Just making the world a better place, my dear." he said gently. "And by that, I mean, for *everyone*." He looked up at her over the top of his spectacles like a schoolteacher telling her she must do better. A tremor of futility shook Vanessa, starting out from the base of her neck and wriggling its way down her spine. She had put up with enough ersatz philosophy and whatever else this smirking little gnome represented. Her curiosity had fled, her higher functions gone with it, leaving her in the midst of more familiar earthy desires. In the absence of a strong pair of hands to ease away her fears and tensions with an oil massage, she stormed off to her room with visions of a deep bath followed by as much wine as her poor body could hold.

DAY FOUR: Thursday

Petersen arrived at the city mortuary fifteen minutes behind time. It would have been to the bewilderment of his neighbours that he spent five minutes on his hands and knees on the pavement outside his apartment, peering curiously under his car with a shaving mirror for signs of a carbomb or other attempts at sabotage. Once in the car, he checked the brakes before setting off, and even on the road he caught himself throwing anxious glances into the mirror to check there were no threatening vehicles pursuing him. It was early morning primal fears making a nuisance of themselves, he realised as he parked outside the city mortuary building, but that didn't make them any the less real. He only hoped that circumstances would allow him to conquer them, before they conquered him.

He hated this place; it looked like an underground nuclear bunker inside, and felt like a polar research station. Though usually possessed of a rational mind, there were nevertheless moments when he felt threatened by the oppressive darkness, and if such things as crashed UFO pilots or zombies existed, they would most likely be found stumbling through those half-lit passages and chilly rooms, thirty feet below the University medical research labs.

But there were no monsters, no ghouls to come lurching out of the gloom today; instead he found Tomas de Carranza sitting patiently on a chair outside Theatre 2.

"Good morning, Kommissar." He grinned at the other man's approach. "I hope you had a pleasant evening?"

"Yes." Petersen said sharply. "And you?" Despite the initial invitation, Petersen had never found it in his heart to address de Carranza on first name terms.

"Very good, yes. I spent the time with my colleague. We had many important new things to discuss."

"How is she doing?"

" 'She'? No, Kommissar. Doctor Khalamanga. The lady-" he stopped, unwilling to drop the bombshell of her revelations. "She was tired, wanted an early night."

Petersen stopped at the Spaniard's side, not listening but looking. "Where's Rosenfeldt?"

"She went out for a cigarette. Said she'd be back in a minute." he looked at his watch. "Five minutes ago. It seems that even Austrians have the same poor estimation of time as every other nationality I've come across. By the way, last night Emanuel and I did some cross-referencing of each other's work and, do you know, that man has an eidetic memory. And he came up with some fascinating new angles-"

"Ah, Dr. Rosenfeldt." Petersen called, grateful to God for sending an angel of deliverance in the form of the little Jewish pathologist. It wasn't that Petersen disliked de Carranza particularly; he was quite sure that the Spaniard probably earned more in royalties in a week than Peterson made in a month, but that in itself he did not resent. He just found the man infuriatingly overbearing and too smug for his own good. Being generous, he could put that down to the fact that they both had to speak in a common language which was not their native tongue. In his more intolerant moments, Peterson had decided that de Carranza was used to always being right, being in control, and having people tell him how incredibly clever he was.

"Kommissar." The pathologist smiled. She glanced aside at de Carranza who, without waiting to be introduced, announced himself gleefully. "Pleased to meet you," She smiled as they entered the mortuary beyond.

"The Professor's assisting us with some of the background to the case." Petersen explained as their presence echoed all the way around the room. "I thought it would be an idea if we both took a second look, in case there was something we missed, especially in the light of recent discoveries."

Rosenfeldt set about removing the body of Siegel for display. The head had not yet been reconnected but was set in place above the neck, the half-inch gap providing a ghoulish sight.

"Here we have him, gentlemen. Take your time, I'll fill in my paperwork while you're at it."

de Carranza approached the trolley tentatively, still having second thoughts. This was a corpse after all, not made up like those lying in their public view before burial to suggest eternal perpetuity, but an emphatic symbol of finality, stark and humbling. And in its raw, skinless and ravaged state, utterly revolting.

"*Madre de Dios*."

"Not a pretty boy, is he?" Rosenfeldt chirped, sensing the disgust in the air.

"How..." de Carranza began, felt a bitter lump of breakfast lodge in his throat. He swallowed, tasting hot chocolate and bile. "How were the fluids removed, Doctor?"

"Carefully. By someone who knows their way around a human body, who probably has had some surgical experience. It's very difficult to completely drain any kind of fluid from a corpse, yet they've come very close to doing so here, leaving only a little residue. It's taken a lot of effort, and patience."

Petersen pulled on a pair of the gloves provided and drew the sheet all the way down to reveal the rest of the crumpled, cracked skin which looked ready to break away at the slightest touch.

"You any further ahead on this one?" Rosenfeldt asked from the workbench at the other end of the room.

"We have...theories." Petersen said, prodding dark, wrinkled flesh which reminded him of the chicken breasts he used to cook up for Sunday dinner, back in the days when he had a wife, and ate real dinners, and Sundays meant something important to him. "We do know Mr. Siegel was up to some very lucrative international antiquities dealing."

"Was he now," de Carranza mused, finding the courage to bring him to the edge of the trolley. "Over the spear?"

"Yes. Three and a half million euros, plus bonuses."

Rosenfeldt chewed on the edge of her pen. "Oh. That does put a different face on the matter."

"Still seems very extravagant, all this." Petersen indicated the severed neck. "Must have taken a lot of effort on someone's part. A bullet in the head I could understand."

"*We* understand it," de Carranza said. "Emanuel and I. Well, we have an explanation, anyway."

"Care to share it?" Petersen asked with a sharp upward glance, his eyes disappearing into shadows from the overhead spotlights.

de Carranza felt uncertain. He didn't like the way voices, and even the tiniest noise, echoed hollowly in this room. He had found one of the few places where he felt uncomfortable hearing his own voice. "Later. It's only a theory at the moment. Let me look here first."

Petersen blew a blast of exasperated breath from the side of his mouth. "Well, I don't see anything new here," he confessed.

"What's that on his shoulder?" de Carranza pointed to a faint blotch on the left deltoid.

"The remains of a tattoo. The heat the body has been subjected to has almost obliterated it."

"Hmm." The other man pondered, taking off his glasses for a closer inspection. Or a 2.5x magnified look, Petersen thought with a fleeting grin.

Rosenfeldt crossed the room from the desk to the door. "I'll be back in a minute. Nature calls."

de Carranza peered at the faded, tattered image. "A tiger's head. It looks like there's a scroll with writing underneath, with two words. Did you manage to work out what this says?"

"Why do you think it's significant, Professor?"

"I don't. It's just one thing your people haven't looked into fully. It may be a dead-end, it may be a lead. We'll never know if we don't look." He pulled from his pocket a digital camera. "May I...?"

Petersen dithered. The man's enthusiasm, or competitive streak, was encouraging, but taking unauthorised pictures of a murder victim did not sit well with his training. He knew he could probably trust the man not to publish them on the Internet, and at least, it might keep him busy for a while and allow Petersen to get on with his job.

"Strictly speaking, this is against procedure. However, if I happened not to be looking at the time..." the Kommissar turned to face the half-open door behind him, clearing his throat as he did so.

de Carranza took the hint. Zooming in as close as he could, he fired off a half-dozen shots with the flash.

"Thank you."

At that moment Rosenfeldt returned, swinging her clipboard happily as she went. "Are we all finished up here?"

"I'm done, thank you." de Carranza said.

She took up the sheet and pulled it back over the body. "Have a nice day now, gentlemen." As they turned to leave, both men heard her whisper, "And it's bed-time for you, Mr. Siegel...no, don't you dare shake your head at me!"

As the two men left the elevator and walked back toward daylight again, Petersen felt the natural warmth gradually return to his body. It was as if that place drew some vital quality out of his mind and psyche, which could only be restored by returning to the upper world of life and colour, away from the underworld and all its Stygian smells and secrets, its hidden corpses and the thick synthetic air of death.

"So what are these theories you two have come up with?" he asked as they mingled with doctors, students and lab technicians in the main foyer.

"Dr. Khalamanga attests to medieval treatises which seem to correspond with certain aspects of the case. We now thoroughly believe the possibility that this crime was motivated by matters as diverse as alchemy, the secret of the Crucifixion, and possibly a modern-day group descended from the original Knights Templar."

This was precisely the kind of crackpot theorizing Petersen had been dreading. The more down-to-earth the case became, the more outlandish the ideas his appointed experts seemed to come up with.

"What the hell are you trying to give me here? Is this what we've waited three days for you to come up with? Alchemy: a ludicrous, obsolete system of recipes to turn pathetic old men into kings. The Crucifixion: an event none of us can ever possibly know the truth about after 2,000 years. Templars: crusaders whose history is now more popular fiction than fact. *That's* your theory?"

de Carranza bit his cheek, fighting back his argumentative instincts. "Alchemy is more than just the search for gold and eternal life. It is a deep, philosophical system which has connections to Gnosticism; beliefs shared by the people who wrote the 'Second Treatise of the Great Seth'."

"Yes, we know this. So?"

"*So*, we decided to work on the assumption that the business with the head and the watch was a kind of calling-card. So we sat until 3 o'clock this morning, searching the Internet for all possible variations on the theme of heads and 1735. Or 5 and 7. After trying every linguistic translation of the word and the numbers, we found half a dozen references to a very obscure group known as Capo 57. 'Capo' is 'head' in Italian. 'Capo' can also mean 'boss', as used by Sicilian crime families; by extension, 'leader'. 'King', even. If we add the numbers we get 12, and putting these together, we find ourselves with Jesus Christ Himself, as the Head of the 12 tribes of Israel, and as leader of the 12 apostles.

"Here we have a group who encapsulate in their name both the temporal and the spiritual kingdoms. A group who operated above and beyond the authority of the Papacy at their height, who were wealthier than most kings of the time, and who have long been imagined to have held the secret of the Holy Grail. Your suspects *are* modern-day Knights Templar, Kommissar, and so secretive that their name is found only in one public document, a strange article relating to an ex-member of their organization who fled rather than suffer their full initiation ceremony."

He pulled a rolled-up sheet of paper from his jacket pocket. "Here. This is from an Italian newspaper, the Florence Gazetta, August 1979."

Petersen took the printout, read it through reluctantly.

'...Three days before his body was found hanging under a bridge over the Arno River, Massimo Constantino had told local police: "They initiate you first by oath, and then by action. They give you a double-edged sword and the Master who presides over the ceremony asks you to tap his neck with the sword, a symbol of the candidate's honour, that he will not injure his Master. After a year and a day the candidate is supposed to allow the Master to return the blow on his own neck. If he has spent the intervening time well - he will then be deemed a full member, and be accepted gratefully into the brotherhood. If the group feel the prospect has not acted well...this is what brings me here to you now. They do not say what happens then, but I fear for my life, and I fear what these men may do."

"Emanuel tells me this idea of the beheading ritual is lifted directly from the great Arthurian romance, 'Sir Gawain and the Green Knight', Kommissar. A work that may have been written by a member of the Templars."

Petersen pocketed the page. He didn't want this angle, didn't need it, and yet it was being thrust upon him from de Carranza, from the crime scene, from Gruber, from everywhere but the victim himself. It had been too much to hope for, a simple case of a theft and an extortion gone wrong.

Petersen removed from his coat the 'Order of the Silver Dragon' subscription letter from Siegel's place. "Well, since mystical societies seem to be in fashion at the moment, let me ask you what you make of this one."

de Carranza took the letter and ran his eyes over it. "Looks like some intellectual's idea of a daring game." He was about to hand it back when something at the top of the page caught his attention, the stylised logo, printed in silvery grey on the letterhead. It was a dragon in outline, curled around a rock or mountain. An image he had seen very recently on Gruber's fireplace.

"What is it?" Petersen asked.

de Carranza looked again, laughing now at his own foolishness. The motif was one he had also seen repeated on the covers of dozens of cheap fantasy novels over the decades. The silver figure Gruber displayed could have been bought in a gift shop almost anywhere in the Western World.

"Nothing. My imagination working overtime, that's all." As Petersen took back the letter, de Carranza asked, "Does this society have an office here, in Vienna?"

"Two, in fact." Petersen replied. "The head office appears to be based in Bavaria. However, the contact addresses are all postal box numbers."

"Two? They must have quite a large membership in that case." And as Gruber had said, a good many respected and intelligent people too, no doubt, comments which got the Spaniard thinking again of the coincidences surrounding Gruber's dragon and the order which bore its name. If Gruber had several unwanted similar ornaments, why choose that very one to display? And in the light of his surprising views upon magic, de

Carranza could not shake the idea that there was still some connection somewhere, however remote.

But that was something he would look into in the future. For the present, he had more pressing matters to attend to.

de Carranza breezed back to Khalamanga's rooms in the Sacher that afternoon, flushed and excited with his new-found learning. "Doctor, I hope you're feeling bright and alert, because we have some more research to do."

"Have a good morning in the mortuary, did you?" the voice of Vanessa caught him off-guard. He stopped, surprised at the sight of her lying stretched out on the cushions at the other end of the suite, a black and white film flickering from the TV set.

"She had a bad night," Khalamanga explained from his seat at the computer.

"Oh. What's the matter, my dear? Why did you not call me?"

"Because last night I wasn't in much of a state to speak. And so far today, you and the Inspector have been busy with Mr. Siegel." She stabbed the 'off' button on the TV remote and tossed it onto the coffee table. "A man dressed as a priest was waiting for me after you left me. Told me I shouldn't be interfering, that this was over all of our heads and we should get out now before we're caught in the crossfire."

"Did he, indeed. And I take it you have given his description to our Kommissar?"

"No, because this whole thing is running out of control now. My mind is made up. I'm leaving, and I'm leaving tonight. It's my decision and not one I've taken lightly. But with the way I've been feeling lately, and how things are going, I know I've overstayed my welcome. I have to be where I know I belong, that's all there is to it. That's the way it's always been, it's just taken me this long to realise the fact."

She pulled herself out of the sofa, collected her bag and strode to the door. de Carranza almost didn't follow her at first, so surprised was he by the change in her movements. She looked confident and bright; head high, her back straight. He put the camera down and hurried to her side, all thoughts of Siegel and his tattoo forgotten. It was the first time he had seen her wearing trousers, smartly tailored by a designer label, and matched by a casual but equally stylish jacket. She no longer looked girlish, vulnerable, *scatty* (whatever that meant), but focused and in control, and the transformation slightly unnerved him.

"Stay in touch." He begged with a heavy sigh. "I absolutely insist."

"You'll be hearing from me, Tomas. Very soon, don't you worry about that. Everything will be okay, I promise." She paused to scribble something on the back of a shopping receipt with an eyebrow pencil and pressed it into his hand. "This is my personal web space, if you're interested in following the facts after I've gone."

She crumpled the paper into his grasp, their fingers entwined for a pleasing moment but, like their lives, destined to be pulled apart again. It had not occurred to him until this very moment quite how much he cared for her, how he needed her now more than ever. He held her tight, not wanting to let her go but knowing that he must, for her sake if nothing else.

"Don't be afraid," she told him. "We're all doing the right thing. That's all that matters. It's all...cool."

Their hands slid apart, reluctantly, and de Carranza pocketed the greasy scrap of paper. "Thank you, my dear. 'Til we meet again...*Voya con Dios*."

"*Lluvia fuerte, casamiento con suerte.*"

de Carranza presented a broken smile. "That's what they said on my second wedding day. It poured non-stop for three days." He paused. "Make that five years."

Just before the door closed completely, she smiled back at him with a gentle wave, a final fulfilment of his desire to see her looking happy and free of fear. He only wished the moment could have lasted longer. He took out his cellphone and toyed with the idea of sending her a text message, then thought the better of it. She had made up her mind, and he would respect her decision. If she was true to her word, he would hear from her soon enough. And in the meantime, there was work to be done.

"Doctor, could I bother you for a few moments please?" he unfurled a cable from his jacket pocket and set about connecting the camera to the computer. "I came away with a few snapshots which may prove helpful to the investigation."

Khalamanga stared at him in disbelief. "You photographed the body?"

"Only a small detail. Petersen was happy to indulge me. He obviously sees me as some sort of bumbling eccentric who longs to be a detective, and will do anything to humour me in my delusions." Khalamanga shifted aside in his chair as de Carranza downloaded the images onto the computer. "There's the remains of a tattoo on the man's shoulder. A tiger's head. It has a scroll and something written within the scroll, and nobody down there has yet investigated it. Now, may I hijack your Internet connection for a short while?"

de Carranza logged on to the global search engine, selected 'Hunt for Images' and typed in 'tiger tattoo'. As he expected, he was hit with over 4,000 results, mostly from tattoo studios around the world, and their customers.

"What do you think you're going to find here?" Khalamanga asked. "Even if you find a match, I'm sure that all tattooists work from stock images. You're not going to trace who did it."

"Maybe it's not a stock image. Maybe it's unique. There's one with a scroll. Look." de Carranza enlarged the image, which linked to a web page about young sailors in the United States Marine Corps. The scroll read 'USS Montana'. "Hm, it's close, but not the same. The tiger's head we have is drawn at a three-quarter angle, not face-on. But we may be on the right track with the military connection."

They searched through more images, each page becoming less and less relevant than the one before.

"How about this?" Khalamanga suggested.

"Yes, that's it." de Carranza placed the two images side by side and, despite the degradation of the skin on Siegel's arm, what remained of the design was a perfect match with the picture Khalamanga had just found within the search results. They clicked on the link and found themselves directed to a web page written in an unfamiliar language, with pictures of men in black combat fatigues and red berets lounging around some sort of barracks. The main picture was a close-up shot of the same tattoo on three of these men's arms, each soldier grinning at the camera, one of them holding up a tin of beer.

"These men are soldiers. Eastern European. Our man was Austrian." Khalamanga pointed out.

"Then let's translate the page and find out who they are." de Carranza clicked on a link. The page refreshed itself, this time in English. The bulk of the website seemed to consist of Serbian nationalist propaganda and the portrayal of the men as heroes during the war in the Balkans.

" 'Some of the men from 'Arkan's Tigers'." de Carranza read. " 'SDG Paramilitary force'...whatever they are."

"Let's find out." Khalamanga said, typing 'Arkan's Tigers' into the web word search. As the screen filled with results, certain words and phrases kept cropping up within the links:

Srpska Dobrovoljacka Garda (Serbian Volunteer Guard)... terrorist/Paramilitary organization, also known as Arkan's Tigers, based upon Serb nationalism and orthodox Christianity ...free reign to loot and murder...war crimes...SDG founder Zeljko Raznatovic, or 'Arkan', hunted for genocide... Arkan assassinated in Belgrade, 2000...

de Carranza stared at the words on the screen, following the cruel and violent tale they told. "My God. Looks like our man was involved in some serious action. Doctor, call Petersen now. This could be vital."

Khalamanga picked up the 'phone. He got through to Petersen's office, was answered by Kupfer and brusquely invited to leave a message. "I'd rather speak to the Kommissar in person. It's important. A possible breakthrough."

As Khalamanga sat waiting on hold, the Spaniard had begun to dig into the bloody past of the SDG; national heroes in their homeland, murderers to NATO and Europol. On a whim, he returned to the main search page and typed in 'Arkan's Tigers+Capo 57'. The PC chugged away to itself as it invariably did when asked to do something vaguely complex, then displayed a small list of results. Top of which was the title of an article: 'Modern-day Knights Doing Battle in Balkans: Capo 57 and the Secret Crusade'."

He navigated to the page which displayed a blank screen behind a 'Loading...' message. As he waited, the page turned to black and the message disappeared. The screen began to fill with a golden glow and an animated sequence unfolded before their eyes. Both men stared as a digitised figure of a man appeared, kneeling with his head on a block.

"I don't like this," de Carranza started.

As he was speaking, an animated sword appeared and severed the figure's head with an extravagant gush of blood, forcing a squeal of alarm from the throat of Khalamanga, who had never experienced a computer game or animated film in his life.

de Carranza hammered the keyboard in his attempt to get the screen to return to normal but the computer had frozen, and the PC's hard disk began to whirr and click frantically to itself.

"Kill the connection, dammit." he yelled, and obeying himself, dashed to the phone socket where he yanked the Internet cable free. A mass of pop-up windows screaming 'Virus attack!' flashed up, then inevitably, the PC restarted itself with a click and some suspicious grinding from the hard drive. Then there was only silence as both men sat and looked at each other in mutual bewilderment.

The unmarked patrol car brought the two academics to the station an hour later where they sat in Petersen's office, awaiting his return from the incident room. The Inspector kept them waiting for less time than they feared, and he greeted them brightly as though he too shared Vanessa's epiphany.

"Gentlemen, thank you both for your patience, and also for your assistance. Let me begin by apologising if I seem to have been rather dismissive of your ideas lately."

"Not a problem, sir." de Carranza assured him, "For people unlike ourselves, who do not live among ancient records and mystical manuscripts day to day, it can seem a large stretch of the imagination to believe that such arcane forces can be at work in our society."

Petersen accepted this. "However, it seems to have been your more down-to-earth research which has provided the most information." he wrestled out of his jacket and hung it on the back of his seat. "Acting directly on your new-found information, we ran every detail we have learned about Josef Siegel back through Europol's databases. We discovered a great deal which we now believe explains the circumstances of the murder."

"Did you track down that Italian newspaper article?" de Carranza asked.

"We didn't need to. Europol have supplied us with a 'black list' they had obtained from members of the Serb Volunteer Guard, what amounts to nothing less than a hit list. In 1996, high-ranking associates of Zeljko Arkan were liquidated by the Serbian State Security Service to prevent their ex-employees from talking about their involvement in war crimes in the Balkans. Our victim, one of Arkan's lieutenants, was one of the few who managed to get away.

"Following our research, we found the victim's background goes far beyond security work. He served with the armed forces for three years during the civil war in the early 1990s. The victim's real name is Gavrilo Silajdzic, a murdering war-criminal and convicted robber who was born in Yugoslavia in 1960. He served in the Serb Volunteer Guard "Tigers", a paramilitary group which recruited its members from the criminal classes. Silajdzic had been on the Serbian State Security Service's hit list for some time, being the one man closest to Arkan whom they hadn't been able to get to. Since 1997, Europol also had Silajdzic on their arrest list. He was, however, taken off that list in 2001."

"Why?" de Carranza demanded.

"He turned up dead one day in Linz, cremated in his car."

"So what was he doing lying around the Burggarten, cooked and headless?"

"Silajdzic knew the police were onto him. The old Serbian guard were after him also, knowing that if we got to him before they did, he could blow the whistle on a lot of very evil men."

de Carranza was confused. "So where does Siegel come in? Did this Serbian war criminal steal his identity?"

"That's what we believe now. Siegel was a loner in his home town. Silajdzic probably chose him very carefully. Portions of Silajdzic's forged passports, other identity documents and samples of his DNA all turned up at the scene of his 'death' - it seemed to be sufficient for the coroner involved to close the case."

"With what verdict?"

"Well, given that the victim was found handcuffed to the steering column, they concluded murder, but no-one was ever investigated or brought to trial. 'Siegel' then moved house, changed jobs, and was accepted at the Hofburg as a security guard with impeccable references in 2001. Silajdzic obviously knew a lot of very clever criminals during his days in Serbia, to cover his tracks so cleanly and to impersonate a man to whom he doesn't bear much physical resemblance."

Petersen slapped down a printout of two passport photographs, one of the Serb, one of the Austrian, side-by-side. Apart from general colouring and build, they had very little in common.

"So what now?" de Carranza asked.

"To be honest, I'd be happy to close the case on the murdering son of a bitch. Whoever cut his head off, did the International War Crimes Tribunal a favour."

"You're forgetting something. The nail and the spear are still missing."

"They are indeed," Petersen agreed. "But that issue falls into the realm of robbery. I am a homicide detective; I investigate homicide, and that is what I have done. The records Europol have of Silajdzic's past in Serbia indicate he had a history of stealing relics and treasures from churches during the war. One such relic, we are told, was an item alleging to be the holy Spear of Longinus. As you are well aware, there has for centuries been more than one claimant to that title, not jut the one in the Hofburg."

"One in the Vatican, one in Krakow, one at Etschmiadzin in Armenia, and a strange one in Montenegro, yes." de Carranza counted them off on his fingers. "The Montenegro spear was believed to have been an identical copy of the Hofburg spear made under orders from Holy Roman Emperor Henry II."

"Exactly, which would correspond to the spear found in the Hofburg on Sunday night. And as you said yourself previously, that basic spearhead could have been reworked to resemble the original at any time since its creation in the 8th Century."

"So, your case is closed?" de Carranza concluded, already sensing hurt and betrayal. "Who killed the Serb? You are a homicide detective, yet you have detected no killer. You can assume Serb hitmen, but such people operate with guns, not swords. The theories my colleague and I have constructed still hold weight. All this means is that somebody else got to him before the Serbs. Why did his head and his body turn up in different places, and a day apart? Why boil and drain a headless corpse? You could have more than one individual involved in this crime – you could have a group or even two rival groups responsible for this act. And now you are willing to ignore these possibilities-"

Petersen cut in, "We have looked into Silajdzic's finances. The bank details we found at his premises show credits in the last four days totalling over three million Euros to one of his accounts. The exact amount for which he seems to have sold the Spear of Destiny to a dealer mentioned in his notebook as 'Vilosivich'. The Spear is gone, very probably out of the country by now, and the task of recovering it is now someone else's problem. Not mine, Professor, nor yours."

de Carranza wasn't listening. "But still nothing has been solved. Tell me how the thief broke into the display case without being seen? You have not solved the mysteries of the spear or anything that happened on Sunday night. You're supposed to be getting paid to solve crimes, yet you-"

Petersen stopped him dead with an angry finger. "Don't try to tell me my job, Professor. This department has been under intense pressure and scrutiny in recent days. Our funding has already been deemed to be in excess. We are having to reassess the whole case in terms of manpower, as well as additional expenditure."

de Carranza finally burst. "You mean, you can't afford to pay us another Euro's worth of expenses to keep us here. Since when was justice dictated to by the flow of money? Or is that simply how it has always been? But if you deem my contributions unnecessary, you should have said so yesterday. That way you could have closed your case, I could have done my book signing today, and everyone would be happy. This investigation makes the Warren Commission report look like a masterpiece of precision and truth. Good day to you now."

The Spaniard stormed out of the office, brushed through Rieser and some other officers returning from the incident room, almost knocked several cups of coffee over a desk as he body-swerved a number of uniforms on his way to the stairs.

The door of Petersen's office creaked as it hung ajar. While Khalamanga and Petersen sat looking at each other, Steinberg popped his head through the doorway.

"Problem, sir?"

Petersen picked up his fountain pen, one of those heavy, titanium-nibbed articles capable of being launched into a dartboard from thirty paces. A birthday present from Maria; a recollection which brought a sour taste to his throat.

"No, Sergeant. No problem. Speak to the press secretary, let her know I'll be holding a conference tonight. I want this matter wrapped up, publicly and internally."

Steinberg closed the door, leaving the other two men to wonder who would speak first.

"Sorry." Khalamanga said with true regret.

"Nothing to apologise for, Doctor." Petersen assured him. "Your colleague is a fine man. Fiery, perhaps, but with a reassuring sense of fair play. If anyone is sorry it is me, for not telling him the truth."

"And what is that?"

Petersen stood up, collected his jacket and walked to the door. "That he's right. He has been all along. But we have not the resources, the time, or the personnel to investigate such an obscure and potentially violent organisation as your Capo 57. The presence of Serbian Security Force hitmen in the equation leaves us in a very difficult position. That side of the investigation will now be handled by Europol. The matter of the spear itself will be taken over by our international fraud offices. For me, at any rate, it's back to the streets."

The realisation of what that meant hit him hard, a terrible sense of familiarity landing upon his shoulders. Back to the torn-up prostitutes, the abused children, the drug gang victims, the cheating spouses. He understood Vanessa's disgust with her old line of work, more than he cared to admit. It had been his idea to install the personal effects of 'Jack' Unterweger in the display cases outside, lest he ever forget what the face of evil can look like, and his own minor role in bringing that same evil to justice. But the events of this second week in April were forcing him to reassess his suitability for that role. It was no longer a foregone conclusion that victims would be avenged and killers would pay, the harsh reality which de Carranza refused to face.

He wished he was able to jump ship into another career, or write a best-selling book and slouch around the world smoking ridiculous cigars and smelling of leather. In the meantime, it was time to clear his desk and wait for the next depressing chronicle of abuse and depravity to land there.

Khalamanga was still staring at him, in that cool, analytical way which made him feel uneasy. "May I show you out, Doctor?"

The Nigerian took the hint. "Thank you, but I shall find me own way. You must have a lot to do."

As Khalamanga became a slim shadow on the other side of the door, Petersen flung the fountain pen down into the desktop, where it embedded itself like a spear, quivering. He did not notice that it had cleanly impaled Vanessa's analyses of the Holy Lance.

The evening continued to pass slowly and dreamily for Vanessa as she set about making her last night in Vienna a comfortable, indulgent experience. She lay in the bath with foam up to her neck, scented candles arranged around the edge, flickering gently to cast swaying, juddery shadows on the walls. The door stood ajar to carry the music through from the hi-fi system next door, one of several souvenirs she had found for herself earlier. It was a CD collection of operatic highlights, currently set to Isolde's 'Liebestod' from Wagner's 'Tristan':

'Ah, behold him...
Can't you see him?
Ever brighter, shining brightly, borne in starlight, high above?'

Her thoughts strayed to pleasant rolling sands of shimmering gold and mysterious, exciting men emerging from Middle Eastern sunsets. As she floated with the music, feeling her fears drift away, she began to fancy that the beloved man Isolde sang of was not her love, but Jesus Christ Himself, walking out of the setting sun and gesturing to her with a gentle shepherd's hand.

The olive-skinned figure came nearer, smiling. She looked upon him with love and devotion, this naked man-god bleeding as he stood before her. She saw herself moving to kiss his wounds, to taste his blood, feel herself absolved of guilt and pain through His eternal sacrifice. Her hands moved over him with passion as she drew him into her and her lips found his, warm and arid like the desert he stood upon. Her fingers pulled back hair from his face, dark punctures and their bloody haloes revealed. She kissed the wounds on his brow, wiping aside the gore, feeling his breath on her neck as she did so.

This was the man she would surrender to, devote her life to, the One who had waited for her. Her true Father, not the man who had abandoned her and her sister at the worst time of their lives, but the one she would willingly serve for her whole eternity.

She began to feel an odd sense of peace with the world, and all the strangeness which had filled it for her recently. She raised her wine glass, drained it, and saw her previous week return in fading memories of sensation, sight, sound and smell. Small details like Petersen's French cigarettes, the vinegary taste of the meat in the restaurant, the thick woven pages of de Carranza's book. She remembered her moment of terror when she fled the police video monitoring room, the mixed emotions as she found herself walking away from de Carranza for the last time, the sense of dread which filled her when she first saw the priest call to her in the lobby downstairs. She thought of the decapitated, castrated Siegel, lying cold and scarred somewhere, a victim of a crime she had once believed she had helped to cause, but which now only tinged her mind with the merest sense of disappointment in herself.

The hands which had wandered so longingly over the skin of her Lord and King now found their way around her own body, fuelling her desires as she felt his mouth upon her throat. His eyes stared into her hers, dark yet light, familiar yet strange – all opposites combined, Alpha and Omega, the beginning and the end. His hands came upon her, running the length of her spine, smearing her damp skin with streaks of blood. He painted her like Himself, bloody and wounded yet deathless. She felt only joy, rapture and the promise of forever as she saw herself slide down into the earth with Him, their limbs wrapped tight and bodies conjoined in one perfect beautiful whole.

It was all over now, she reminded herself, smiling. It was a sad-eyed smile, coming as it did to the song of Isolde's Transfiguration, the doomed heroine's passing from earthly pain to sublime majesty, strings and brass under the direction of Sir Georg Solti elevating the soul of Vanessa Descartes. To her, this music was holier than Wagner's holiest work, 'Parsifal'; holy in that it put her in touch with sensations and thoughts she rarely encountered in everyday life. It was music which had served her well as stress-relief, helped her through her periods of depression and self-loathing, offered her a glimpse of the eternal splendour that could one day become hers, when all fears would be cast aside and there would be only joy as she sank, fulfilled and glorious, into the arms of highest love and warmest light.

And, as she knew she would before the end of the music, she began to cry, tears of hot salt which fell in her wine as the music reached its climax, and she reached hers.

Khalamanga turned off the volume on the television, unhappy with what he had just heard. He sat at the far end of his room, staring not at the TV set but at the window, refusing to acknowledge the presence of the messenger which had just brought such miserable, yet not unexpected, news. That it had come in his splendid luxury suite made the news all the more unacceptable. The crystal chandeliers above sparkled with the flickering light from the television screen, mere tinsel in Khalamanga's eyes. Plush rugs and velvet drapes did nothing to insulate him from the fact that his time in Vienna had been mis-spent, three days of a busman's holiday which had been neither pleasurable nor especially edifying. Not through any mistake on his part, as he had once feared, but due to circumstances beyond his control, which made the situation even more frustrating.

The pale peach decor, for all its supposed restful qualities, went nowhere towards calming de Carranza. He had blazed with indignation since they reconvened at the Sacher to discuss the premature conclusion to their investigation. Khalamanga had listened while de Carranza thundered and lightninged around the suite, bellowing his anger through rolling clouds of cigar smoke and spurts of brandy, until the TV news publicly announced what the two men had already been told in private. Petersen look tired and drained in front of the cameras, fielding questions from the press with the mannerisms of a man longing to go home, get drunk and go to bed.

"That's that, then." The Nigerian concluded. "The case is closed, and Inspector Petersen has washed his hands of us like Pontius Pilate."

"de Carranza is going nowhere," the Spaniard retorted. "He came to this city on a mission. And he will leave only when that mission is accomplished. I have made a promise, and it shall be kept."

Khalamanga shrugged helplessly. "But what can we accomplish ourselves? We are only two men, on the wrong side of middle-age. We'll be lost without Petersen and his people."

"No, Emanuel. You're wrong. Petersen is lost without *us*. The case may now be closed, yes, but it will never be solved. Not until we do what we came here to do. I intend to pursue this matter privately, financed from my own pocket, in the hope that I too may be able to pay to see justice done. A man was hung under a bridge over twenty-five years ago in Italy. Was anyone brought to justice for that? How many other men have Capo 57 slaughtered in their time, without punishment?" he was on his feet again, fists and fingers punctuating his speech as he prowled his well-worn path around the furniture. "If you want out, Emanuel, I won't think any less of you. But-"

The telephone rang, stopping him in his tracks. Khalamanga stared at the handset, as though unsure what to do with it at first. Shaking off his surprise, he moved to the bedside unit and picked it up. "Hello?"

After a few seconds the call ended, leaving Khalamanga with a puzzled look on his face and an intriguing silence lingering in the room which de Carranza lost no time in shattering.

"*Well*, Emanuel?"

"I don't understand. That was Petersen, saying we should meet him outside at once. It sounded urgent."

The two men walked in the path of the streetlights, mingling with the small groups of tourists who flitted like moths in and out of the amber pools and cast incredible shadows across the white walls which bounded the Michaelerplatz. It was unusually quiet for the time of night, and de Carranza found himself gravitating towards the towering marble statue of Hercules wrestling with Cerberus, the triple-headed watchdog of Hades. The purity of the sculpture, the glowing white marble, made a subconscious beacon for the anxious Spaniard, as much as its representation of strength conquering darker forces.

Petersen emerged from the shade of the Imperial Palace, one hand holding a cigarette, the other in his coat pocket. He looked like a character from one of those old thriller novels, de Carranza fancied, or a shot from 'The Third Man'.

"Thank you for coming," Petersen said quietly once they were within speaking range. "I must apologise for this rather clandestine meeting." He stubbed his cigarette out under his foot and began looking for a new one. "But things seem to be moving very fast suddenly."

"I cannot explain everything, but if I say that some things are beyond my control, that there is pressure being exerted not only upon my department to come up with the *right* conclusions, as well as the pressures upon me personally, then you will know why. Dr. Steiner has been pushing us to wrap up the murder, or to at least keep it out of the papers. Says he doesn't want war criminals and murderers associated with his museum. I think some people need to get their priorities sorted out."

de Carranza asked, "This may be indiscreet of me, but are you aware if any of your colleagues or superiors happen to have ties to certain groups that we are investigating?"

Petersen sucked smoke and smiled. "It may be indiscreet to ask, but I couldn't possibly make any comment. All I have been told, by the commissioner, is that certain matters be left to the counter-terrorism units. Or brushed under the carpet. One way or another, it is to be taken out of my hands."

"But you won't deny it either," the Spaniard said. "I understand. Are we in any danger, at the moment?"

"No. But I know you're dedicated to this case, and I thought you had a right to know some of the facts that I could not discuss in public. The Capo group are involved, but not in the way any of us imagined. There is another group at large, a third party we know nothing about, and they seem to be in direct conflict with Capo 57. You mentioned this before and I, of course, ignored it."

"This has already been confirmed," Khalamanga agreed, "Vanessa and I had an illuminating discussion this morning."

Petersen asked, "What about?"

"She had met a man in her hotel - a priest – last night. He spoke to her about a war being fought invisibly through the centuries. I would doubt that Serbian terrorists have been involved in such an affair, so it was reasonable to assume the existence of a third, hitherto undiscovered, organization." Petersen visibly paled under the warm streetlight. "She mentioned battles fought at Jerusalem, and most significantly, at Montsegur - one of the last fortresses of the Cathar heretics, who very active in the South of France in the twelfth and thirteenth centuries."

Petersen asked, "Why has she not come to tell me any of this?"

"She's already made up her mind to leave Vienna. From the sound of it, she's also afraid for her life and wants no further part in a case which she says she helped to create. Her research into the spear, and the nail especially, has been somewhat... overshadowed."

"How very good of us all to share this valuable information with each other. Would you care to give me the abridged version of this new revelation?"

Petersen listened, frowning, as the Spaniard passed on Vanessa's story of the phonecalls and the crucifixion nail, the priest and the recurring commandment to 'do the right thing'. "That's all," he said in conclusion. "I had planned to mention it to you, but only after she was safely back home. I didn't want her getting involved any deeper."

Petersen stepped aside to throw his cigarette away, swallowed momentarily by the night, the shadow which Vienna had cast upon them all. "She already is *very* involved, Professor. For God's sake, this priest character demands investigation for a start; he's obviously an agent of Capo 57 or their rivals. When did she say she was leaving?"

"Sometime tonight. I don't know when exactly."

Petersen gestured to the Audi Estate parked at the edge of the precinct. "Get in. Let's hope we're not too late."

"I really don't want to drag her back into this." de Carranza protested.

"You're not dragging her anywhere, and you're damned lucky I don't intend to pull all three of you down the station for withholding vital information."

They got into the Audi estate and Petersen turned the ignition key. Too late, he realised with a startled sense of relief, to have checked for hidden bombs or traps underneath the vehicle. The engine turned over quietly, pulsing gently through the floor beneath his feet. He took a deep breath into his chest and peered into the infinite blackness of the sky ahead. It was blackness that seemed not only impenetrable, but intimidating, threatening him with its endless obscurity, punctuated at this tiny local level only by the dim haloes of the streetlights.

He stomped on the accelerator, a little too slow off the handbrake to prevent a screaming wheelspin as he tore up the city side streets and onto the Operngasse, following the one-way traffic system to Margaretenstrasse to the South-west. As he drove, his fingers idly fiddled with the volume knob of the radio, and the 'Dies Irae' from Verdi's 'Requiem' filled the car:

*'Quantus tremor est futurus,
quando judex est venturus,
cuncta stricte discussurus!'*

"Louder!" de Carranza enthused from the back seat, and Petersen obliged, finding a strange exorcism of his emotions through the rumbling kettle drums and breathless excitement in the swirling, relentless chanting.

They marched three abreast through the main doors of the Holiday Inn and into the lift at the end of the silent lobby.

"Room D27..." Petersen thought aloud. He stabbed the button for the 4th floor and slowly, with a gentle sigh, the lift bore them upwards.

de Carranza closed his eyes against the uncertainty he now felt, the fear of heights he'd always had since a small boy, of falling, of being too high above the ground for his own safety. He had never used the lift at the University, always taking the stairs even when it meant he would be late for class or lunch. His relief was audible when they arrived on the fourth floor and the doors opened into a deep-carpeted hall with framed abstract art on the walls amid bland, calming decor. It was a pleasant scene, the distant sounds of music, televisions, conversations assuring them that elsewhere in the world, and even here in Vienna, things continued as normal.

They found her door without any difficulty, Petersen going first to knock. "Music playing inside," he reported to the others. "Maybe I should call on her." He rapped loudly on the door, stepped back, waited. "She's unlikely to be asleep with that lot blaring out. I just hope she'll hear us." He knocked again.

"Try the door." Khalamanga suggested.

"I don't think-" Petersen began to object, having images of three unwanted men entering a ladies' room and the reaction that would be likely to elicit from her, then went against his normal judgement and followed the Doctor's advice. To everyone's surprise it opened, flooding the hallway with Wagner. "Frau Descartes? Hello." The bed was rumpled but unoccupied, bags, clothing, CDs and books lying around the place. The music was Isolde's 'Liebestod'.

"Vanessa?" de Carranza tried. When no answer came, he moved to the stereo stack and turned down the volume. He waved at Khalamanga to close the door. As the music died, all three became rapidly aware of how quiet the room had become. "Hello?"

Petersen hung back by the front door, unwilling to invade too quickly. He searched the room with his eyes, finding nothing amiss, yet unsettled by the piercing silence and the sound of his own breath. de Carranza walked to the back of the room and tried the handle of the bathroom door. "Are you in there?"

When the handle turned, he was surprised to find the door give beneath his gentle pressure. The heat and steam hit him, forcing him to retreat and almost falling into Khalamanga who had followed on behind. de Carranza cried her name again into the stifling darkness and pulled on the light cord.

The walls were running with water, the floor awash with puddles which the Spaniard almost slipped in as he twisted around to get out of the bathroom as quickly as he entered it, this time running into Khalamanga and throwing them both onto the bed in a clumsy clinch. The sight made Petersen smile for a moment as the two men struggled to untangle themselves from the middle of the bed which creaked and heaved beneath them.

"She's-" de Carranza spluttered. He curled into a half-sitting, half praying position on the edge of the bed as he fought to regain his senses. "Gone," he sobbed, blew his nose and wiped his face on the bedsheet beneath him.

"What do you mean?" Petersen bawled, enraged at the stupidity of the man. She couldn't just have *gone*, leaving her room unlocked, her valuables and everything else lying around the place. Nobody leaves a room with the stereo blaring, unless they simply dash across the hall for a few seconds to the drink machine, the cigarette dispenser.

He pushed his way through to the bathroom to find some sense. Confused, Khalamanga dashed to his side and hovered on the threshold beside the detective, taking a minute or two to comprehend the image which lay in front of them. The burnt-out candles lining the bath, the pale, pink-skinned ghost which floated under a thin shroud of bubbles and lavender-scented foam, the peacefully closed eyes which did not see the men, the half-open mouth which spoke no words of greeting or surprise.

de Carranza heard the bathroom door click, felt the bed buck beneath him, heard the sighing, groaning weight of Khalamanga flop beside him. He heard Petersen's heavy tread move deeper into the bathroom, then come back out again, crashing the door shut behind. de Carranza opened his eyes and stood up, confronted Petersen face to face, silently demanding the answer he already knew. The Kommissar shook his head with a sad finality.

"I'm sorry."

de Carranza leant his weight against the computer desk, feeling now that he was not a real person, that his consciousness was somehow present in a strange existence which was not the world he knew, not even the alarming, sinister world he had found himself forced to deal with in the last few days. This was a sense of detachment from any sort of truth or certainty which was not frightening, sad or infuriating, just *wrong*, and which therefore could not be true. He hadn't really seen the bleached shape drifting, Ophelia-like, in the room next door. Some morbid element of his overworked imagination had decided to create that scene. As his fingers flittered unconsciously across the computer desk, a page of writing slipped from its position on top of the computer monitor and fluttered across the keyboard beneath. As he picked up the page, he saw it was written in her own semi-legible hand, slithering across a single sheet of hotel notepaper. The writing trickled to an increasingly squint diminuendo as it went on, forcing him to rotate the page as he scanned the lines. He read the words, the first few of them, without any comprehension of what he was seeing. The characters may as well have been in Greek, or Coptic, or some kind of code for that matter:

'My dear Professor... the strain is all too much. I need to get out, and I couldn't think of any other way. I promised you I'd be in touch again, so here it is. I'm sorry to have left you with this, but please don't be sad. You know that I worked in police forensics for nearly two years before I retired from that line, having seen my own impending disintegration lie ahead of me. It was bad enough then, dealing with the day-to-day realities of physical crime, picking through the private parts of innocent corpses to help apprehend killers, murderers, creatures so inhuman they do not even deserve to be called 'animals'. I thought I could have escaped all of that when I went on to archaeological research, but I couldn't. If the years of my career have told me anything, it is that people have never stopped being vile to each other through the ages - that a murder victim from the Roman Empire, from the Dark Ages or the Medieval times is as much a victim, as much a human being, as someone whose life is taken yesterday, or last week. The old fears and the helpless need to right these wrongs still burned me up, except that I could no longer affect what had happened. I would not see anyone brought to justice, my testimony would not condemn any beast to rightful sentence, I would not see families smiling and celebrating retribution.

With Josef Siegel, all these emotions came to a head, pun intended this time. That a thing so barbaric could happen in the middle of one of the most beautiful cities I have ever seen makes it even worse, like the cruelty of the Ancient Romans - so civilised and yet so wicked, lions and Christians, and crucifixions. You may wonder why I've done this thing, why I decided to take this easy route out of the big scheme - why I'm swallowing two or three of these pills at a time as I'm writing this, no doubt getting increasingly incoherent as I do so. No doubt Inspector Petersen will spend time puzzling over it too. You'll all wonder why I didn't jump on the first plane home, like I always said I would. Well, you'll keep on looking, and if any of you live up to my expectations, you will discover why, and you will understand. I have no family to contact now, only friends, and colleagues, and though we knew each other for only a short time, I know I have you, too. This is why I wish my personal effects here to be kept by you, Tomas - and Doctor Kalamanka.

'But think of this, that by the time you read this, that I will know for sure the secrets of the afterlife - the truth of heaven, hell, and the hereafter - the secrets that men have agonised over since the beginning of human thought, and which kept me so awake at nights when I was younger. Feel no sadness for me, my dear Tomas. I hope that you go on to break this case open and uncover the true criminals here. I know that one day we shall all meet again, and all our answers shall be there to share. Until then, I remain forever yours, Vanessa Descartes.'

The signature was tiny, and scribbled at the bottom of the page was the message, 'Dr Yuri's behind the truth!!', like some kind of cryptic afterthought.

After a minute or two of staring at the smudged ink on the paper and the blotches of red wine which had soaked through from the desk beneath, de Carranza saw that the letter was specifically addressed to him. The unreality of the situation melted around him at this realisation, and gradually the need to act grew within him; the need to fulfil his duty, to investigate the situation, establish the facts, help the police. It was a need he no longer felt capable of fulfilling. He turned toward the bed, where Khalamanga sat stiff and rigid, and passed him the letter.

Khalamanga looked long into de Carranza's face to see his own terror reflected there. "We shouldn't have left her."

"Left her?" de Carranza found tears in his throat, "Nobody *left* her. She seemed perfectly stable the last we saw her, happier than I had ever seen her. Does this seem right to either of you? Should we not question why, on the eve of her departure from Vienna, she should..." he waved his hand in the general direction of the bathroom, "...suddenly do *that*?"

Khalamanga tried hard to focus himself and form a practical opinion, but found his thoughts troubled and fractured. The image still floated uppermost in his mind's eye, sickening him, making him feel guilty and ghoulish for even having been there, seeing her lying there and his first view of a naked woman for nearly thirty years. But he had no answers. There had been so much conjecture lately, it all seemed so irrelevant and useless when faced with a cold pale corpse which had only hours before been a trusted colleague and a breathing human being. He sighed, shuddered, took off his spectacles and rubbed his eyes. "I don't know. I don't know what 'right' is any more. All I know is, we're dealing with dangerous and obsessive people who seem capable of anything now."

Petersen's thoughts had been running in different directions during the other men's dialogue, hearing their words but not listening. "Dangerous," he repeated. He found himself grabbing at the telephone, his mind already contemplating possible scenarios. The note would have to be analysed, the body thoroughly examined, the scene photographed, a scene that the three blundering men had already helped to disturb - thoughts which scattered as he picked up the handset and found himself listening to silence. He rattled the cradle. He tapped the keypad urgently, relaxed at the result. She had left it off the hook, that was all. Nobody had sabotaged the line.

As he waited to be connected to his own department's number, he wandered to the window, the slats of the blinds painting black stripes across his face. Something flickered across the street, drawing his attention to a parked car full of suits and expensive foreign overcoats.

"Kommissar Petersen's office, how-"

"It's Petersen here. Look, get two patrol cars, and paramedics to the Holiday Inn on Margaretenstrasse, Room D27. Suicide, possible murder. Probably directly connected to the Holy Spear case."

There was anxious sounds of activity at the other end. "Er, just a moment, sir. Give me those details again."

As he repeated the address, Petersen saw the back door of the car open and one of its occupants step out. It was a Mercedes, he thought absently to himself; a good 100,000 Euros of anyone's money, and only then did it occur to him that the car's occupants appeared to be watching the hotel.

"Okay, sir. We've got cars 21 and 37 heading your way now, ETA four minutes. Paramedics have been notified."

Petersen continued to watch. The man outside lit up a cigarette with a trembling left hand as he moved away from the car. He noted, for future reference, that the man was about 6 feet tall, thin and spectacled, looked about 60 years old and had thinning silver-grey hair. He walked stiffly and slowly, hunched at the shoulders, his left arm bent behind his back as though trying to hide the evidence of the shake.

"Good, Steinberg. Look, stay on the line, will you? We may have a potential situation here."

"What sort of a situation, sir?"

Petersen took a deep breath as he prepared to explain when, as if on cue, the man outside threw his cigarette aside into the gutter and began to walk across the road. At the same time, all four doors of the Mercedes flew open and another four men stepped out, a huddle of fluorescent white shirts, trailing scarves and swirling coats. "Just tell them to move it." he bashed the telephone down and jerked the blinds shut, turning to the others with a face full of panic. "Can any of you see the key for this room?" The others shrugged, looking confused. He jerked a frantic finger at the window. "There's a gang of characters coming across the road, and I don't like the look. Now we're going to lock ourselves in and wait for my officers to turn up."

de Carranza asked, "Who do you think these men are?"

Petersen rummaged deeper, casting aside clothing, personal belongings, pulling open drawers with a lack of respect which de Carranza would have found obscene had it not been the middle of a crime scene. "I don't know. It may mean nothing. I may just be jumping to conclusions, panicking, over-reacting..." Another bedside drawer was yanked open, so hard that it separated from its runners and spewed its contents across the bed. Khalamanga's long jaw unhinged itself in horror as an eight-inch pink phallus landed squarely in his lap amid torn tissues and crumpled shopping receipts. For a moment, his traumatised mind conceived the grotesque notion that it was Vanessa who had been responsible for the murder and castration of the corpse in the Hofburg, the missing member hidden in her bedside cabinet, until now. That a thought so terrible could even enter his imagination alarmed him as much as the notion itself – that the quiet, nervous young woman could have somehow been responsible for that outrage.

Petersen grabbed the articles back and stuffed them away out of sight again. "...I seriously hope I am, in which case we'll soon be able to deal properly with the body," he continued, feeling a flush warm his face as Khalamanga's quizzical gaze followed his hands back to the drawer.

"*Body?*" de Carranza retorted, "You mean – she has a name –Va..." He stopped before the tears of anger and confusion broke onto his face. To utter her name in the context of that sentence meant to admit aloud that she was dead, and he was not willing to accept that, not yet.

Petersen spotted the keys on a ring, grabbed them in triumph, just as the door rattled from a heavy knock.

"*Room service?*" a voice asked in German on the other side. Petersen dropped the keys to the floor with a rattle, realising the game was up. He dashed back to the window, peered hard through the gap between the edge of the blind and the window frame but couldn't see any other movement outside. de Carranza and Khalamanga stared at each other, the situation now almost too surreal to be true. Petersen moved back to the door, flattening himself against the adjoining wall. He gestured to the others to move to the other side of the room, away from the doorway.

"Room service."

Petersen stretched out to reach the door handle. He flung the door wide to the wall and without waiting for any reaction, launched himself toward the figure now entering. There was a clatter and a half-strangled scream as Petersen wrapped himself around the man in the dark suit. There was no attempt to fight back, no struggle, just a trembling, instant surrender.

"Who the hell are you?" Petersen demanded.

He dragged the figure backwards through the room and found himself holding by the collar a young waiter, barely twenty years old, his face filled with spots, and panic.

"I'm Room Service, sir. You ordered another bottle of wine..." he checked his notepad. "For Frau Descartes, at half-past ten." He glanced worriedly at his watch. "Sorry I'm a little late. Please don't report me."

Recovering from his embarrassment quickly, Petersen pulled out his police ID wallet and flashed it in the man's face. "Who placed that order?"

"A gentleman did, sir. I thought it was yourself." The waiter glanced past Petersen's trenchcoated bulk and saw de Carranza and Khalamanga sitting on the far edge of the bed. Khalamanga forced a nervous smile and waved timidly back, trying to look friendly. "Is there something wrong, sir?"

Petersen flicked a napkin off the trolley and wrapped it around the top of the bottle. "I'm taking this as evidence," he explained, removing the wine onto the television cabinet. "There'll be policemen here in a minute. I want you to stay here and give a full statement. I want you to think, and think hard about the man you spoke to. Okay?"

The waiter nodded, terrified. "Yes. Of course. Has something happened?"

"*Something* has happened, yes."

Outside, they heard the descending whine of patrol car sirens, and de Carranza rushed to the window. Two cars had parked across the road, disgorging their uniformed contents in the direction of the hotel.

"Is the lady alright?" the waiter begged, getting excited.

"Stay here." Petersen warned. "And don't touch anything." He stepped out into the hallway, listening hard. After a moment, he recognised the faint crackle of radios followed by the dull flurries of feet on the stairs. Within half a minute, a sea of black uniforms came surging down the corridor towards him, and with a visible sense of relief, Petersen stepped out to meet them.

"Body's in the bathroom," he said miserably. "There was this note." He passed Vanessa's letter to the leading officer, a good man, Petersen recalled, by the name of Weinhof. Other officers filed past into the room, where de Carranza and Khalamanga now found themselves feeling rather intimidated. Turning to the waiter, he added; "This character just appeared while we were waiting. Said a man called room service and ordered a bottle of wine for her."

"It's true." the waiter protested. "All that happened was, I got a call from this man at about nine o'clock. Said he wanted a bottle of our best red for the lady at ten-thirty. That was all, I swear."

"Get a statement," Petersen instructed Weinhof. "Have that new bottle of wine checked over as well. And did you happen to pass anyone acting suspiciously downstairs?"

"Can't say we did, sir. Our priority was to get here as quickly as possible. Is this the situation you mentioned?"

Petersen stepped back into the corridor, glancing both ways for a sign of the five suited men. "Not entirely, no. I'll be back."

He dashed to the stairs and descended to the ground floor. The restaurant was closed, but the Bistro was still open, and he took a quick scan of the guests there before moving on to the front lobby, shoes ringing off the strip of dark brown tiles which led to the exit. He followed the beechwood curve of the reception desk around until he found a female assistant at the far end, doing something with a notepad. No, she was quick to assure him, she hadn't seen any group of men in suits enter the hotel within the last few minutes.

Petersen ran out into the street for further proof that he wasn't getting completely delusional. He checked both ways, jogged past parked patrol cars, scanned the road a hundred yards in every direction. There was no expensive Mercedes to be seen, no trace of the five mysterious men. Acting on more of a whim than anything, he crossed over to the vacant spot where he had seen the car parked, and began to look for hard evidence.

As he was busily kneeling in the middle of the road, hands brushing over the rough tarmac, the headlights of a fast-approaching ambulance swung around the corner of Kettenbruckengasse and nearly blinded him, soaking his crouching figure in twin jets of light. Throwing out a hand to steady himself, he felt his finger touch something soft and damp on the ground and, looking down, he saw the cigarette butt discarded by the man with the trembling hand. It still felt warm to the touch, and he collected the dog-end with growing excitement. The ambulance slewed to a halt at the doors of the hotel and Petersen dashed back to explain the situation to the disembarking crew before they got inside.

Hurried footsteps in the doorway of room D27 heralded his return, flushed and out of breath from his effort to make it upstairs before the medics.

"How's it going?" Petersen asked as he squeezed himself back inside.

"I've called Rosenfeldt," Weinhof explained. "We're not seeing any obvious signs of foul play, to be honest. But we'll make sure they cover every angle."

Petersen nodded his approval. "Good. I've told Reception what's happened. They didn't look too happy. In fact, I can see the local tourist agencies starting to ask us for compensation soon."

The paramedic team appeared outside, rattling a gurney into the doorway until they discovered too many people in their way. "I think things are going to get a bit cramped in here," Petersen turned to Weinhof. "You keep an eye on things. I'm going now."

"Are we treating this as suicide, or murder, sir?"

"Assume the worst. This is too coincidental for my liking. Oh, and while you're at it..." he handed over the cigarette end, now sealed in a small plastic pouch. "Get this analysed. Full database search, Europol, the works."

Weinhof looked sceptical. "A cigarette, sir?"

Petersen patted his shoulder reassuringly. "Humour me, Sergeant. I need to get home, get some rest." He caught the attention of the two academics who were both doing their best to ignore the impolite activities taking place around them. "And so do you two gentlemen. Come on, let's get out of here."

DAY FIVE: Friday

Petersen was back in the office at half past nine the next morning, and reading reports at his desk by ten. Several cups of coffee and a cold pastry served as breakfast while he digested routine emails, read the morning newspapers, cursed at several articles which took a very negative view of his own abilities and debated his department's reasons for closing the Holy Spear case. Whether anyone wanted to or not, however, it seemed that this case was one that would not allow itself to be closed.

By the end of lunchtime, the results he had demanded were brought to him by Weinhof, who looked as though he had been on constant duty since the night before. His eyes were dark and his chin shadowy, yet the information he revealed was sharp and clear.

"Here we go, sir. The handwriting analysis on the suicide note shows a definite disintegration throughout. All indications are that she was becoming increasingly under the influence as she wrote it. Dr. Rosenfeldt's report doesn't show anything shocking. We saw no perceptible rigor at the scene - even allowing for the submersion, she had been dead less than six hours."

"I knew that. She was with de Carranza and Khalamanga earlier that day."

"Post mortem does show a massive overdose of barbiturates. Specifically: methylphenobarbital, commonly used to treat epilepsy or stress. We found a few 200mg tablets at the scene. Looks like she had really meant to do away with herself; going by the normal prescription for that dosage, she had swallowed more than a week's worth of pills. The alcohol of course greatly worsened the situation. Report suggests she has been a habitual user for several years now, and probably needed larger and larger doses due to the usual tolerance that develops over time. Some significant liver damage also, bordering on cirrhosis, definite signs of alcohol dependency for a prolonged period." Weinhof flicked over a page. "Not the first time she's tried this, either. Clear scars on her arms, some going back nearly twenty years perhaps, show that she's previously cut her wrists, and pretty deep too." Petersen groaned aloud, not wanting to hear any more, but knowing he must listen. "All going the correct way, as well...running up the arm, not across it. Some evidence to show she may have tried to have the scars removed with surgery."

"I never realised she was that ill." Petersen rubbed hard at his forehead, wishing he did not feel like crying openly. He blew his nose into a paper handkerchief, failed to notice that he hadn't quite caught it all, resulting in a blot on some documents on his desk beneath. "Is that everything?"

"Er, not quite. Report also states there are a number of contusions and marks on her back, shoulders and buttocks - some were recent, some several days old."

Petersen screwed up his face, uncomprehending. "Meaning what? She's been beaten up?"

"Not those kind of marks, sir. More likely she's been whipping herself. The angle of the injuries all suggest self-inflicted religious flagellation, according to Rosenfeldt."

Petersen added grimly, "Or sexual sadomasochism."

Weinhof shrugged broadly. "Maybe a bit of both. We did recover a leather strap from underneath the bed in her room."

"So what's the official cause of death?"

"Respiratory paralysis, perfectly normal for a barbiturate-induced overdose. Analysis of the pulmonary system confirms this. No signs of struggle, and we found no other DNA or print traces at the scene - other than your own, and that of the two foreign experts."

Petersen felt his stomach tighten. He felt ill now, upset at hearing the woman he once liked and respected being reduced to a series of medical terms and statistics, pieces of her now residing in jars and phials in that black, desolate chamber of cold still air beneath the University laboratories, where dismembered corpses lay in chilled vaults and threatened Petersen in his weaker moments.

With that thought, he completely understood Vanessa's disgust with the whole business of prodding, dissecting, and peering at the dead, especially when compounded with the innocence of many of the victims she must have had to examine. In the past there had never been any emotional connection for Petersen between a body and the analysis. He might feel sympathy, outrage, anger or sadness but there was no personality for him to identify with, nothing to remember, or look back upon. His first contact with previous victims had always been as corpses, whose sole purpose to him was to help bring their killers to justice and, the judicial system allowing, see their deaths avenged.

He felt that he could never again look at another body or study anatomical photographs without his mind drifting back to the charming fox-haired, grey-eyed woman who had never wanted to be involved in this whole mess in the first place.

"Okay. What's Rosenfeldt's conclusion then, definite suicide?"

Weinhof nodded. "Absolutely nothing to contradict that view, sir. I know it's tempting to assume otherwise, especially after seeing those photographs we received this morning-"

Petersen raised a hand to brush aside that comment, a new development he had refused to think too hard about yet. "Or, unless someone else knew of her fragile state of mind, and predicted this would happen. Maybe even persuaded her to do it. Pushed all the right buttons."

Weinhof puffed his cheeks. "That's another matter altogether, sir. But I thought you would want to know the facts. Moving on to the other things we found at the scene, the wine bottle shows only the prints of the waiter we interviewed. The call for room service came from outside the hotel, at about nine-thirty, from an unknown number. The wine itself tested negative for any poison or drug. The dregs of the wine she drank earlier were also completely negative, and there is nothing in any of the tests to suggest she ingested anything other than the drink and drugs that were found in her stomach." He pulled another page to the top of his file. "Reports from the patrols around the

Hofburg and the Burggarten have brought in a few witness statements from Sunday night. Couple of people have stated they saw a man in a dark uniform with a small group of other men, before midnight. The descriptions are hazy but one of them said she did recall seeing some kind of package being passed over - a long, thin item wrapped up in rags."

Petersen's excitement raised his usually deep voice by a semitone. "What? Possible eyewitnesses to Silajdzic's deal with Vilosivich?"

Weinhof smiled. "Looks that way. As for that cigarette butt you gave me..." he trailed off suggestively, holding the Kommissar's gaze. "Where did you find that, sir?"

"Outside the hotel, in the middle of the road. I saw a man throw it away while I was waiting for you to arrive."

"And why did you ask us to check it with Europol?"

Petersen realised how ridiculous he had been the night before. Where he had seen five potential assassins, kidnappers or terrorists climbing out of a car purchased with embezzled funds or the profits of war, there may have only been some professional men passing through Vienna on a business trip. It was strange how they had disappeared almost as the police had shown up in force, yet there could be numerous reasons why. Had he not decided to over-react and assault the innocent waiter, he may have seen exactly what happened from Vanessa's window. He shrugged and broke the sergeant's inquiring stare. "I had a hunch, that was all. I was not thinking clearly."

Weinhof turned the page around and handed it across to Petersen. "Then you'd better look at this. A partial print on the butt, and a 100% DNA match on the saliva to this individual."

Petersen took what he now realised was an Europol criminal file, mug shots attached which killed the scepticism that had filled him a moment before. It was the silver-haired man with the shaking hand he had seen smoking beside the car.

"Xiomar Rubelli," he read, "Gun-running, drugs-trafficking, bribery, embezzlement..." he gawped up at Weinhof, disbelieving. "What the hell have we got here?"

"This man has been in the top twenty European 'wanted' list for years. He was an associate of Licio Gelli in the 1970s, and has had a career almost as colourful. Under the name of Ralph Hesse he founded and led an extreme right-wing group, Sonderbehandlung X, or SB-X, with his 'associate', Karmen Brandt. The pair of them have been on the run for nearly thirty years; and yet he turns up in the middle of all this last night, then just vanishes again?"

Petersen was barely listening, trying to take in the facts in the file before him. "I could have nailed this bastard. If I had only telephoned a few minutes sooner." He banged his fist into the middle of the page. "God damn it."

Weinhof went on, "The DNA data on file is, according to Europol's experts, 'corrupt' in some way. They couldn't quite explain how. But the fact remains that the DNA on the cigarette you gave me is corrupt in the exact same way..."

"What do you mean, 'corrupt' ? Impure? Polluted?"

"No, nothing to do with the quality of the samples, sir; but the actual DNA data itself. As if there's something inherent in this man's genes which they haven't been able to identify. Something unique. Don't ask - if you want my opinion, I think they're a bit embarrassed. About not being able to explain it. And there is just one other anomaly, sir." Weinhof passed another document across the table, a copy of part of a dossier from Nazi Germany. The picture showed a man clearly in his mid-50s, dressed in full SS regalia. Petersen peered at the text, studied the portrait hard. It bore an astonishing similarity to Xiomar Rubelli; the most glaring case of a throwback, or a forgery, Petersen had ever seen.

"A relative? Father or uncle maybe?"

"Er, not sure, sir. Europol say that the original Ralph Hesse was an Ubersturmbahnfuhrer in the White Wolves division of the SS between 1941 and 1945. He trained as a medical surgeon and operated in the Eastern front a lot, spent time in Yugoslavia, Poland, the Balkans. He organised various Einsatzkommando units for unspecified missions, something to do with medical experiments at prison camps there. Last known whereabouts, Berlin - just before the fall of the city. Seems he also had a hand in commissioning quests for holy relics, and was best friends with Himmler."

Petersen laid the old and the new dossiers side by side. The likeness in the photographs was astounding, but the chronology, if true, would make Xiomar Rubelli probably the world's oldest man. "Rubelli probably stole his identity when this war-criminal disappeared, or perished. Perhaps even tried to continue the Nazi's work. Anyway, what about this Karmen Brandt character?"

Weinhof produced another Europol document. The picture showed a woman in her mid-fifties, much of her face hidden beneath expensive Italian sunglasses and a heavy blonde bob. With her hard jawline and chiselled cheekbones, Petersen fancied she would not be a pleasant individual to cross swords with.

"Some sources have speculated that she may currently be the brains behind SB X. She certainly fits the bill; born in Bavaria, she stood in a local election representing her own right-wing, anti-immigration party in the early-1970s. Scorned and attacked in the press, she left Germany and seems to have met up with Rubelli at some time before '75. She also has had strong links in the past to a number of underground occult societies, mostly following the teachings of Dr. John Dee, Crowley and the like."

"Black magic?"

"Not necessarily. From what I can gather, more focused on the summoning of spirits and angels, that sort of thing. She now runs her own magical society called the Order of the Silver Dragon."

Petersen pondered. "Does she now." He removed from a file the subscription letter taken from Silajdzic's apartment, held it up. "This crazy bunch, you mean?"

"Yes, that's right sir. I thought the name sounded familiar. I guess whatever they might have been planning last night, we probably stopped them. And it must have been pretty important to bring Rubelli out of the woodwork like that. We may have saved people's lives. Perhaps even yours." Petersen didn't like how that sounded, although he appreciated the sentiment.

"Thanks, Weinhof. That's good work. And as for your SB-X group, I think I know a man who will be able to help us fill in some details..."

Petersen stood in the lobby of the Sacher, peering at his watch in between puffs of his cigarette and occasional glances at the smartly uniformed staff and their even smarter, rich guests whom they scurried after like obedient pets. Compared to them all Petersen felt and looked like a scruff, yet he knew the job he was doing was vital, a job that none of those beautifully-coiffeured tourists could ever handle for even a day. The lift doors opened behind him, spilling out a little group of laughing Japanese women, followed by the unmistakable duo of de Carranza and Khalamanga. Seen objectively, the pair of them looked rather comical; the shorter, rounder one balanced by the tall thin one. He greeted them with a nod and turned, indicating they should follow him outside, through the bright afternoon sun and into a now too-familiar Audi estate car and its odours of French cigarettes and take-away food. Petersen waited until the two men had closed the back doors and made themselves at ease. Khalamanga began trying to fit the seatbelt together, but Petersen called a halt to his activities.

"No need for that, Doctor. We're not going anywhere. I just happened to be passing by, and I have some troubling new evidence which I need your help with. This is off the record just now, hence this rather hasty meeting."

"What is it?" de Carranza asked nervously. He was still seeing fragments and flashes of death from the night before, and doubted he would be able to face anything new on top of all that.

"I've just picked these up from the lab, where they were being analysed. It's unnerved me, I must say, and I have no wish to unnerve you also, but I think you have a right to see these."

Petersen dug into his inner coat pocket and threw something into the back of the car. de Carranza fumbled it, not knowing what it might be, and Khalamanga collected it from the floor. It was a large plain envelope, a Wien postmark and the address of Petersen's department at the police station typed on the front.

"This turned up this morning," the Kommissar explained. "Look at them all. We don't understand what they are supposed to mean. We initially thought it was just a crank, but I would like to have you either confirm or deny that, so we know where we all stand."

Khalamanga carefully opened the envelope. Inside were a number of black and white photographs, standard six by eights. The first one was a candid picture of Vanessa sitting on a bench by the banks of the Donaukanal. Scrawled across the middle of her face, in red ink, was the word, "Endura".

Petersen looked hopefully over his shoulder. "Well?"

"The word refers to ritual suicide," Khalamanga explained nervously, true fear taking hold of his voice. "Practiced by the medieval Cathars. When a member of their elite priesthood had decided their time on earth was up, they took their own lives. Some have argued the method used was the slitting of the veins of the arms whilst lying in a bathtub."

He looked through the other contents of the envelope. The next picture showed de Carranza waiting to cross a busy road with a familiar expression of scornful puzzlement on his face. Scrawled across his body were the words *Auto da Fe*, and above his head was a sketch of what looked like a snake wrapped around a hatchet.

"Oh, very clever." de Carranza snorted. "So somebody fancies me as a heretic, do they? Well, I haven't seen any members of the Inquisition in town, so until then-" he grabbed the picture from Khalamanga, shredded it into quarters, then eighths. "-I say, to hell with the lot of them."

"Professor!" Petersen's mouth gaped, more astonished than angry that the man had just ripped up a piece of police evidence.

"Sorry. But that is a personal attack against me, my work, my own heritage. And I don't like it."

"Can you explain the meaning of the words then, please?"

de Carranza muttered, " 'Act of Faith.' The term describes lavish ceremonies organized by the Church at which heretics were traditionally punished, the highlights being burnings at the stake. I suppose they helped to keep the peasants' minds off other things like clerical corruption, plague, and taxes."

"What about the symbol?"

"No, I've no idea."

Khalamanga took out the third picture; himself, looking awed and slightly bewildered as he stared up at the facade of the Nationalbibliothek building. Written across the picture was the name 'St. Maurice'."

Khalamanga explained, "The commander of the Roman Theban Legion during the rule of the Emperor Maximian, the patron saint of Crusaders and originator of the code of chivalry. An African and a devoted Christian, he refused to honour Maximian as a living god and was executed for it. The silver wrap on the Spear of Destiny is dedicated to him; *Lancea Sancti Maurici Sanctus Mauricius*. He was the first knight I ever read about as a very young boy, and I have been fascinated by stories of chivalry and romance ever since, thanks to him."

"Is this something you've ever made public, Doctor?"

Khalamanga sighed inwardly. "I've written papers and the occasional book on the subject. Fairly dry, academic stuff, long out of print. It would have taken a fairly diligent researcher to track down that little fact about me, I would say."

"I think someone is trying to play with us, Kommissar." de Carranza suggested sourly. "Upset you, mess with your mind."

"Then they have succeeded." Petersen unfurled another photograph from inside his coat. "This was the last picture in the batch. And it is the only one that I understand." The other men stared at the image, shocked at what they saw. It was Petersen, standing smoking on a street corner. Dotted across his body, chest and arms were half a dozen red ink 'X's, and the written tag, 'St. Sebastian'.

"My God," Khalamanga groaned. "This is turning into some kind of horrible game."

"Well, I don't intend to play." Petersen said. He stuffed the picture back into his pocket. "All of these have been dusted, analysed, tested. There are no prints, no forensic evidence of any kind. The photographic paper is of the most common variety found in Europe. The handwriting analysis identified two completely separate hands; one on Vanessa's, another on the rest, and suggested different educational backgrounds as well. Whoever took these has been shadowing our every move since this case began."

"And now you fear that you will be shot to death with arrows, that the Professor will be burned alive, and I be decapitated?" Khalamanga concluded.

"Why not?" Petersen said. "They already seem to have described the events of last night, going by your explanation, Doctor. Why shouldn't they predict the end for the rest of us?"

"The poor woman did not slit her wrists." Khalamanga replied, "There was no blood. Just a peaceful passing."

"No, Doctor. She didn't cut her wrists last night, but she definitely had done so at least once in her past. Post-mortem examinations showed clear and deliberate scars on both her inner forearms."

"But I doubt that she was a Cathar of any sort. They held extreme views on lifestyle, and kept a very high moral code when compared with the established church of the time."

Petersen went on, "Perhaps not. But I've looked at her background. Her sister Francesca committed suicide at the age of nineteen. Vanessa was the one who found her, when she herself was only a young teenager. She had slashed her wrists in the bath and also consumed a large quantity of sedatives and alcohol. Her grandmother on her mother's side killed herself in the same fashion, as did her aunt Eleanor. So the precedent was already there in the genes, and in her mind."

de Carranza groaned in his despair, seeing the dark truth behind her final words to him. Where he had seen her relief at leaving Vienna and returning home, she had instead already planned her final exit with the hope of rejoining her beloved sister, and being free at last of the ghosts which had haunted her for so long. He cursed his own ego which had brought him to this city, this intellectual playground, the city which had brought them together and just as quickly, torn them apart again. Had he never come to Vienna it would still have happened, but he would never have known her, nor begun to spend the rest of his life regretting it. His face disappeared behind clasped hands, beyond words.

He recalled their dinner together, a warm, exciting evening which, in another place far distant from here, could feasibly have led somewhere. He remembered her difficulty in cutting up some of her meat on the plate, the laughter they had shared, and his imagination substituted the meat with her own dissected liver, scarred and half-eaten by alcohol, bathed not in sauce or dressing but in her blood, fresh and crimson.

Petersen checked his watch, started up the car. "Well, thank you both for your assistance, gentlemen. I must be getting back to the station now, but rest assured I'll be treating this new evidence very seriously indeed. Oh, and there was just one other thing. Be on your guard for these two individuals. It's unlikely you will see them, but if you do, call me at once, okay?"

"Who are these people?" Khalamanga asked as Petersen displayed the photographs of Rubelli and Brandt.

"Karmen Brandt and Xiomar Rubelli. Two very dangerous criminals, with links to radical political and magical organizations. We believe they are active in some way behind the events of the past week."

"Magic," de Carranza laughed, "What sort of a fool-"

His gaze fell on a familiar-looking typeface sticking out the top of the file. He grabbed the folder from Petersen's hand, threw aside the pages and watched as a flyer for the Grand High Order of the Silver Dragon fluttered onto his lap.

"This..." his trembling hand held the flyer up to Petersen. "Are these people connected to this group?"

"Brandt runs the organization," Petersen explained. "She's the founder, and the leader."

"May I keep this for a while?"

"After the way you shredded that photograph, I should say no," Petersen said with a half-smile. "Why, can you cast any light on this?"

"I don't know." The Spaniard murmured. He drew a hand across his brow, feeling hot sweat smearing beneath his palm. "I...I'll get back to you on this one."

"Good luck, then." Petersen replied and started the engine to indicate the meeting was now adjourned.

The two men got out of the Audi and exchanged glances as Petersen drove off.

"Something bothering you?" Khalamanga asked.

de Carranza shook his head, unwilling to voice his fears yet. "No, not really. A coincidence, I'm sure." He unfolded the flyer, studied it again in the hope that his imagination was getting the better of him. Khalamanga adjusted his spectacles and studied it with him, his long finger tracing the dragon design.

"Interesting," he observed. "The dragon has its own tail in its mouth, like an ouroborus; in ancient alchemy, the symbol of the cycle of birth and death. The Gnostics used it to represent the unity of opposites."

The Spaniard raised his eyes to the misty sun. He felt a dim light penetrate his thoughts. "*Unity of opposites*. Like the spear left in the Hofburg. Like the corpse of Siegel. This is our second group, Emanuel – the rivals of Capo 57. And I've got a horrible feeling I know who may be able to tell us more about them."

"What? Who?" Khalamanga babbled, not understanding. de Carranza was already dashing down the street in the direction of his parked Peugeot. "Tomas – wait. Where are you going?"

Without stopping, de Carranza yelled back, "I'm going to see a man about a dragon!"

Driving one-handed, swerving in and out of traffic like a suicidal drunkard, de Carranza held his cellphone to his ear with his other hand as he awaited a reply from the University Ancient Languages department. His mind was heaving with countless possibilities – fragments of conversation, phrases, images combining in a horrible Dali-esque nightmare. *Salome with the head of John the Baptist.* The circular dragon ornament above Gruber's fireplace. His colleague's throwaway reference to the Egyptian god Thoth, who helped resurrect the dismembered Osiris and who was connected to the 'Sethian' spear via the distinctive dialect of the inscription. Teasing, obscure hints or *ennoias* which suggested Gruber knew more than he had so far been willing to say.

"Come on...answer, *answer*, damn you."

Finally the ring tone broke. "University languages department, how may I-"

"Finally. Is Gruber available? Professor Gruber?"

"What? Who is this?"

"Professor Tomas de Carranza, that's who. Is Gruber there?" he paused to swing around the front of a truck which had just nosed out of a side street in front of him, "Tell him it's urgent."

The Peugeot slammed to a standstill at a set of pedestrian lights. He waited while the receptionist clicked away into the distance, then returned a minute later. "I'm sorry, Professor Gruber went home at lunch time, complaining of feeling unwell."

A loud honk behind him alerted him to the fact that the lights had changed, and he was holding up the traffic. He kicked against the accelerator and jerked the car forward.

"What was wrong with him?"

"Sorry. I don't have any more information, sir."

de Carranza let the cellphone bounce into the passenger's seat as he tore sharply down a one-way street to get onto the outer ring. Friday afternoon traffic was beginning to build-up; for many Viennese the weekend had already begun. For de Carranza, his nightmares were seeping through into reality. For almost the first time in his life, he seriously hoped that he would be proved wrong.

The priest sat behind the wheel of his Volvo, idly flicking the safety catch on the Glock-17 semi-automatic. Something was brewing in the air on Laudongasse. He didn't know what form it might take, but he had glimpsed enough traffic, both human and vehicular, in the vicinity of No. 177 to know that he would have to be ready for anything. Events were starting to slip out of his reach, and he would need to take control very soon to have any hope of keeping the equilibrium. He couldn't be everywhere at once; he had already cruised past the Sacher and the police station several times that afternoon to reassure himself that things were normal with the other players.

Since the death of Vanessa Descartes, the ante had been raised almost beyond the priest's means. Now he knew he would soon have to do things the hard way, the messy way, the way he had been trained to do all those years ago, and that would mean more killings.

But this was, after all, war.

de Carranza brought the car to a sharp halt outside Gruber's home. His satchel flipped end over end to land on its side in the passenger's footwell, but he did not notice. For a moment he sat breathless behind the wheel, feeling his chest reverberate with dread and expectation. What was he going to find - a man genuinely ill in his bed, or something far worse? Had Gruber even gone home at all, or was de Carranza grossly over-reacting?

He got out and walked up the drive, trying not to move too quickly, hoping his heart rate would decelerate by the time he reached the door. Such stresses were not good for him, advice from his doctors which he had tried hard to ignore despite the continual pandering of Pablo Sandoval.

He banged on the door. "Ka-Hache? Hello?"

He squeezed the button of the bell, stooped to rattle the letterbox, then noticed the door was not fully shut. He weighed up his options in the space of a moment. He considered against calling Petersen, summoning squad cars to the street. He resolved to get the suspense over with as quickly as possible, and face the consequences later.

He pushed the door inwards and stepped into the hall.

"Ka-Hache?"

Silence wrapped around his ears, increasing the volume of his own heartbeat. He strode into the living room. The chess table was set up, a game in progress. de Carranza flicked through photocopied pages beside the board. It seemed Gruber was playing through an historical match, Fischer v Spassky, 1974.

He moved to the sofa. There was a slim folder on one of the cushions, half-open, cuttings and newspaper articles inside. The Spaniard collected them and looked through them. All were taken from different publications, and each one had a headline or title more alarming than the last:

'Polish Industrialists Executed in Racial Murders?'

The text described three prominent Jewish businessmen in Warsaw who had all gone missing at the beginning of March. They had turned up a week later, each with a single bullet to the back of the head, their bodies burned inside a car, apparently to hinder identification. de Carranza sniffed with distaste. He recalled that Gruber never had much time for Jews, but could not understand his associate's interest in such a story.

'Civil Bank Executive Found Dead in Own Pool' cried the next article, and de Carranza quickly learned of the recent case of Hungarian banker, Igor Venka, an executive in the First Civil Bank of Vienna who had been found drowned in his swimming pool on the night of March 12th.

He flicked onwards to the next piece. 'Archbishop Strauss of Paderborn dead: Prelate Drowns in Beer Vat', and fought back a nervous, guilty snigger at the thought of a German ending up in a vessel of beer. The next article Gruber had salvaged was from *Der Standard* and entitled, 'English Diplomat Butchered by Neo-Nazis?' A photograph of a man in his 60s was juxtaposed by stock images of a 'Totenkopf' - an SS death's head emblem, illustrating the story of a gruesome and brutal butchering that seemed without motivation or meaning.

The last clipping was a half-page taken from *Der Kurier:* 'Spanish Heiress Was Buried Alive, say Experts!' Now gripped by curiosity, he read with distaste the tale of a wealthy businesswoman who had been discovered dead, nailed inside a wooden casket: '...Alfreda Reina, 54, widow of millionaire entrepreneur Carlos Reina, was found by police on Thursday in the garden of her own holiday home near Prague. She had been dead for almost two weeks according to official statements, having suffered a cruel death by suffocation within a coffin laid in a shallow grave...'

The rest of the report went on to make a fuss over the copper coins that had been taped over her eyes and the large chess piece, a King, which had been inserted deep between her legs: '...police are at a loss to explain the thinking behind these acts, and have warned that a sexually-motivated serial killer may be stalking the area."

Gruber had run a yellow highlighter pen over the word 'king' and de Carranza's gaze wandered back to the chess set, wondering again why he should be interested in such lurid news. He would study these articles and ponder their relevance with Khalamanga and Petersen, but first he had to find Gruber.

As he crossed back across the room in the direction of the hall, he realised there was something missing, a disruption in the neat, symmetrical perfection of Gruber's living room. There was a gap on the wall where he recalled something having been before. He ran his hand over the smooth papered surface and brushed the sharp protuberance of a picture hook which had only days before held the print of Salome and John the Baptist.

On a whim, he glanced across to the fireplace. The silver dragon had vanished too, the very thing which had sparked his suspicions in the first place, and de Carranza found himself forced to grab at the wall for support. His wildest, most paranoid fears were making a conspirator and possible murderer out of his old study partner, and drawing cold pellets of sweat onto his forehead as if from some invisible magnet.

"Ka-Hache?" Again, expecting no response. This time he was answered by a dull thud from the back of the house.

"Who the hell's that?" a familiar voice shouted. "Tomas?" The bulky shape of Gruber appeared in the doorway to the kitchen wearing a t-shirt and shorts. He carried a cordless telephone in one hand, a piece of paper in the other.

"Ka-Hache..." the other man gasped with relief, almost sobbing. "I thought-"

Gruber stomped into the room and bashed the phone down into its charger.

"Dangerous business that, thinking. What the hell are you doing here?"

So relieved was he to see Gruber alive and well, de Carranza didn't bother to question the frosty reception he received. "I was worried. I called the University...they said you went home sick."

Gruber peered at him quizzically. "I am sick. I'm sick of this place, and I'm leaving the country for a while. I've just been reserving my ticket." He pointed to the file in de Carranza's hands. "What are you doing with my research?"

de Carranza realised he was still clutching the document folder to his chest. He guiltily put it down on the sofa again. "Sorry, I...I'm an academic, you know. I have an enquiring mind." He shrugged. "Or a very big nose."

"I noticed." Gruber sat down at the chess table and studied his visitor over the top of the pieces. "Why this sudden overriding concern for my safety?"

de Carranza pointed to the fireplace. "What happened to your dragon?"

Gruber's beard tore apart in an incredulous sneer. "You came all the way out here to quiz me about my stupid ornaments? Good God, man. Some women from the Church came around during the week, looking for junk for their charity sale this weekend. I gave them that, and all the others."

"You gave away your ouroborus?"

"It was a bloody *dragon*, Tomas, one of a series of fantasy characters. Don't get clever with me."

The Spaniard sat down on the sofa. "Very well, I'll resist that temptation for a moment. But what about your painting? Did you donate that to the Church women as well?"

"What? Tomas, of the two of us, I'm the one who's getting worried. Yes, I gave it to them. If you must know, this whole thing at the Hofburg has spooked me. I would never be able to look at the picture again without thinking of that murder, that whole head on a plate business."

"You recommended me onto this case because you felt it was too close to home. Didn't you?"

" 'Fraid I don't know what you're talking about, old man."

"You knew exactly what I was getting myself into. You know more about this case than you could ever tell anybody. You couldn't be involved because of your connections to certain groups or individuals."

Gruber's chin sank into his palm, incredulity pouring from his gaze. "Carry on. But this had better have a damn good punchline, I'm telling you."

"Who are the Order of the Silver Dragon? And what do you know about Karmen Brandt?"

Gruber continued to stare. But no longer in anger or indignation. His gaze softened, his fingers ran through his beard as he realised there was no place to hide. He looked away.

"Dangerous, to answer both your questions. Main reason why I'm getting out of here."

"Tell me more."

"No, Tomas. Because I know what you're like. I can't have you running around sticking your head into every nook and cranny, because you don't know who's waiting in the dark with an axe."

"Or a sword?"

"I'm warning you - leave it. I already have. I've submitted my resignation to the order this very afternoon. There are things going on out there that worry me. In the last six months the membership of the Order has quadrupled. 14 persons were raised to the 5th degree last month alone - the third highest rank in the Order. I myself, after nearly 20 years service, have barely scraped it to 3rd. I came to the conclusion that too many of the wrong sorts of people were beginning to fill the ranks at the higher levels."

"So what are they and what do they get up to?"

"On the surface, a group with an interest in furthering the intellectual and philosophical study of magic as an alternative system of belief. I joined in the late '80s. Well, there wasn't much to it back then, was there? We got a newsletter - had meetings - there were trips to significant sites like the Externsteine in Germany, public lectures and the like. It was all very above board and respectable."

Gruber walked to the window, gazed out idly onto the manicured square of lawn in front. The sun fell through the sash window and painted his face with the shadow of the cross from the window frames.

"So why your sudden fear?"

"Let's say I started to read between the lines. I did some research of my own, outwith the order's recommended reading list. Between Brandt's strange announcements about the group's destiny and the way things seemed to be going in the Hofburg case, let's just say I saw the traces of something I didn't like. Though I still can't put my finger upon it."

"How many meetings have you been at lately?"

"Not many. The last one I attended was in January."

"Was Josef Siegel there?"

"You missed your calling, Tomas. You should have been a policeman. You would have enjoyed sticking your nose into people's grimy secret lives. And yes, he was. It was his initiation to the 7th and highest degree. I didn't see most of the ceremony, only the 6th and 7th degrees took part in that. We were there only for the beginning of the moot. I didn't see Brandt, assuming she was there at all."

"And what happened exactly? Something involving heads, perhaps? - in imitation of John the Baptist, the reincarnation of Elijah who gave the Gnosis to Christ. To embody the power of life and resurrection in the head, which the Templar Knights worshipped and were executed for. Or am I just whistling in the wind?"

"God dammit, Tomas. Get out of this case. Go home, go back to your University, while you still can."

"You invited me onto this case in the first place, Ka-Hache. You let me get involved – you sat there with Petersen, and Vanessa, and you said nothing-" as those words left his lips, they triggered a barely-repressed primal force in the Spaniard's mind. He flew against the other man, pinning him to the wall by his collar. "That English girl's dead, damn you – *because you didn't warn anyone what we were dealing with!*"

de Carranza squared his shoulders, fist raised in the air. He had done a little boxing in his student days, and even now was still game for a quick one-two if the circumstances demanded. He had nearly punched a particularly cheeky reporter who wouldn't let him off the aeroplane at Vienna, and he was certainly prepared to lay one on Gruber if need be. The gold signet rings on his right hand were more than capable of blackening an eye or bursting a lip on their own without much effort, but seeing Gruber weep with remorse did not make him feel any better. He relaxed his grip, Gruber sagged beneath him, sobbing.

"Then perhaps you should come to the police and explain to them exactly *what* we are dealing with?"

"No." the other man raised a tear-streaked face from his hands. "They *own* the police, don't you understand? That's why I'm leaving here."

He pulled himself across to the drinks cabinet, began stirring himself a Martini. de Carranza used the following silence to collect his thoughts.

"So if you're running, Ka-Hache, and the police are infiltrated with spies, and this Silver Dragon gang are likely to use violence against anyone they think could threaten them...then this leaves me in something of a tight spot. Pinned down from all sides - a checkmate, you might say."

Gruber downed his drink in a single gulp and poured himself another. "You're not a king here, Tomas. You're barely a pawn."

"Then perhaps this lowly pawn shall stand up for his King, and do battle against the Satanic windmills."

Gruber smiled sorrowfully. "You always were the idealist, Tomas. Let me drink to your success." He raised the glass just as his left eye burst out of his face like a rotten tomato. Gruber spiralled sideways across the room, crashed through the chess table and dragged a bloody smear across the wall with the back of his head. Sparkling splinters of glass dropped from the shattered window behind de Carranza, unseen, tinkling onto the window ledge.

de Carranza watched as the white satin wallpaper dripped with the decor of an abattoir, the rattling of displaced chessmen now the only sound in the room. For a heartbeat, all time and motion was suspended.

Then he was racing for the front door, beyond fear now, beyond even anger, his mind teetering on the edge of madness. He dashed outside, skidded to a halt on the front doorstep as a slim man in priest's clothing stood facing him from the middle of Gruber's lawn. His right hand was buried out of sight inside his coat. His face screwed up in horror at the sight of de Carranza whose white sweater had been sprayed with Gruber's blood, as yet unseen by its wearer. Both men faced each other, neither knowing what to do next.

"*Shite!*" the priest swore, and hurdled the garden wall.

By the time de Carranza had pulled his leaden body into Gruber's petulia beds, all that remained of the sinister visitor was the sound of a rapidly accelerating engine and a diminishing cloud of exhaust fumes. de Carranza wanted to give chase, to scream, to retaliate, to run after that long dark car as it careened around the corner towards the Alsergrund.

Instead he fell to his knees on the gravel path and howled like an abandoned dog.

Five hours after the horror at No. 174, de Carranza sat in Petersen's car with the Kommissar outside the police station. He had been nursed and fed sandwiches and coffee in between the necessary formalities of dictating and signing witness statements, under the direction of Petersen.

"I still say you should see a doctor. You're in shock." Petersen advised him from the driver's seat of the cigarette-scented Audi. "First Vanessa, and now this."

"I need no doctor." de Carranza growled. "I'm just sick, sick and angry. Ka-Hache was dabbling in things way beyond his control. He didn't deserve to end like that, but he knew he was playing with fire. I'll have the rest of my life to rue his passing. As for now, I need to be strong, if I am to stand a chance of being able to help bring his killers to justice. And to think that I stood face to face with his murderer - *this close* - that little swine masquerading as a man of God. Lucky for him he can run, or I would have torn him to pieces with my bare hands."

"Professor - if it's of any interest to you, we've had the ballistics report back already. I made sure there was no time lost on this."

"And?"

"*And* - the fatal shot was a high velocity 7.62 mm high explosive rifle round. Standard NATO issue. It was also fired at an elevation of something like 70 degrees from the horizontal through the living room window. Meaning the priest could not have been the killer unless, like Superman, he too can leap tall buildings in a single bound.

"Our forensic team have checked out the empty house opposite Gruber's, no 177, the only place where the shot could have come from. They found an empty shell in the upstairs bedroom, and footprints two sizes larger than those of the priest we found in Gruber's garden."

The two men sat in silence for some time. de Carranza wondered why Petersen wasn't making his excuses to leave, when he guessed that the Kommissar was probably glad of the peace, a few minutes when he wasn't expected to run around doing several things at once and ordering other people to do the same.

"I re-read some more of your book today." Petersen said at last. "Specifically, the section on how Jesus is portrayed in popular culture and re-designed according to nationalist, political and other interests. And one modern-day group in particular caught my attention."

"Sonderbehandlung X." de Carranza concluded. "Those idiots who view Christ as a blonde Aryan?"

"I'm afraid so. You do realise they are involved in this, don't you?"

de Carranza nodded. "When you showed me the file on Xiomar Rubelli, I recognised him straight away. A distinctive name, reminds me of German Measles. But because one bunch of fascists is as uninteresting and offensive as the next, I'm afraid my research came to a halt very quickly. In the end, it didn't warrant much examination other than as an unpleasant footnote."

Petersen pulled a crumpled sheet of photocopy paper out of his pocket, spread it out against the steering wheel. "This is a copy of an old SB-X propaganda flyer." His finger traced the symbol on the page, two 'X's joined vertically, one on top of the other. "This symbol is a pagan Norse rune, representing the god of fertility. I couldn't understand the connection myself at first." He shook a cigarette out of his packet of Gauloises and lit up. "Then I had some ideas of my own, that these people might be following some fantasy based on the bloodline of Christ, the 'holy blood' and all that jazz. It occurred to me that genetic science, on some level, is playing an increasingly important part in this case. Like a recurring leitmotif, it keeps turning up in my investigations." He flicked ash out the window. "Jesus Christ is supposed to be the product of a virgin birth, right? So genetically, He would have inherited only the chromosomes of his mother, the female double 'X' chromosome. And like the Nazis who liquidated 'inferior' types in their prison camps, I think these neo-Nazis hope to liquidate the old Jewish-based Christian orthodoxy with their superior Aryan variety."

de Carranza's head began to hurt. "Or it could represent two Christs...the first, and the Second Coming. While it may be a fascinating parlour game, it still doesn't make much sense in the real world."

"It doesn't have to make sense to us, Professor." Petersen said. "It only has to make sense to Brandt, Rubelli and their friends, and be attractive enough to gain initiates at the lower levels. The Silver Dragon is clearly a gateway for the potential hierarchy of SB X, with some kind of filtering process in place to keep the chaff in the bottom ranks – no offence intended to your late colleague." He blew twin trails of smoke down his nose, dragon-like, de Carranza thought absently. "But there's a big difference in saying something, and having the wherewithal to go out and do it."

"Of course. But we can never underestimate fanaticism, and the will to power. All extremist acts are impossible until they happen, after which, they seem inevitable in retrospect. Who ever could have predicted the mass extermination of the Jews of Europe, 70 years ago? Or the attack on the World Trade Centre in September 2001?"

Petersen agreed silently. "Anyway, you've had a dreadful day, Professor. Can I give you a lift somewhere?"

de Carranza shook his head. "No. There's still something I need to get off my chest. All this talk of nationalists lately... it's forcing me now to confess something that I would much rather have kept a secret, but I think it ought to be known. If only to offset any threats of blackmail that may soon be coming my way."

Petersen tried not to look shocked. "Blackmail?"

"That symbol drawn on the photograph of me. The entwined axe and serpent." The Spaniard bowed his head, looking as sheepish as he sounded. "I didn't want to have to explain this in front of Dr. Khalamanga. It's the symbol of ETA, the Basque terrorist group. Whoever sent you that has done a lot of digging into my background. And that is not only disturbing, Kommissar, that scares the hell out of me."

Realising he was about to be privy to a secret, Petersen stubbed out his cigarette and raised the electric window. "Go on. I assure you, whatever you say will be held in strictest confidence."

"Then let me explain. I was born and raised in Navarre, on the border with the Basque Country, and my father was a Basque, though my mother was not. He spoke Euskera and imparted to me the need to keep alive this tongue which was fast disappearing, and so he made it his duty to teach me the language whenever he was able to find an hour or so out of his working day. When I was seventeen years old, I joined ETA. That was when the group started, in 1959. It wasn't violent back then, of course, but even after the first killings I still thought, in my own angry young way, that it was somehow justified. Franco had been hard on the Basques. For most of my young adult life I was a Marxist-Leninist, in theory at least, and so the aims and policies of ETA were perfectly in tune with my own thinking.

"It was only when I left University, and found myself travelling to big cities that I realised my radical views were not compatible with a promising career. Reluctantly, I rejected my partisan ideals before the government decided to investigate me, or worse. But despite all this, I'm sorry to say I still drank a toast to ETA when they got Luis Carrero Blanco in '73. That act saved us from a fascist dynasty and Franco was forced to hand power over to Juan Carlos de Bourbon. I remember calling my father, who was in his eighties at the time and in a nursing home, to tell him the news. He told me he would be able to die happy now, knowing that democracy would finally be restored after all those years, and that Franco had been beaten at last.

"And as things got more violent, I found myself losing all sympathy for their cause. I had already lost my faith by this time, so what did it matter now if I lost my principles too? I can only thank God for my education, or I too could have ended up dying in a police cell."

Petersen smiled at the man's emphatic invocation of the name of God. No matter what he said on the subject, it was clear de Carranza's faith was not entirely lost. "Well, I can't arrest you for being a radical young student. If that was the case, the prisons of the world would be overflowing, and the universities all vacant." He turned to face his passenger. "May I take you home?"

This time, too hurt and too tired to object, de Carranza agreed.

"I'm very sorry to hear about your friend." Khalamanga told de Carranza in the Sacher restaurant as they relaxed over dessert. When he received the call from Petersen telling him that his Spanish acquaintance was now an eyewitness to a murder, Khalamanga had wanted to pack up and go home there and then. But as the hours passed in anxious anticipation, he realised that was the easy solution, the cowardly solution, the unjust solution which would leave even more crimes unsolved. He knew he should stay on in Vienna but he had de Carranza's wellbeing to consider as well as his own. "To have lost Vanessa is bad enough, but at least her passing was somewhat peaceful."

"He was not so much a friend but more of a study partner, a rival, even." de Carranza sniffed. His mind replayed again the moment when reality had inverted itself, when blood and brains had flashed across Gruber's living room, and he winced at the image, drawing Khalamanga's attention.

"Was he the one you feared would have information on the Silver Dragon group?"

"Yes, he was. And I was right. What I had hoped all along had been silly little coincidences, turned out to be very relevant symbols."

"Are you still sure you want to stay? Things seem to have become very complicated suddenly."

"If they had wanted me dead, I'd be dead. There was one shot, that means one target. And if they kill me, they'll have to kill Petersen too, since I spent several hours repeating to him and his sergeants everything Ka-Hache had said to me." he refused to tell Khalamanga about Gruber's fears that 'they owned the police'. He was growing increasingly distrustful, he realised, but with good reason. "And in any case, if we go, then we make Petersen's job impossible. He needs us, and he knows it."

"You're right. There may be evil in this city, true. But I sense also a force for good at work, and we must not turn our backs on it, and run away from the shadows. The truth must not be forsaken in the face of fear."

"Bold words." de Carranza pondered. "And I'll take inspiration from your example. Thank you for inviting me here for dinner by the way, although I don't understand why you didn't order a main course."

"I'm not hungry."

"And what have you eaten all day?" de Carranza squinted through a hazy veil of cigar smoke. "I don't mean to pry, but starving yourself is not wise, Emanuel. Nor does it help to make up for what was inflicted on your people in Biafra."

Khalamanga felt flustered that the Spaniard had succeeded in realising this fact. It had never been so much a matter of guilt, as one of remembrance. His own immediate family had lived and eaten well in their new lives in England, while other relations had foraged for scraps with the animals in the dust during the civil war; images and stories Khalamanga wanted never to forget, lest he allow himself to become complacent in his own life and forget the mercy shown him by God.

"I...I don't..." he spluttered vainly, but the look in the other man's eye ended his protest. Khalamanga rested his long face between his hands. "Well, we've had a terrible week of it so far," he reflected. "What little appetite I have has left me. I just thought that you deserved some sort of a treat, and this was the best I could think of at short notice."

de Carranza loosened his belt. "And much appreciated it was too. Thank you."

A long shadow flitted urgently across their table. "Sir?" their waiter announced, "The gentleman over there asked me to pass this to you." he indicated a folded note on the tray alongside the bill.

de Carranza stared, trying to follow the waiter's eye. "What man? Where?"

The waiter pointed to an empty table across the restaurant. "Er, an Englishman. A priest. He seems to have left now, actually."

de Carranza leapt to his feet, and through the French windows he caught sight of a figure in a large black hat and coat moving off into the street outside. As he kept looking, the man turned in his direction, revealing a glimpse of a clerical collar and a shockingly familiar face.

"You..." he started, then felt the twinge in his chest which forced him back down into his seat again. The waiter departed and Khalamanga grabbed up the note from the tray. Written in an educated, elongated hand, was the message; *'Pie Jesu Domine, dona eis requiem.'*

"What's it say? Emanuel." but the Nigerian was already gone, leaving the Spaniard alone at the table with the priest's message in one hand and the bill in the other.

Outwith the restful world of the Sacher's restaurant, Khalamanga felt the reality of his situation hit him on the winds of vehicle noise and human traffic, bodies pushing around and against him like a tidal wave. Unheedful of those who stood in his way, he burst onward, bouncing and skipping his way through the throngs to keep the priest in view.

"Father." He shouted. "Father, wait."

But the priest was already on the run, coat flying out behind him like the wings of some giant carrion bird as he flew towards the Capuchin Church at the far end of Tegetthoffstrasse. Khalamanga put on a spurt, felt his breath burst in his throat as he sprinted harder, arms pumping him along like the pistons of a dark, slim locomotive. His feet barely connected with the concrete, his old white sports shoes skimmed the pavement, and still the masses seemed bent on blocking his path at every step.

"Father - 'scuse me - sorry - Father? Excuse - Father! Please, stop."

But this priest ignored his pleas, and the human sea still refused to part for him. Khalamanga crossed the road, narrowly missing a cyclist who swerved to avoid him and was blasted by angry car horns for his trouble. Darting on and off the pavement to dodge puzzled pedestrians, the priest swerved wildly to avoid horse-drawn carriages and those who turned to stare after him, then disappeared from view down a side street onto Spiegelgasse. Khalamanga had to grab a drain pipe at the corner to slow himself down, swung his body around to see the dark shape fluttering toward the far end of the street. He felt scabs of rust flake off beneath his sweating grasp and the pipe rumbled above him as he let go, and threw himself back into the chase.

The priest's running was awkward, one-sided, due to his right hand firmly holding his hat in place on his head as he went. Despite his ungraceful movements, Khalamanga recognised hidden reserves of power and stamina in the stranger, for he continued to draw further ahead with every stride, and hurdled clear across several sets of stone steps with the ease of a commando on an assault course.

"Who are you?" the Doctor heard himself cry above his own thudding pulse. He leapt briskly across puddles, body-swerved piles of packing crates and boxes but by the time he emerged onto the main thoroughfare of Spiegelgasse there was no sign of the man.

Khalamanga stared left and right, wandered across the road to the back end of the Dorotheum auction house where a rank of Mercedes and BMWs stretched the length of the road in front of him. Rich and well-dressed art lovers brushed him aside as they passed, diamond and gold jewellery flashing in the sun and adding to the Nigerian's confusion as he struggled to guess where the priest could possibly have fled to. Like a rat, he had slipped away from under Khalamanga's feet, his destination unknowable. There were over a dozen churches and St. Stephan's cathedral within spitting distance of the Hotel Sacher, Khalamanga recalled glumly. He could be in any of them by now, or in any department store, or in a taxi, a tram, or climbing the stairs to a city apartment. As he emerged into the main street, weaving a path through the passers-by, he thought he caught a flicker of something dark moving down the side street opposite him. But then it flew up into the air and out of sight, separating as it did so into three large crows.

Khalamanga stood for a moment, glancing to his left and right. The smell of his own sweat mingled with vehicle fumes and the odour of Greek cuisine as his breath slowly returned to him. Stiffly, with hands pressed deep into his lower back to fight the attack of a painful stitch, he turned away and retraced his steps to the Sacher where de Carranza would no doubt be cursing him black and blue for running off and leaving him to pay the bill.

"Dammit, Emanuel," de Carranza scolded as they reunited outside. "I was cursing you black and blue there for running off and leaving me to pay the bill. I hope it was worth it."

"No, I lost him. He obviously knew exactly where he was going."

"Where did you last see him?"

Khalamanga leant himself against the wall. "Up that way," he pointed, "Towards Stephansplatz. It was very busy...he was too fast, and I'm not the athlete I was once."

The Spaniard looked down at the note in his hands. "Well, we do at least have a sample of this nosey creature's handwriting. Something I'm sure our dear Kommissar will be very interested to get his hands on."

Petersen pulled at his tie, trying to loosen the garment's stranglehold upon his breathing as he studied the new evidence de Carranza and Khalamanga had just presented him with. His office had been a dry, stale repository for Gauloise smoke and ill temper before the two men arrived, and the air was now thick enough to force even Petersen to open the window.

"I really need to kick this habit," he confessed to no-one in particular. "I always keep saying 'After this case is closed' – and then another one pops up. Like a perpetual bloody toaster, except the toast is always black and burnt." He ground his current cigarette into the blackened silver tray and compared the handwritten note to the 'Endura' photograph of Vanessa. "Anyway, I'm not an expert on handwriting but I have studied it in the past. And this is definitely a real match. I'll have it analysed for DNA traces as well, should help tell us some more about this individual."

The door of the office swung open and Kupfer entered, eyes drooping in the way that told Petersen he had been spending a long time staring at computer screens. "Got the file on the British priest, sir."

Petersen leapt to his feet in excitement. "Speak of the devil. Go ahead, then."

Kupfer gently closed the door behind him. He glanced worriedly at the two other men in front of him.

"I said, go ahead." Petersen repeated, showing more irritation than usual.

"Sir, this is potentially sensitive information." The sergeant gestured vaguely towards Khalamanga, suggesting this would not be suitable for his ears.

"Sensitive?" de Carranza erupted without turning around, "This man has tormented Vanessa, Karl-Heinze Gruber and all of us currently in this room...so explain 'sensitive', please."

Petersen raised calming hands. "Alright, Professor, relax. Anything that's in that file can be made known to all of us, Kupfer. There are no secrets in this case. Not to any of us, at least."

Reluctantly, Kupfer threw down the thin card document onto the desk. "Fair enough, but you're not going to like it."

Petersen grabbed the folder, sat back eagerly in his seat. "Here we go, gentlemen," he chuckled with a knowing smile for the two academics. "We've nailed him, that's what matters for the moment." he flicked open the cover. "This clever little bastard-" his voice trailed off, lingering on that word as he stared at the front page, then looked up at Kupfer, building rage upon his face. The other man shrugged helplessly, silently saying 'I told you so'. Petersen looked back at the page in front of him, flicked it over, stared at the next page. He looked up again. "Who is taking the piss out of us?"

Kupfer's face offered all the apology he was capable of. "Sir, this came directly from Westminster. I can't even begin to explain the hoops our people have had to jump through to get that far."

Petersen looked back at the two-page document, a mass of black strikethroughs, crossings-out and 'classified' blanks. Only the photograph at the top of the front page was visible; even the name was blacked out.

"So what is this?" he slapped the folder, spun it away across the desk where it was saved from becoming airborne by de Carranza's outstretched hands. "English humour? What is this character? Army? Special forces?"

"No, he's higher than that. Maybe secret service or black ops, but we're only guessing."

de Carranza opened the file. The man who stared out of the photograph was in his mid-thirties, crew-cut, inscrutable, taunting him with his anonymity, but it was the same face he had seen in Gruber's garden, that was beyond doubt, and the wounds of recent hours re-opened. Poor Vanessa, tormented and harassed, and Gruber, similarly threatened no doubt. Everyone whom the nameless Englishman had come into contact with had died horribly, and he was unable to shake the idea that he and Khalamanga would be next, cursed by the black-clad angel of death.

"Professor?" Petersen asked curtly, expecting the confirmation.

de Carranza nodded, subdued and sour. "Yes, it's him. Younger, but definitely the same."

Petersen turned himself away to face the window. He stared out at the dark, blank windows of the offices across the road and found himself longing for an ordinary 9 to 5 job. "Well, it's a start. We have his face now, and by God, I'll make sure this picture is pumped out of every TV station, 24/7. Whatever this secret little mole was, he won't be very secret any more. Our people will be sick of his face by this time tomorrow."

"That was the other thing, sir. Officially, we can't touch him."

Petersen's chair squealed like a kicked cat as he spun it back around to demand an explanation from his sergeant.

"Excuse me?"

"If we find him, we have to hand him over straight away to the British Embassy. That's the condition we agreed to that allowed us to get the file in the first place."

Petersen's fist battered the file into the table beneath. "This is bullshit."

"I know, sir. His presence in Vienna suggests some level of covert operation on behalf of the British. And with your permission, I'd like to lead an investigation to make his arrest an immediate priority."

"Quite right too," de Carranza agreed loudly. "Before the rest of us end up dead."

Petersen stood, stretched his back. "First the Serbs and now the British. Why do I feel we're just getting pushed around here?"

"Not necessarily, sir. They didn't specify we had to hand him back intact, or even *alive*." Kupfer cracked his knuckles dramatically, a rare show of bravado which set Petersen's mind racing.

"What's got you chomping at the bit so suddenly, Sergeant? Getting bored with desk work again?"

Kupfer opened the door behind him. "Major suspect, isn't he? If we can catch him on the hop, who knows what he might let drop about Capo 57 and SB-X." he turned away into the open doorway. "Let me know what you think, sir. I have just the men for the job. But don't take too long over it. We don't have a lot of time."

The priest sat behind the wheel of his car, idly drumming his fingers against the dashboard in time to the Viennese waltz on the radio. Khalamanga had given him a damn good run for his money earlier, he reflected, forcing him to call upon all of his old training to get out of sight before half the city became alerted to his existence. He assumed that the agents of destruction would know of his presence in Vienna now. If they didn't, they were a lot less perceptive than he had ever given them credit for, but that didn't matter anymore. The time for secrecy was at an end. The disaster at Gruber's could have cost him dearly, allowing himself to be caught out in the open, but desperate measures had been required. He had failed badly, and only hoped that next time he wouldn't be so slow to react. Colonel McPherson would not have been impressed.

As he watched the street ahead he saw a pair of figures stroll along the pavement from the direction of the police station. The thin black man with legs that looked ridiculously long in proportion to the rest of him and the stockier, shorter figure with the silvery-grey ponytail. When they had just disappeared out of view around the bend in the road, he started up and slid out cautiously into the traffic lane. They were probably heading back to the Sacher. In that case, he calculated that the walk would take them about eight minutes at their normal pace, given the Spaniard's shorter stride, his extra forty pounds of weight and general lack of fitness following his double heart bypass operation in 1995. It would give the priest plenty of time to get on ahead and park somewhere inconspicuous. He had noticed the police presence following the assassination of Gruber, and knew he would have to be very careful to avoid arrest himself. Yet the risk was necessary, if his presence in Vienna was to have any value at all for anyone.

Petersen bade goodnight to the rest of his duty staff and switched off lights, locked drawers and gathered up personal files before leaving the incident room for the night. As he trotted down the stairs to the front office, only a few dozen yards away from the door and freedom for the rest of the evening, he found himself being approached by a shirt-sleeved officer who clearly did not share his superior's desire to leave the building. "Kommissar Petersen?"

"What?" whatever it was, it would have to wait until the morning. He had suffered a long and tiring day, was in need of rest and a hot meal, and he was not willing to sacrifice another moment of his time to the Holy Spear or Siegel or Silajdzic, not tonight.

"Er, they need you downstairs in Interview Room 4, sir. Straight away."

Petersen began to feel uncomfortable again, that sensation which usually meant he was about to be hit by another bombshell, another unavoidable distraction hurtling in his direction. "I'm going home, Kaufman. Tell them-"

"A man came in earlier, sir. Said he murdered Silajdzic on Sunday night, and that he'll speak only to you."

Petersen didn't even break his stride. He cast a single lingering, hateful glance at the front door, standing half-open and inviting him to walk out, teasing him, but he ignored the blatant seduction of freedom and kept walking in the direction of the stairs.

The door of the interview room flew open two minutes later as Petersen entered, having paused only to snatch a coffee and some chocolate bars from the basement vending machine on the way. Inside the drab, blue-grey walls of Room 4 he found a baggy-eyed Kupfer and a couple of sergeants sitting opposite a thin, equally tired-looking young man with untidy facial hair and a vacant look in his eyes. He was dressed in a sheepskin coat, jeans and a faded T-shirt, completely nondescript in every way. He looked like a typical student, the kind Petersen was used to seeing in left-wing protest marches. As he studied the man closer, Petersen began to wonder how so sickly an individual had even been able to pick up the massive murder weapon, never mind wield it with such devastating accuracy.

"Kommissar Petersen?" the man asked, laughing disconcertedly as if he expected to be horribly disappointed.

"He was insistent." Kupfer explained as the Kommissar approached the table.

"Yes, I'm Petersen." he sat down opposite the young man, feeling uncomfortable. He was tired, itchy little spasms running up and down his spine as his body cried for rest. Yet here he would need to be strong, alert, professional. This wasn't going to wait until the morning. "What is it?"

Interview Room 4 had been the scene of some of Petersen's most satisfying victories and most frustrating defeats, the hard teak table a silent witness to long hours of interrogation, tearful confession and bitter wrath. Petersen noted the brown smears of faded blood on the spot where he had broken the nose of a child killer against its surface six years earlier. The bottom of the door still bore a three-inch dent where Petersen had put his boot after watching a sneering wife-beater walk out with his lawyer, a free man, due to insufficient evidence.

"I want you to arrest me. I've killed a man. I'm also risking my own safety by coming to you now. I came under cover of night, but I suspect someone, somewhere will have noticed. They always seem to. They have always been two steps ahead of us - as if they knew exactly what we know."

"Who is 'they' ?"

"You know the answer to that, Inspector. You're smart enough to have figured it out by now, I hope."

"Why don't you just confirm that for me, then? Make sure we're both reading from the same script."

The man laughed tiredly, as though finding himself obliged to take part in a child's silly game. "You'd know of them as Sonderbehandlung X. An extremely dangerous organization whose leader is currently walking about this very city." The young man smelled of vinegar, and was sweating heavily, just the way Petersen wanted him to, though the overbearing scent in the room was a stale unwashed one, not so pleasant.

"I know. And the best counter-terrorism units in Europe are working to apprehend him. Take it from me, we know a lot more than you think."

The man shook his head. "No, you don't know enough. They may have named themselves after Nazi terminology, but their roots date back centuries. Rubelli did not found the group, he *reformed* it; gave it a new name, a modern political and racial dimension. At the top level, SB X consists of over 900 people in thirteen countries, including members of several current governments."

Classic conspiracy theorist, Petersen thought. He decided it was time to lay some cards on the table.

"Do you know this lady?" he tossed a copy of Vanessa's passport photo across the table. The young man picked it up, showed vague recognition.

"I've seen her. British scientist, did the work on the Holy Spear last month."

"Do you know why Rubelli and four other men should have been hanging around outside her hotel on the night she was found dead?"

"I guess she probably knew something she wasn't willing to talk about. Let's face it, she obviously knew a lot more than she let on."

Petersen pulled himself out of his coat as the heat in the little plaster-walled room brought a skein of sweat to his face. The lack of windows helped to make most interrogations a damp, sweaty business at the best of times, which was good for grilling suspects but not so good for interrogators when things got difficult. "What makes you say that?"

"Well, she screwed us over with the nail that we requested she send to us. She probably thought we were a bunch of crazy fanatics."

"You asked her to break the law. To give you something that was not yours to have, nor hers to give away."

"I'm sure my brothers asked her nicely."

Petersen found himself wanting to hit this man, felt his old primal urges starting to seep through his pores. All this back-stabbing and mayhem over a couple of bits of metal. What the hell did it matter to anyone if they had been used to crucify Jesus? What relevance did that have to modern man, half way through the first decade of the 21st Century? Did it matter a damn if Jesus himself ever existed at all?

"How does this sound, then. Perhaps 'lying' was the only way she could hope to get nutcases like you and your 'brothers' off her back?"

The man's voice hardened. "Maybe, but we felt it was worth it. Because if we fail..." he twitched his head bird-like, the thin grin cracking his face with a glimmer of white teeth. "Well, let me just say, you'll all have a lot more to worry about than some scientist who didn't want to reveal the truth and got a guilty conscience about it later on."

"Will we, now. And if we do sit back and do nothing, what earth-shattering event can we all expect to wake up to?"

"You do know about the old Biblical prophecy, which says that when the Jews all return to Israel, then we'll see the dawn of Armageddon?"

Petersen nodded impatiently. "I watch trashy American films too, yes."

"Well, this is what is happening, if you look at your news. More and more immigrants are returning to their spiritual and cultural homeland. The Middle Eastern crisis will never be resolved for so long as the boundaries of the occupied territories are pushed further back, and the Palestinians keep retaliating-"

"So now it's all the fault of the Palestinians and the Jews, is it? Because some people want to make a new life for themselves, Rubelli is going to trigger Armageddon and conquer Europe with his magic spear?" Petersen laughed out loud. "Are your people the only ones who take all this James Bond nonsense seriously?"

The man shrugged with his eyes. "Well, you're the one who said the best counter-terrorist units in the Continent are currently on Rubelli's case. That sounds pretty serious to me." Petersen could find no answer to that. "The prophecy becomes self-fulfilling. Rubelli only has to wait for his racial enemies to gather in one place...all his bad eggs in one basket, and then-" he mimed a massive explosion with his hands. "-he drops a brick into the basket. *That* is Armageddon."

Petersen said nothing, refusing to fill the silence, suddenly fearful for the world around him. It was as though a hole was opening up in the world and the life that he knew, to offer him a glimpse of the appalling alternatives that lay just behind the thin curtain of possibility. Like a fortune-teller gesturing to his crystal ball, this man conjured up images Petersen had no wish to deal with. He scratched himself under the chin; he could feel beard stubble beginning to prick through his skin. He needed a shave, a bath, a drink, a warm bed. The wall beside him slithered and glistened with condensation, the sense of anxiety now a tangible presence in the soggy air.

"So how does that result from your friends not getting the so-called Holy Nail from Vanessa Descartes?"

"You can't expect me to know the secrets of our enemies. Did the Russians who died in their thousands at Stalingrad know anything of Hitler's designs for all of Europe? I'm only a foot soldier, Kommissar. I am here only so that together we can all do the right thing, and save ourselves from the Black Sun."

That phrase 'the right thing' rang out in Petersen's head. He had heard mention of that before, in some conversation recently concerning the mysterious English priest. "What is the Black Sun?"

"Rubelli, or whatever it is he's become, and also what he will unleash. He stands poised to distil the celestial fire, to restore the holy pillar of the Saxons and to unify the ancient opposites."

Petersen sniffed, unimpressed with the pseudo-mystical waffle. "Does he, now. He looked like a Parkinson's victim in the process of having a stroke when I saw him."

"That's right," the young man snapped. "Laugh at him. Millions of people once laughed at a little man with a silly moustache as well, until the day he wiped the smile off everyone's face. I'm trying to help you, Kommissar. Look around you, read your newspapers. You're so wrapped up in this case, you can't see how it relates to the bigger picture. He's putting in place his power structure, and gathering the symbols of that power. Not just here, but all over Europe."

Petersen grabbed his cigarette pack out of his shirt pocket, shook out its final remaining occupant onto the table.

"Kupfer, do me a favour and get another packet, will you?" he shoved a cluster of coinage into the sergeant's hands. As Kupfer left the room, Petersen asked, "Well, let's not get sidetracked. You came here to confess to a murder, so let's begin with your name, shall we?"

"Names aren't important. Mine least of all. But if you must, it is Dragan."

"Fair enough, Dragan. I take it these 'brothers' you refer to are the men of Capo 57?"

"Yes. I have served them faithfully for the last three years by working for them as an undercover agent within the ranks of SB-X."

Kupfer re-appeared with cigarettes, passed them to his boss, sat down again. He unscrewed the top of the bottle of cola he'd picked up for himself. It was going to be a long night, and he would be needing all the energy he could get. Petersen lit up the cigarette, coughed, and began to feel a little more relaxed.

"Those things will kill you one day," Kupfer remarked.

"I doubt that." Petersen replied darkly. "Now, from the beginning," he signalled to Kupfer to start the audio/video recording machine which sat at the end of the table.

"I killed a traitor, a murderer and rapist on Sunday night, underneath the Hofburg Schatzkammer."

"Josef Siegel?"

"I don't care what name he's using now. He knew we had been chasing him across Europe for years, thought he would be safe in Vienna."

"Why were you chasing him?"

"He had once been a..." Dragan swallowed hard as though afraid his next words would choke him. "A *brother*. A leader of men in Capo 57, whom he betrayed and killed during the Balkan civil war. We also knew of his ties to the Church of Dragovitsa, which is sponsored and run by the highest ranks of SB-X."

"What is this church?"

"A modern heresy, a re-birth of medieval Bogomilism. They believe in two deities - a good power who created the heavens, and an evil one, Satanial, responsible for the corrupt earthly world, symbolised by the Roman Church. They also held sacred a relic which its followers said 'laughed at the Roman Church and at Christ', and made fools of all true Christians without their knowing it.

"Somehow, this murdering traitor got work at the Hofburg, and we knew we would have to watch him very carefully. When the research work on the spear was completed and we were sent a very obvious fake nail, we knew we would have to use any means to obtain the True Nail before Silajdzic got hold of it. Coincidentally, SB-X had by this time, made plans of their own for Silajdzic. From those I was closest to within the enemy ranks, I heard that he was 'the sixth'."

"The sixth what?"

"I don't know. I'm sorry."

Petersen dug half-chewed fingernails into his brows with frustration. "Okay. Do any of these stories ring a bell?" he pulled out the cuttings Gruber had collected and spread them out on the table. Dragan peered at the articles, mouthed the words as he read. His eyes skimmed the texts, then lifted once again to meet Petersen's through the curling threads of smouldering Gauloise.

"No."

Feeling the tiredness wash through him again, Petersen stretched himself back in his seat. This wasn't going as smoothly as he had hoped. "Carry on, then."

"The edict was given within SB-X for the liquidation of Silajdzic, as he had sole responsibility for security in the area around the Holy Spear. He had been ordered by Rubelli to steal the spear, but they got wind of some plan of his to double-cross them and sell it to a third party. I applied for the right to take him out, and was accepted; maybe because they viewed me as expendable.

"I told my brothers in Capo 57 of the plot I was involved in. They decided this was very convenient, and so on Sunday night I prepared to kill Silajdzic, and to steal the Holy Nail while I was at it. And that is what I did."

"So you killed him, hacked him up, boiled his body and siphoned out his internal fluids? For what reason?"

"I castrated the bastard and cut off his head – that was enough for me. I can't say what happened after I finished with him, Kommissar. When it was over, I only wanted to get the hell out before I got caught."

Petersen turned to his sergeant and silently mouthed an obscenity. From hoping to hear the whole bizarre story, he was to be left with only a small part of it, and still no understanding of what had really gone on in the Hofburg that night. He had the 'who' and the 'how', mostly, but was still far from knowing the 'why', the most important part.

He got up and paced the room, shirt-sleeved, hoping that his physical movements would keep his mental process going as well. "So explain why you killed him as you did. Fair enough, he betrayed your brothers, you say. But why go to those extreme lengths?"

"Why? You must understand, this was never supposed to have been personal. I was doing it for the greater good, for my brothers, not for myself. But when I realised how our paths had crossed, I thanked God for having the chance to bring the revenge I had nursed all my adult life-"

"Revenge?" Petersen's interest was aroused again.

"-but only now, do I understand this was not destiny. This has been *planned*, contrived, at such a high level by unseen minds who move human beings around like chess pieces - I cry at the manipulation, for I had served their purposes, not my own."

Petersen's hands gripped the table, hungry for answers. He could smell the result now, oozing through the man's skin as his secrets began to spill onto the waiting tabletop. His fingernails carved the beginning of another notch into the scarred and rugged woodgrain, that well-trodden battleground of the past.

"Dragan. What did Silajdzic do to you? What was this revenge?"

"I allowed myself to be used. I let my vendetta drive me - not my need to do the right thing. But at least I saw that my mother's soul would finally rest in peace." he wiped at his eyes, the first signs of emotion he had shown all night. "She wasn't old. Not even 30. I had watched her suffer a dozen times - she had never cried, never begged for mercy from any of them, the abusers. She was silent with Silajdzic right up until he ripped her throat open and threw her body at my feet in the Church of St George that day, all those years ago, in a place you've never heard of called Zvornik."

And Dragan told the story of his first meeting with the man from Arkan's Srpska Dobrovoljacka Garda, and how it led to their second fatal encounter.

"Fair enough," Petersen said as the story ended. "Now tell us what happened at the Hofburg?"

"On Sunday night, I hung around the Burggarten waiting for my chance to get inside. I hadn't seen anyone come out, but at about 11pm, I saw Silajdzic walking past me toward the museum. I knew this was my chance, so I caught him at the front door and presented him with the sign."

"Which sign?"

"The endless knot. The secret sign of Capo 57." he raised his right hand before him, and drew a deliberate shape in the air; from his right hip to his left shoulder; then to his right shoulder; down to his left hip; up to his forehead, then back to his right hip again. "The 'pentangle'. The ancient holy symbol, borne on the shields of the Knights Templar."

"Like a Masonic handshake?" Kupfer proposed.

Petersen sketched out the pentangle on a piece of notepaper in front of him, along with a rough crucifixion diagram, a stickman superimposed on a cross. He added a spear in the figure's side. As Dragan continued his story, Petersen found himself doodling drips of blood coming from the spear.

"He knew then that I had exposed his identity, his murdering past. He told me he would be willing to hand over the Spear of Destiny, if I would spare his life. I guessed he was playing for time, but figured he might make my job easier so I agreed and followed him inside. He told me to follow in his steps exactly, as he had created blindspots by adjusting the security cameras. We swapped clothes and he asked me to walk around to make it look like he was going about his normal duty. I pulled his cap down low to hide my face, while he disabled the alarm and removed the spear."

"Did you see him cut the glass?" Kupfer asked.

"I didn't see exactly what he was up to. But when I came over, I saw the hole in the case, and he was removing the spear. As I approached, he brought out a gun and I ran for where I thought the main door was, but it turned out to be the stairs leading down to the storerooms. The doors were all locked, apart from one near the far end, and I hid inside, waiting for him to find me. I had my own silenced weapon with me, a Beretta, but instead I took down a medieval sword from the wall."

"You carried a gun, yet you killed him with a sword? We understand that Capo 57 initiate their new members with a sword during a mock beheading."

Dragan looked at Petersen and a hint of respect coloured his pale face. "Well, you're right there. I thought it fitting that the blow be returned upon him, for all his crimes against his brothers, and against humanity."

"And you just left him there? Lying in the storeroom with blood and guts for anyone to stumble across?"

"Yes. I was told it would be collected later - it wasn't any of my concern, I'd done my job."

Petersen tapped the end of his pen against the table, prodding dents in the worn and blistered varnish. There were still gaps in the chronology, worrying gaps at that, meaning persons unknown had been active in the museum, removed the remains to another location, then dumped it to be found the following day.

"What about the head?"

"SB-X had ordered me to place his head on a silver tray, and hide it. I wasn't told why, and I didn't ask. I did it so not to raise their suspicions, but I took it onto holy ground to face the true Lord he had denied throughout his life. There I left the watch set to point to the fact that Capo 57 had been involved, a little sting in the tail for SB-X should they have bothered to look.

"When I got back upstairs I pulled apart the spear that he had given me, and took the Holy Nail. I felt a strange sensation as I did so, a surge of power. In a flash, it all made sense - why the artefact was called the Spear of Destiny - not for the spear itself, but for the great and holy power contained in the True Nail. I took the old pin the English woman had fobbed us off with, and left it behind with all the other rubbish. Just as a way of throwing it back in her face."

"But it wasn't rightly yours." Petersen objected, feeling his temperature rise again. In some twisted way Petersen felt himself wishing that she had actually been murdered, just to allow him the chance of nailing the bastard who did it and throwing the book at him. In the current situation there was no sense of justice, nothing to retaliate against, only a sad loss which could only be accepted and left unclosed. Like Maria, four years ago; the accident blamed on a wet road and a freak occurrence which left her completely decapitated in the crash. "You stole it. And what about the spear?"

"That ridiculous thing, made by one of Charlemagne's smiths? Although I do know Rubelli's people believed the legend, mentioned in some of the Holy Grail stories, that the spear would have the power to lay waste to the Kingdom of Logres, the land of their enemies."

"So you believed the analysis of Frau Descartes, in this case? You were happy to accept that the Spear of Destiny, this awesome, famous artefact of myth and legend that can destroy lands and grant victory, was not the genuine article? You admit your colleagues knew that she lied about her work lately. Yet you were all prepared to believe that particular analysis without question?"

Dragan shrugged off the insinuation. "Capo 57 had studied this work intensely. We read every scientific journal, every report in every language we could find. This research, in addition to knowledge possessed by the Grandmasters, convinced us that the Spear of Destiny was not the authentic article."

"We found blood in the museum near the Holy Spear display case, blood which was not that of the victim."

"Don't call him a 'victim'," Dragan snarled. "You make him sound pitiful. And I don't know about any blood around the case. Maybe someone had a nosebleed?"

Petersen lit up a cigarette, took his seat again. "Well," he said slowly as he built up his next statement in his mind; "I am sorry to put a damper on your glory here, Dragan. I don't know what great and holy power you felt on Sunday night, but it was not the power of the True Nail."

"You're not religious," Dragan laughed. "Not a believer. I can see it in your eyes, from the moment you walked in. They're pale and dim, like your aura. You're a fading man, Kommissar...though it's still not too late for you."

Petersen felt those words ring through his head. He wanted to dismiss that last comment as drug-induced New Age claptrap, but something about the tone of the man's voice gave them a more serious, truer meaning. He pushed that disturbing idea to the back of his mind and hoped he would forget it.

"Yes, you're right about that. I'm not religious. But the fact remains, you didn't have the right nail. Because the Spear of Destiny had already been removed by the time you met Silajdzic outside the museum. People we interviewed recently say they saw men in the Burggarten that night around the Hofburg - one of whom seemed to be carrying a bundle of rags, about the size and length of the Spear. That would explain why you met Silajdzic *returning* to the museum."

Dragan began to look worried. "What are you saying?"

"That the spear which Silajdzic was willing to give you was a copy, the same age as the original; probably the one previously kept in Montenegro which 'laughed at the Church and Christ'. You were too late, Dragan." Petersen apologised, feeling genuine regret now. He didn't know why he should feel that way, but something in his soul felt pity for the unhappy figure now slouching opposite him. "Don't feel bad about it. Your brothers don't have the True Nail, but neither does Rubelli." Petersen stood up and signalled to Wolz. "Suspending interview, at 2234 hours."

He tapped Kupfer on the shoulder and led him outside into the corridor, closing the interview room door behind them.

"What do you reckon, sir?" Kupfer asked quietly. "D'you think he's on the level?"

"Yes, I do. But there are things I don't understand. Like how he managed to wield that massive sword to decapitate a man in a single blow. Especially a tough, battle-hardened criminal like Silajdzic."

"Hmm, I wondered that myself. Not exactly Schwarzenegger, is he?"

"He's also invisible, if his story is true. In fact, so is Silajdzic - if the theft and vandalism happened before the decapitation. The cameras show nothing happening at the Holy Spear display until they run out, at midnight. The facts still don't add up with the tapes."

Kupfer groaned, "We have to go back to the security men then. Grill them all, one at a time, start all over."

"No, not yet. I've just had a radical thought. I'm going to pull in Weber."

"Weber?" Kupfer echoed, excited, as he chased Petersen towards the stairs.

"Yes. He has to know something." Petersen punched his fist into his palm. "Dammit, I should have done this days ago!"

Within forty-five minutes, Dr. Weber was sitting opposite Petersen and Kupfer in Interview Room 1, looking as content as any man could be after being dragged out of bed at his home by two pushy policemen who were both far too tired to bother with pleasantries.

"We have a man next door who has confessed to the murder of Josef Siegel," Petersen announced to the anxious assistant curator. "Now I need some answers from you. You pushed Frau Descartes to analyse the pieces of the spear, specifically to rule out the idea that any of them had been substituted. Why? What made you think this spear was not the original Spear of Destiny?"

Weber looked down at his fingers, fidgeting and caressing his knuckles. "It's not fair. Shouldn't have to go through all this...it wasn't his fault."

Petersen lunged to his feet, brought his fist crashing down into the table only an inch from Weber's hands. It had the desired effect, knocking the other man back in his chair as if he had been shot.

"Not fair?" Petersen's voice continued the assault, "I'll tell you what's not fair - a woman who felt that taking her own life was preferable to putting up with the twisted theatrics going on around here – and a respected professor of ancient languages who got his brains blown out for even daring to investigate them. Now don't talk to me about 'fairness', Doctor, and start giving me some answers."

Weber's self-control crumbled. "I...I...I'm so sorry about Frau Descartes. You can't imagine...how...." he stopped to spare the policemen a pleading glance. "Can I have a coffee please?"

"Sergeant Kupfer will fetch you one, as soon as you've answered my question. Do you know this man 'Dragan' ?"

"Yes. Yes, I do." Weber took his spectacles and tossed them onto the table in front of him. He fell back in the chair, arms hanging at his side, eyes cast up at the ceiling directly above him in a gesture of exasperated defeat. "He's my son."

Petersen saw the glistening streaks worming their way down the older man's face, saw his eyelids flittering shut as he began to sob and shudder. Kupfer noticed the urgent glances Petersen was now throwing in his direction, and quickly left the room to fetch coffee.

"The last few weeks have seen a lot of excitement over the Holy Nail," Weber explained quietly as he sipped his drink. His glasses steamed up but he didn't notice; his stare was beyond anything in the room at that moment. "I found out that Dragan had been assigned the task of recovering it for Capo 57. And I felt proud of him, honoured. You see, Dragan is not my own son – he was orphaned during the civil wars in Eastern Europe, and given to me by the charitable men of Capo 57. In return for raising him to become an initiate to the brotherhood, I was given a salary and higher status within the society."

Petersen understood. Another exercise in Masonic-style back-scratching. "So what made you draw so much attention to the possibility of the substitution?"

"When Dragan brought us the nail, it was taken to a private laboratory on Monday morning," Weber explained. "Our analysis did not match the data we had seen from Frau Descartes' original work. The nail we had in our possession showed no evidence of 1st Century fragments - the earliest they could pin it down to was the 10th Century, around the time of Henry II. Then we knew a double-cross had occurred."

"So what did your brothers want the nail for?"

"The Grandmaster and the Three Knight-Commanders of the Cross are the only men anywhere who will understand the overall strategy. And they live in Paris, Jerusalem and Dusseldorf."

"Were you aware of the fact that men from Capo 57 had intimidated Frau Descartes with phonecalls, demanding that she give them the nail?"

Weber shook his head. "No. The first I learned of the plot to steal the nail was about a week ago, by which time it had obviously become considerably advanced. I could do nothing myself, for I had been under the scrutiny of Dr. Steiner ever since the original work began." he leaned eagerly over the table, eyes widening above the rim of his glasses. "Is there anything else you want to know, Kommissar?"

"Just two things," Petersen replied. "You are a member of Capo 57, yet you allowed Silajdzic, a known traitor to your group and member of SB-X, to work in your museum, with responsibility for the very artefact you were trying to keep from him and his allies. Why?"

Weber smiled. "Keep your friends close and your enemies closer, the Masters said. That way we could keep an eye on him, and wait for him to make his move."

"Hmm. And what do you know about changes made to the security cameras in the Schatzkammer? Dragan says he was told by Silajdzic that he had altered their position to allow him to move around unseen. Yet Silajdzic's decapitated head is seen on screen, at a time when the Holy Spear is still visible in its case. So either Dragan's lying, or someone-"

Weber cut in, "I didn't want Dragan being caught on film and prosecuted for this act. I set up a looped recording of the Holy Spear display on two of the cameras to allow the theft to proceed. I'm sorry to have caused you all that extra work, Kommissar, but I hope you can understand my situation. It's been a horrible dilemma for me lately, but I'm happy it's over. Can I get to see him now?"

As he stood up to lead Weber away, Petersen turned to Kupfer with grim satisfaction. "Inside job. I damn well *knew* it."

The door of Interview Room 4 opened and Petersen peered inside.

"Dragan? We have your father here to see you."

Petersen held the door open and Weber rushed into the room to be beside the younger man. "How are you, Dragan? Have they treated you okay?"

As the pair embraced and sobbed into each others' shoulders, Petersen and Kupfer drew back into the corridor.

"Your thoughts, sir?" Kupfer asked. The pensiveness on Petersen's face had been unusually stark.

"My gut reaction is to throw the book at Dragan, and charge Weber as an accessory."

Kupfer waited, seeing an objection to this forming behind the bigger man's face, one he was reluctant to share. "*But*, sir...?"

"But, part of me is almost thankful to Dragan for ridding the world of Gavrilo Silajdzic. Just a shame he had to go about it in such dramatic, headline-grabbing fashion."

"And Weber?"

"Well, what else could he do? He couldn't challenge the Masters of Capo 57. He couldn't stop the Schatzkammer being robbed. Men far more powerful than him had already cast the die. He must have gone through hell, with all this drama so close to home."

An officer had appeared behind them, coughed to get Petersen's attention. "Yes?"

"The blood test results from the suspect, sir. Thought you'd be interested to know. He's O negative, the most common type."

Petersen stared at Kupfer, anxiously considering more possibilities.. "And the museum samples were B-type. Thank you," he said quickly, dismissing the constable. He pulled Kupfer aside. "Got any ideas, Sergeant?"

"We get a sample taken from Weber straightaway. No matter the result, it's going to prove someone a liar – whether Dragan, Weber, or Pfeifenberger's boys." He gestured to the two men across the room, now laughing together quite merrily. "What about them?"

"We leave them here overnight. I need to sleep on this, and I'm not going to make any decisions at this late hour. Before I go home, I need to do one final thing." Petersen summoned Sergeant Wolz and requested a photocopy of the entire 'Dragan' interview.

"I'm going home to study this," he explained to Kupfer as they waited outside the small office at the end of the corridor. "There's a lot of stuff in there I didn't understand and I need to cross-reference it with the theories of our experts."

Wolz emerged from the office with a thick bundle of pages, still warm and tingling to the touch, fresh from the photocopier. "All done, sir."

Petersen took the transcript and filed it away inside his overcoat. "Thanks. Kupfer, I'll have to ask you to break up the happy family reunion. Separate cells for them both, as far apart as possible, and 24-hour security on Dragan. The boy may be paranoid, but he has every right to be. And get someone to call me when Weber's blood test is done." he patted his colleague on the back. "Thanks for the support, by the way."

Kupfer smiled. "It's what I'm here for, sir."

DAY SIX: Saturday

Petersen sat in front of a muted television programme into the early hours of the morning, some scientific documentary on the history of astronomy. Cold coffee and an overflowing ashtray sat by his side, the remains of his attempts to stimulate his dwindling creativity. His body still cried for sleep but his mind refused to allow him that luxury, not yet, not when he was so close to finding answers. There were so many pieces of evidence dotted around, there had to be enough there to start making some connections.

He flicked through the script, running a yellow highlighter pen over strange or difficult passages. He took a final draw of his cigarette before crushing it out, grabbed up his personal case file from the coffee table and rustled through the dozens of pages, notes and photographs within. A meaning of some sort was prodding at the edge of his consciousness, struggling to break through to his higher mind. He felt it as a physical sensation which tingled and burned along his nerve endings, searching for an opening. His eyes lifted heavily toward the television screen where maps of the constellations were displayed, fanciful pictures of their symbolic representations sketched over the top - a strong bearded man, a mighty bull, two dogs. Petersen recognised Orion, Taurus, Canis Major and Canis Minor, when he felt that sense of understanding begin to penetrate the dark mists of his tired mind.

He slid out the crime scene picture of the bloodstains, rotated it through ninety degrees. The more he looked at it now, the more he saw a recognisable pattern emerging, a diagram, a schematic. He pulled out the crucifixion doodle he had made during the interview and laid it beside the photograph. He grabbed up a pencil and began joining together the blotches of blood on the photograph. When he was done he looked at his work and smiled broadly to himself. The smile widened, became a low snigger, evolved into a full-blown laugh which was ended by a fit of coughing. As he thumped himself in the chest to try to clear his airways, the telephone rang.

He cleared his throat harshly, mucus rattled in his chest. He grabbed up the phone and waited. "Kommissar?" It was Wolz. "Blood test result on Weber, sir. He's Type A, I'm afraid. So still no match on the museum blood. We're fast running out of options."

Petersen cleared his throat, brushed cigarette ash away from his case notes. "Okay, Wolz. Thank you."

"Er, there's something else, sir. On a bit of a whim, I called through to the lab, and asked if they could retest the original museum samples for me. They kept me waiting, and when they came back on the line I was told those samples were no longer there. Missing, vanished-"

"*Vanished?*"

"Okay, stolen, perhaps. They were confused and couldn't explain it. Sir-?"

Petersen's anger distorted his voice to a crackle down the telephone line. "Thanks for that great news, Wolz. Just when I thought I was getting somewhere."

He crashed the telephone down and considered his next course of action over a fresh mug of coffee.

Khalamanga and de Carranza had been standing around in the Sacher's lobby for more than ten minutes when Khalamanga recognised Petersen's Audi Estate pull up in the street outside. Petersen had telephoned the suite, begging their urgent assistance with the arcane details of Dragan Weber's confession. de Carranza had been vocal in his reluctance to leave the comfort of the armchair, until Khalamanga explained the urgency in the Kommissar's tone and the suggestion that they could be on the verge of cracking the case.

"Here he is," Khalamanga said with a nod, and walked to door. While de Carranza was more interested in following the path of a female hotel guest whose skirt was much shorter than one might have expected for one of her age group, Khalamanga went outside to greet the policeman. Only when the black mini-dress disappeared into the lift, did the Spaniard finally motivate himself to move after his colleague.

Petersen met them both in the street, looking furtive. "Good evening again, gentlemen. I'll get straight to the point. I want you to have this." he handed de Carranza a bundle of paper. "This is the typescript of the entire interview."

de Carranza was astounded. "But isn't this strictly confidential police information?"

"You're also a vital part of this investigation. It would take too long to explain it to you. There are things this man has said which I know you two will understand, but we do not. Study it and get back to me tomorrow with your findings, because I don't think we have a lot of time. After speaking to that man..." he glanced over his shoulder as if expecting Dragan Weber to be standing there. "Well, it's a lot to take in. He corroborates a lot of things you gentlemen have mentioned, but there are still mysteries." he pocketed his hands. "That's why I'm cutting you in on this. So outsiders will know the truth, and we won't risk this case being buried."

"I don't understand," Khalamanga said. "You sound as though you don't trust your own people."

"Let's just say, we can't assume anything. The blood samples we took from the museum floor have suddenly gone missing. I stopped by the lab on my way here. I looked in the storage room myself, and all record of them has gone. The technicians there can't explain it. The doctor is very upset about it all." Petersen handed a sealed plastic bag to de Carranza. "I want you to take these as well. It's some of Vanessa's personal effects. She did say in her note she wanted you to have them. I don't know what you want to do with them, but I feel I owe it to her to carry out her last wishes. I hope you don't mind."

de Carranza nodded sadly. "No, I understand. Thank you." He put the bag away inside his satchel, thinking he would bury the items once it was all over.

"The final thing I have to say, is...I know this confession is all very illuminating. But something about that man has disturbed me from the moment I saw him. I sensed that he knows more than he's letting on in some respects. That he's deliberately saying enough to lead us somewhere, but no further."

"In what way, Kommissar?"

Petersen stepped closer to Khalamanga, about to divulge his fears when something slapped de Carranza across the stomach and, looking down, he saw splashes of bright red on his shirt. He was shot; hit in the gut and would die within minutes, shot down, assassinated just like Gruber.

"Kommissar." the Spaniard spluttered. "I'm...shot!"

But Petersen wasn't listening. He continued to stand, bewildered, staring at Khalamanga who stared back at him.

de Carranza raised his fingers in front of his face, seeing his own blood look strangely unreal, like paint or dye. He had never imagined that it would end like this; his life, his Viennese adventure, his quest for greater glory and the challenge of a lifetime which he hoped to prove to himself, to Pablo Sandoval, to Gruber, his ex-wives and everyone else just how clever Tomas Emilio Baltasar Bartolomé de Carranza was. Now all they would know was that he died, just another mysterious and sensational death among all the others. *If they kill me, they'll have to kill Petersen too,* he had said only hours ago, though he had never imagined it could all have happened so fast, beyond their control, beyond police protection, beyond hope.

At least it didn't hurt. It wasn't so bad, after all. He felt himself smiling at the thought; here was Tomas de Carranza, lover of life, actually embracing death. He turned to Khalamanga to say his final farewell, but the other man wasn't looking at him. He was staring at Petersen, who suddenly jerked as the next of the silenced gunshots tore through his chest, throwing a cascade of blood up the broken glass behind him. He managed only a tight, gasping sound from the back of his throat before the third, fourth, fifth and sixth shots tore his shirt apart. As Petersen tumbled hard against the wall, Khalamanga shrieked in disbelief and turned his last, despairing glance toward the street, the source of the sudden silent death. A tall man in a grey serge suit stood there in the space between two cars, a semi-automatic pistol raised to shoot again.

The gunman twitched and from the road behind him something screeched into the night, a horrible, piercing scream that was not human, not natural but mechanical. de Carranza watched the man flip up into the air and tumble onto the bonnet of a long dark car which had just arrived in the middle of the parking space. A crack shot across the lower part of the windscreen where the man's head struck, pushing the glass inwards. As the limp figure in the grey suit bounced into the road, the front door of the vehicle flew open and the face of the English priest appeared from the darkness beyond.

"Petersen-?" the question lay stillborn, answered by bloody holes in the glass, the glistening streaks and smears and the open, sagging mouth which spewed gore like a flooding gargoyle. The priest cursed himself blind. He had arrived ten seconds too late, but at least he had managed to save two other lives. "Get in the car."

The other men stood dazed on the pavement, unable to react to this latest intrusion to their world. Too much had happened too soon. Life was playing out at a terrifying speed, a runaway train neither wanted to be on in the first place, yet from which they could not escape.

Rattus rattus: black rat, carrier of bubonic plague

de Carranza was still staring at the blood, confused. He reasoned now that it wasn't his, but Petersen's. He was alive, still breathing, the witness now of two shootings and a suicide in two days. He resented that; if this was life, then he would gladly prefer death. If his future days were to be spent seeing others die and be slaughtered around him, then he wanted none of those days. Something tugged on his arm, drawing him to a place he didn't want to go. He couldn't see beyond the bloodied fingertips of his own hand, detached points of vital tincture standing out in the black of night.

"No," he cried against the forces of chaos and motion, "Leave me be."

A distant and unfamiliar voice yelled, *"Get in the bloody car, you idiots!"*

Khalamanga made a break for it with the still-stunned Spaniard behind him, who barely registered the events as they occurred, reality passing him by until he saw the fallen semi-automatic lying in the gutter. He grabbed and pocketed the weapon as he was pulled into the back seat of the Volvo. It might come in useful, he thought vaguely.

"What in God's name is going on?" Khalamanga demanded as the priest stomped on the accelerator.

"God has nothing to do with this," the Englishman replied emphatically. "Things are moving faster than I could have anticipated. I need to think, plan our next move. And until then, there will be no questions. Because, for the first time, I don't have any answers. Okay?"

"I have one, Father." Khalamanga said. "May we know your name, at least?"

"You can call me Father Rattus. It's a pseudonym I've used for many years, since my early days as an army chaplain."

de Carranza laughed harshly at that, tears and emotions staining his voice. "So, you identify yourself with filth-carrying vermin found in sewers?"

"No, Professor. As in, a dweller in the underground, unseen, but always under your feet, listening and watching in the darkness. I would love to be more forthcoming, but in my position I have to be very careful. And as to what motivates some of the people out there just now, I'm as confused about a lot of what's happening as you are."

"Oh, I doubt that, Father. You seem to be a good few steps ahead of everyone, if your little note in the Sacher means anything at all."

"It meant exactly what it said." Rattus replied. "A prayer for all those who have died this week. What ever else I may be, I am first and foremost a bona fide member of the Church of England clergy, and a soldier of God."

As the journey took them out of the city and it became clear to all three men that they were not being followed, whether by gunmen or policemen, the priest eased off the accelerator and the roads grew narrower, quieter. Ambient lights diminished, the night became blacker and the shadows in the back of the car grew deeper, enveloping Khalamanga and de Carranza.

Rattus turned to the men behind him. "Are you two okay?" For a minute, nobody spoke. The passengers stared dumbly out their respective windows, looking like a pair of matching bookends. "Look. I'm-"

"No." de Carranza broke in. "It's never going to be *okay* again, don't you understand?"

"-I was going to say, I'm sorry about Petersen. I really am." His mouth tightened, fingers gripped the wheel. "Third time this week I've done my best to protect somebody – to save them – third time I've failed." he bashed his fist into the dashboard. "Thank God I managed to save you two. Now at least we may have a chance."

Still trying to deny the last half-hour's events, de Carranza shook his head vehemently. "We? *We*? What is this 'we' ? You're the one behind all of this." he stretched between the seats and pressed his mouth to the priest's ear. "You were there at Gruber's when he was killed – you badgered and harassed Vanessa until the woman killed herself – you show up like an angel of death just as Petersen is ripped apart in front of us. What are you doing to me?"

The priest turned his head away to avoid the other man's anger and spittle. "If you'll let me explain…"

"Yes, explain please." de Carranza rooted through his satchel and located the photographs sent to Petersen. He threw them down onto the front passenger seat. "Explain 'Endura' and 'St. Sebastian'. Explain why you felt you had to make Petersen and the rest of us even more paranoid with this stupid game of yours."

The priest glanced aside at the scattered prints, their written warnings clear and plain. He mouthed a silent query at the sight. "I don't understand."

"Really, Father? Well here's a shock for you – neither do we. So stop the car and let's all have a chat about this, shall we." he removed the fallen automatic from his pocket and jabbed it against the driver's ear. "Now."

Khalamanga cried out in his alarm. "For God's sake, Tomas."

The priest's unruffled demeanour broke with a deep, ragged sigh. "Okay, you win. I'll tell you what I can." He pulled them over into the entrance of a farmer's field, turned off the headlights and the engine. "You can put the gun down, Professor. I came to Vienna to save lives, and to take them only in self-defence or to save others. *I'm on your side*, but you have to trust me." de Carranza withdrew the gun, a silent sanction. Relieved, Rattus collected the prints and sifted through them. "Yes, this is my work. But this vandalism – these messages – this is not my writing."

"Wrong. Look again at the picture of Vanessa. Petersen confirmed the handwriting there is the same as that on the note you left us at the Sacher. So try again, *Rata*."

The Englishman switched on the inner light, screwed his face up to study the picture in close detail. "That looks like my writing." He studied it hard under the light, casting white reflections across the windscreen as he did so. Slowly, the priest lowered the picture onto his lap. He looked long and hard into the black night ahead, felt the night looking back into him. A terrible realisation had started to filter through his consciousness. "Somebody is playing with me. And yes, I can explain what's happened."

He leant aside and opened the glove compartment, drew out a bundle of pages and a hard-backed writing pad. "This is the dossier I've kept on all of you; Vanessa,

Petersen, Professor Gruber, and I do believe I was writing up my findings on Vanessa's family after I had selected the picture of her to send to the police." He traced his finger over the surface of the picture. "Look here. You'll see the imprint of my written notes there quite clearly. I now recall I used the photo and some other pages to lean on at the time. The imprint must have gone through the pages, and onto the surface of the photograph beneath."

de Carranza snatched the picture and peered into it intently. Across the whole width of the photograph could be seen half-formed letters, curls and lines, numbers, all weaving and writhing within each other. He recognised several complete words, some of which merged with the inked 'Endura'.

"So what are you saying? That someone else simply filled in the appropriate word with ink? Sorry, I don't buy it."

"Then maybe you'll buy *this*."

de Carranza and Khalamanga studied the handwritten page that was thrust toward them, saw the word 'Endura!?' written in the midst of scribbled details of Vanessa's family suicides. Khalamanga took the photograph and compared the lettering side-by-side with that on the page. Several other indented words clearly revealed themselves on the surface of the picture, and the more they looked at them, the more they saw the likely truth. There were small portions of the letters which had not been inked, but were still indented, suggesting that whomever had filled in the letters had not managed to see them in their entirety.

"Petersen did say the other messages had been written in a different hand," Khalamanga reminded his colleague.

"But you're accusing the police of altering evidence, and intimidation," de Carranza argued. "They would also have needed to know the significance of that particular word, and studied very closely the backgrounds of the rest of us. And you still haven't explained why you sent those threatening images to the police in the first place?"

"I sent the pictures to establish a precedent, that was all. To make the police aware there was an independent observer out there, someone watching over all of you. Not an angel of death, Professor, but a *guardian* angel. And in any case, I explained it all in the letter I sent with the pictures."

"What letter?" Khalamanga asked, confused. "Petersen didn't mention any letter."

The priest said, "Well, it was there, I swear to you. Whoever wrote over my photographs, probably destroyed the explanatory note too. Which confirms what I've thought all along."

de Carranza could feel a sensation of dread slithering up his spine, something he had been trying hard to suppress since his last moments in the company of his old friend Karl-Heinze Gruber.

"Share it, please."

"That Petersen, or someone in his department, is working for the other side."

The Spaniard bowed his head in horror, all fears confirmed. "Gruber said that as well. He said the Order of the Silver Dragon 'owned the police'." The car rocked as he pounded his fists into the door panel beside him, his frustration and anger boiling over. "Bastards!"

Khalamanga offered a calming hand. de Carranza took it, held it, reminding himself of the moments he had held Vanessa's hand in his, memories which seemed to belong to another lifetime altogether, another world which seemed good and kind and filled with hope in comparison to the one he inhabited now, the secret underbelly of Vienna which no tourist would ever uncover. The 'Nightside of Eden', Khalamanga had called it.

"Can we go now?" the priest asked. "I'd like to get moving."

"Not until you give me the truth about Vanessa." de Carranza insisted. "What were you trying to do to her? Drive her over the edge?"

"I studied all of you, your background, your careers, in an effort to learn if any of you could be at risk of being 'bought' or compromised in any way by the enemy. Due to her terrible family history of suicides, Vanessa was top of my list. I feared greatly for her own safety, and sanity, in the midst of all this. My feeling was that she should never have been brought into this case in the first place.

"You see, her sister Francesca had joined a small Gnostic group in her home town of Stockport, the 'Community of the Inner Light of Jesus Christ', and we are left with the likelihood that Francesca was unbalanced, depressed, at a most difficult time of life - made worse by the separation of their parents. At such moments do young people reach out to grasp at straws, and seek even more dramatic solutions to their problem. Therefore, on a psychological level, I anticipated the risk that Vanessa may have been likely to follow her sister's, aunt's and grandmother's course of action at a time of extreme stress, especially given the trigger of the Gnostic aspect of this case."

de Carranza tasted the bitterness in his throat. "Then she was compromised from the outset. And she probably knew it." he sank back in the seat, shut his eyes, found himself feeling alone suddenly, estranged from life and the world despite the close presence of the other men. He needed rest, yes, but knew he could never sleep, knowing that the darkness held only bloody ghosts; Petersen and Gruber, oozing gore, Vanessa clean and drifting but bloody on the inside, a frail mind haemorrhaging in its final torment. Now he understood the reasons why mankind's primal fear was of the darkness; the world from which anything could emerge, where demons and fallen angels may dwell, and the souls of the unavenged screamed and bled eternally.

The Spaniard's eyes flickered open and focused on the expectant face of the driver. "Get us out of here. *Please*, Father."

"Breakfast, Tomas?" Khalamanga asked smiling, a tray of fried bacon, toast and eggs held before him. Since arriving at Father Rattus' rural cottage the night before, de Carranza had said nothing, slept fitfully on a sofa that was a foot too short to contain him comfortably and now, with the spring sun lancing through the blinds of the kitchen-cum-sitting room, he sat at the circular table, deep in thought over the terrible turn of events which had brought him there. With his hair down and dressed only in vest, shorts and socks, he looked so far removed from the proud, flamboyant celebrity author Khalamanga had met less than a week ago.

The cottage was a late 19th-Century affair 30 miles or so outside Vienna, encircled by forests and farms. It was a basic two-room farmer's house with an outside toilet and an integral coal shed which had been transformed into a shower room. The kind of place de Carranza had often longed to retire to, an isolated retreat in the middle of nowhere, although at that moment he would have given anything to be back in his apartment in the middle of Madrid with only enthusiastic Real fans in the street to upset him.

He muttered in vague approval at the idea of food, and Khalamanga set the tray down in front of him. Mechanically, the Spaniard added salt, garnish, prodded the bacon with his fork, tried hard not to associate the blobs of tomato sauce with the idea of bloodstains. The kettle began to whistle on the stove, and Khalamanga went to attend to it.

"Coffee in a minute," he announced cheerfully. "How did you sleep, by the way?"

de Carranza chewed slowly, his gaze fixed on the wall opposite and the framed Tyrolean watercolours which reflected lines of daylight. He refused to even contemplate answering such a stupid question.

"St. Sebastian," he sighed.

Khalamanga stopped pouring water with an irritated sigh. "Leave it, Tomas. You're looking for evil patterns, where none exist."

"Am I? Four photographs turn up, bearing four prophecies. Two of those prophecies have already come to pass. Do you still want to deny the fact, Doctor, that somebody is *making* an evil pattern out of all this?"

Khalamanga continued with the coffee-making, stirring and milking. "That's only if you decide to interpret Vanessa's suicide in that way. Yes, Petersen was shot. But in the modern world, most political murders and assassinations are carried out with bullets."

"And what is a bullet but the descendent of the arrow? It's all the same, Doctor."

"*No*." Khalamanga banged his coffee mug off the draining board to end this speculation. "No, it's not the same. Yes, St. Sebastian was shot with arrows. But - he *survived* his shooting." he gestured meaningfully with the mug. "Diocletian had to have him beaten to death."

"So what are you saying – Petersen may not be dead, after taking half a dozen bullets in the chest?"

"No, *no*, Tomas, quite the opposite; I don't think the deaths of our colleagues are linked at all, despite these pictures with their ridiculous threats."

"Yet we have gone on the run with the man responsible for taking those very pictures. Taken without our knowledge, or consent. So please excuse me, Doctor, if after having faced four corpses this week so far, three of which I knew previously as walking, talking human beings, I begin to get a little godamn *terrified-*"

The kitchen door burst open and a ruddy-faced Father Rattus appeared, almost unrecognisable at first due to his being dressed in hiking boots, camouflage trousers and a heavy waterproof jacket. Broken open over one arm was an old fashioned double-barrelled shotgun, hanging over the other shoulder were half a dozen rabbits. He smelled of fresh sweat and the country, gunpowder and spearmint chewing gum.

"There we are." he deposited the dead rodents on the bench in front of Khalamanga. "Ought to see us alright for dinner tonight. Stew, anyone?" he noted Khalamanga's unease as he finished his coffee duties. "Don't worry, Doctor. These bunnies don't have a vicious streak a mile wide. You fellows enjoy your breakfast. Or lunch, should I say, given it's nearly one o' clock. I'm off to commune with Groucho, Harpo and Chico, so I may be a while." Sensing silent puzzlement, he added, "They're the three computers on my wireless network here. I just named them after some of my favourite philosophers."

As the kitchen door creaked shut behind him, Khalamanga understood the origins of the man's surreal sense of humour, and de Carranza saw his life being taken over by agents of chaos and destruction. No wonder, he thought grimly, Vanessa took the easy path out.

"You must know that script off by heart," de Carranza said, the first words spoken in the room for over ten minutes since lunch was served. "I thought your memory was…"

"It's nothing to do with my memory," Khalamanga replied sharply. He held up Petersen's sketch of the crucifixion and the photograph of the museum bloodstains, which Petersen had joined up to form a recognisable pattern. "Look at this. Five bloodstains, forming a graphic representation of the five wounds of Christ: three nails, crown, spear. This isn't a random configuration of blobs, Tomas. Now, I've done some calculations. The line forming the crossbar of the cross bisects the vertical at exactly one third of its height. Both ends of the crosspiece are exactly equidistant from the line forming the vertical, and the fifth blot, representing the spear wound, lies off to the left of the vertical." he pulled a copy of one of the crime scene pictures from his own file and placed it beside Petersen's diagram. "Exactly five inches away from the tip of the spear of Seth. The spear is pointing directly to the fifth bloodstain...pointing to *itself*, if you will."

Sighing, and with his joints creaking from a very uncomfortable night's rest, de Carranza leant over the table and spun the diagrams around to face him. He looked at the lines, checked the distances against the scale given at the bottom of the pictures.

"It's good," he admitted. "As good as the fact that we can multiply the height of the Great Pyramid by ten million, or whatever, and get the circumference of the Earth. But it still doesn't help us understand what the hell is going on."

"Maybe we don't need to anymore. Maybe we're out of the realms of scientific analysis, and we have to trust now to our instincts, our subconscious...our *belief*, Tomas. That word you dislike so much."

"And in so doing, what conclusions will that allow us to draw? That holy blood rained down from heaven in perfect formation to encourage our intuition, and get me back into Church again?"

Khalamanga lifted his spectacles and rubbed at his eyes. There were moments when de Carranza's sense of the melodramatic made him almost furious, a condition Khalamanga rarely experienced. "No, Tomas. I'm not. But the blood does not come from anyone known to have been in the area of the Spear of Destiny on Sunday night. Somebody took care to arrange these blood samples in they way they did. I'm not suggesting stigmata, but it is something we should store in the backs of our minds, I think. Especially as the 'bleeding lance' is a common feature of the Holy Grail processions featured in the medieval romances, with the blood which flows from the lance into the Holy Grail cup often interpreted as being that of Christ Himself."

"Very well, Emanuel. I'll file that theory alongside my thoughts on flying saucers and the Loch Ness monster. Is there anything else you think you've discovered?"

"Yes, actually." the Nigerian said excitedly, his boyish enthusiasm undimmed by de Carranza's doubts. "You see, there are portions of this interview which suggest some advanced esoteric learning. There's the bit where he says Rubelli, 'like Prometheus, distils the celestial fire and unleashes his power'. " Khalamanga flicked pages, peered over the tops of his glasses until he found the passage. "Now that's a sophisticated concept, and has much bearing on the Great Work of alchemy."

"Does it? Enlighten me. Because to me, it sounds just like a poetic description of a nuclear attack, the 'brick' that Dragan suggests Rubelli will drop on the holy land."

"Yet distillation is one of the key stages in classical alchemy. The first alchemist, Zosimos of Panopolis, wrote of a vision in which he saw men in a bowl of boiling water, mortified, during a process of spiritual transformation. Dragan has already said Rubelli is following 'a sequence, a process...' Celestial fire is how the mystical 'ether' is often described - quintessence, or the fifth element; as in the familiar quartet of earth, fire, air and water. The substance of quintessence is never fully explained or described - it is a nebulous, mystical substance, yet essential to the success of the Work."

"Meaning?"

Khalamanga smiled. "Meaning, Tomas, that our man understands that Rubelli is performing an alchemical transmutation. It is my belief that Rubelli has interpreted the meaning of 'celestial fire' as being none other than the blood of Christ. That is why SB-X wanted the nail, and why Capo 57 have tried so hard to stop them."

"What - to synthesize - *clone* - the blood of Christ? Is that where you're going with all of this?"

Khalamanga didn't share de Carranza's sense of outrage. "Why not? If the nail was genuine, the possibility remains that there may be minute fragments of DNA still attached-"

"Rubbish," de Carranza snorted, "You've been reading too much cheap fiction. Any trace of human material would have been utterly destroyed during the smithing process, never mind the decay and degradation of 2,000 years."

Khalamanga cut in, "It's irrelevant what science says. Faith alone is what has brought us here, through all of this past week. Faith in the spear to have the tests take place. Faith in the possibility of the nail, which stopped that research. Faith which has driven Capo 57, and their enemies, through centuries of war. What this tells us is that human beings, ones more worthy and significant than us, have invested this nail with the essence of belief; that somehow, trapped within the fragments, lies the very blood of Christ - the belief that His blood somehow is superior to mortal men. That it is the very essence of life and birth, able to heal, restore life, give sight to a blind Roman soldier and to prevail for ever, despite all that science says, and what people like you think."

de Carranza decided to take offence at that last comment. "And what, Doctor, do *you* think? Do you have faith in the slivers of metal wrought into an 8th Century tree-nail? Looking at this in the light of the day, I find myself wondering why it took me so long to lose my faith in the first place, a faith that is wrapped around myth and fabrication. Here I find myself cursing this notion of faith as the most destructive power ever unleashed by man upon the world - and now, you beg me to trust to that very power?"

Khalamanga was silent for a moment. He heard the words as those of a man who lived too long in the glare of publicity and deliberate controversy, inviting argument with his strong opinions which often seemed to be borne out of a desire to create discord rather than intellectual stimulation, to provoke rather than to educate. He was one of those writers who made money out of fictionalising the life of Christ, like the Bible Code-breakers and the Holy Grail discoverers. Khalamanga understood enough of the other man's nature to know that nothing short of a miracle would restore faith to the soul of Tomas de Carranza, and even then only if he allowed it to do so.

"We've already agreed to disagree on this point," Khalamanga said through a nervous smile. "Let's not fall out over it." But he could sense the lingering chill in the other man's voice as he replied,

"And we'll continue to disagree, Emanuel. We've digressed enough already – please, carry on."

Khalamanga rummaged through the breast pocket of his jacket and produced a black marker pen. "I'm gong to need space to write all of this down," he pushed stools away beneath the kitchen table just as their host returned, silently wondering why Khalamanga was so keenly adjusting the seating arrangements.

"Ah, Father. You don't mind if I write on your floor, do you? I have a lot of explaining to do here." Taking the continued silence as an affirmative, he spread Gruber's cuttings and Petersen's notes beside him and scribbled down words on the butter-yellow linoleum: *fire – lead – iron – zinc.*

"Did they never teach you to write on paper at Oxford?" Rattus enquired. "Or did they spend so much on feasts and drink for the dons that they couldn't afford it?"

Khalamanga stopped. "This is the crux of the case. *Alchemy*, Father. The greatest and most terrible transmutation the world has ever seen."

"The search for gold, and eternal life?"

Khalamanga hitched up his trousers and knelt back on the floor. "Yes, but in many different ways. Pure alchemical work exists on three levels at once - mind, matter and spirit. If I'm wrong, then I'm wrong. I'll clean your floor and then we can make rabbit stew. But if I'm right..." he scrabbled back to the beginning of his list. "I'll begin with the first operation in the process, which is Calcination. This is represented by fire and lead, and here we are dealing with the basest, most impure matter." He rustled through Gruber's news cuttings. "And it has parallels to this case of the men who were shot and burned in Poland last month."

de Carranza shrugged. "They were businessmen. They could have stepped on someone's toes; Poland can still be a harsh country."

"Maybe, but let me break this down for you. We'll assume SB-X were behind this, and that the act had some significance to them. If we look at the two agents of destruction - fire and lead - we find the first stage in the classical process represented. If we accept SB-X's horrible racialist views, we can interpret the bodies of the three men as representing what they would view as the basest form of living matter. If you're not convinced, two of the men also had considerable financial interests in a major shipping firm which handled industrial exports." He looked aside to the other men for a reaction. Seeing none, he went on.

"The second operation is Dissolution, and is symbolized by tin, and water." The pen squeaked on the linoleum as it scribbled more symbols. "Here we have the case reported a week later of the banker drowned in his pool. The man died in water, and the First Civil Bank ran the country's second largest import operation of *tin*, among other things. Now here I believe I've found a candidate for the third operation of Separation - in which an English diplomat, Sir Alexander Fotheringay, was found hacked to death in his apartment in Dortmund. The police seem to think the murder weapon was a very large and sharp implement - an axe, a machete - maybe even a sword. They're pursuing it as a politically-motivated attack, given that an iron SS 'Totenkopf' - a death's head badge - was found pinned to the man's chest. And they're right...just not in the way they think."

"How, then?" de Carranza challenged.

"Iron and weapons of war such as swords and axes, symbolize this stage in the process. The death's head, or skull, is also an alchemical symbol known as the Caput Mortuum in Latin. It refers to the dross left over from a process."

"So they're saying that the Englishman was dross, in some way? Like the other men they've killed - inferior, impure?"

"Yes. And looking at the report, it seems Fotheringay had a controlling share in a major oil company, and also ran a small but successful airline. Do you believe this is a coincidence so far?"

de Carranza laughed. "For all I know, you're making this up as you go along. Now who's looking for evil patterns, Emanuel?"

Unperturbed, the Nigerian continued with his exposition. He knew he would convert the sceptics, and soon, because the best was yet to come. "Conjunction is our fourth stage in the process, represented by earth and copper." he threw a photocopied news report onto the Spaniard's lap. "The Conjunction is the unification of opposing archetypal forces, often depicted by the symbolic figures of a King and a Queen. Are you still doubting, Tomas?" de Carranza caught the page and found himself glancing over the strange and horrible story of Alfreda Reina again.

"The burial in earth, the coins...the chess piece." he grimaced, threw the report back on the floor. "And in Spanish, Reina means 'Queen'."

Khalamanga nodded and grinned, triumphant at last in having broken de Carranza's scepticism. "The fifth stage is Fermentation, symbolized by sulphur. Here we have the Archbishop of Paderborn, drowned in fermenting yeast in his own cellar." Khalamanga pointed to a typed page taken from one of Petersen's files. "This is part of the coroner's report on the man's death, which mentions among the dull scientific data the curious fact that the levels of sulphur dioxide present in the beer were nearly a hundred times higher than normal."

Rattus said, "So despite the official story, the Archbishop was the fifth stage of the process; not a suicide at all?"

"And our headless friend in the Hofburg is what Dragan calls 'the sixth', eh?" de Carranza concluded. This was no longer a string of coincidences being jumped upon by an over-zealous student of esoterica, but the meticulous unravelling of a plot that lay almost beyond human comprehension. Khalamanga had beaten de Carranza, just as Gruber had done in the chess game. But this time the Spaniard did not feel inferior, but honoured, to have been able to assist so worthy an intellect in solving the diabolical puzzle. He was only ashamed it had taken him so long to stop doubting the other man's abilities.

"Yes, Tomas. Well done. The sixth process is Distillation, and is symbolized by silver. And what is distillation but the separation of various volatile substances - in this case, bodily fluids?"

"Dragan says he was ordered to leave the head on a silver tray." de Carranza added.

Rattus said, "Silajdzic happened on Sunday night. Do you think Vanessa may have been the seventh?"

"No, Father. I believe the seventh stage is yet to come – and will be the biggest, and most significant event in the whole sequence, for that will be the grand conclusion. The Seventh and final stage is Coagulation. The goal of all alchemists, the end result of the Work...the transformation into pure gold."

"Then we're in a race against time," Rattus suggested. "And we need to understand why they chose these high-profile, influential persons to murder and mutilate. Maybe they all represented something opposed to SB-X and their agenda or beliefs, or had something Rubelli wanted control of."

"Possibly, but I think it's simpler even than that. He's using the human body as the object of transformation." Khalamanga stopped to slap himself on the forehead. "Oh my, it's so simple. They began with the basest human form; through to Silajdzic, one of their own – probably a sacrifice, after all – and ultimately..."

"...the Son of God, reborn." Rattus concluded. "The spiritual gold, behind which lurks the physical Black Sun of Rubelli."

de Carranza's face contorted in disbelief. "Then if you're right...that Rubelli is trying to bring back Christ...he must truly be insane."

"Or inspired." Khalamanga turned to the priest. "What do you say, Father? You must have some ideas of your own. I would even wager that you're here on behalf of Capo 57. Am I right?"

"Half-right, Doctor. I don't work for Capo 57, but I know of them only too well. The only reason they haven't dared kill me is because I know where the bodies are buried." He laughed dryly. "They have members in the British Government and they practically run the MOD and the FO through the ranks of the civil service. I came into contact with them while serving out in Iraq, during Desert Storm. But that's another story altogether. I could tell you more, so much more, but I really would have to kill you, I'm afraid." The cheerful smile vanished. "No, seriously. I'm one of the few men alive who has read the complete Black Chronicle of Capo 57, first written down by Kastadiz of Tyre in the 1300s."

"So what *is* Capo 57?" Khalamanga begged. "We found references to them on the Internet, which someone went to a lot of trouble to stop us from looking at."

"Yes. That 'someone' was me. I wrote the virus which stopped your investigations, because I didn't want you making yourselves targets. I didn't know how far Capo would go to protect themselves at this time. And much as I may agree with most of their principles, I know from experience that they are capable of being just as ruthless as their enemies."

"Then what can you tell us about them?"

Rattus pulled himself up a stool at the kitchen table. "What I can say is, that at their height during the 1200s, the Knights of the Order of the Holy Temple of Jerusalem were a great and noble institution who possessed colossal wealth and power. But there were some within the order who wanted more, who planned to overthrow the ruling Kings of Europe and even unseat the Pope of the day. This enclave was known as 'Mors Stupebit' - 'Death strikes', from a line in the 'Dies Irae'. Their mission was to replace the Grandmaster of the Templars with one of their own, and bring the Day of Judgement down upon their enemies through war.

"You see, the Templars had long held a sacred and famous relic taken from the Holy Land, a cloth bearing the imprint of the face of Christ. But the Mors Stupebit took their reverence for this article further and they worshipped it instead of the Cross. They called it the 'Baphomet', and with it, the Mors knights intended to resurrect Christ, and follow Him into a final Crusade which would allow them to rule all Europe and the Holy Land in triumph."

de Carranza asked, "Tell me how these knights intended to bring back Christ with a holy cloth." But Khalamanga was already nodding in silent understanding, his wild theories all but confirmed now.

"Because the cloth held traces of His blood, sweat and tears. And these samples could be distilled, reproduced through some secret recipe which would restore Him to life. Perhaps even the very recipe you've uncovered here today, Doctor – this diabolical scheme which Rubelli may have *discovered* or *inherited*, rather than conceived."

de Carranza was astonished. "Are you saying the Templars understood the concepts behind DNA, 700 years ago?"

"Far be it from me to suggest anything so explosive," Rattus replied. "What I can say is that according to the Chronicles of Kastadiz, following the dissolution of the Templars, the surviving factions would later evolve to become SB-X and Capo 57. The conflicts between them continued to be sporadic up until the 1960s, when, after the discovery of the genetic codes, SB-X's numbers increased dramatically, and have continued to do so until today. I'll let you draw your own conclusions from that, gentlemen."

Khalamanga rubbed his long chin. "Then – truly - my instincts had been correct all along! - that the Templars, the cult of the head, the secret of the holy blood, the Resurrection - have all been linked for centuries, and are converging now as we speak." He pointed to the manuscript on de Carranza's lap. "And those pages there hold the key. We must try to comprehend the clues that Dragan and Petersen have left for us. Tomas, what else has Petersen highlighted?"

de Carranza flicked pages, ran his finger over the blocks of German text. "There's a line where Dragan talks of the Spear of Destiny laying waste to a land. Is that relevant, or another of your fancy metaphors?"

Khalamanga explained, "Yes, that is a reference to the Grail Romances, where there is a prophecy that the holy lance will destroy a land called Logres. The name is a poetic invention, but it has also been strongly identified with England."

"England," de Carranza repeated nervously. "The nation who helped defeat Germany in two world wars, and who seem to be the breeding ground for Capo 57. Revenge against the hereditary enemy, would you say?"

"Wouldn't surprise me," Rattus said. "They've been looking for revenge ever since Hurst scored that dodgy goal in extra time." when he found himself the subject of curious stares, he dutifully pulled himself behind the laptop computer on the kitchen table which bore a photograph of Chico Marx pasted on the outer lid.

"There's another bit, about rebuilding the holy pillar of the Saxons." de Carranza went on. "I take it that was some kind of pagan fertility symbol?"

Khalamanga arose, stretched his legs, feeling the need to exercise his body again. Unable to embark on one of his usual runs, he made do by pacing the room from end to end. "The central pillar of the world, which also features prominently in several of the Holy Grail stories." The pacing became heavier, Khalamanga's fingertips began to knead and rub his upper shoulders and his lower neck, a habit he had often found helped to stimulate his thought processes. "The holy pillar..." he thought to himself, whispering half-formed words under his breath, giving life to ideas which were quickly silenced again. "The centre of Europe..."

"Well that could signify just about anywhere, geographically or politically." Rattus said.

"No," Khalamanga argued. "No, it's not. He's being very specific. He's referring to a single place. The centre of the world, at least what was believed to be so, by the heathen Saxons."

"If you're talking about the axis mundi," de Carranza went on, "Most Indo-European tribes erected pillars and columns to represent the central axis – all over England, France, Germany."

"But only one, built by the Saxons, was destroyed by Charlemagne; and we already know the Holy Roman Empire, the 1st Reich, is being invoked here. And that was a pillar known as the Irminsul, which was demolished in 772."

"But such a symbol is pagan, not Christian. Why invoke that as the centre of his proposed new Holy Empire?"

"He's inventing his own mythology. He's going to begin at Year Zero, with a symbolic and mythical genesis couched in symbols and ideas which will appeal to his followers and strengthen his authority. He's combining imagery from the Germanic heathen past; the Saxon symbol of the centre of the world, with radical modern Aryanism to produce a very potent concoction. Just like Himmler, he's cross-breeding this heritage, these fictional concepts of a noble Saxon warrior-race with strict Christian, though not *Judaeo*-Christian, morality. He's outdoing Charlemagne, usurping Napolean, bettering Hitler to produce something even bigger. *A Fourth Reich*."

"But did this Irminsul ever actually exist?"

Khalamanga raised his eyes to the ceiling, drawing a list of memories from the back of his mind. "Our Irminsul was said to have stood near the ancient rock formation known as the Externsteine. Carved with Christian imagery from the medieval period, it is also said to have been a cult centre for ancient pagan practices. It lies outside Detmold, in Horn-Bad Meinberg at 51°52'8N, 8°55'3E. I was out there on a field trip with the University in July of '75." de Carranza saw the other man's long, lantern jaw fall as he finished his explanation. "Wait a minute...that's it. My God. This is starting to fall into place. Father, how long would it take to get from here to Westphalia?"

Rattus clicked a few buttons on Chico's keyboard and pulled up an online road atlas of Central Europe. "Depends on whether you want to cut north through the Czech Republic then head west, or travel the length of Austria to the west then cross the Bavarian Alps. Driving, at normal pace, I'd say a couple of days, since you're looking at about six hundred miles of road."

Khalamanga slapped the printed page in his hand. "I believe the final stage in the process will be unveiled at the site of the new Irminsul. It was in 1093 that the monastery of Paderborn bought the land containing the Externsteine, and those holy rocks would still be owned by that Archdiocese, whose last administrator has recently been found drowned in his own beer. We have to get there, and soon."

de Carranza stared, open-mouthed. "What? You're saying we just all jump into a car and blast off into Germany, without a clue what we're going to be facing when we get there, nor what we intend to do?"

"Well, what good is sitting here being clever going to do us?" Khalamanga stopped pacing. "We know we have to stop SB-X. If we can get there ahead of Rubelli, we have a chance to end it all. All I know is, we are running out of time the longer we sit here."

While the two academics set about preparing for their departure, Rattus sat in solemn silence while the television news began. As expected, the events of the previous night made the opening feature. 'Police Inspector Shot Dead' ran the subtitle, bringing grim expressions to the faces of the three men as the familiar facade of the Sacher appeared, obscured by incident vans, uniformed police and crowd barriers.

A picture of Petersen was flashed up, looking stern and handsome. The newsreader reiterated the known facts; that he had been hit six times, no assailant had been seen nor traced, no weapon recovered but that Hotel Sacher guests and staff did recall seeing the two distinctive academics in the hotel lobby prior to the murder, and their own disappearance.

Unflattering portraits of de Carranza and Khalamanga appeared to the left of the newsreader as she continued her announcements. "My God," Khalamanga groaned. "Where did they find that terrible picture of me?"

"This is Professor Tomas de Carranza of the University of Madrid, and Doctor Emanuel Khalamanga of the University of Oxford, England, who were assisting Petersen with the Spear of Destiny theft. Kommissar Kupfer of the Viennese Police Department refused to comment upon whether the missing men were directly involved in the murder of Petersen, but did say that he was making it his urgent priority to trace them..."

"Kupfer?" de Carranza repeated, "Since when was he a Kommissar?"

Rattus replied, "Probably since Petersen ceased being one last night."

Live footage of Kupfer outside the police station, surrounded by microphones, appeared on the screen. "We are currently doing everything we can to uncover the motivations behind this despicable, dreadful crime," Kupfer assured the thronging mass of cameras. "Wilhelm Petersen was a close friend as well as an excellent policeman, and the apprehension of his murderers is now our utmost priority."

"Herr Kommissar," someone shouted, "Is this in any way linked with the Holy Spear case? And the deaths of Professor Karl-Heinze Gruber and Vanessa Descartes?"

"I have no comment to make on that point," Kupfer replied. Turning straight to the camera, he said sternly; "The men who are on the run now have been working very closely with Kommissar Petersen, and may have vital knowledge regarding his death. I appeal to them both to turn themselves in, if only so we can eliminate them from our enquiries."

The report moved back to the studio, with a stock picture of the Holy Spear and a passport portrait of an unfamiliar, square-faced man in his sixties.

"...in another bizarre twist in the already sensational case of the Holy Spear of Destiny," the newsreader went on, "Police today discovered the dead body of international antiquities dealer Miko Vilosivich, near Vienna International Airport. Vilosivich had already been linked with the theft of the Holy Spear, and police believe he had paid over three million Euros for the Spear ..."

Rattus switched off the television. "God dammit. This has really raised the stakes now. We daren't hope that Capo 57 were responsible for killing Vilosivich – we have to assume the worst. If Rubelli was responsible for that, he now has the original Spear of Destiny in his possession, along with the true nail of the Cross."

de Carranza coughed, drawing their attention. "Gentlemen," he announced, "I've been looking through these news stories of Gruber's." He put down the cuttings and picked up his notepad. "And I've done some calculations of my own. Silajdzic was murdered last Sunday night, April 9th. Archbishop Strauss disappeared after evening mass the week before on Sunday, April 2nd, and was found on the Monday morning by his housekeeper. Alfreda Reina was found on April the 4th, but she disappeared on *Sunday* the 26th of March. Fotheringay was murdered on the night of *Sunday*, March 19th."

Rattus pressed his hand across his face, sweat-wiping. "He's working on a seven-day cycle, isn't he? His process advances one step each Sunday. Seven separate operations, each seven days apart, totalling forty-nine days altogether. He's invoking the power of seven as a magical and occult number."

Khalamanga agreed. He realised the implications. "The seventh and final stage will happen tomorrow." he sucked in a sharp breath of air as though struck by a severe pain. "What date is tomorrow?"

"April the 16th." de Carranza replied. "The date of my planned book signing in Paris, which my secretary had cleverly contrived to fall upon..." the realisation cast a dark cloud across his face. "...*Easter Sunday*."

Silence flooded the cottage kitchen again as all three men suffered through various stages of anxiety. Rattus was first to break the troubled peace as he moved over sighing floorboards to the window. He tilted the blinds back and looked at the distant sun which bled across the horizon, cowering beneath long black scars of altostratus which slashed the bronzed sky.

"Did you hear that?"

de Carranza felt his ears twitch. There was a low rumbling from somewhere distant, a deep throbbing which was felt, rather than heard, vibrating on the fringe of their perception.

"Yes. What is it?"

"A large number of vehicles, coming this way. Get the hell out of it now, both of you. Take the jeep. Just get to Germany and do what you can to stop this madness. Don't worry about me. Go on. Now."

de Carranza dithered, thought about objecting or uttering a random expletive, then decided to save his breath for the toils ahead. If God was intending him to regain his faith by some series of tribulations, then this was a strange way of going about it. He stumbled through the front door and felt his way through the encroaching night to the priest's jeep as the keys grew slick with palmsweat.

Through the hall window, Khalamanga saw the dimming light dancing on a line of heavy vehicles, distant headlamps slicing through the trees in their direction. "Thank you, Father. I pray we'll meet again."

"Me too, Doctor. Now buzz off, okay?"

Khalamanga did as he was told.

The night was rushing down fast, and before long it would be black from east to west. de Carranza wiped his beard, feeling moisture gather there. The car bumped and shuddered, a pot hole catching under the nearside wheels. de Carranza dimmed the headlights and hoped they would not attract attention.

When more than five minutes had passed and the rough farm road still rumbled on beneath them, de Carranza flicked the lights onto full beam to show briefly a silvery streak stretching into the darkness and a broken wooden gate sagging on its hinge on their left. As his eyes lit up with the after-image, it seemed as if they were enacting some cosmic rite of passage. The darkness felt tangible, a physical substance through which he had to continually force the car. His eyes strained ahead for a reassuring burst of normality, only to be confronted with a crucified, headless body. A scream of horror died in his throat, choked off only by his sucking in a breath of precious air. He stamped the brakes, jerking the jeep to a growling standstill.

He had to have imagined it, he told himself and yet there it was, lurching out of the night toward them, ragged and raven-pecked but now not so terrifying. A scarecrow, he realised with a childish smile. A straw man the farmer had propped against the fence, presumably to be fitted with a new head to replace the rubbery remains of turnip which clung to the wooden neck. He groaned into his beard at his own fallibility.

Leaving the track at last, the main road beckoned them onwards. He shifted up into higher gear and switched on the radio. It was a discussion programme, obviously with a humorous theme, to judge from frequent laughter from the studio audience, but the words and content were unimportant. In its own way, it helped to reconnect him to some form of civilisation again, remind him of the normal, mundane world out there which he had seen so little of in the past forty-eight hours, and reassure him that there was more to the universe than unknown threats sneaking up behind, and endless blackness lying ahead.

The image of the headless scarecrow returned, bringing with it a replay of the terror he had felt at that first glimpse. He knew there was a deeper, more fundamental truth which was yet to be found, a truth whose surface had been barely scratched by his most recent bestseller. The scarecrow faded from his mind and was replaced by a blood-drenched image of a man on a crucifix, sagging in agony as a Roman *pilum* sank deep between his ribs.

de Carranza snatched his hand off the wheel and rubbed at his eyes, hoping the physical act of clearing his sight would erase the mental vision, but it only sharpened the focus of the scene. He saw every detail of the scourging, every blemish, every laceration of the skin, the dark crusty streaks of blood which had hardened from the wounds, covered in sand and dust and plant seeds and stuck with fibres from the whip. He saw his own self pick up a mallet and drive in a nail, felt the warm gush of blood across the back of his hand until he too began to share in the pain of the victim, feeling the agony within his own body. The blood on his hand was not that of the other man, but his own. He felt the metal spike probing his side, choked and coughed as his diaphragm began to compress under his own weight, his arms aflame with the pain which burned from his punctured wrists to his bleeding heart, the agonizing end which as a child de Carranza had been taught to reflect upon and always keep in mind. He understood now the true meaning of the word 'excruciating', from 'cruciare' - 'to crucify' - the most terrible pain that could be suffered by man, or even the Son of Man.

The car wobbled, de Carranza saw the verge rushing up at speed, and spun the wheel just fast enough to avoid ploughing through a fence. A lay-by ahead offered rest and recuperation, and he gratefully pulled in to a standstill.

"Emanuel?"

He switched on the interior light and glanced in the rear-view mirror. Khalamanga lay curled up across the back seat like a child, his knees under his chin, mouth open as he slept, and dreamt.

The Spaniard switched the light and radio off, hoping that he too might be able to find half an hour's rest before he resumed the longest and most important drive of his life.

DAY SEVEN: Sunday

The morning sun rested on the brow of the hill as they drove on toward the Southern German border. Following the road map's advice, de Carranza had steered them along a route parallel to the Danube, passing Linz to the North and along the mountain roads which led past the Attersee on the way to Salzburg. By Khalamanga's reckoning they had travelled a little less than 200 miles. The roads weren't conducive to cruising at full speed, nor to relaxed driving. They twisted and turned, rose and fell and threw up surprising junctions and unmarked crossroads which had resulted in several wrong turnings and a near-collision with a farm tractor.

   Seven days ago, the Spaniard reflected, he was sitting in a radio studio in Barcelona in preparation for a live interview and the promised start of a European tour to promote 'Who Was Jesus?'. Had anyone told him that exactly a week later he would be driving across half of Europe in the hope of saving half the world from the plans of a genocidal fanatic, he would have laughed them out of existence.

   However, seven days was a long time. God only took six to create the world and everything in it, after all.

Khalamanga leant against the passenger door of the cabin, chin sunk into his palm as he stared through his own reflection at the passing countryside. There was so much beauty and wonder in the world, he thought, such joy and peace to behold, that the events of the last six days seemed so distant, fanciful even. Cattle grazed as they had done for thousands of years, clouds drifted and mountains stood, eternal, unyielding. There was nothing in the world around them at that moment which even suggested the evil madness which pushed them to their destiny, and Khalamanga could not escape the fear that everything he had ever believed and assumed about this case was wrong, founded upon supposition, coincidence, and that de Carranza was correct in all his cynicism. He half-expected to find nothing when they reached their destination, to hear the alleged world-conquering plans had fizzled and expired. He would have a hard job returning to his old life in that case; at best, he would have a lot of explaining to do to the Viennese police, and even more to his colleagues and family back in England. He had already begun to mentally script his responses to the questions he expected the police to put to him, when his mobile telephone startled him out of his daydream.

   The line crackled with terrible interference, and Khalamanga could just make out a voice over the rushing noise in the background. "Hello...Doctor? Rattus here. What's your status?"

   "Father. Why, hello. We've come through the Bavarian Alps, passed Hallein a little while ago. We're making good time. What about you?"

   "Don't worry about me. I made it out OK. Look, I've just heard the news. The Viennese police department is in uproar at the moment. Petersen's body has been stolen from the city mortuary. No signs of forced entry, and the press are swarming."

Khalamanga stuck a finger in his other ear to cut down the engine sound at his end. "Stolen? I don't understand."

"That's a shame, Doctor. I was rather hoping you'd have had an explanation for that one, because I'm pretty sure it's got something to do with the last stage in your process. And I for one am all out of ideas."

Khalamanga thought hard, tried not to be distracted by the whooshing in his ear and the uncomfortable sensation in his head he always got when using a mobile handset. "Let me think about it. I'll get back to you on that."

"Don't think too long, Doctor. Kupfer made another announcement, said he's stepping up the manhunt for the pair of you. Believes you to be his prime suspects. Be careful out there." And with that, the line went dead.

"News, Emanuel?" de Carranza asked.

"It's not good. Petersen's body has been taken from the mortuary. It's beginning to look as if there's someone on the police force, or very close to them, who is secretly working for Capo 57 or SB X."

"Why does that not surprise me? Strange how his second-in-command suddenly is promoted into his place, and decides to pursue us as suspects, eh."

Khalamanga bit his tongue, unwilling to speak his mind. He knew he would find strength in God to help him through these moments of doubt, but he could not rely upon de Carranza doing the same. The Spaniard's well-being was as essential as his own, and if keeping him in the dark meant they still had a chance of reaching the site of the Irminsul ahead of Rubelli, then so be it.

de Carranza slowed down as they approached a tiny village, a few dozen houses and a couple of shops clustered around the road. A filling station lay at the far end, a welcome sight to the driver who had been fretting about the ever-diminishing fuel supply for the past fifty miles.

"One thing's for sure," he said as he pulled to a halt in the forecourt and released his seatbelt, "We should find out pretty soon."

As he began to fill up the tank, he glanced over to the shop. There was wurst and salami for sale among the ubiquitous drivers' essentials of boiled sweets, over-priced drink and special interest magazines. de Carranza decided that he was hungry enough to buy four sticks of salami to occupy him for the next leg of the journey. The rumbling of the pump and the quiet buzz of the countryside led him to disturbing thoughts, and to consider the reality of what he could be driving into. He could be running headlong to his own death, or that of the man in the car beside him. Common sense and all de Carranza's life experience told him to turn around and get home as quickly as possible, as Vanessa had wanted to do and as Karl-Heinze Gruber had tried to do.

But were he to run now, he would be a failure, who had ducked out at the last moment when things got nasty, as he had suspected early on they would; a loser, who cared only to save his own skin rather than that of others, who had just wasted the last five days of his life and would be returning home to suspicion, unanswerable questions and even more accusations of publicity-seeking than usual. He might write a book to set the record straight but it would seem cynical in the wake of the tragic events in

Vienna. His only option was to push on ahead regardless, face the storm and take whatever further kicks in the teeth the Great Unknowable could conceive for him. If nothing else, he owed it to Gruber, to Vanessa and to Petersen.

Pondering on his immediate future, he failed to notice the petrol tank overflowing and spilling fuel across his boots.

Khalamanga turned his face toward the sun and felt it wash over him, casting arrows upon him, *through* him, filling up his dusty eyelids as he closed them tight against the North African dawn. He knew what it meant to be a citizen of Rome, a foundation of the greatest empire the world had seen, but even more than this, he knew what it meant to be a soldier of God, a member of the greatest empire the world co*uld ever* see - the eternal kingdom of God and His son.

Sweat tickled the side of his cheek, seeping from beneath his helmet. Another battle was soon to arise and once again Maurice of Thebes would be caked in the familiar raiment of blood, dust and tears. Every battle he entered was dedicated to the name of his Emperor, and every battle he won he dedicated to his God, though it was not the God of the Emperor, who himself dared to assume that position. For Maurice there had been only one time when God clothed Himself in human flesh and walked the earth, and would remain that way until He decided to revisit. But were He to do so, He would be unlikely to choose as His representative a fat, balding egomaniac of suspicious parentage.

For Maurice, war was simple - men lived and men died. The battles that took place within his soul were another matter; the conflict between his duty to his Emperor, and his submission to the will of God. It was a conflict he knew he would be unlikely to win. But for today, there was of a simpler kind to be waged - with sword and spear he would once more lead the legion of Thebes against the troublesome tribes who clamoured at the Empire's door.

It was a hot day, the light unfiltered by any cloud or mist, and the enemy wore the sun upon their backs. Yet Maurice trusted in the power of the spear he wielded, the spear whose secret was known only to his men, for it alone had tasted the Holy Blood of the Messiah two hundred and fifty years before, and would spit the unholy blood of many heathens before this afternoon was done.

As the horses thundered and thudded through the ragged, dusty lines of the enemy, Maurice prayed for the souls that they crushed. Where his spear flashed, ribbons of crimson whirled in the air like festival streamers, screams of dying men sucked into the swirling storm of battle as metals clattered and bodies broke and burst upon the desert floor like old fruit. The Theban Commander cried the name of his Saviour as the tribesmen turned to flee, waving the banner with the red cross of Christ to cries of victory. The Outpost was again secure; his superiors would be pleased.

Maurice pulled up on the reins of his steed and opened his gaze onto the reflected face of Emanuel Khalamanga in the side window of the jeep. He rubbed some life and feeling back into his numb legs, sore from sitting so long, and he smiled. The daydream filled him with the guilty pleasure of wish-fulfilment, a scene from a life that for all its remoteness he still felt connected to, more than any outsider would ever know, more so than he himself could even understand during his waking hours.

Driving on into the mid-afternoon sun and passing signs for Heidelburg and Odenwald, de Carranza had become fed up with the endless noise of the engine. He did not want music to distract him, so conversation was his only option to break the monotony. He crumpled up the wrapping of the last salami into the cigarette bin and belched deeply.

"You're being very quiet again, Emanuel. That usually means you're thinking about something. And right now, anything worth thinking about is worth talking about."

Khalamanga's nose wrinkled as he inhaled another blast of petroleum from de Carranza's leather boots. He pumped the Scooby Doo air freshener on the dashboard to release sickly perfume into the cabin and felt slightly nauseous as the smells mingled and prickled his nasal passages. "I've been wondering why Rubelli calls himself the 'Black Sun'. In classical mysticism, the familiar golden sun of heavenly perfection has its dark twin – its shadow – the Sol Niger. We already believe that Rubelli is planning to perform some kind of ritual designed to hasten the Second Coming of Christ."

"So what are you saying, that Rubelli thinks he's the *antichrist*?"

Khalamanga realised how silly it sounded when spoken out loud, yet the signs were there to be read. "As the true sun rises at dawn, the Black Sun rises at dusk, to rule the night, the symbol of Saturn and destruction. The Book of Revelation says *'and the sun became black as sackcloth of hair, and the moon became as blood...'* "

"Bloody prophecies," de Carranza sneered. "St. John was out of his head on hallucinogens while he wrote that stuff. Give me something tangible, Emanuel – something we can grasp."

"Very well. In reality, the Black Sun is a symbol of three interlaced swastikas, found as a floor decoration in Wewelsburg castle in Westphalia, which Heinrich Himmler hoped to use as the centre of the Third Reich. Ever since, it has been adopted as a mystical symbol by neo-pagan and occult Aryan groups around the world. I'm thinking that Petersen's corpse is part of the seventh and final operation in the alchemical process. In the previous six operations, life was taken away. I believe – I'm *convinced* – that the seventh will be different. That before nightfall on this Easter Sunday, Petersen's corpse will be used as a vessel to embody Rubelli's vision of a strong, Nordic Christ and Rubelli, the Black Sun, shall arise as the master of this new order."

"Great. That's all you had to say, Emanuel – *'Step on it, Tomas!'* "

So saying, he squeezed the accelerator so hard it threw Khalamanga back in his seat and crashed his papers over his feet.

"Oh my God...please don't drive so fast."

"Why, Doctor? We either get there with all haste, or we give up now. I'm not even doing two hundred. Close your eyes."

Khalamanga nearly vomited with terror. He couldn't have meant two hundred miles per hour - that couldn't be possible, surely? He risked a half-glance toward the speedometer, and realised the Spaniard was counting in metric kilometres, though the position of the needle and the rising tone of the engine were still frightening enough.

"You're not going to subject me to this all the way to Horn-Bad Meinberg. I'll be a nervous wreck."

de Carranza swung in hard in front of the lorry, prompting the driver to express his disapproval with a flash of his lights. de Carranza shook his fist at the back window, swerving as he did so and prompting Khalamanga to invoke the name of God again. And as the Nigerian's blood pressure rose, the Spaniard's seemed to decrease, as though he were exorcising all his demons through the steering wheel.

"Stop fretting, Emanuel. I like driving. I always have, since I was 19, when I got my first ever car." de Carranza fought the wheel, feeling the torque begin to push them in undesirable directions. It was a powerful force, like a raging crosswind, and the recollections of pleasant times past helped to keep his mind off the imminent danger. "It was a tiny Fiat, had a 1 litre engine. I thought it was magnificent. I felt invincible...I used to drive around the streets of Navarre at night looking for girls, racing other stupid young men around the back roads."

"That's wonderful, Tomas. This is a great time to learn that you have forty years of maniacal driving behind you."

The jeep swerved again to avoid an onrushing series of potholes, pushing Khalamanga hard against the door with the force. With trembling hands, the Doctor tried to collect his notes in an effort to divert his attention from the madness around him, but he knew he would be unable to concentrate. As he chanced to glance up through the lower part of the windscreen, he saw a sign go past for an approaching intersection where the rural road met the busy, multi-lane highway, dusty flashes of lorries, caravans, trucks and buses moving past in the middle distance.

"Oh my God."

"Emanuel, if I had a Euro for every time you've shouted 'oh my God' since we got in this car, I'd have enough to buy an Aston Martin."

"This isn't funny, I'm not laughing, and if I come through this alive-"

" 'If', Doctor? What's happened to *your* faith all of a sudden?"

"If I..." Khalamanga tried again, before realising his mind had turned black with fear. de Carranza saw the intersection looming. As the white lines rushed onward, he stomped the clutch into the floor and snatched the gear stick back into third. The engine howled its protest, blotting out all other sound and Khalamanga found his stare settling on the instrument display. He saw the rev counter flickering wildly around the 7,000 mark, buried in the red zone. He didn't know what the readout meant but he knew it didn't look, or sound, promising.

"Stop talking." He begged. "Please don't distract yourself - and in God's name, stop trying to humour me. Accept that I am absolutely - utterly - shitting myself!"

As the speed began to drop, de Carranza shifted off the throttle and began tapping the brakes, gently at first to avoid losing control, then harder to force the revs down manually. The vibration through the floor rattled through Khalamanga's body, shaking his teeth in his head and forcing him to squeeze his palms over his face.

de Carranza laughed. "It's okay, Doctor. You don't have to apologise for it. And I'll be honest with you – right now, I don't care. Because if God has a plan for us, he can't let it all end here. And if it does all end here then we weren't destined to save the world anyway. So sit back and just enjoy the ride."

Khalamanga pulled his sweater up over his head and pressed his hands against his ears, presenting a comical sight to any passing drivers who cared to look. Once this was all over, he would never let himself be driven anywhere in a car by anyone else ever again.

"Left at this junction," Khalamanga mumbled as they passed the latest sign for the Externsteine. Khalamanga had done his homework and knew that the caretaker would not be present at this time on a Sunday, but there was the worrying chance that new-agers, tourists, hippies or furtive lovers might come wandering to the famous site. As they drew along the final bends of Externsteiner Strasse with grassy fields around them and beautifully-cultivated forests ahead, they saw the first signs of unrest. Empty police patrol cars sat facing into the road. Fluorescent tape stretched around the perimeter and it occurred to de Carranza that with the thick wooded hills at one end of the rocks, and a river at the other, escape would prove difficult for SB X's members. There would be no innocent members of the public around now, at least.

The megalithic outcrop stretched up into the sky, nearly 40 meters high, growing out of the ground like the remains of some giant's fairy-tale castle, and even at that distance de Carranza was struck by the ageless authority those rocks commanded.

"Looks like the police have things under control," he observed cautiously. "Perhaps we shouldn't get any closer in case they decide to jump on us."

"Why would they?" Khalamanga parried, "If they've already arrested Rubelli, they must know he would have been responsible. And if they haven't, then why are they still here? We need to get closer."

"The police are in control here. There's nothing we can add to this. I'm turning back–"

A firm hand on the steering wheel begged to differ. "No, Tomas. We've come all this way. You damn near killed me back there - I need to be involved, even if only in some minute way, to see this nightmare through to the end. If you don't want to join me, let me out now and I'll walk the rest of the way." He looked into the other man's eyes with a stern sincerity, which managed to make de Carranza feel small and cowardly in a way he couldn't quite explain.

Unhappily, the Spaniard turned the jeep up towards the base of the rocks and parked about fifty metres away from the grove. For a few moments both men sat and looked out at the prehistoric site of worship and mystery, which even now drew men to its sacred heart and inspired the most impassioned devotion.

"It's beautiful," de Carranza said as the engine died and the sounds of nature took over.

"It's even better up close. The carvings and reliefs are some of the most amazing I have seen. The only example of Byzantine stone relief in all of Germany is here, showing the Irminsul being crushed under the power of Christianity."

de Carranza glanced worriedly around but saw no policemen, no signs of human life. "I suppose we should get out now and have a look, eh?"

He stepped out and threw the door shut behind him, slightly harder than he intended, as he realised from the echo which rebounded around the clearing and scattered flocks of birds resting in the nearby trees. Khalamanga appeared at his side, face wrinkled up against the bright sun as he gathered his bearings at the edge of the grove. The Spaniard pointed to a ten foot tall wooden pole that stood just in front of the megaliths. "What's that?"

"A big wooden post."

de Carranza fought back the impulse to make a scathing remark. "I meant...was it here the last time you visited this place? Or is it a new addition?"

The Nigerian adjusted his spectacles. "No. That may be their attempt at rebuilding the Irminsul. It's not very impressive, if it is."

"Do you feel something here?" de Carranza asked, feeling disturbed again. "It's like what I felt back in Vienna, when we were in the biergarten on Tuesday. Only stronger – more powerful – *closer*. Like an energy, a kind of force in the air?"

Khalamanga agreed. "There is something; this place has been a holy site for thousands of years. Prehistoric men, pagans, monks, hermits, Nazis and New Agers have all gathered here to pray, to hold sacred rites." he pointed to the top of one of the rocks where a metal bridge was visible. "There is an ancient observatory aligned exactly with the rising midsummer sun. Strange that the monks left that intact."

"People once lived here?"

"Yes, in the caves at the bottom - there, look. There are wonderful carved steps as well, leading up to the top."

While they were admiring the wonders of the rocks, a movement from the other end of the site attracted Khalamanga's attention. A group of people had just emerged from one of the caves and were now looking in their direction.

de Carranza returned the gaze of the silver-haired man in the Italian white suit and leather overcoat. He was flanked by a smallish woman wrapped in black velvet who was currently flicking cigarette ash lazily into the breeze. She seemed dressed for a funeral rather than a spiritual and temporal rebirth, every part of her body covered apart from her head and face, which looked icy pale above her rich gothic clothing. One earring was a gold sun and a silver moon pendant hung against her chest, confirming in Khalamanga's mind that she was the individual responsible for the last seven weeks of human butchery in the name of alchemical transformation. She stood erect and stiff, making the most of her average height and the high-heeled boots just visible beneath the hem of her flowing skirt. Her slim waist was narrowed even further by a tightly-laced leather bodice, which de Carranza surmised had a medical purpose as her neck remained tilted at a constant angle, bent slightly towards her left shoulder.

In contrast to Karmen Brandt, Rubelli looked sick, even terminal; his left hand exhibited a noticeable tremor, suggesting Parkinson's or a similar condition. A number of younger men dressed in expensive suits and coats skulked around the edge of the treeline where a large white van, resembling an unmarked ambulance, sat incongruously. The seeds of terrible doubt had already germinated in the Spaniard's mind before the first policemen appeared from the trees, pistols and rifles raised, but not towards the leaders of SB-X.

"They're *arresting* us, Tomas. I…I don't understand."

"Oh, I do. I told you this was a terrible idea."

The old man gestured happily to the two visitors as they found themselves being pushed forward at gunpoint by half a dozen members of the local polizei or at least, by men wearing their uniforms. "Gentlemen. How wonderful to see you both. Please, come and join us."

"Xiomar Rubelli." Khalamanga announced miserably. "First and current Grandmaster of Sonderbehandlung X, forty-ninth Grand-Commander of Mors Stupebit, a position in which he succeeded Heinrich Himmler. President of the European Crusade for True Holy Relics. Patriarch of the New Reformed Church of Dragovitsa, sometime member of the Italian fascist group P2 and the man referred to in the Chronicles of Capo 57 only as 'The Black Sun'."

Rubelli applauded with genuine appreciation. "I'm very impressed, Doctor. Thank you for taking the time to study my career." He pulled a cigarette from a silver case and lit up. "Tomas de Carranza." he grinned, "I've read so much of your work. Your new book overwhelmed me." He fumbled with the cigarette for a moment, passing it from one hand to the other, then finally placed it in his mouth for safe keeping. "Please, allow me-" he stretched out his right hand, expecting it to be shaken. de Carranza was too surprised by the gesture to do anything but stare at him in return; was this the man who was single-handedly trying to destroy the Middle East and reform the entire continent of Europe?

"You're not going to get around me that easily. Whatever it is you're up to here, people have died this week, people I knew and respected; murdered in front of my eyes by your bloody butchers and I cannot - *will not!* - accept these atrocities."

The other man sighed and put his hands out of sight behind his back. "I apologise, Professor. I admit, I'm disappointed though maybe not surprised. I know you are a genuine man of very strong personal beliefs, and I respect that." He nodded to Khalamanga. "Don't know much about you, I'm afraid."

"Emanuel Wole Khalamanga. Master of Arts with Honours, Jesus College, Oxford. 1978."

"Oxford." Rubelli repeated. "Ah. The *other* English University, eh? Ha ha!"

"It's the only one I'm aware of." Khalamanga retorted.

"Enough joking, perhaps?" Brandt interjected, her mouth a slash of dark red lipstick. Even her smile looked like a bloody wound, and for the first time in his life de Carranza felt fear in the presence of a woman.

"She's so impatient," Rubelli informed them. "Always wants things done yesterday." He walked back to her side, shaking as he went. "Now we're all together, perhaps Miss Brandt can reveal the purpose of our Great Work to you...after all, you must be curious, no?"

Taking her cue, Brandt began. "Well, here we stand at the holiest site of the Saxons, reconsecrated for a new age, the fusion of the old and the new, the very centre of the universe where nothing is impossible. From this place will arise a new empire which will empower its allies and destroy its enemies. And the first of those to succumb, Doctor, shall be England. That pompous little dumping-ground for the anally retentive. Oh they'll suffer, alright. For their betrayal of their origins, from being a noble Saxon kingdom, they degenerated into a cesspit filled with the worst kind of mongrels - scum from every corner of the world, a melting pot of the basest matter known to mankind; nothing but the dross left by their own putrefaction."

"The Caput Mortuum." Khalamanga surmised.

Rubelli grinned sideways at his female friend. "I told you he was good, didn't I? Never underestimate an English University man. But please, let's return to the present." He gestured to the group of men who stood beside the parked van. They opened the back doors and proceeded to rattle and clank around inside before emerging with a wheeled gurney, on which lay a horribly suggestive shape beneath a heavy sheet.

"No - that can't be-" de Carranza began, but found himself without the courage to complete the sentence. Rubelli strolled to the side of the trolley and gently pulled the sheet down. "I suppose he was a good man, as far as policemen go." he reflected sadly. "At least, until the morning of December 18th, 1999, when he and his excitable colleagues shot down my nephew Frederick in cold blood." He prodded a finger into one of the black holes in the corpse's chest. "Glad to say that our retaliation was not so inaccurate. The lack of a serious police inquiry was one thing - the failure to discipline this bad-tempered cowboy was something I refused to swallow."

Khalamanga saw one of the final pieces in his 'evil pattern' drop into place. "December 18th is the feast day of St. Sebastian," he groaned aside. "It was true, after all."

"He *knew*." de Carranza replied, suddenly comprehending. "He understood his time was short. That's why he was so desperate to keep us informed, so we could carry on the investigation after him."

Rubelli looked up to his captive audience, happy again, his arm trembling with more than excitement. "But today, he gets what no other man has ever had: a second chance. To be reborn and to rule the world as the Son of Man; strong, tall and fair."

Behind him, Brandt's face was smeared with a nauseating smirk. She pawed the naked body, out of sight beneath the sheet. "Yes, very fair."

"And as the holy spirit of Christ once entered the body of another, so it shall again: *'I visited a bodily dwelling...I cast out the one who was in it first, and I went in...and all the archons, as well as all the begotten powers of the earth, were shaken when it saw the likeness of the Image, since it was mixed. And I am the one who was in it, not resembling him who was in it first. For he was an earthly man, but I am from above the heavens...'* "

"So you know your 'Second Treatise of the Great Seth'. I'm impressed." de Carranza noted.

"Thank you, Professor. For resurrection of the imperfect is the only way to reach perfection. As was predicted by John the Baptiser, the Messiah who gave Christ the Gnosis 2,000 years ago; the same gnosis which has been stored and distilled in minute quantities within the Holy Nail - the heavenly fire which transcends all known matter. This, gentlemen, is the true quintessence of the alchemists – often mentioned but never explained."

Two of the suited men removed a metre and a half length of wood from the back of the van which they placed solemnly at the foot of the wooden pillar, whose true purpose was now revealed. At Brandt's signal, they lifted the body down and spread its arms out upon the crossbar. They held the legs together, bound them at the ankles so one foot lay above the other in the traditional posture of crucifixion which de Carranza could not help but comment upon: "I see you subscribe to the late triclavianist interpretation, rather than the words of your own Gnostic gospels. Hmm."

Brandt shot him a penetrating stare. "What?"

" *'And the world became poorer when he was restrained with a multitude of fetters. They nailed him to the tree, and they fixed him with four nails of brass.'* " de Carranza pointed to the bound ankles. "For I, too, know my 'Second Treatise'. *Four* nails, madam. Not three."

"The presence of the holy blood is all that is required. This is a work of transformation, not of literal re-interpretation, Professor."

"What you mean is, you could only find three possible True Nails and fudged your already screwed-up doctrines accordingly. You can't honestly believe that this disgusting pantomime is going to have any kind of result?"

Rubelli shook his head, denying the possibility of doubt. "Oh yes, Professor. The power of quintessence is beyond imagination. The same blood which will soon be within this vessel here-" he indicated Petersen, "and therein it will flow through him and restore Him to life. As Christ was the first Aryan, fair and golden, brighter than the sun and purer than life itself, so now He'll bring vengeance against the Jews who crucified Him, a vengeance which will be carried on by His people until His kingdom is built here on earth, temporal and eternal. The tribe of Judah - or of Judas - shall finally be no more."

de Carranza could only laugh, more in sorrow now than indignation. "I've come across some ludicrous dogma in my time but I think this one tops them all. There were no blond, blue-eyed speakers of Aramaic living in Judea in the 1st Century."

"Now, Professor, who is showing his ignorance? You've already stated in your very fine book that Jesus Christ was not one single person. If you argue that He was not crucified, then I argue that He was, though He did not rise again - that moment has still to come. For He was himself a follower of the Gnosis, and He understood the need for His own death, and the need for His return. And now all we aim to do is to hasten that final rebirth. And it is such a shame your lady friend did away with herself - she knew so much, believe me. So much so, I had insisted upon talking to her personally over a bottle of vintage...1945, a pretty good year." He half-laughed, half-sniffed, as if from a private joke."

Brandt moved around the trolley and pointed behind Khalamanga and de Carranza.

"He's here," she told him. "Perhaps we might begin at last?"

Behind him, de Carranza heard a commotion among the policemen, and turning, he saw another couple of uniforms step out from a silver Mercedes. They were followed by the figure of Kommissar Kupfer, carrying a small briefcase and walking no longer in the long shadow of Petersen, but upright to the point of arrogance. He greeted Rubelli like a brother and kissed the hand of Brandt through her velvet glove. The three of them shared in hushed conversation before Kupfer placed his briefcase on the gurney and unlocked it.

"Finally," Rubelli stared upon the contents. "The five True and Holy relics from the crucifixion, together again, for the first time in 2,000 years." Like a surgeon preparing for an operation, he removed each of the relics from the case and placed them aside on the trolley. "The three nails - from the Holy Spear of Vienna, from Aachen, and from Nuremburg. The Spear of Destiny itself. And five of the remaining thorns from the crown..." he glanced meaningfully at de Carranza. "Courtesy of Oviedo Cathedral, Professor."

The Spaniard shook with helpless outrage. "How dare you help yourself to relics from my country. Or anybody else's, for that matter. For these things - manufactured by human hand, with ordinary tools - are what you would kill and steal for? Fakes and fabrications."

"I know of your problems with faith, Professor." The older man laughed. "Trust me; I shall solve them for you." He took out a heavy carpenter's mallet from the case and placed it alongside the other artefacts. "Pick up the hammer, and drive in the first Holy Nail. Restore your faith, prove to yourself that I - *we* - are right."

The Spaniard looked at the expectant faces, each one as deadly serious as the other. Rubelli looked back at him, the ash growing long at the end of his cigarette as he waited.

"No." Warm trails seeped from the Spaniard's eyes, like blood from an open wound, for it physically hurt him to look down upon the pale, still face of Petersen; the man he had known for less than a week but who had changed his life forever, and who was now very close to bringing that life to an end. "No, I will not. And you can do what you like to me, it will make no odds, because your dream is a nightmare, and I refuse to take part in it."

A gun appeared from Kupfer's pocket and prodded the back of Khalamanga's head. "Perhaps the messy death of your sidekick may change your mind. After all, was not St. Maurice executed for refusing to acknowledge his true lord and master?"

With those words, did de Carranza see the answers to all the anomalies which had plagued the official investigation of late. Petersen's paranoia had firm roots, and they went even deeper than he had ever suspected. It was Kupfer himself who had written the threats and warnings on Rattus' pictures, Kupfer who had destroyed Rattus' letter, and who had fed back information to his secret superiors, keeping SB-X seven steps ahead.

"Why?" he begged, wanting an answer, any answer, some justification for all the murder and treachery.

Kupfer replied, "Why what? Why am I here, doing all this? Well, I guess it all goes back to that stupid Pope of yours we helped take care of, back in '78. Eh, Mr. Rubelli?"

de Carranza felt his body grow cold underneath his clothes, shuddered as patches of sweat grew upon his back, between his shoulders, on his neck. "John...Paul?"

Rubelli smiled, nodding, trembling. "Well done, Professor. Yes, that was only the start of our program to rebuild the power structure of Europe. But after your Basque terrorists took out Franco's successor in '73, we had no fascist leaders left to support us. We infiltrated the Italian government and it's economy, but your smiley Pope tried to put paid to all of that too. You see, every so often there comes a man so dangerous, so radical, that he simply cannot be allowed to live. John Paul I knew what he wanted, and he planned to get it. Unfortunately that meant liberating millions of Catholics, giving them the Papal approval to actually think for themselves."

Brandt continued, "All you Catholics need to be kept under; it's the only way to control so many tormented souls. And when we finish here today, they'll see the truth with their own eyes, that their Lord is returned and walking among them. Then, that army of rosary-rubbing sheep will be in the pocket of Sonderbehandlung X."

"And you think those people are all willing to support you in whatever atrocities you decide to commit now, in the name of racial purity?" the Spaniard fumed. "You really are insane."

Kupfer shook off his words with a laugh. "No, they'll see the truth. They know who was responsible for killing Christ - it's in all of them, it's part of their creed. They took Judas Iscariot, the archetypical Jew, and they made him their eternal adversary. Now they'll have the chance to satisfy their darkest longings against all of their Christ-killers. And what would you know about purity, Professor? You're part Arab, part Jew, part Basque; no wonder you're so confused. I wouldn't be surprised if there was even gypsy blood festering under that filthy dark skin of yours."

"Please, Kommissar." Rubelli interjected, "I won't have you insult our honoured guest." A heavy scowl flickered over his face. "This is a man of much wisdom, as proven by the fact he stands here now with us, having deciphered our Great Work in a mere few days."

But the Spaniard's hackles still prickled. He refused to allow Kupfer's sneering slights go without reply. "For your information, *Sergeant*, Archbishop Bartolomé de Carranza y Miranda of Navarre was the wisest man in Spain of his time. I know how great my family are. The Jewish doctors, the Moorish astronomers, the *conversos*, the *moriscos,* the Catholics, and I am proud of all of them - as proud as I am to stand before you and defy you, as a Spaniard, as a citizen of the free world."

Kupfer clicked back the safety catch. "Of course you are. Now pick up the hammer and do as you're told."

Khalamanga closed his eyes, tears oozing from beneath his lids. "Tomas, don't you dare do this."

de Carranza took up the first nail, the one from the Holy Spear, the artefact that had spilled more than just the blood of Christ in the past week. He set the tip of it on Petersen's right wrist in the gap between the ulna and radius.

"*Tomas!*"

But de Carranza did not hear his friend's shriek of despair. "Forgive me, God." He sighed, and brought the mallet down as hard as he could.

The nail slid through the flesh of the arm, grinding against bone as it thudded into the wood beneath. He looked up at Rubelli, Brandt and Kupfer through his veil of tears, their faces blurring and melting into a watery illusion before him.

As he raised the hammer again, the spectators cried out as one in varying degrees of excitement and terror as the corpse's left arm twitched and spasmed in the air. Rubelli clutched the edge of the trolley with trembling hands. The whole scene had already pushed de Carranza to the edge of his mental abyss, and he seized the True Nail and wrenched it free. Petersen's arm twitched once more and flopped back onto the wooden bar, as soft and lifeless as it had been moments before.

"Professor!" Rubelli sounded like a grandfather scolding a wayward child. "Put that nail back."

Men in police uniforms had begun to converge upon him and de Carranza knew the game was lost. Like the chess game against Gruber, he had worked himself into a corner against a superior force. It was not for himself that he felt sorrow, but for Khalamanga, the well-meaning pawn caught up in the endgame. The nearest uniformed man pointed his gun into the Doctor's face and for a fraction of a second, de Carranza was aware of the sound of something cutting through the air, hurtling in his direction, unstoppable and deadly. The sudden appearance of a metal arrow protruding from the gunman's shoulder brought with it a scream of shock and glancing up, de Carranza saw a dark figure duck out of sight behind a tree on the hillside.

The other policemen and gunmen scattered, seeking cover in the cave entrances. As all attention shifted from the Spaniard to the bushes, the trees, and the rocks for signs of the unseen crossbowman, the battle began. While Rubelli ran, Brandt found herself on the receiving end of a hefty push from Khalamanga which knocked her sprawling against the trolley and rattled the relics to the ground.

"Get your dirty hands off those." she warned, but Khalamanga's long fingers had already found the nails. They both went for the Spear at the same time, Khalamanga seizing one end while she grabbed at the other, and the artefact was wrestled up into the air between them. Brandt pulled, twisting her body to lever it out of his grasp, when her fingers slipped. The point caught in her shoulder, ripping through fabric and flesh and for that brief moment Khalamanga saw himself as St. Maurice, the first knight and wielder of the very spear which bore his name. And in a blinding burst of insight, Khalamanga realised what had brought him to this place. The 'hunch' he had felt seven days ago was nothing to do with his work, his research, or a lucky guess on his part. He had been imbued with the spirit of St. Maurice of Thebes since the day he handled that heavy old cloth-bound book in Charing Cross Road, with its romantic Victorian illustrations of the tall black man dressed as a Roman general who carried the *lancea et clavus domini* to victory, by the will of God.

"*Deus vult!*" he cried, echoing the battle cry of the Crusaders as his enemy fell beneath his blow, whether by true divine intervention or a lucky accident. Before the wound spewed out its blood, he caught a glimpse of magical and astrological symbols tattooed into Brandt's pale skin and recognised them as wards against dark spirits, fallen angels, *Nephilim*. She screamed in outrage more than pain, a harsh crow-like sound which brought henchmen running.

"You black filth," she spat, her mucus spattering across the lenses of his spectacles. "I'll make you suffer for that." Khalamanga saw her thugs closing in, knowing his only option was to flee for the safety of the stones. "Shoot the bastard." She told them, and guns were raised, seeing a clear and easy target.

Tomas de Carranza saw this too. Twenty metres of open ground still lay between the sprinting Doctor and the edge of safety. Without thinking, he slid his hand inside his jacket and found the stock of the semi-automatic he had collected from outside the Hotel Sacher. Now was the time for courage, strength, cunning; now was the time to take up arms. His actions would not secure independence for his beloved Basque homeland, but they might help toward an even greater goal. For now, de Carranza was no longer a Spaniard or a citizen of the free world. He was an angry teenaged Marxist Basque student again, and he was armed. His mind's eye lit up with slogans in his native language, Euskera, eurekas.

"*Bietan jarrai!*" His finger pumped the trigger, the gun kicked out a volley of lead over the heads of the crouching, running gunmen.

Seizing the opportunity for himself, de Carranza fled in the other direction, hoping to reach the cover of the trees before fate, or bullets, caught up with him. There were voices close behind shouting in German, and a frantic glance showed Kupfer and his officers in close pursuit. His chest grew tight, his breath sputtering in harsh bursts in his throat. He would have to stop soon, and trust the unseen marksmen, if they happened to be looking his way, or God guided their hands.

"Halt!" Kupfer sent a bullet into a tree a metre to the Spaniard's left. de Carranza stopped, turned, willing to surrender, just as the three men around Kupfer crumpled and dropped in perfect unison, no crossbow bolts this time, spurts of blood spiralling out of arms, thighs and shoulders from the impact of high velocity rifle rounds.

He managed another thirty metres or so up the slope, between the side of the Externsteine and the trees, when he found himself unable to move any further, slipping and slithering his way to a giddy, pain-induced standstill. For the first time in years he was acutely aware of his weakened heart, felt the blood surging through his veins in his temples and heard again the words of warning from his doctors. The doctors Pablo Sandoval had said he should have paid more attention to.

Kupfer cocked the .38 revolver as he stood over his cornered quarry. "Pointless running," he laughed. "Now hand over the nail."

"Don't have it. Threw it away."

Kupfer started to laugh. "Not much use in keeping you alive then, is there?" But his merriment died as de Carranza's gold signet rings broke his left jaw in two places. The Kommissar fell back down the slope, stunned at first by the pain, then angered by the fact he never saw it coming.

"That's for the Catholics," de Carranza spat.

Kupfer pulled himself back out of the raging Spaniard's reach, too slow, as de Carranza delivered a sharp left to his other cheek. Kupfer's head burst with a million multi-coloured points of light, his vision momentarily obscured by the grey mist of pain. Through the fuzz and the ringing in his ears he heard the other man shouting, saw his mouth opening, but his brain interpreted no words, only a distant, distorted human noise. Kupfer scrambled further down the slope, consciously trying to give himself time to steady his aim.

"Going to shoot me, are you?" de Carranza laughed, on fire with bravado now. "Well, this one's for the Arabs and the Jews..."

He launched another attack, a hard jab straight into the middle of Kupfer's face. The bone in his nose gave way with a moist crunch and Kupfer tasted warm blood at the back of his throat, felt it welling up on his lip, his chin, saw streaks of red on the back of his hand. Much as de Carranza had always been taught to fight fair in the boxing ring, there were times when such rules were but a distant ideal. With Kupfer on his knees and his face dripping from the assault, he knew he would have to disable him, and quickly. The Austrian reached out for the fallen .38 just as the Cuban heel of de Carranza's boot ground his fingers into the earth.

"And that...is for my *Pope*, you fascist bastard." The heel descended again, this time across the knuckles, and Kupfer spat dirt and blood.

"Stop now, Professor." a strong French accent announced. "We don't want you wasting your energy, do we?" Looking up the hillside, both men saw a tall figure dressed in camouflage clothing, its head wrapped in a thick scarf. A light assault rifle pointed down at them.

"Thank you," Kupfer wiped the blood away from his face. "Let me explain. I'm one of you – an undercover mole, Central Europe division." he paused to cough up some blood, spat it aside on the earth. "I know what they plan to do here, and in the future. I can tell you everything."

"Don't listen to him." de Carranza panted. "He's a liar - a murderer - he killed Kommissar Petersen, he's one of *them*."

The stranger waved at de Carranza to be silent. "Show me the sign, brother." The Frenchman said. "Then there'll be no doubt."

Kupfer stepped back, raised his right hand, and made the symbol of the endless knot which de Carranza recognised from the transcript of Dragan's interview. His heart began to sink. The cunning swine was using Capo's own secrets against them, and would be very likely to shoot the Frenchman as soon as his back turned.

"Very well." The stranger replied. "You've proven what you are. That's enough for me."

de Carranza could see no way forward. He fell to his knees, the tightness in his chest turning to pain which danced down his left side. If it got any worse he knew he would pass out, like he did back in the early 1990's when his heart condition was first diagnosed, and in this situation he would probably stop breathing altogether.

Kupfer laughed quietly to himself. "Thank you, brother, for saving me from this maniac. I thought he was about to kill me."

"No he wasn't." The Frenchman explained. "Because *I am*." he lowered the gun and Kupfer's parietal bone disintegrated in a gush of red and grey as the body tumbled away to lie, a blood-streaked mound, at the bottom of the hill.

His ears whining from the hard crack of the shot, momentarily stunned, de Carranza could only whisper in his broken, wheezing voice. "I don't understand. He made the sign...?"

The stranger crunched down through the undergrowth and squatted at de Carranza's side. "He made the sign wrong. And no true brother would ever share our most holy symbol with an outsider. Whoever showed him that was protecting our secret." he tapped the side of his nose, and de Carranza fancied he felt the warmth of a smile from beneath the other man's bandit-style scarf. "You wait here, Professor. And keep your head down, eh?"

As the man dashed off, the Spaniard heard himself groan, "I'm not going anywhere. Nowhere in this world, anyway."

High above on top of the Externsteine, Khalamanga sprinted furiously along the walkway with the collection of relics clinking and jangling in his pocket. The points of the nails prodded him in the hip with every step, reminding him of the strange and terrible scene he had witnessed beneath; the hammer and the nail, de Carranza and the twitching arm. He didn't have time to think or reflect, he just had to keep on moving, knowing only that he was heading towards the edge of the rocks with nothing but a sheer 40 meter drop into the water beneath.

It was a strange return to his personal past, he thought, as he struggled to ignore the sharp stitch that was growing in his side. It had been over thirty years since he trod this same path of prehistoric rock, the view of the countryside surrounding Horn-Bad Meinberg just as it had looked back in his young University days, and the field trip during which he had met his first and only girlfriend. She was local, was named Anna, and introduced herself to the 20 year-old Nigerian in perfect English while he was sketching the view over the prehistoric observatory. She told him that her family would never accept her speaking to someone like him because he was black, but that she found him fascinating and wanted to know more about him. When he returned to Oxford they stayed in touch by letter, until she came to visit the following year and stayed with him for a month in his room in Abingdon. Khalamanga found himself revisiting those first moments of his relationship as he pounded onwards, the pain coming sharper now, his desperate thoughts interrupted by fragments of gentle conversation, her high-pitched girlish laugh, the thrill he felt when she first touched his hand as they both looked out from the top of the tallest pillar to see the evening sun go down. He wondered what Anna Abendroth was doing now, and what she would make of him.

"Stop." the frantic cries of Rubelli blew past him, forcing him to glance back. The old man had managed to get up the twisting stone steps and was giving a creditable chase as Khalamanga found himself rapidly running out of space. "Give them up," he panted. "You can't do this. Not after all this time."

Khalamanga removed the nails from his pocket and moved as close to the edge of the wall as his bravery allowed. If Rubelli decided to tackle him, or shoot him, the nails would still fall into the river beneath, irrespective of Khalamanga's own fate.

"Give them to us," Rubelli panted. "You can't deprive us, not now."

"Yes, now. And for *ever*-" he turned, his right arm coming up in a perfect cricket bowling action to send the holy Spear of Destiny spinning high and far into the air. It flipped end over end, crashed down into the waters to plunge through fifty feet of murk and mud to the bottom, taking the hopes and desires of Xiomar Rubelli and his followers with it. The old man stood and stared, his eyes blinking with disbelief as the nails went scattering in the spear's wake, one after the other, to create fading ripples upon the reflections of vernal twilight.

Rubelli bowed his head. His left hand trembled uncontrollably. The spasm spread to his shoulder, causing it to twitch under his coat.

"That's a bad shake you have there." Khalamanga commented, unsure how best to humour the madman. Now that the dramatic moment was over, he began to consciously fear for his life and the consequences of his actions.

"A risk I was prepared to take. We had known for so long, you see, that the holy genetic code was the answer to everything. The true alchemist's dream." Khalamanga noticed a third figure charging along the top of the rocks toward them, visible just over Rubelli's left shoulder. "The answer to eternal life. My time in the SS had been well spent. It took effort to capture a little of his tissue...scrapings of skin, dandruff, and the like, before the Russians burned him, before his remains were lost to the world forever." His right hand gripped the left, squeezing it, trying to physically wring the nervous tremors out of his body. "His Parkinson's had become so advanced in his later years, you know."

Khalamanga squinted into the light, seeing Rubelli's eyes fixed on the sky, somewhere over the horizon. He was no longer speaking to Khalamanga, but recalling or confessing now, a terrible or incredible secret.

"Who? *Whose* remains?"

"The gene-splicing was a triumph, though. No scientific journals ever proclaimed its success, yet it came only a few years after the supposed discovery of the double helix. The knights of Mors Stupebit had known the theory centuries before Crick and Watson - strange how knowledge can lie buried until it is given a new face and a clever name, eh?" And as he continued, his voice began to escalate in volume, thickening and darkening. "I carried his passion, his power, his blood within me for 40 years, much longer than I should have lived. I was a vessel, a carrier of the great man's soul, his strength..." his head began to shake, not with palsy but with rising fervour, his right hand forming a fist which pounded into his breast. He was no longer speaking to Khalamanga. He was making a speech to tens of thousands of hypnotised followers, his eyes alight in the burning fires of a torchlit parade. "Through my work, the Wolf of War would live on, to lead the noble few into a new dawn. And I realised, if I could do it with him - I could do it with anyone, even the Son of Man..." he gestured wildly down at the remnants of his New Golgotha, where Christ nearly arose for a second time. "And I was right. Was I not, Doctor? Was that not the spark of a new and perfect sun which could have burned the world with its greatness?" the fist had become a claw, tearing at the fabric of his coat. "They said he was mad - maybe I inherited some of that as well. But I succeeded nonetheless. As I succeeded here today, for that brief moment. And that, Doctor, is why I know I can at least die happy now, as the oldest living man in the world, who nearly became its ruler...*again*..."

And just as suddenly as it began, the infected voice dropped into a sigh and Rubelli's physical frame sunk in on itself. No longer stirring, now spent and limp. His breathing came heavy, his gaze lost beneath sagging eyelids and the shake in the arm was back, more noticeable than before.

"The game's up, Rubelli." A clipped English accent announced behind him. Khalamanga had been so wrapt in the other man's words that he had completely failed to notice the appearance of the black-clad figure with the crossbows. As Rubelli shuffled around to confront the new arrival, the tip of the loaded weapon prodded him in the chest. "Now we're going to walk back to the steps, you and I, and then safely down to the ground, alright? We don't want you taking a dive at this height. You're going to stand trial, my friend."

As Rubelli laughed in reply, Father Rattus pulled up his balaclava with his free hand to throw a wink at Khalamanga. "Nice to see you again, Doctor. Damn glad you made it."

Khalamanga could only smile, a thin, sad smile as the Englishman led away Rubelli the Nazi, the mystic, the alchemist, or whatever he really was. And with a heavy breath he turned his face toward the descending sun and listened as Anna whispered words of enchantment into his ear.

At the foot of the Externsteine, the small group of soldiers from Capo 57 stood smoking and whispering to each other as they held Karmen Brandt and her associates at gunpoint. Bleeding, torn and bitter, she made a pathetic figure despite her lavish attire and accoutrements, a human canvas painted in red, white and black, face smudged with her own blood and watered with the tears of her rage. Most of the German policemen nursed bullet or crossbow wounds and only Rubelli himself stood out unscathed among the carnage, unrepentant, unbowed. Brandt stared through him with a loathing that was not good to behold.

"I hope you don't expect our operations to crumble now." she told Rattus, masked and anonymous once more. "We have massive holdings and investments, we have members in positions of authority so high and cloistered that they are untouchable. I am but one head, and my organization is a Hydra."

"That's as may be," Rattus replied , "But before you kicked my door in the other night and smashed up my friends the Marx Brothers, they succeeded in transferring over 950 million Euros from your group, and its subsidiaries' bank accounts, and deposited it all in the accounts of a Swiss-based charity who provide guide dogs for the blind. True, I have committed Internet banking fraud on an awe-inspiring and hitherto unprecedented scale, but the really good bit is-" here he stopped to prod the vacant-looking Rubelli, "It was all done in *your* name, using your passwords and your security credentials. Mr. Rubelli, Sonderbehandlung X has kicked the bucket. It's shuffled off it's mortal coil, run down the curtain and joined the choir invisible. This is an *ex-Sonderbehandlung.*"

Rubelli shrugged, barely aware of his surroundings now as he shuffled past his consort, Brandt. Her top lip curled, looking like an angered snake as Khalamanga smiled at the joke. "You haven't heard the last of this. You will all regret this day, and soon, I promise you. Bloody *Üntermensch.*"

Khalamanga heard her words but the fears they brought were of a far more immediate kind as he realised that de Carranza was nowhere in sight. He searched with his eyes and hoped with his heart as he scanned the milling groups of gunmen and their prisoners but there was no swarthy Spaniard in sight.

And then he saw him, halfway up the hill at the other end of the stones. de Carranza was lying on the ground, and he wasn't moving.

"Tomas." Khalamanga sobbed into the older man's face. "Talk to me. Please."

The Spaniard lay propped against the tree, arms wrapped tightly around himself as though in the process of freezing to death. His face was grey, his stare held firm by the setting sun. Khalamanga leaned closer and heard the words of the Lord's Prayer whispered in Spanish.

"Tomas, snap out of it. Speak to me."

"Too late," de Carranza laughed. "My mind's all clouds." He tugged at Khalamanga's jacket. "But we won, didn't we, my friend? Though God knows how." He closed his eyes with a gentle grin. "Perhaps I'll ask Him when I see Him."

The only pain he felt now came from the knowledge that Pablo Sandoval would be distraught, and would blame himself for not stopping his beloved Professor from embarking on his final adventure. He didn't see his life flashing before his eyes, he saw no tunnels with strange lights ahead, but nor did he feel unhappy with his time on earth. He was glad he had lived it as well as he had, without fear or restraint.

"That's a pretty sunset over there. The nicest I've ever seen." He thought he felt his heart laugh at him from within his own hollow breast, the offbeat cadence of a staggering pulse. It reminded him of the modern jazz which had played in the Sigmund-Freud-Park café as he dined with Vanessa, exuberant but unresolved and complicated, a fitting theme for the woman herself, and for his own life in general.

Khalamanga stared helplessly down into the clearing, the scene which only minutes before had been a war zone. He couldn't leave de Carranza now. Silajdzic, Gruber, Vanessa, and Petersen had all entered his life and departed again to leave indelible marks upon his life. He looked down at the blasted, bloody mess of Kupfer, and he trembled at the sight. Violent death had become commonplace so recently that Khalamanga still refused to accept the finality of it all. Why should he alone live, while others fell around him?

"*Tomas?*"

de Carranza uttered a low groan and clasped his hands across his chest in a final gesture of submission to the will of God, leaving Khalamanga with the prospect of facing the death of a third colleague in the space of four days. It was not turning out to be a very good day, but it was the first Easter Sunday he had ever not spent in a church.

EPILOGUE: Three Days Later

The glare of publicity surrounding the spectacular conclusion to the case of the Holy Spear had begun to recede, and its two most prominent protagonists had sought refuge within the walls of Khalamanga's home in Oxford. Students, fellows and colleagues alike had clamoured at the Doctor's door for answers, revelations, even autographs, mixing freely with excited reporters and curious locals who were enjoying the media circus. Refusing them all, Khalamanga saw them off with characteristic dignity, saying he had nothing to add to what he had already told the world's press, and throwing into the bin several written offers from British tabloid newspapers to tell what really happened under the holy rocks of the Saxons.

The affair at the Externsteine had been wrapped up as swiftly as it started. Three Europol helicopters put down in the clearing soon after the battle's end, the whole scene efficiently sealed off by agents within minutes of their landing. Khalamanga watched helplessly as de Carranza was stretchered off into the medical chopper along with the wounded. The masked gunmen had all vanished, Rattus similarly gone into the underworld from whence he came, and Khalamanga made it clear to the investigators that he was more concerned about the fate of Tomas de Carranza than in answering questions about who or what had been responsible for the whole military-style operation.

Following an overnight stay in hospital, de Carranza had been discharged the next day with a clean bill of health, his chest pains and breathlessness diagnosed as a bad case of indigestion probably brought on by his unusual exertion at the Externsteine. The doctors had taken note of his history of heart problems and advised him to cut down on the rich foods and consider a less stressful existence, stern advice which de Carranza humbly agreed to consider.

"Damn German sausage meat," he had joked to Khalamanga as the pair of them left the St. Catherine's hospital foyer. "That's the last time I eat salami from a Bavarian petrol station."

Their subsequent detention and questioning by Europol had caused them both to miss Petersen's funeral, a grand and fitting tribute which reduced them to tears when they eventually got to see the recorded footage afterwards. Before their departure for England, both men caught a flight back to Vienna to lay a wreath on the tomb of Kommissar Wilhelm Frederick Petersen and to pray for the peace of his soul.

The other surviving players in the drama had each found their own destinies by Wednesday afternoon. Weinhof took over the role of Kommissar recently vacated by the deceased Kupfer and promised a full enquiry into the alleged infiltration of the Viennese police force by Sonderbehandlung-X. Dragan Weber was charged with the murder of Gavrilo Silajdzic but recommended for psychiatric assessment, a decision which would see him escape prison and potentially be a free man again within a few years. His adoptive father, initially charged as an accessory to the crime under Kupfer's brief rule, had all charges against him dropped by Weinhof and was granted a period of paid leave from the Hofburg by Steiner. Xiomar Rubelli died just before midnight on the night following his arrest, seemingly from a self-administered cyanide ampoule as he sat in a German maximum security cell. This action left Karmen Brandt to face the impending full force of the law along with her associates, and Khalamanga read with some anxiety her renewed threats against the individuals who had helped to apprehend her.

Of Father Rattus, neither Khalamanga nor de Carranza heard a word, and no mention was made in any report concerning Capo 57, nor the activities of a small band of heavily-armed gunmen in Westphalia. Europol took full credit for the operation, a fact which made both men wonder just how influential Capo 57 really was.

"I have to say, friend, it's going to take us quite a while to return to any kind of normality after this." de Carranza announced as he settled himself in the largest of Khalamanga's two mismatched armchairs.

"We'll get there, Tomas." Khalamanga assured him as he set the other man's coffee cup down on the table in front of him. "In a few weeks the papers will be full of something else, and we'll be forgotten. Brandt and her friends will be locked up for a long time, I hope. People will return to the Hofburg to see the Spear, as they always did..." he trailed to a halt, shook his shoulders in a pantomime of guilt. "Well...they'll see *a* spear. With Vanessa's phoney old nail set in it."

"But you were right, Emanuel. It did all come down to faith in the end, didn't it? Dragan had the faith to believe that the nail he took from the Seth Spear was genuine, even to the point of feeling a surge of power from it."

"Don't be so quick to dismiss these things, Tomas." Khalamanga warned as he took his seat opposite with a cup of tea. "There was something in that nail. We all saw Petersen's arm come to life."

"Post-mortem spasm." de Carranza laughed with a dismissive wave. "The phenomenon is not unknown among undertakers and mortuary workers. There is nothing that cannot be explained rationally in all of this, looking back on it now and with time to think clearly. The only irrational elements are the minds of Rubelli and Brandt."

Khalamanga thought again over the words of Rubelli, those few sentences which suggested such awful possibilities. But that was something Khalamanga refused to consider too deeply, having had those words haunt his dreams since Sunday night, as much as anything else he had seen or heard in the preceding week.

"Yet still the original mysteries remain." de Carranza reflected. "The blood on the floor, the contradictory spear of Seth. In a way, I feel that we've failed somehow. We were hired to answer those questions, help solve the case, and in the end, we are all as confused as when we set out on this journey."

"At least it was a journey that we managed to learn from. Even if neither of us reached our true goals - you still reject your faith, I still feel like I need to justify my existence in some way. Perhaps it has set us both upon the right path to those goals, at least."

As they sipped their drinks and relaxed in the sparsely-furnished surroundings of Khalamanga's study, the Nigerian reflected upon his own life. He had been important, he realised; for the first time, he had done something for others, for himself, and for the world as a whole. He had seen the worst cruelty, the most frightening madness, the extremes of humanity. It had terrified him and invigorated him, like a ride on a rollercoaster and in a strange kind of way, he felt sorry that it was all over. Those few days in Vienna and those vital hours in Germany had made him feel more alive than his previous fifty years combined.

de Carranza raised his cup of coffee with a wry smile. "Well then, let's drink to staying on the right path."

Khalamanga leaned in and they chinked china. Normality, even banality, was once more seeping back into both their lives. de Carranza had spoken to Pablo Sandoval at some length about his future engagements, insisting that he cancel all planned appointments. While he himself still lurked just beyond the public stare, sales of 'Who Was Jesus?' had tripled literally overnight, and he had found himself seriously contemplating retirement from the University. The writing royalties were still rolling in and he was determined to enjoy as much of their benefits as he could, while he was still able to do so.

Khalamanga's future had never seemed less clear to him. From decades of predictable research and study, to being involved in a plot so incredible and far-reaching that the world's press were still discovering new aspects of it after ten days, his personal world had turned upside down. He hated the faded, formal portraits of himself that he kept seeing reproduced on television and in the newspapers, pictures which looked more like prison mug shots than passport identification. He couldn't stop thinking how sombre and uninteresting he looked in them. He knew in his heart that the events of the past week had changed him forever, and it was now up to him to make that change one for the better. It would be a difficult time of transformation for a man in his fifties, but one he knew would bring its own rewards. Although one part of that transformation was already beginning to unfold itself, a beautiful white and yellow German butterfly re-emerging from the cocoon of the past; for earlier that morning Khalamanga had awoken to a message on his answerphone, and a voice that spoke to him through thirty years of time:

'Hello, Emanuel Khalamanga, my dear, dear friend. This is Anna Abendroth. I've just finished watching Fox News and your name and face have been all over the screen, again. I hope you don't mind me tracking you down like this. I was so sorry how we lost contact after those wonderful weeks we spent together in Oxford. I know I promised you I would return, but things happened that were beyond my control. My parents moved to America and that's where I've been for the past thirty years; Houston, Texas, in fact. I know you'll be very busy and probably won't even remember me, but seeing those pictures of the Externsteine on TV brought back so many wonderful memories. I've been longing to see England again, and you might just be the

best excuse I've had to get out of this dustbowl for a while. I'll call you again when I arrive, if you're still interested. We have a hell of a lot of catching up to do. Well, that was all. God bless you, darling.'

As private thoughts played out through the minds of both men, de Carranza's left hand slid into his trouser pocket, idly shifting through spare Euro coinage and tattered remnants of his Viennese adventure. He had found no souvenirs of the city to bring home, and those few pieces of loose change, shopping receipts and restaurant bills were all he had left from those turbulent days. He found something crumpled there, another bill. He pulled out the paper and unfolded it, trying to deduce its meaning. It wasn't in his writing, and seemed to relate to an Internet website of some kind: 'www.spacenet.org.uk/journals/v_descartes'.

"Emanuel..." he passed the second-hand scrap across the table. "Take a look at this. It's Vanessa's. She gave it to me before she left us in the Sacher on Thursday afternoon." his face furrowed as he remembered those last few minutes together. "I recall she said...if we were 'interested in following the facts'. I thought it an odd thing to say at the time."

Khalamanga picked it up and thumbed it thoughtfully. "Should we?" he displayed his large impacted teeth with boyish enthusiasm.

"Why ask me? You'll only go and look it up yourself anyway, with or without my assent. So go ahead, get a virus and crash your PC. And I'll laugh and say 'told you so'." he drained his coffee and began exploring Khalamanga's study, peering at books on shelves, tutting over the dusty collection of porcelain statuettes of Jesus and the holy family.

Khalamanga chuckled to himself as he logged on to his Internet connection and typed in the address from the piece of paper. "What exactly is this?" he asked as he skimmed the text on the screen.

de Carranza peered over his shoulder to read the welcome screen. "It's a private online journal. A 'blog', I believe." The text on the screen read: 'Archaeological Metallurgy and Unveiling the Truth: One Manchester Lass and Her Investigations into Weird and Ancient Stuff.' Below the title was a separate box: "This journal is closed to public access. Please enter your username and password to continue." and blank fields in which these details could be typed.

Pointing to these, de Carranza said, "It's secured, and we don't have the login details. That's a shame." As he turned away, he heard the Doctor whisper something behind him. "What now, Emanuel? You're never going to hack her password, you know."

" 'Doctor Yuri's behind the truth'. The last line of her suicide note."

de Carranza spread his arms wide in a dramatic shrug, urging clarification.

"And...?"

"Well, if he relates to the truth protected by the username and password on this web page, perhaps that's a clue to her login. No?"

The Spaniard thought about it for a moment. He was willing to dismiss the whole idea - the case was over, the woman dead, with her service due the coming Friday. Yet there were still questions to be asked, and nothing could divert de Carranza from the opportunity to be clever and solve a puzzle.

"Maybe so. Who knows. Do you have any idea who Dr. Yuri might be?"

"I assumed one of her colleagues, maybe someone she worked with on the original tests on the spear."

de Carranza raked through his satchel to find the collection of Vanessa's belongings given him by Petersen. "Let's see what we have in here." He took out the plastic bag and burst it open, scattering a small bundle of things over the coffee table, looking to find an address book. Khalamanga joined de Carranza in his search and picked up her purse. Getting over his initial distaste, he opened the purse and emptied the loose change out. It was more of a wallet inside, with fold-out sections and compartments. There was an ID card behind a plastic pocket on one side, on the other a photograph of a handsome, dark-skinned man with a thin moustache.

"Recognise him?" Khalamanga asked, holding the purse wide open.

de Carranza studied it for a moment, searching his memory. "Omar Sharif," he said. "From about the time he made 'Doctor Zhivago'."

"Doctor who?" Khalamanga asked, not quite understanding. He had never devoted much time to films, preferring the purity of the written word instead.

"No, Doctor 'Zhivago'. Probably his most famous role." de Carranza kept looking through the other personal effects. There was a diary of some sort which he began to flick through, hoping for more beyond the usual memos for birthdays and holidays. As he searched on, Khalamanga went back across to the computer and hammered a query through the search engine.

"I'm not seeing anything here," de Carranza reported miserably. "Maybe we should-"

Khalamanga's hand descended over his shoulder and lifted the purse off the table, pulling de Carranza's enquiring gaze with it.

"What are you doing, Emanuel?"

Khalamanga stood back and removed the portrait of Sharif from its plastic compartment. He flipped the picture around between his fingers and held it in front of de Carranza's face with a triumphant grin. "Doctor Zhivago's first name is Yuri. I'd bet that the username is 'Doctor Yuri', and this here is the password."

Written on the reverse of the picture was the conundrum 'arabstallion69' in a small, nervous hand. de Carranza laughed aloud as he read it. "Well, I don't think I would have guessed that one too easily."

They went back to the computer desk, the Spaniard sitting himself down with burning excitement as he typed in the details. "Fingers crossed," he said and hit the 'enter' key. For a moment, nothing happened. Then the hard disk clicked, the screen refreshed and flashed up a message: 'Welcome to Spacenet, doctoryuri.'

"My God, we're *in*, dammit."

The two men exchanged high fives and cries of excitement. As they did so, the message disappeared and redirected to a list of online diary entries, ordered according to date, which showed the last entry had been made on Thursday. And a moment later both men found themselves reading the words of Vanessa Descartes:

'*My dear Tomas, I hope you managed to take my hint today. Sorry if I end up being a bit obscure about all this. My head's a mess at the moment, and I'm maybe not thinking too logically. So if you've had to jump through a few hoops to get this far, I'm sorry. I only hope you have managed to get here at all, and that it's not too late. If you haven't...well, pants. Otherwise, read on.*

'*I'll start off with a few confessions for Kommissar Peterson. I'm afraid I've ended up being less than honest with everyone recently. Partly through my own fears, possibly unfounded, partly through fears caused by very real things beyond my control - men phoning me up and demanding holy relics from me, for example. When I was first working on the spear and the nail with Doctor Reed last month, I did some things I shouldn't have. I thought Steiner was being a prick the way he treated us, refusing to let us perform any valuable invasive testing on the relics. Since we were dealing with two artefacts alleged to have pierced a human body, I thought from an archaeological and a forensic point of view that such surface analysis as he requested would be pointless. So I decided to be a naughty girl. I cut minute samples out of the supposed fragments of the True Nail, and I subjected them to everything I could think of, and just when I thought I was getting nowhere - BOOM*

'*There it was, right there in front of me. For a start, the pieces of the older nail were composed of brass, not iron. And attached to them - God knows how - were microscopic fragments of human tissue. It was exciting, of course, but it hardly meant anything. It could have come from anyone over the centuries. But I ran a full DNA test on it anyway, just to have some results. Though I had no way of knowing at the time, this, my dear friends, is my reason for the decision I have taken. This Monday morning when I returned to the Hofburg and the crime scene, I sneaked a swab of the blood from the floor for some reason I couldn't fathom at the time. It was only when I was back in Lab 9 later that day, I even remembered what I had done, and I ran a quick check of my own against the results I had secretly taken from the nail previously. I can't say I knew what I expected to find, or even why I did what I did. I just did it.*

'*My last act as a forensic scientist - the profession I abandoned years ago for the sake of my health - is what has brought me to this state, this wonderful state of knowing that nothing else I do can match this. Nobody could ever lay claim to having discovered anything so incredible as an identical match of DNA in two samples of blood, 2,000 years apart, which my analysis proves unequivocally belong to the same man. From those tiny fibres on the nail, to the fresh drops on the floor of the museum - they contained the identical genetic blueprint, B-type negative blood.*

'*Now here comes my other confession. I managed to get into the labs where you fellows kept your samples, and I removed the phials of the blood stored there. I'm afraid I rather had to charm the old bloke who was in charge - and he ended up giving me slightly more access than he realised. Anyway, I grabbed the samples and I burned them. If they was truly what I thought they were, then it was too great a secret to end up in the wrong hands. I knew men would kill for such a secret, and though I felt very wrong for doing it at the time, I knew in my heart I was helping to save countless souls in the future.*

'My greatest work has been in these, what have proved to be the last days of my life, for now I know that there are wonders and glories beyond this life which we cannot hope to understand in our waking hours. By the time you read this I will already have entered His realm, to rejoin my beloved sister Francesca, happy in the knowledge that, like Him, we too will be eternal.

"I hope now you understand. I know you will accept this revelation with the joy and relief that such a wonder can bring.'

de Carranza wheezed, unable to speak now. As he read, his fear deepened, his hand shook, he covered his mouth. When he had reached the end of the passage he was weeping openly, his beard dripping with tears.

Standing behind the Spaniard, reading the words with him, Khalamanga began to cry as well, but with relief, and joy. The adventure had been greater than either of them could have realised, and he felt proud to have known so brilliant and insightful a woman as Vanessa Descartes, she who had managed to show them all the truth behind the mysteries.

"She was right about the blood in the museum," Khalamanga managed through his tears. "She said at our first meeting she thought there might be a Jewish link to the bloodstains."

de Carranza pointed out a passage on the screen. " '...the pieces of the older nail were composed of brass, not iron'..." his usually rich voice trembled as he repeated the line from the 'Second Treatise of the Great Seth'*: "They nailed him to the tree, and they fixed him with four nails of brass..."*

"There you have it. The answers, Tomas. The answers to our questions, the end of our quest. It's magnificent..." he rubbed at his eyes, wiping away the salt which stung and half-blinded him. For a long time, de Carranza didn't move, didn't speak, just stared at the screen and read over and over again what was displayed there. His right hand hovered above the mouse button, longing to click on the arrow which would continue Vanessa's entry, yet fearful to do so.

At length, he found his voice.

"Answers?" he croaked, head-shaking. "No. There are no answers in this quest, Doctor. Only more questions. Your medieval writers knew that 800 years ago, when they wrote that the solution to the quest for the Holy Grail is to ask the secret question. By asking the questions, we don't get the answer, but we do succeed in our quest. And through the history of our Church, that is what the problem has been. Nobody asks any more. They just believe. This is the message that I have tried to put forth in my books, the fact nobody has actually sat down with their enemies, their heretical foes, and asked them why they think this way, *why* they follow one path and not another."

He sucked a long, shuddering sigh deep into his chest. The button clicked and the screen scrolled, revealing the last half of Vanessa's entry.

'Additional: My dear Professor...this is my last revelation to you. I'm afraid to say that once again, things have rested with me, but I hope that this time I have done the right thing - if not for me then for all of us.

'The fact is I also lied about the Spear of Seth. When Weber asked me to confirm the dating of the thing the day after the murder and break-in, I ran all the tests again that I had done on the original Spear of Destiny. And the fact revealed to me in the laboratory was this: that the Spear of Seth dates to no later than the end of the 1st Century AD, a genuine Roman pilum used during the days of the Empire. Whether it belonged to a blind soldier named Longinus, we will never know, nor if it was ever carried by St. Maurice, Constantine, or Charlemagne. I knew this data would be explosive, so I fudged it. I didn't want any more threats, or decapitations, and I hope you can understand how I saw this as the right thing to do.

'Now obviously the spearhead has been physically altered over the years with the space for the nail, the inscriptions, and so on. I can't even try to explain the contradiction of its nature. My first theory was that it's Gnostic graffiti - an attempt to undermine the value of what may be a true relic of the Crucifixion. But now, having come to the end of my process of transformation, I wonder if the early Christians and the first Gnostics understood more of the mystery of Christ than their heritage of warring factions would lead us to believe. Maybe back then the Passion and Crucifixion were viewed by its witnesses in different ways. The whole event could have been a nebulous experience that offered many explanations, even to those who saw it first hand. What I found when I analysed the engraving in detail, was that the edges of the engraved characters showed minute signs of wear consistent with the true age of the spearhead, ultimately proving your assertion, Tomas, that the quote from the 'Great Seth' could be contemporary. The nature of this inscription is highly consistent with the kind of engraving processes used in the early centuries AD, though I would suggest that the work was of an exceptionally high quality, such as would be fit for a prince, or a King.

'To prove all that you have just read, there is a single copy of the metallurgical scans, and X-ray fluorescence data which I have stored in a safe-deposit box in Vienna. There are also some old journals and diaries there that you may find interesting – other things I have discovered in the past which have proved to me there is more, so much more, that lies beyond this world of ours – things so great and terrifying I can't even hint at them here, or you would think me insane. I have lived with some dreadful knowledge these past few years, which this week's events have finally helped me to come to terms with.

Anyway, I have mailed the key for the box to the main police station in Stockport, Manchester, with the order that it be given up only to any of you three gentlemen with proof of your identity. If you do decide to use that knowledge in some way, I trust you will do so to ease tensions, not create them - to stop wars, not prolong them, and to save human life, not end it. The men who asked me for the original nail knew that it was genuine - that it contained shreds of Our Lord's blood - and they knew that such knowledge and proof could heal, restore the Holy Land - and all because of these old bits of metal which we all laughed at.

'Well, I for one got the biggest shock of all, I can say. I thought I would truly die when I found my dearest sister dead all those years ago, so I could say that I've been living on borrowed time since that day. If so, then I have been spared by some divine power to carry out the work that you find concluded here, work so great that it would render the rest of my life meaningless, make every day an anti-climax.

'So let me try to return to the Spear itself, and offer my point of view on the whole matter. Maybe that is the secret behind the Spear of Seth - that all his followers who came after Him can only interpret one small part of so great an event, like the blind men trying to describe the elephant to each other. If Christ was truly the Son of God, then he could be all of these things. The half-blind man who inscribed that spear may have seen more than the blind who unquestionably accept what they're told is gospel truth. We're all blind, and we all interpret what we think is the truth, but the fact remains that none of this changes His life or message. It's ironic that it takes an agnostic like me to deduce these facts, and only now at this stage in my life and career. But I'll stop trying to reconstruct the Crucifixion now - that, I'm sure, will be Professor de Carranza's next job.

'I feel happy to leave you all now, knowing there is hope for the future of us all. But I feel I am not really going anywhere - we will remain together, the four of us, linked intrinsically by our associations with this incredible series of events, and the knowledge that the four of us now share. Yours forever,

Vanessa.'

"So, the Spear of Seth..." Khalamanga began, then shook his head in wonder. "My God. If it is true, then that explains why Dragan felt the buzz he described in his testimony – when he ripped the false nail from the heart of the *true* spear."

de Carranza laughed darkly to himself as he walked away across the room. "You know, at any other time in my life, I would have done exactly what she says - written a book about the whole affair. I spent my life scratching through desert sands, peering through magnifying glasses at cracked parchment and papyri, trying to unearth a fraction of the revelation that we have here. But, if anyone should be the guardian of these secrets, Emanuel, it ought to be you."

Khalamanga blinked. "Why?"

"After a career like mine, my audience will be asking how I can follow a book like my last one. It will become a blockbuster, but for the wrong reasons - not because people want to find the truth about Jesus but because they're bored with the last controversial theory they have read, and want some new and even more radical story to amuse them. We have learned things that could set the religious world alight. But with so many popular myths and radical interpretations these days, I will be looked on as just another greedy bandwagon-jumper. Nothing else can possibly compete with what I've just come through...my spiritual re-awakening means far more than mere money.

"These secrets, these great truths, ought to remain in your hands only. You can throw them away like you did the nails, and the Spear. Or you can keep them all your life and die, knowing you are one of the few men in the world to know what you know. The choice is yours, for the quest was yours. Me? I only stuck around for the thrill; for the personal gain of being involved in something that would help to sell more books, further my career and maybe, if I was lucky, my life experience. Well, I certainly got the latter. But you were there from the start."

Khalamanga stood up. "Maybe we should both forget all about it for the meantime, and go somewhere for a drink. I know I could certainly use one."

de Carranza lost no time in accepting that offer. Collecting their jackets, they left the house and headed out to the nearest pub through a quiet side street edged with high wooden fences and elderly oak trees flourishing behind. The golden disk of the sun immersed itself in blood-red pools of cloud, drawing the Spaniard's gaze upward to distant heaven and beyond.

"This'll be my first time in an English pub," he mused as they approached the mock-Tudor facade of 'The King's Arms'. A few young people, probably students, sat sharing jokes and drinks in the adjoining beer garden, enjoying the first break in the relentless downpour which had drenched the city for the past seven days. Their humour turned to hushed excitement as the two distinctive celebrities passed by, as large as life and just as fascinating.

Khalamanga pushed open the front door and allowed a trickle of conversation, music and laughter to drift past them. "By the way," he enquired, "What did you do with the holy nail, after you pulled it out of Petersen?"

de Carranza shrugged casually. "Well, I spent a week in Vienna and never found the time to buy a souvenir, so..."

The End of

'MARANATHA'

Tomas de Carranza and Emanuel Khalamanga will return, in

'THE KEYS OF HEAVEN, THE ASHES OF HELL'

The Trinity Chronicles continue, with

'VENUS IN SATURN'

www.ingramcontent.com/pod-product-compliance
Ingram Content Group UK Ltd.
Pitfield, Milton Keynes, MK11 3LW, UK
UKHW041439180426
11947UKWH000078/519